The New York Times, July 3, 1937:
AMELIA EARHART
FORCED DOWN AT SEA;
WORST IS FEARED . . .

The official story went out the next day—

The popular heroine, on a routine flight, had encountered engine trouble, crashed into turbulent seas, and presumably drowned. The stunned world mourned a daring, courageous woman.

But the official story was a calculated lie.

What really happened involved a top-secret mission, dangerously incriminating photographs, the deadly alliance of two megalomaniacal super-powers, and a bizarre kidnapping that would lead to the most horrifying conspiracy in history.

By order of eight U.S. presidents, the truth had been hidden.

Now, the best-guarded secret of the century is about to be revealed . . .

Ghostflight

William Katz

A DELL BOOK

Published by
Dell Publishing Co., Inc.
1 Dag Hammarskjold Plaza
New York, New York 10017

Dell ® TM 681510, Dell Publishing Co., Inc.

ISBN: 0-440-13269-X

Printed in the United States of America

First printing—June 1980

Ghostflight

The New York Times, July 3, 1937:

MISS EARHART FORCED DOWN
AT SEA, HOWLAND ISLE FEARS;
COAST GUARD BEGINS SEARCH

Washington, July 2—Coast Guard headquarters was advised tonight that Amelia Earhart was believed to have alighted on the Pacific Ocean near Howland Island shortly after five P.M. Eastern daylight time today . . .

CHAPTER 1

Los Angeles Airport, December 2, 1982

The green glow of the radarscope reflected on Ed Stanton's face, giving him a sickly, moribund look. He had eight hundred thirty-five lives on his hands, symbolized by six dots floating gently across the screen. A few were separated by as little as thirty seconds' flying time. If Stanton gave the wrong order, two of those dots would merge, then melt away. It had happened to another controller the year before.

"United six, go to eighteen thousand and hold," Stanton said into the mike on his headset. His voice was steady, with the matter-of-fact correctness that repetition brings. An instant later a United Airlines captain brought one hundred fifty-three people a thousand feet closer to Earth.

Stanton was thirty-two and looked forty. His bloodshot eyes bulged, as a controller's do after eight years, and he knew the mainspring that kept him going was rapidly wearing down. He gazed at the round scope, studying the hypnotic drift of the six dots as they traveled in circles, waiting to land. Then he cleared his throat to speak.

"United six . . ."

He froze.

"Stand by."

He jutted toward the screen.

There in the upper left . . . a seventh dot!

It cut across the sky, heading straight for the stack of circling planes.

Stanton's headset crackled.

"American four-five here. What the hell's going on?"

"I'm checking, four-five," Stanton answered. His fingers began to tremble.

"United six here. That's a twin-prop job. Pre-war Lockheed Electra, out from . . . Whoa! It just came under me! Number NR 16020."

Stanton jotted down the number. He was an aviation buff and it stuck in his mind. Beads of sweat coated his forehead as he clicked on his radio.

"NR 16020, this is L.A. control. Come in."

Silence.

"NR 16020. Answer!"

NR 16020 veered over downtown Los Angeles heading for the airport. Its pilot looked down. My God, it had changed so completely in forty-five years.

When Stanton realized the intruder wouldn't turn away, he pressed a red button on his console. Instantly a warning flashed in every key airport office. Stanton relayed the details.

Sirens wailed. People in the terminal paused. Fright crossed the faces of those whose relatives had just taken off or were landing. For most, though, the sirens meant excitement. Some rushed for positions at the windows facing the field.

* * *

Jack Dahlquist had a great poker hand when the red phone buzzed. His huge fingers grabbed the receiver and placed it next to his equally massive ear. The Chief of Airport Security barked an order. Dahlquist threw down his hand, splashing his chips on the cement floor.

"Craps!" he said. "Some weirdo up there. Lez move."

He raised his two-hundred-forty-five-pound frame out of the wooden folding chair, revealing the khaki uniform of an airport police sergeant. His partner threw open a screen door and they piled into their Dodge patrol car, heading for the runway. Dahlquist, a fifty-eight-year-old former Navy petty officer, clicked on his transmitter and ordered other units to converge. He spoke in the raspy voice of a three-pack-a-day man, whose lungs wore a protective coating of tar.

Most of Dahlquist's cases involved drunken passengers or pickpockets working the terminal. This was a first.

The Dodge stopped. Dahlquist squeezed himself out. By now scores of security men were gathered at specific points along the runway. All were armed, some with automatic weapons.

Suddenly, Dahlquist heard engines. Then, out of the smog, the Electra appeared and began its approach. On the field, idle chatter stopped. Every eye was on the twin-engine plane now only fifty feet off the ground and closing.

The intruder touched the runway with both wing wheels, then settled back on its tail and rolled to a stop. Every vehicle on the field raced toward it.

Dahlquist arrived first. Slowly, he walked forward of the right wing, pistol in hand. He looked into the cockpit, but the pilot had gone back to the fuselage. Dahlquist lifted his bullhorn and flipped the on switch. There was a piercing screech before he hurriedly adjusted the volume.

"You in there," he ordered, "come out!"

He heard a metallic clunk from inside the fuselage door. His finger touched the trigger of his pistol as he breathed heavily.

Another clunk.

A small crack opened where the door met the fuselage. Dahlquist dropped to one knee, his gun pointed at the top third of the rectangular door, where a head would be.

The door swung open. A figure appeared in the shadowy inside of the Electra, then jumped to the ground.

Dahlquist slowly lowered his gun.

There he stood, face to face with a slim woman in her late forties. A slight smile formed at her lips. She wore tan slacks and a short leather flight jacket, topped by an orange scarf. Her hair was clipped short. She hardly seemed a threat.

"Who the hell are you?" Dahlquist barked.

The woman's smile grew.

"My name . . ." she said, "is Amelia Earhart."

CHAPTER 2

BULLETIN
LOS ANGELES, DECEMBER 2 (AP)—A WOM-
AN CLAIMING TO BE AMELIA EARHART
CUT THROUGH THE SKIES OVER LOS AN-
GELES TODAY AND MADE AN ILLEGAL
LANDING AT INTERNATIONAL AIRPORT.

THE WOMAN, WHO BORE A STRIKING
RESEMBLANCE TO EARHART, FLEW THE
SAME TYPE PLANE IN WHICH THE AVIA-
TRIX VANISHED IN THE PACIFIC IN 1937.
THE PLANE'S NUMBER WAS ALSO THE
SAME.

THE FLIER SEEMED ABOUT FORTY-
EIGHT. THE REAL AMELIA EARHART IN
THIS YEAR OF 1982 WOULD BE EIGHTY-
FOUR.

Washington, D.C.

Richard Sovern stood at his bulletproof window reading the AP dispatch. Director of the Critical Research
Group (CRG), an intelligence unit reporting directly
to the White House, Sovern was, in effect, the President's personal troubleshooter in the spy business.

He walked to a three-foot-high gray safe in the corner of his office and removed a manila file. Inside was a letter addressed to the United States ambassador in London. Sovern reviewed it, slipped it back in the file, then returned to his desk and flipped on his intercom. "Frank, would you come in please." He sat down and tossed the file in front of him. Its label read:

EARHART, AMELIA MARY
OPENED 1937
CLOSED ———

Sovern slumped in his oversized leather chair, waiting for his aide to enter. He was only forty-nine, but, like Ed Stanton in Los Angeles, the strain of work was aging him. His hair was streaked with gray and there were a few lines chiseled in his face. His blue eyes showed unmistakable fatigue, even behind his black-rimmed reading glasses. Ironically, the changes added to his cool, distinguished look. He liked to wear a brown wool sweater under his suit, and with his narrow frame and Sherlock Holmes pipe he looked more like a British professor than an American agent.

The door swung open. Franklin Foreman, his twenty-nine-year-old aide, strode in.

"Look at this," Sovern said.

Foreman read the dispatch.

"Okay," Sovern ordered, "get fingerprints, voiceprints, pictures, TV tapes, and medical charts on this woman."

"Why?" Foreman asked. "She's in her forties."

"You saw the London letter?" Sovern inquired.

"Yes."

"Then the answer should be obvious. I want you to

contact our L.A. office and have them search that plane for cameras."

Foreman had a skeptical look on his face. "Look, Dick," he asked, "shouldn't the FBI do this? If it's a hoax, which is what it looks like, and we get involved, we'll look like fools."

Sovern leaned back, forcing some of the springs in his chair to squeak. He took a long draw on his pipe and smiled in amusement at Foreman's chronic concern for self-image. "Frank," he said, "if it's a hoax I'll send out a memo saying the investigation was *my* idea and that you opposed it with all the persuasive power at your command." He took out a yellow authorization form that Foreman would file with his orders and leaned over to sign it:

RICHARD A. SOVERN, M.D., DIRECTOR

The signature was unique, for Sovern was the first medical intelligence officer to rise to a position of power.

Foreman took the paper and left quickly.

Sovern waited expectantly for the reply from California, but turned immediately to other work. For him the lady flier's landing couldn't have come at a more feverish time, for he was in charge of the growing American efforts to combat the rise of neo-Nazi groups in West Germany. These groups had become increasingly open and aggressive as more and more Germans yearned for the order, the spirit, and the discipline of the Nazi period. Although this new fascism had suffered a temporary setback after the showing of the American television film *Holocaust* in 1979, it had quickly revived. Still small in number and under constant legal attack by the West German government, these neo-Nazi groups were, in Sovern's mind, a convulsion waiting to happen, a political time bomb that could explode at any moment of stress.

There were other pressures on Sovern as well. His career was under general assault by the Washington intelligence establishment, which didn't much care for his unorthodox methods. True, Sovern was a legend among intelligence men and had the commendations to prove it—those secret citations given at closed ceremonies, awards the outside world would never see. They read like a dictionary definition of achievement in his profession:

COMMENDATION: for penetrating a Soviet air base with commandos and flying out a MIG-25.

COMMENDATION: for infiltrating into East Germany to perform emergency surgery on a defector hiding from the police.

COMMENDATION: for smashing a spy ring inside NATO.

COMMENDATION: for inventing a bed that secretly monitored the medical condition of visiting heads of state.

The commendations meant little now, for Sovern had broken one of the writs of the Washington establishment. Soon after becoming CRG director he learned that some agents were plotting illegal assassinations of foreign "enemies." Similar plots had been exposed at the CIA and had led to the intelligence reforms of the 1970's.

Sovern could have crushed the plot quietly, but he knew that if word of it leaked, no one would believe it had been destroyed. So he called the chairman of the

Senate Committee on Government Operations and
asked to testify "on an urgent matter."

> I come before you with a sense of deep sadness. I
> come to reveal a plot within my own agency, to
> name those involved, some of them friends of
> mine. . . .

It was a bombshell. *The Washington Post* called
Sovern "one of the few security men not afraid of
his own people." To idealists he was a new Elliot
Richardson, a Sam Ervin. But to hardliners who saw
loyalty to the organization as the equal of loyalty to
the country, he was a traitor. Richard Sovern, in their
view, was an oddball whose appointment as CRG director was a correctable error.

Pressure grew on Sovern to quit. He refused, and his
public stature had made him unfireable.

One night someone shot at his office window.

Despite the danger he refused to resign and as a
result faced the possibility that his opponents would
deal with him in the classic manner of the clandestine
service.

While waiting for the data on the woman pilot to
flow in, Sovern reviewed the EARHART file. Reading
about the past triggered thoughts of his early years.
His mother, a nurse in Chicago, gave him *Microbe
Hunters,* a book mothers gave sons to stimulate their
interest in medicine. In Sovern's case it worked. He
earned a medical degree from Wisconsin and interned
in Boston. Then he served with the army in Hawaii.
In a letter to his mother he wrote: "I'm going to become a physician in the CIA. . . ."

Mother's image: her son, after all that education,
looking into the ears of shady men in trenchcoats.

But his actual job was evaluating the medical condition of foreign leaders from pictures, newsfilm, visual observation, and the reports of American diplomats. His performance was brilliant. He predicted the death of President Pompidou of France and traced the deterioration of a Soviet Army corps to the ulcers of its commander. He was the first to describe the failing health of Chairman Mao Tse-tung. The CIA let him branch out into other roles and sent him overseas. His exploits, especially the "removal" of the MIG-25, guaranteed his future. When the Critical Research Group was formed, his record made him the ideal man to head it. A search committee said:

> He understands that his first allegiance is to the nation, not to a policy or agency. In that respect he differs from many officials, who routinely alter their reports to suit the current point of view.

It was that quality that got Sovern in trouble with most of the intelligence establishment, trouble he wore as a kind of badge of honor.

His intercom buzzed. "Sir," Foreman told him, "the information is coming in from L.A."

Sovern quickly took the file and turned it inward so no one would see. Then he left his office and walked down the carpeted hall to the CRG lab.

The lab was a forty- by sixty-foot room crammed with electronic instruments. The walls were polished-white tile for cleanliness, and the ceiling was soundproofed. Filtered air flowed in from vents and was kept at seventy degrees. In one corner was a communications cell, sealed off from the rest of the lab by windowless walls. Inside, connected with forty-five CRG stations around the world, were three gray consoles that could receive any form of transmittal—teletype, pictures, voice recordings, satellite transmissions, videotapes, and codes.

Sovern asked all but three technicians to leave. The other sixteen understood that they weren't cleared for the work about to begin. Indeed only seven people in all of CRG were cleared for the EARHART file.

The data from Los Angeles flowed into the communications cell, beginning with fingerprints of the mystery pilot. Sovern took them to an illuminated magnifier and compared them with the prints of Amelia Earhart. As he worked, pictures of the pilot came across. A bearded technician compared them with pictures of Earhart, using special gauges to measure the size of facial features, bones, and limbs.

Received next were the medical and dental X-rays. Sovern went to work on these assisted by Dr. Mark Robertson, a radiologist. Using X-ray illuminators, they compared the films to X-rays of Amelia Earhart, making detailed notes as they progressed.

Sovern and Robertson glanced at each other when their examinations were finished. They said nothing, but there was apprehension in each man's eyes, fear coupled with confusion.

A recorder started taping a voice transmission. It was part of a short meeting between the woman flier and reporters. Sovern watched as an IBM printer that "read" voices made a transcript of the tape:

"Okay, lady, if you're Amelia Earhart, tell us where you've been all these years and why you look so incredibly young."

"I'm afraid I can't tell you where I've been or how I managed to remain preserved, so to speak. I will ask to have contact with certain people in the government, though, and the truth will eventually come out."

When the transmission ended, Sovern took two sound cassettes from the EARHART file. The first was marked AMELIA EARHART AFTER FIRST SOLO TRANSATLANTIC FLIGHT, 1932. He clipped it into a playback deck and turned it on. He and his aides listened carefully, comparing this voice to the one they'd just heard:

"It's much easier to fly the Atlantic Ocean now than it was a few years ago. I expect to be able to do it in my lifetime again, possibly not as a solo expedition, but in regular transatlantic service, which is inevitable in our lifetime."

Sovern clipped in the second cassette. Its label read AMELIA EARHART DISCUSSING LAST FLIGHT, 1937:

"The contemplated course covers about twenty-seven thousand miles. It will be the first flight, if successful, which approximates the equator. The plane I'm using is a transport plane. It is the Lockheed Electra, normally carrying ten passengers and two pilots.

"If the flight's successful, I hope it will increase women's interest in flying. If so it will be worthwhile as far as I'm concerned."

With a technician's help Sovern was able to generate oscilloscope "pictures" of both the voice on the cassettes and the one on the Los Angeles tape. Each looked like the jagged line of an economics graph. Sovern visually compared the two.

The lab's red phone rang. It was connected directly to the White House. Foreman quickly picked up and listened, then turned to Sovern. "It's Elmer Rose. The Chief is concerned about the lady in L.A. He wants your call as soon as you finish."

Sovern nodded a yes and felt the tension inside him grow. The President's concern only added to his own. He could sense the crisis building.

A teleprinter began tapping out a message:

STAND BY FOR FILM TRANSMISSION. FILM RECOVERED FROM LOCKHEED ELECTRA NUMBER 16020 TODAY. EMULSION OLD AND BRITTLE. EASTMAN STOCK DISCONTINUED AS OF JULY, 1939. RUSH PROCESSED.

A buzzer on a video receiver sounded when the film started coming across. Sovern watched a Sony seventeen-inch monitor as Franklin Foreman and the technicians crowded around him. Simultaneously a video-tape machine made an instant print of the film. The men watched in total silence as faded images appeared before them. Their faces flickered with each sudden change of light and tone. The only sound was the whirring of the machinery's motors.

The film ran two minutes twenty-one seconds.

When it was over, Richard Sovern walked slowly to the red phone and asked to be connected directly to the President. In a few moments the soft, shy voice came over the wire.

"Yes, Dick, what is it?"

"Mr. President," Sovern replied, "Earhart is back."

CHAPTER 3

Sovern walked into the small yellow room in the basement of the White House. Six pairs of eyes greeted him. He felt the chill.

Seated at a round teakwood table were the secretaries of state and defense and the directors of the CIA, FBI, Defense Intelligence Agency, and National Security Agency. Together they made up the National Operations Board (NOB). Its role was to oversee the most sensitive activities of American intelligence. These men were the cream of the Washington establishment, scrupulous protectors of tradition and style. They did not regard Richard Sovern as one of them, and he rather enjoyed that.

Sovern discreetly glanced around at them as they spoke with each other. He knew they would try to nail him on the Earhart question. He saw a few of them look at their watches with the motions of men who thought their time was being wasted. They were typical, he thought, of executives trained in a system of set standards and respectable points of view. They had little time for the bizarre, little comprehension of the unusual.

Sovern felt ready for them.

His eyes wandered around the bare walls, which were broken only by a world map. Suddenly the door swung open and the President entered. A thinnish man of fifty-two, he had a slow gait and a look of singular unimportance. He wore plain gray trousers and a striped shirt, open at the neck. The members of NOB rose, but not with the snap that would greet a more commanding figure. Most considered themselves superior to him.

Sovern knew, though, that the President's casual manner hid a razor mind. But he also knew that the man could be both great and petty, with no way of predicting which way he would react. After more than a year in office no one could really say *what* he believed, if anything. Herblock, the cartoonist, depicted him as an octopus with tentacles reaching out to embrace every group. And Mort Sahl, noting his folksy manner but vague principles, insisted on calling him Harry S Nixon.

The President slumped in his chair as if ready to watch a football game. "I want to thank you all for making it over here so quickly," he said. "We've got kind of a problem. . . ." His voice trailed off, adding to the impression of a man without conviction. "Dick Sovern tells us that Amelia Earhart has come back . . ."

"Mr. President!"

The voice cut through the room like a knife. It belonged to Rudolph Peddington, director of the CIA, whose birdlike face was dominated by thick glasses.

"Sir," he said, "I don't like to throw a monkey

wrench into the works, but I want it known that CIA believes this is completely ridiculous. People don't return from the dead. Furthermore . . ."

"Uh, Rudy, I wish you'd hold that for later."

"I just wanted it in the record," Peddington answered.

"Fine, but let Dick brief us, then we'll see if we go along." He nodded to Sovern. "Go ahead."

Sovern opened the file. The same skeptical eyes that greeted him now glanced at the folder, as if wondering what tricks the CRG chief was hiding. "As you know," he began, "a lady landed in Los Angeles today. Before I talk about her, I've got to go back in time a little. I'm sure you've all heard theories about the disappearance of Amelia Earhart."

Everyone nodded that they had.

"Well, now I'm going to tell you the *real* story."

Heads darted forward in surprise and anger. Why was *Sovern* the one to know the truth?

"This has been kept from almost everyone in government at the order of eight presidents," Sovern explained. "It's been handed down since Roosevelt and given only to those who would need it if Earhart showed up. I was told by the President soon after his inauguration, when he gave me the EARHART file."

"I object," Peddington snapped. "I don't think we should be given material selectively. It endangers the Board's role as a check on illegal operations."

"I'll take the rap," the President said. "But we can discuss it another time." He gestured for Sovern to continue.

Sovern could still feel the resentment, but he also sensed anticipation and excitement, a belief that a deep secret was about to be unlocked.

"As you know," he said, "there had always been rumors that Amelia Earhart's last flight was a spy mission. Well, the rumors were true. President Roosevelt had asked her to photograph new Japanese bases in the Pacific. She agreed. So did her navigator, Fred Noonan.

"She took the pictures on the last leg of her trip. Suddenly she came under antiaircraft fire."

"Japanese shore guns?" Peddington asked.

"No. German destroyers. That's the strange thing. The Germans and Japanese were starting to cooperate about this time, and the ships were on a good-will visit. Earhart tried to evade, but a shell got her wing and she ditched near Howland Island."

"Why did the Nazis shoot?" a Board member asked.

"Possibly as a gesture of support for the Japanese," Sovern replied. "Or maybe they saw Earhart as a kind of prize."

"How do we know all this?" Peddington wanted to know.

"I'll get to that," Sovern answered. "Fred Noonan was probably executed, and Earhart was taken back to Germany. There was apparently some friction with the Japanese over this point, but the Germans weren't about to give her up. She was interned at Dachau . . ."

Most of the Board stiffened.

". . . but not in the extermination section. She was housed in a compound for foreign prisoners. She was supposed to be kept from anyone who'd tell the world she was there, but she was able to make contact with a Swiss consul. He was secretly working for the U.S. as a spy."

"How did she make contact?" the FBI director asked.

"We don't know. The consul wouldn't even tell our people. State thought there was probably a Swiss ring working inside the compound and that they arranged for notes to be passed from Earhart to our man."

"Why wasn't this made public?" Peddington asked.

"President Roosevelt thought public disclosure would harm the country. We'd have been admitting that we let a national heroine be captured, then did nothing to get her back. More important, the Germans would've wondered how we knew Amelia was being held. The Swiss connection might've been blown.

"And there was something else. The Germans wanted the capture kept secret. If Roosevelt had announced it, Earhart might have been executed."

"Why *did* they keep it secret?" someone asked.

"We never knew. Roosevelt thought there might be ransom involved, but the Germans never brought it up."

"How do we know those notes to the Swiss guy were genuine?" the Secretary of Defense inquired.

Sovern reached into the file and took out a cellophane packet containing many slips of paper. "We checked the handwriting," he replied. "Also there was a code that Roosevelt gave Earhart. She was known as HPH. It stood for Hyde Park High in Chicago, her alma mater."

Sovern took one slip of paper from the packet. "Here is one of the notes," he said. The others stared in fascination. Even Peddington quickly breathed on his glasses and cleaned them so he could see the note clearly.

"Notice here, in the lower left . . . HPH."

There was a long silence, broken only by the whoosh of an air conditioner and the occasional thump of a footstep on the floor above.

"You'd better tell 'em what she wrote," the President said.

Sovern took a deep breath, then adjusted himself in his chair. "Even though Earhart was under arrest," he said, "she was allowed to speak to some top Nazi brass. They apparently thought they could pick up something from loose talk and they liked speaking with the celebrity. Through these conversations Earhart pieced together data on new German fighters. The information was extremely valuable. But that wasn't the most important thing she did."

Inquisitive looks crossed the other faces as Sovern reached again into the packet. He removed a note tagged DOCUMENT 53—TOP SECRET—NO DISTRIB.

"In September, 1938, this note was delivered by the Swiss Embassy in Washington to the State Department: 'From talks with Nazi officers. Hitler planning Blitzkrieg across Europe starting with Czechoslovakia. Will include mass exterminations of enemies in camps like Dachau. Believe only assassination of Hitler can prevent this. Officers think Japanese will follow with attack in Pacific starting with US Naval Base Pearl Harbor.' "

Shock filled the room.

"My God," the FBI director said softly. "We knew."

"Yes," Sovern replied.

The men around the table stared at each other with a strange sense of embarrassment. They felt a kinship with their predecessors. They were part of the same club. Now they knew that these men whose portraits hung in their agencies, in some cases behind their own desks, had blown it.

A question had to be asked, but all were reluctant to ask it. Chester LeVan, the large, powerful-looking Secretary of Defense, finally elected himself. LeVan was formerly president of a shipbuilding conglomerate and spoke with the biting, steely rhythms of a fast-talking executive.

"Who ignored the warnings?" he asked bluntly.

Sovern looked toward the President.

"We're not here to discuss that," the Chief answered.

"Seems in this corner it's relevant," LeVan countered. "You've got dirt here. Maybe it was forty years back, but it's still dirt and even more messy than Watergate. The war might have been avoided had we listened to the lady."

The President's eyes suddenly glared. "As I said, we're not here to discuss that," he repeated. "Dick, go ahead."

"When the war began," Sovern went on, "the United States lost track of Earhart. She was presumed dead and the file was put into storage. That was until some weeks ago when a letter arrived at our London Embassy. It was ignored at first—they didn't know what to make of it—and it reached CRG through routine channels. Fortunately, someone who knew the EAR-HART file saw it. The letter reads simply, 'I'm coming home. HPH.' "

Every mind in the room focused on the lady in Los Angeles.

"When that flier landed out there today," Sovern went on, "we immediately tied her to the letter. We checked her fingerprints against Earhart's.

"They matched.

"We checked her voice against recordings of Earhart.

"They matched.

"So did dental charts and medical records."

There was a stony silence. The faces of the NOB were tense. Sovern read into those faces a grudging willingness to take the matter seriously. He knew he hadn't convinced these men, but no one was looking at his watch any longer.

"In the plane," he said, "we found the camera that our people had given Earhart in thirty-seven. Inside was the same film. Of course it was faded after all this time, but it did yield an image."

He took a videocassette from his briefcase and walked to the videotape player. It was hooked to a television set mounted on a table next to it. Sovern clipped the cassette into the chamber as members of the Board turned their chairs to see.

"This is a tape of that film," Sovern said, flipping a switch.

The scratchy leader came on, with the usual countdown of numbers printed backwards: 10-9-8-7-6-5-4-3-2-1. Then an image. It flickered at first, but an ocean was visible. The film had been taken from the air, the lens pointed straight down.

Then the outline of a beach appeared, barely discernible on the old film. Trees. Palms. A tropical island. Concrete.

The concrete continued. A runway. The wing of a plane in the upper left, but only a tiny part of it. Another plane. Single-engine fighter. A circle on its wing. Japanese.

The members of the Board squirmed.

The film went blank for a moment, as if the camera had been shut off. Then a new image faded in—badly churning seas, visible as the plane banked.

But then three antiaircraft shells burst close by.

The plane lurched, its camera still aiming down.

Three dots appeared on the ocean.

Sovern hit the rewind button, then spun a knob that magnified the image. The dots grew. So did two swastika flags.

German destroyers.

"Just beyond the horizon was Howland Island," Sovern said. The image began to shake and the horizon spun around. "She's hit." More shakes. Smoke. The plane leveled off and dove toward the water. The camera ran until the Electra ditched.

"She might've made it to Howland had they not fired," Sovern said. He shut off the machine and returned to his seat.

"Impressive," Peddington conceded. "But Dick," he went on, his tone patronizing, "we all know that the lady in Los Angeles is in her forties. Explain that."

"I can't."

"Try."

"I'd be guessing," Sovern said firmly.

"Then let's have some guessing."

The President turned to Sovern. "Dick, you must have *some* theory."

"I don't," Sovern replied. "Mr. President, one of the greatest mistakes we make is to expect quick answers, right or wrong, good or bad. We wouldn't want our doctor to guess, but some people enjoy guesswork in the White House."

Peddington turned beet red. "I wasn't suggesting . . ."

"I'll take the medical approach," Sovern said. "The answer to Earhart's youth awaits further study. It may even lie beyond our understanding. I rule out nothing."

Peddington sensed an opening.

"You think she was sent by the Divine Chief Pilot?" he asked with a wink.

Slight smiles of ridicule formed on some lips. Peddington's eyes rolled, a gesture he made sure that others saw. The President looked around to test the winds and found them blowing unfavorably for Sovern. He, too, now smiled lightly.

"Mr. President," Peddington inquired, "may I comment?"

"Yes."

Peddington jotted some notes, then tossed his pencil on the table. "Look," he said, "I admire Dick's imagination, but he's been had and ought to admit it. I think I can offer some explanation for what's happened."

Rudolph Francis Peddington was the consummate Washington insider. He had come to prominence as an assistant secretary of defense under Truman when only twenty-nine. Magazines featured him as a whiz kid. They reported how he had gone through Yale and the Harvard Law School with perfect grades, how he had won a Rhodes Scholarship and impressed Winston Churchill with a critique of British foreign policy.

He had been born to a Main Line Philadelphia family, which never hurt his chances for advancement. But no one could say that Rudolph Peddington leaned on family connections. He was eminently fit for every government position he had held, including ambassadorships to Moscow and Paris. His appointment as CIA director cleared the Senate without a dissenting vote.

When not in government Peddington was a partner in the New York law firm of Howell, Ruppert, and Peddington, whose clients included thirty-six of the Fortune 500 firms. He had been married to a descendant of John Hancock, but she died in 1972.

Peddington was neither easygoing nor a soft touch. He was precise, thorough, and combative. He dominated meetings of the Board, just as he had dominated every agency in which he had served. The thick glasses and high dome added to the impression he gave of

being an intellect. Richard Sovern couldn't stand more
than a few minutes of Peddington—few could—but he
agreed that he was one of the best men in federal
service.

"Now," Peddington said, "let's begin by examining
the plane in which the woman landed. Is it exactly
like the plane in which Earhart vanished?"

"It is," Sovern answered.

"But it *could* be a duplicate."

"It could, but the serial numbers on all sections
check out."

"Numbers come from files," Peddington argued.
"Files can be stolen."

"True," Sovern said, "but the camera . . ."

"That can be duplicated too. And as for the film,
you agree that any Hollywood special-effects man
could've produced it?"

"It's conceivable, but a check of the emulsion
showed it was more than forty years old."

"There are stocks of old film lying around," Peddington said. "The CIA has some, as you know from
your days with us." He stressed his next words. "They
come in handy for making pictures look old." He
paused, waiting for the message to sink in, then continued. "Now for the woman. She, or someone, sent a
note with the letters HPH. That, too, comes from a
file. I suggest—don't take this personally, Dick—that
CRG has a security problem. Possible?"

"Possible," Sovern conceded. "But you haven't dealt
with the fingerprints, voice, appearance, dental
charts . . ."

"Let's get to that," Peddington agreed. "If the
woman *is* Amelia Earhart, then she's been made
younger by plastic surgery."

"Our doctors checked that out," Sovern countered.

"There's no sign of it. Besides, surgery couldn't change bone age, and this woman has the bones of a thirty-five-year-old. Earhart's would be old and brittle."

Peddington quickly reviewed his notes. He had lost the point. "All right," he said, "then the lady is a fake. I attribute the fingerprints and the rest to advanced science. This may be a stunt by some doctors who've learned to rebuild parts of human bodies. I mean, there was the TV show, *The Bionic Woman*."

"And of course," Sovern shot back, "these same wonderful folks duplicated the plane, the film, cracked CRG's security to get Earhart's code, and knew *where* it was kept. You're stretching credibility to the torture point."

"I'm proposing ideas. It's possible someone in CRG is involved."

Sovern knew it was a cogent thesis, but a poor one. In fact he was struck by *how* poor it was. It required a combination of circumstances that was almost mathematically impossible. Was Peddington, he wondered, grasping at straws just to embarrass him?

"Even if Rudy's idea has some kick to it," the President asked, "why would anyone want to duplicate Amelia Earhart?"

"To make a bundle," Chester LeVan replied. "I've got a hunch about a cosmetics company. No kidding. If someone could copy a real body, imagine what they could do for dames."

Laughter. But it was laughter tinged with tension. It was possible. *Anything* was possible.

"What about a foreign power?" Sovern asked.

The question wasn't odd, but the source was. "I thought you told us-this was just little ol' Amelia flyin' home," LeVan said.

"That's right," Sovern replied, "but where did she come from, Shangri-La?"

The meeting was interrupted by an army sergeant who opened the door and moved quickly into the room. He walked to the President, handed him a paper, then left. The President read the bulletin, then looked up.

"Earhart just made a statement out in L.A. She says the only person she'll talk to about why she's here and what she wants is . . . Richard Sovern."

Surprise swept the room. Sovern looked the most surprised of all. "Why?" he asked.

The President examined the note further, then looked directly at Sovern.

"She says . . . *you'll* believe her."

CHAPTER 4

Los Angeles

Sovern walked into the small, dusty detention room at International Airport, a sense of electric anticipation running through him. The lady pilot was seated on a shaky wooden chair at a table covered with graffiti. Sovern had no doubt who she was as soon as he saw her; the cool, gray eyes, the short, tousled hair, the high, graceful cheekbones—unmistakably Amelia Earhart. The slim figure and stately bearing that were evident even as she sat gave further proof that this was the woman from the past, the international mystery, the legend who had returned. Sovern saw that she was intently reading an article in the newspaper about the takeover of a West German youth group by some neo-Nazis. As he entered she put the paper aside and looked up. He walked toward her and extended his hand.

"Richard Sovern," he said.

"Amelia Earhart," she replied. A chill went up Sovern's spine as she spoke her name. It intensified when she took his hand.

"Not used to meeting ghosts, are you?" Earhart asked.

"No," Sovern replied, expressionless. But he retained a healthy suspicion regarding her purpose. The fact that she was a heroine in the thirties, he knew, did not mean she was one now. "I'm glad you're back," he went on, trying to establish some rapport. "Welcome home."

"Thanks. It's good to be back," Earhart said with characteristic grace. She watched as Sovern looked her up and down, his medically trained eyes concentrating on her face, trying to find some hint of what had kept her so young. "Would you like a closer look?" she asked.

"Absolutely." He stepped nearer.

She turned her head from side to side. "I want you to look closely," she said. "It's very important that you see exactly what's been done." She now extended her hands so Sovern could study them. "Remarkable," she asked, "isn't it?"

"It certainly is. Would you explain?"

"We'll get to that," she said. "But there's something I want you to know first. You *do* believe I'm Amelia Earhart, don't you?"

"Yes," Sovern said, "unless I'm convinced otherwise, and I'm always willing to look at new evidence."

"Understandable."

"But I'm afraid I'm the only one who *does* accept you."

"I figured as much," Earhart sighed. "But it's important to dispel those doubts, Mr. Sovern—not only for my sake, but for the sake of our country, for *everyone's* country."

"What do you mean?"

"Everything in its time."

Sovern felt the tension starting to rise. He realized that Earhart would not be hurried, that she would orchestrate the details of her return. She gestured for him to sit.

"I prefer to stand," he said, asserting his refusal to lose control. He continued to stand, and gazed into Earhart's strong, resolute eyes.

"Mr. Sovern," she said, "I called for you because you have the best reputation in your business. People are likely to believe something if it comes from you that they might not believe coming from others. And you're likely to hear out a story that more limited men would reject."

"That's kind of you, but please be specific," Sovern said.

Earhart got up and walked slowly to the barred window looking out on the airfield. "You must promise me to keep an open mind . . . a *very* open mind."

"Of course."

"Does the date January thirtieth mean anything to you?"

Sovern thought for a moment. The date rang a bell that returned him to his youth. "That was Franklin Roosevelt's birthday."

"By coincidence. Anything else?"

Again Sovern searched his memory. "No," he replied.

Earhart looked directly into his eyes. "January thirtieth 1933," she said.

Sovern tensed. Immediately he knew. "That's the date Adolf Hitler took power in Germany."

"Correct."

"So?"

"Next January thirtieth—1983, less than two months from now—will be the fiftieth anniversary."

"And there'll be a commemoration," Sovern said sardonically.

"Yes."

"How do *you* know?"

Earhart paused. Some chatter in the hallway outside made her suddenly uneasy. "Look," she said, "this is very sensitive. You wouldn't want it to get out . . . prematurely." The movement of her eyes toward the walls said she knew something of electronic eavesdropping.

"Would you feel more comfortable in another room?" Sovern inquired. "Or we could go outside the airport."

"No, I've got a better idea, and it provides for absolute security. We'll talk in my plane."

"Fine," Sovern said, starting to walk toward the door.

"In the air."

Sovern was startled. The suggestion was odd, almost flippant, and it disturbed him. "That's hardly a place for an earthshaking announcement," he said wryly.

"Perhaps," Amelia replied, "but it's the one place I feel absolutely secure."

"Frankly, we have much better places. We've guarded the most sensitive people without incident. An old plane isn't the place to be."

"Throw a guard around the plane if you like," Earhart said firmly. "That's where I want to be." Then she walked briskly toward Sovern and suddenly pointed to her face. "Mr. Sovern," she declared, *"this* is Nazi science. You're going to learn a lot about it soon. And it's going to explain a great deal about what's happening now."

Sovern continued looking at this determined woman. Her request for him to fly with her made him hesitate a moment. Obviously certain risks were involved. What if she *was* a hoax, despite his belief? He could be in danger, perhaps the target of a kidnapping. He would have to be armed, he reasoned, and other planes would have to fly cover. And there might be some strange threat he couldn't anticipate, possibly linked to the bizarre science that retarded Earhart's aging.

But there was the other side. He was still convinced that this *was* Earhart, and the hint of her special knowledge of the Nazis, combined with a possible neo-Nazi threat in West Germany, was a mixture too powerful to be ignored. Besides, Sovern mused, he could hardly turn Earhart down and simply return to Washington with nothing more. He wasn't afraid of Rudolph Peddington and the other vultures, but he was realistic about keeping his guard up.

Earhart's penetrating eyes continued gazing at him, waiting for an answer. His finely honed instinct for risk and survival, nurtured over the years, told him that the benefits outweighed the liabilities. The instinct was helped along by a healthy dose of curiosity.

"All right," he finally said. "I don't like this but we'll fly."

Earhart's relief was evident in her grin. She snapped her full five feet eight inches to a mock attention. "I'm ready," she replied.

Sovern ordered Earhart's plane fueled and arranged for it to be followed by Navy Trackers from the carrier Ranger, cruising off the Los Angeles coast. He also arranged for radar stations to follow the Electra and keep watch for aircraft that might fly nearby.

An hour later the plane was ready. A baffled, yet fascinated ground crew rolled it onto the apron. Ear-

hart and Sovern then walked out to the Electra alone.
There were no loading ramps small enough for it, so
they were raised to the fuselage door by a cargo lift.

Sovern was immediately taken with the inside of the
relic. He had never been in a plane with a tail wheel
before and found it weird to walk uphill to the cockpit. The fuselage had no seats, only extra fuel tanks,
life preservers, and some bright yellow kites that had
been sent along on the final 1937 flight to be used as
emergency markers. The plane smelled of oil and gas-
oline and was dark except for a few glints of light
coming in through tiny windows. The feeling was
claustrophobic, like being inside the Alaska pipeline.

To Sovern the cockpit was a toy, and the clunky instrument panel had a Model-T quality. The two
pilots' seats were well-worn brown leather. This cockpit was not a confidence-inspiring control center, and
for a few moments Sovern felt a touch of rare fear
about having his life depend on it.

Only as Sovern watched Earhart go through her pre-
flight check did his concern subside. In addition he
was becoming aware, powerfully aware, of how for-
midable this woman was. She was out of the past, yet
almost an ideal model of what a modern woman
should be. She was thoroughly in control, yet retained
a quiet dignity, a softness, that was disarming. She
refused to raise her voice when making a point and
would not permit emotion to creep into her conversation. Sovern knew she had been a medical student,
nurse, social worker, teacher, businesswoman, lecturer,
flier, adventurer. She still showed the bearing, the
worldliness, of a woman for all seasons.

Earhart made a final check of the instruments, then
started the two engines. She taxied down the runway,

waited about three minutes for clearance from the Los Angeles tower, then roared into the air.

Sovern swallowed hard as the plane rose, the crushing in his ears reminding him that this was an unpressurized cabin. He felt the same tingling as he did before propellers were replaced by jets—the intense vibration that made parts of the plane buzz and excited the blood flow. There was always the sense that the plane would shake apart.

As the Electra banked, Sovern saw that Earhart appeared enveloped in a halo, outlined by the sparkling reflections bouncing off the Pacific. As she leveled off at seven thousand five hundred feet, cruising at one hundred ninety-five miles per hour, she eased back and relaxed a bit, reducing the engine speed. The vibrations quieted.

Sovern looked back through his side window to see, six miles behind and off to the right, three Grumman Trackers, twin-propeller Navy patrol planes.

"Where are we going?" Sovern asked.

"Nowhere special," Earhart replied, "but at least we can talk alone now."

"Okay. Shoot."

"I want to tell you something right off," Earhart said. "I don't know whether you will accept it or whether you *can* accept it. But it will color everything else I tell you, and I have a feeling it will change everything you do from this moment on." There was a forbidding pause. "Mr. Sovern," Amelia Earhart said, "Adolf Hitler is alive."

Maybe it was the shock of what Earhart said, maybe it was the sudden sense that he was being made a fool of, but Richard Sovern instantly discarded his pledge to keep an open mind and turned icy, almost contemptuous.

"That's ridiculous," he said firmly.

"And true," Earhart retorted with equal firmness.

"Look," Sovern went on, "Adolf Hitler committed suicide in his Berlin bunker in 1945."

"Did you see the body?"

Sovern stared at Earhart, but remained silent. Of course he hadn't seen the body, but he was not about to play this woman's rhetorical game.

"Maybe," Earhart suggested, "it would be easier to accept if I started at the beginning, back in 1937. Then you'd realize that Adolf Hitler is about to re-take power in Germany—on the fiftieth anniversary of his first takeover."

Sovern took a deep, pained breath, the breath of a man who didn't know whether he was present at a moment in history or a milestone in deception. "I'll hear you out," he said somewhat distantly, "but this had better be good."

Earhart moved around in her seat to a more comfortable position. Her eyes swept the instruments and looked about the sky automatically, watching out for other aircraft.

"I'm sure you don't remember much about 1937," she began.

"I was in grammar school," Sovern replied.

"Well, I was 39 and enjoying a marvelous flying career. I was internationally famous, had been decorated by governments, and was a friend of President and Mrs. Roosevelt. I decided, though, to end the adventurous part of my flying and to do it with something spectacular that had never been done before—flying around the world at the Equator.

"My husband arranged the flight. You may remember that he was George Palmer Putnam of the publishing family. Of course, George had sold his

interest in the book house years before to become an
executive at Paramount Studios and by 1937 was on
his own, a kind of promoter.

"I'm afraid 1937 wasn't a swell year," Earhart went
on. "President Roosevelt had just begun his second
term, but the depression was still going full blast. He
was furious with the Supreme Court for striking down
so much of his New Deal program and was trying to
have the law changed so he could appoint some new
justices.

"The Nazis," she continued, "had been in power
four years and were building up their forces. The
surrounding countries pretended not to notice. People
were living in a dream world. Then there was the
Japanese situation. I became involved in that in Febru-
ary of 1937 when President Roosevelt asked me to
come to the White House. He was his usual charming
self, which meant he wanted something.

"He told me about the situation in the Pacific. The
Japanese—he called them Japs—had been given some
islands by the League of Nations, and we suspected
they were building illegal bases on them. Information
was hard to get because they wouldn't let our planes
or ships near. The President thought that if a well-
known female flier on a publicized flight happened to
drift near a base and snapped pictures, the Japanese
wouldn't risk an incident by shooting her down."

"You got the hint," Sovern said.

"Between the eyes. And so, my navigator and I took
off on May seventeenth. We arrived on the other side
of the world at Lae, New Guinea, at the end of June.
We prepared there for the longest part of our trip,
almost three thousand miles over water from Lae to
tiny Howland Island, which is two thousand miles
southwest of Hawaii. We planned to fly in an arc,

skimming along the southern rim of the Japanese-controlled islands.

"The flight progressed well enough, and we were able to shoot our film without opposition from the Japanese. After the photography we headed into miserable weather. It was overcast, impossible for navigation, and we were having radio trouble. We were lost, running north and south, and running low on fuel. Then we passed over this line of destroyers and assumed they were Japanese. As you know, of course, they actually were German. I don't know why they shot us down, but we were so low it's possible they thought we were photographing them. Or maybe they read my wing number, which was famous, and decided they wanted me as a prisoner.

"I was forced to ditch and they took us aboard one of the destroyers. They also recovered the plane."

"Your navigator, Fred Noonan," Sovern asked, "how did he die?"

Earhart lowered her eyes. "Fred didn't survive the trip to Germany," she said. "They told me he died of internal injuries caused by the ditching, but I know he suffered no more than a jolt. I think they just considered him surplus."

"Go on," Sovern said.

"I arrived in Germany and was held in a private apartment at Dachau until 1943. I was often visited by high German air officers, who seemed to regard me as a curiosity. They tried to pry information out of me about American planes and boasted about their war plans and relations with the Japanese. That's how I pieced together the warning about Pearl Harbor.

"In 1943 I was taken to a vast underground medical complex near Berlin. There I was told about a so-called fountain of youth project."

"Explain," Sovern requested.

"The Nazi doctors were working on techniques to retard aging. They assumed it was a curable disease and had developed a machine that they attached to the bloodstream, something like today's kidney machines. It wasn't completely effective, but they believed they could add ten or fifteen years to a life span through regular treatments, and more through total treatment."

"Total treatment?"

"They wanted to attack all the major symptoms of aging at the same time."

Quickly, Sovern's medical mind began to click as he silently catalogued the steps in the aging process. He knew that many of the major symptoms of old age involved deterioration of the circulatory system. Mental failings, an inability to move with ease, the fading of sight and hearing, were often caused by an insufficient blood supply. The Nazis would have had to attack that problem in ways far more advanced than even the known techniques of the 1980's.

Sovern also knew that the Germans would've had to suppress the gastrointestinal disturbances of advancing age. And they would've had to retard the changes in bone tissue that make aging bones brittle and susceptible to fracture, as well as develop some technique for combating the diminished lung functions of old age.

Finally, Sovern realized, the Nazi doctors would've had to unlock the mystery of how body cells age and why the aging cells are more susceptible to malignancy and to the accumulation of calcium, cholesterol, and other chemical substances that attack the system.

"Tell me about this so-called total treatment," he asked Earhart.

"A person would be attached to a special machine,

put to sleep, and treated. The treatment could last weeks or even months at a time. You'd be awakened, exercised, studied by the doctors, and maybe given a few months of non-treatment in the medical complex. Then you'd be put back on the machine. One of the first things you'd notice, by the way, was that the treatment had a jarring effect on memory. It was a selective effect—you'd remember some things and forget others; there didn't seem to be any particular order. The problem continues to this day. There are things I remember about that period and there are things that are blanks."

"I see," Sovern said in a studious, doctor's manner. "I assume by what you just said that they gave you the total treatment."

"Yes. And you can see that it worked."

"Who ordered it for you?"

"Adolf Hitler."

"Are you sure?"

"They reminded me of it every time I was awakened."

"Why would Hitler order this for you?"

Earhart paused and looked out at a low-lying cloud below. "I don't know," she finally replied. "I heard the phrase 'politically useful' a few times, but I don't know quite what they meant. I do know that Hitler was fascinated with me, especially by the fact that I have German blood. I do have a theory as to the real reasons he might have had to preserve me with the new machine."

"Shoot," Sovern said.

"Let me get to that in a moment," Earhart replied. "It needs a little background." She paused once more to collect her thoughts, some of them blurred by the memory-dimming effects of her treatment. "I recall

being awakened on the machine one day and being
told that the war was about over and that Germany
was defeated. We were being moved, someone said."

"Where?"

"South. That's all I know. The 'National Redoubt,'
one of the doctors called the place. Do you know anything about that?"

"Yes," Sovern replied strongly, his eyes alive with
recognition. "At the end of World War II the Allies
believed that much of the Nazi leadership escaped to
a secret hiding place in the Bavarian region. It was
known, presumably, as the National Redoubt. In fact,
one of the main reasons the American army swung
south in the last days of the war rather than going on
to Berlin was to try to find this place. They didn't,
and eventually our intelligence people concluded that
it never existed. Obviously we were right the first
time."

"I wish they had found it," Earhart said somberly,
as if suggesting what might have been. "When we arrived there I heard a lot of talk about the Reich eventually regrouping. No Fourth Reich, mind you. They
said the Third would return. I kept hearing the German equivalent of Reich Reborn."

Sovern instantly recognized this as the name of the
largest, best organized, and most violent of the emerg-
ing neo-Nazi groups in Germany.

"They continued your treatment there?" Sovern
asked.

"Yes, although the doctors were very weary from the
war. They looked older every time I awakened from
the treatments."

"How come they looked old if they had this machine?"

"That," Earhart replied, "is the most important

question you can ask. They had only two machines. A doctor told me they had trouble getting a rare alloy needed for a critical part . . . I don't remember its exact name. They only had enough to build the two before their supply was cut. And each machine had to be available at all times to the patient, even when he wasn't connected to it, in case of emergency."

"Who got the other machine?" Sovern asked tersely.

"Guess . . ."

"Can you be *sure*?" There was a sternness, almost an anger, in Sovern's voice as he confronted the possibility that Hitler had survived.

"I saw him getting the treatment," Earhart replied. "It was through a glass partition, but it was him. And maybe that's why I got the treatment first."

"I don't understand," Sovern said.

"My theory," Earhart answered, "is that Hitler wanted the first machine used for me to be sure that the treatment worked before he went on it."

"Why you?"

"Frankly, I think it was a question of Hitler's ego. If I died, that would have been it. But if the treatment worked, *he* would have been the one to preserve Amelia Earhart. Please don't think I'm immodest, but Hitler was becoming totally contemptuous of those around him. I think—if I may say so—that I represented a kind of heroic purity to him."

"Interesting," Sovern said. "That's a very good analysis of the way the man thought. Did you have much contact with him?"

"None. Not in all these years. And no one ever talked about him."

"Then how do you know he's still . . ."

"I saw him late last year before my escape. They led me to a glass-enclosed room where the other ma-

chine was kept. I looked in for a few minutes and saw
him lying on a table. His eyes were open . . . and
unforgettable. He's older of course, but the equipment
has retarded his age. Remember, Hitler wasn't that
old in 1945 when the world saw him last. He was only
fifty-six. He's ninety-two now, but when I saw him he
looked like a healthy man in his seventies. Many active
leaders are that old."

"You aren't giving me evidence," Sovern insisted.
"That could've been a fake, an imposter. They may
have been setting you up."

Earhart turned solemnly to Sovern. "Look at me,"
she demanded, "and see what these people are capable
of doing. Do you really want to take the chance that
the man I saw was a fake? Consider what's happening
with those neo-Nazi groups in Germany, consider what
could happen if the Third Reich is reborn there."

There was no rational, informed answer Sovern
could give. The only real evidence he had that Hitler
was dead was submitted years before by the Soviet
Union, not necessarily the best source of reliable information. He was determined to press on, to gather
more facts.

"The treatment you received," he asked Earhart,
"was it the same as Hitler's?"

"From what I saw of the equipment, yes."

"Did they stop your treatment at any point?"

"Yes. Last year. They said they were going to re-
orient me to modern society. I was to be trained to
serve under the leadership of—they never used his
name or title, they just called him the greatest man
who ever lived. I went through educational briefings
during which I learned about developments that had
occurred since 1943: television, the atomic bomb, jet
planes, and the like."

"Did they tell you specifically what they planned to do?"

"Only that the Third Reich would retake Germany on January thirtieth."

Sovern leaned over toward Earhart, once again studying her closely. His eyes focused on her hairline and then on her hands. The youthfulness of her skin was incredible, but he did, when looking intently, notice the beginnings of some age lines. He seemed to hesitate before asking his next question, as if embarrassed.

"Go ahead," Earhart urged him, understanding.

"Did anything . . . happen to you when they stopped the treatments?" Sovern asked.

"Yes," Earhart replied firmly. "I began aging. I noticed it almost immediately, especially around the eyes. And some hairs started turning gray at the roots. And . . . I began moving more slowly. Nothing dramatic. But I noticed."

"Is there anything you can do about these things?"

"Nothing I know of. The Nazis never told me. They probably didn't even know the aftereffects of the treatment."

"No, probably not," Sovern agreed. He pondered for a few moments, assessing the implications of what Earhart had just revealed. "If they take Hitler off, then, and try to return him to power, then he too . . ." He stopped. He realized he was onto something critically important. Earhart looked over at him, understanding what was going through his mind. If Hitler was in fact alive, Sovern reasoned, and was now preparing to try to retake power, then he would begin to deteriorate. Logically, Sovern knew, he would deteriorate more dramatically than Earhart since he was in much worse condition and was much older when his treatments first started.

But there was one problem with this theory. "Could the machine be moved?" Sovern asked.

"It was big—about twice the size of an old iron lung," Earhart replied. "But I guess they could move it."

"So no matter where Hitler traveled during his return to power, he could be put back on it . . ."

Earhart shook her head negatively. "You don't understand," she said. "In the time between treatments you couldn't think clearly. There were even periods of incoherence. A man trying to seize power—or do *anything* besides simply exist and move muscles—would have to be taken off permanently."

"I see," Sovern said. He had a vision in his mind of Adolf Hitler deteriorating and finally dying. He tucked the idea in the recesses of his mind, determined to relentlessly pursue the rest of the Earhart saga.

"How did you end up here?" he asked bluntly.

"The details are vague at this point," Earhart replied.

"Vague? You said it was only last year."

"It's the effect of the treatment. As I said, there's no logic to the clouding effect it has had on my memory. I only remember there was this scientist. I don't recall his name. He was very old. He had worked for the Nazis since before the war. I remember him last year saying how bitter he was, and some of his friends too, because they were passed over for top positions, excluded from the decision-making, and kept in the dark about future plans. He had grown disillusioned with the movement's leadership . . . he felt betrayed."

"And to get back he let you escape?"

"Escape may not be exactly the right word," Earhart said. "I was let out one day. The next thing I knew I was being escorted aboard a TWA flight from Munich to New York. My passport was in the name of a Mary Conway."

"Who put you aboard?"

"I believe they were two of the people from the lab. They must've turned against the Nazis too. We flew to New York and then on to Denver. We were picked up by car at the airport and driven to the outskirts of Reno, Nevada."

"Why Reno?"

"That's where my plane was. One of the men with me explained that the dissidents who decided to free me to get back at the other Nazis, also decided to get my plane to America. Apparently they felt its presence would help attest to my authenticity. It had been stored in sections somewhere in the south of West Germany, and the dissidents simply had the crates shipped to a small airfield near Reno, listing the contents as antique aircraft parts destined for a private collector." Earhart turned to Sovern and smiled. "The private collector was Mary Conway."

"Nicely done," Sovern conceded, hating to give a compliment to Nazis even if they were dissidents.

"These people gave me an apartment, a bank account, and registration for my plane, which they had arranged to have assembled. The registration was falsified, of course, and the plane did not yet have my old I.D. number. I painted that on later."

"What happened to the dissidents?"

"I have no idea. They just disappeared. I'm sure they were afraid of being found out, and I don't think they had much use for me personally. They just saw releasing me as a means toward retaliation.

"I knew the Nazis would be hunting for me," Earhart continued. "I wanted to make contact with the U.S. government fast. I went to a local FBI office and told my story. They threw me out and accused me of being emotionally unstable. I was tempted to cause some trouble just to attract attention, but I was afraid that would just draw some Nazi assassin.

"I tried a local office of the Defense Department. Even when I offered to prove my identity with fingerprints, they laughed. The plane, I realized, was the key to establishing who I was. My only chance was to do something quick and spectacular with the plane, something that would ensure putting me under Federal protection. That's when I got the idea to fly into Los Angeles unannounced."

"How did you learn about me?" Sovern asked.

"I did library research in back issues of newspapers. I tried to find the name of someone I could trust who might understand the medical work done on me."

"Go on."

"My main concern was whether I could still fly the plane even after it was checked out mechanically. I went through my routines on the ground, refamiliarizing myself with the controls. My lax memory didn't cause any problems. It seems the treatment only affects the memory of things that happened after the machine is first connected.

"I took off and made some practice flights. I was wobbly at first, but soon regained my confidence. Finally I flew to a deserted airstrip at the edge of the Mojave desert to paint my old registration number on the plane, and flew on to Los Angeles. And the rest, Mr. Sovern, you know."

There was silence.

Neither Sovern nor Earhart said a word as the Electra headed back to the airfield. Earhart sensed that Sovern was choosing his strategy, and she was right. He wondered how the National Operations Board could be convinced that Earhart was genuine or at least was worth investigating. She had not, after all, presented any proof that Hitler was alive—only claims and recollections. Sovern himself could not reasonably accept much of what she had said, only that it should not be ignored. Once on the ground he cabled the President:

REQUEST YOU CONVENE MEETING OF NATIONAL OPERATIONS BOARD AT CIA HEADQUARTERS LANGLEY TONIGHT. WILL PRESENT EARHART'S STORY. HAVE VERY DIFFICULT SITUATION.

II

Sovern and Earhart flew east in an Air Force transport. During the flight Sovern reviewed the highlights of a speech he was scheduled to make on political conditions in West Germany before the Foreign Policy Association. Since the topic was of obvious interest to Earhart, he gave her a copy of the speech to read. She studied it, seeing in its thrust the potential for the tragedy she had come back to prevent:

The new Nazi problem should not be exaggerated nor should it be minimized. We saw in Germany in the early thirties just how quickly a functioning regime can be toppled. We saw the same in Iran in 1979.

Certainly the historic German obsession with order was made more insistent by the terrorist activities of left-wing students in the late seventies. As West Germans have been subjected to the kidnappings and murders of the Baader-Meinhof gang, the hijackings of airliners, and the bombings of buildings, some have recalled a time of enforced law and order under the Führer.

The partial collapse of the economic miracle that made Germany a major world economic power in the decades after its loss in World War II has contributed to the present condition. Inflation has risen; many students cannot find jobs that equal their qualifications; many others question a society that seems to be going nowhere. The Mercedes-Benz and the large house have become the reigning symbols of success. Under Hitler, some recall, there was a national spirit.

False nostalgia, reaction to terrorism, a search for something more than materialism—these are the ingredients of what one international magazine has called "Germany's new Hitler wave." Small, perhaps; seemingly feeble, perhaps—but remember that the same was said of the little band of Nazis in the late twenties. We are trying, through the West German government, to counter the neo-Nazi groups. No one can guarantee success because no one knows for sure what is in the minds and hearts of the German people.

At the same time the Soviets have repeatedly warned that Russia will move decisively, militarily, if the Nazis ever come even close to returning to power. They may, of course, be much closer than anyone imagines. After all, only the lack of a single charismatic leader prevents them from unifying their various groups and making a serious stab for control.

After she read the speech, Amelia Earhart re-read that last sentence over and over.

The time, she knew, was almost at hand.

CHAPTER 5

Langley, Virginia

The National Operations Board met on the seventh floor, the director's floor, of the Central Intelligence Agency at nine that night. Richard Sovern sat at one end of a long, teakwood table, opposite the President.

The room, like many in the CIA, was gun-metal gray, with no windows. The steady whoosh of air conditioning seemed stronger than usual here. Fluorescents softened everything, but a defective one gave off a steady, grating buzz. At each place on the table aides had put a yellow lined pad and several sharpened pencils. Behind the President was a red princess wall phone for emergencies. The carpeting was industrial-quality, deep blue, new, and shedding, leaving deposits of fiber on the shined shoes of the board. It was also sizzling with static electricity.

The atmosphere was urgent, the feeling magnified by the advisory that had just arrived from the CIA station chief in West Germany:

CHANCELLOR FRANZ HOLMUTH OF
WEST GERMANY MURDERED BY GUNFIRE
OUTSIDE RESIDENCE IN BONN. KILLER
ESCAPED, BUT SMALL NAZI FLAG LEFT
AT SCENE. MESSAGE FROM CLANDESTINE
TRANSMITTER STATED HOLMUTH
FOUND GUILTY OF PRO-COMMUNIST AC-
TIVITY BY NATIONAL SOCIALIST PEO-
PLES COURT.

Sovern, particularly, was stunned by the news. The
Nazis had engaged in some petty violence and occasionally in the murder of minor figures. The idea
that they would assassinate the leader of their country
seemed impossible, far-fetched, perhaps the work of
some bizarre unit on their fringe. Sovern wondered,
though, whether this was the first reaction to the public emergence of Amelia Earhart in Los Angeles, the
first sign of panic by those Nazis surrounding Hitler,
the first indication that they were prepared to act on a
vast scale . . . before being trapped by information
Earhart might provide.

And Sovern wondered about something else. He
wondered about Hitler's physical condition. If he had
been taken off the machine to prepare for a takeover
attempt, how much had he deteriorated?

The Nazi attempt to seize power that Earhart had
reported in her strange flight with him might, Sovern
knew, come earlier. The telling combination of Earhart's surfacing and Hitler's possible deterioration
could advance the timetable dramatically, providing
little time—or no time—to counter it.

As the Board was seated, the first repercussions of
the West German chancellor's murder started coming

in. The red phone behind the President buzzed. The Chief picked it up.

"Yes?" he asked.

"Hotline coming, sir," was the message delivered tersely by the CIA watch office a few doors down. It meant simply that a note from the Soviet Government was coming through on the hotline and would be delivered to the President within moments. There was no point in starting the meeting without first knowing what the Russians would say.

About a minute later a CIA clerk entered with a sheet of paper, delivered it to the President, and left promptly. The President read out loud.

"This is from Moscow. Quote. It is apparent from the murder of the West German chancellor that you are incapable of controlling events in that country. The Soviet government looks with continued dismay on the continuing permissiveness toward these Nazi groups and warns that it will not stand idly by if a Nazi regime is restored or even threatened. We are prepared to shed blood to protect our security against the Nazi barbarism. Unquote."

The President looked around the room. "That pretty much states the issue, doesn't it?" he reflected. The members of the Board could see that he was deeply disturbed by the note. The Russians had become increasingly threatening, and the President wanted no part of military confrontations.

"Mr. President," Sovern said, "I ask to be recognized to report on my conversation with Amelia Earhart. I'm afraid it won't make the situation any better."

"She has stuff on the Nazis?" the President inquired.

"Stuff is putting it mildly."

"Well," the President responded, "I guess there's

really nothing to say about the Russian note. We know how they feel and we'd better solve this thing. Go ahead, Dick."

Sovern pulled his chair closer to the table, cleared his throat, and proceeded to give a twenty-minute briefing on every important detail of his talk with the lady flier. He outlined the story of her capture in the Pacific, her imprisonment, the daring medical experiments, the secret National Redoubt in the south of Germany, and her escape with the help of Nazi dissidents. The members listened in tense, if skeptical, silence, each man fascinated, if less than overwhelmed by the lack of substantiation. And then, at the end, Sovern dropped the bombshell, presenting Earhart's incredible claim that Adolf Hitler was alive and would seize West Germany on January 30, 1983.

There were a few gasps and a snicker or two. Mostly, the Board members simply stared at Sovern. No, they couldn't accept the claim at face value, echoing Sovern's own belief, but few were rejecting it outright. Even Rudolph Peddington, Sovern's chief nemesis, listened carefully, weighing each statement. The Soviet note, the reality of neo-Nazism, the medical proof that Earhart was indeed Earhart, the fact that no *American* had ever seen Hitler's body, combined to make these men consider the chance that Earhart's story might be true.

Sovern was determined to make the best possible case for Earhart so that at minimum an investigation of the Hitler story could go forward. "I think," he told the Board, "that there's a chance her story about Hitler may have substance." He looked around. The glances were doubting, but the Board was continuing to give him a hearing. "Consider these facts," he went on forcefully. "First, we know that Earhart was held by the Nazis. So she had *access* to information.

"Second, many of her details are checkable. We've already checked her story about the plane being shipped back to America in parts, and customs records confirm it. My people in Germany are already interviewing the German shipping agents who handled the transaction.

"Third, and most important, there's no reason for Earhart to give us the warning about Hitler unless she thought it was true. Of course, it's always possible she's been brainwashed, but we've seen no evidence of it. Her own youthfulness suggests the Nazis did have some kind of device as she claims. I admit, as a physician, that this kind of thing sticks in my throat. I'm not very high on science fiction. But the Nazis were advanced in many areas, and although I'm sorry to say it, their medical experiments in concentration camps may have given them some insight into the aging process that we still don't have today.

"The key question is, if they *did* have an age-retarding device, who else did they want to preserve? The answer is fairly obvious.

"Look," Sovern concluded, his audience still riveted, "I can't prove Hitler is alive, but I strongly recommend we pursue the possibility. We can't responsibly avoid it. The benefits of going all out on this thing far outweigh the costs."

He leaned back and once again eyed the faces turned toward him. Most were blank. No one was jumping to conclusions or making commitments.

"It bothers me," Peddington said.

"Of course," Sovern answered. "It's not a cut and dried thing. It bothers me too."

"No, no, no," Peddington retorted. "You don't understand. It bothers me because it's too easy. Now you're not a lawyer, Dick, but we lawyers are trained to suspect easy stories. Her escape, if you call it that, was too easy. Having the plane conveniently brought to America was too easy. Learning to fly again, the same. Avoiding getting caught by the Nazis . . . too easy. I think she's involved with the Nazis, too, but on *their* side. Maybe she's a plant."

"Maybe," Sovern agreed. "As I said, we don't rule anything out. But remember that we weren't on the inside of the Nazi business. We're in no position to know."

"Have you set a lie detector test?" Peddington asked.

Sovern knew Peddington was trying to rattle him, but he retained his usual cool. "I've been thinking of it," he replied, "but what good would it do? They're only eighty percent accurate, and the treatments she's received may make her responses different from a normal person's."

"All right," Peddington conceded, "what about hypnosis?"

"Again," Sovern replied, "her responses might be abnormal, yet we'd never know since we've never had experience with such a person."

"So there's no scientific way of checking her out?" the President asked.

"Mr. President," Sovern answered, "there's no scientific way to check *anyone* out. If there were, there'd be no need for trials. All the gadgets, including the new voice stress analyzer that detects lies by stresses in the voice, are only partly accurate. You wouldn't base national policy on them."

"No," the President agreed. "We could get creamed."

Chester LeVan, his European-cut Cardin shirt making his chest muscles more prominent than ever, shuffled some memoranda before him, a skeptical look on his oversized lips. "Well, it's tough to believe this tale," he said, "but we all know what's been happening in Germany. Damned if I'd recommend we just shove this in the file." He raised his bushy eyebrows and turned them on Peddington.

"Well," Peddington said, "I'd hate to have this administration make a fool of itself. Of course we should pursue the Nazi thing and we *have* been. But Hitler? I mean if he *is* alive, where is he?"

"Earhart didn't know," Sovern replied. "It could be Germany, Latin America, almost anywhere outside the Communist bloc."

"You don't think he's *here*, do you?" the President asked.

"Why not? This country's made it awfully easy for Nazi war criminals to get in since the war. I suspect there'd be a means of getting Hitler in and hiding him."

"Now wait," Peddington said, "let's talk turkey on this thing. Even if Hitler got back to West Germany, who said he could take over?"

"No one," Sovern said tersely. "But do you want to chance it? After all Hitler is becoming glamorized again in some parts of German society. It's possible he could take power by perfectly legal means if there's some kind of convulsion over there, just as he did in thirty-three. With the right manipulation of the public and a few more murders of top officials, we couldn't predict what would happen."

Rudolph Peddington leaned back and smiled from

behind his thick glasses. It was an ugly wince, but it expressed the self-satisfaction of one who believed himself on the verge of winning an argument. "And if Mr. Führer did take over," he said quietly, "my CIA boys would simply blow his head off and end the whole thing."

"Wonderful idea," Sovern replied, his eyes wide but filled with sarcasm.

"Well," Peddington asked, "so what's our big problem?"

"Our big problem," Sovern answered, "is that we might not get to him. He could be protected as solidly as Castro is. And your boys tried to get that one, didn't they? Also, killing him once he goes public could produce a backlash from his followers with a lot of American troops getting killed. Then there's the Russians. Who knows what they'd do if Hitler actually came back? We've got their threats in writing," Sovern continued, gesturing toward the hotline report in front of the President. "The missiles could be over Munich and Bonn before we could act. Let's not forget that we've got a treaty to defend West Germany, even if it has a fascist government."

The President glanced at each man, then at Sovern. "We're sittin' here talkin'," he said, "and the damned thing'll be over in less than two months. I say we go at the Hitler thing full steam. Christ, I've got an election in a couple years. If we sit on our hands and old Adolf comes goose-steppin' out of some forest, I'm licked."

Sovern was not surprised that this President saw the issue in personal terms. He was an obsessively political man. But if it meant coming to the right decision, he reasoned, it didn't much matter.

"Dick," the Chief continued, "go to it." He looked around with a devilish grin. "Anyone disagree?"

"Abstain," Peddington said. "Let the record show it."

No one, of course, would actually try to counter the President's decision.

"What's step number one?" the President inquired.

"First," Sovern replied, "I'm going to make sure of Earhart's security in Washington. I don't want any blunders. Then I notify the Russians."

"Whoa!" LeVan objected. "Leave them out of this."

"We can't. They declared Hitler dead in forty-five and later presented evidence to back the claim. We've got to confront them. If they give us something overwhelming to prove their point, then Earhart's wrong."

"I buy," the President commented.

"Next," Sovern went on, "we check the brown boxes in the Archives." There were nods of recognition.

"What brown boxes?" the Chief asked.

Sovern took a long draw on his pipe. "At the end of the war," he said, "we captured millions of Nazi documents. They're stored in brown cartons over at the Archives. Many have never been touched."

"So?" the President asked.

"It's possible there's something on the age-retarding work over there. Those documents have revealed incredible things before. For instance in 1977 some Archives researchers discovered the plans for an elaborate Nazi energy program that included synthetic fuels. It's actually been helpful to our own efforts. Of course, I'll need an army of intelligence people to go through all that stuff."

"You've got what you need."

Sovern had won. Although the room was laced with skepticism and Peddington was openly contemptuous, the CRG director had the President's support to proceed with the Earhart mystery.

He left the CIA building, heading for the most critical assignment in his career—a possible confrontation with Adolf Hitler.

CHAPTER 6

Williamstown, Massachusetts

"The Earhart defection has changed everything," Willy Haas said as he sat at the head of a long, early-American table in the farmhouse along Route Forty-three.

At the table were five other men, almost all in their sixties, who made up the Council of Rebirth, the ruling body of Reich Reborn. Haas was operations director of the organization and president of the council.

"Poor security," Haas snapped in his moderate German accent, "always poor security. That was the problem when they tried to kill Der Führer in 1944. That is the problem now." The lines in his narrow face reflected his sixty-seven years, most of them spent in service to the Nazi cause. "So she got to the American, Richard Sovern," he went on, "and is telling everything she knows. And because of her the symbolism of January 30, 1983, the date we have looked forward to for a generation, must fall. But, as in the past, we shall be made stronger by applying our own will."

The lines in his face tightened. Haas wore a look of iron. "Prepare to leave Williamstown at once!" he ordered. "We are going *home*."

Although the change had been brought about by a disaster, the others broke into spontaneous applause. Two younger people, aides to the council, peeked in from the living room and also applauded. They could sense the electricity, the determination of the men around the table.

Willy Haas, American citizen, member of Rotary, former Scout leader, New England farmer, had been born in Leipzig during World War I, the time of the first German humiliation of the twentieth century. His father had died in that war. Haas had always bragged that his father was a hero who had fallen for Germany in a charge against the French army of Marshal Foch. Actually Gunther Haas had been shot for desertion. Willy had tried to compensate for the family shame by fanatical devotion to national service.

He had been a minor postal official when he joined the Nazi party in 1938. Party leaders quickly became impressed with his loyalty and his ability to run a small office. When war came he was made a captain in the Waffen SS and assigned to organize security for one of the sections in Hitler's Berlin headquarters. After the war he came to the United States, his way paved by the strange network of immigration officials and sponsoring organizations that seemed to have great difficulty detecting former Nazis. Haas had no surviving family. His wife and only son had been killed in a British air raid.

When Haas arrived in the United States he had already been given a mission by the postwar Nazi hierarchy: recruit sympathizers and train them for sabotage, espionage, and military administration. At the same time he was to become a farmer in Massachusetts as a cover. The party provided him with all the money he needed. He worked his way up, becoming director as the older Nazis died off.

He was not a particularly "Nazi-looking" conspirator. He was partially bald, but the remaining hair was dark brown, not blond. His height was medium with a slight bulge around the middle. Haas's voice, for a man who had routinely participated in mass murders, was soft and grandfatherly, broken occasionally by a smoker's hoarseness. Everyone in Reich Reborn, though, was aware of his sadistic nature. He had once beaten a man to death with a shovel because the man had delivered a secret message twenty minutes late.

The council itself was a remarkably capable group. Its members had been chosen by Haas because they possessed the skills that would be needed by senior administrators in a new Nazi regime. They were experts in law, government, defense, and science. All had been junior party officials in the days of Nazi glory. All had met one of the demanding prerequisites for council membership: carrying out an act of terror in which at least two civilians died.

Besides Haas and the council there was one more senior Nazi, by far the most important. He was simply called the Chairman, for the use of Nazi terminology was strictly forbidden for security reasons—and "Führer" was the most Nazi term of all.

The Chairman resided in a room at the end of a corridor inside the farmhouse. The room was protected by an iron door and a steel gate outside. It had no windows and was fully furnished with the medical equipment the Chairman needed to retard his aging.

"Have our people in Munich been informed of the acceleration in plans?" a council member asked Haas in the clipped, military manner of these meetings.

"General Gottes has been notified," Haas replied with authority. "He assures me the change can be carried out with the usual efficiency."

"The last report, though, mentioned deficiencies in weapons and ammunition."

"That has been rectified," Haas announced. "We recently broke the programming code on an American Seventh Army computer and are buying our supplies directly from American firms. The bills are going to the West German Defense Ministry."

"Excellent work," a council member stated.

"That is the minimum we expect," Haas retorted.

"The Chairman's condition?" asked another member.

Haas glanced in the direction of the sealed room. "He is in reasonable condition," he said. "Obviously, there are still tired spells and memory lapses, and there has been some aging in his face since we reduced the treatments to return him to normal functioning. But his spirits are good. His brain as always is superb." Haas hesitated. "He was very upset about Amelia Earhart. Those responsible for this problem shall be hunted down like the common criminals they are. I myself will be glad to fire the shots and watch their heads explode."

Haas gestured for the two young aides to go to the Chairman. "See if he needs medicine," he ordered. The two were Greta Berndt and Helmut Pflug. Both had joined Reich Reborn in West Germany as a reaction to the terror of young leftists. They were now in their early twenties and completely trusted by Willy Haas.

"They will remain behind," he told the council. "They will take care of the house and maintain our network in America."

"Is any attempt being made to get Earhart back?" a gray-haired council member who had flown in from Chicago inquired.

"Of course," Haas replied. "There are operations underway in New York. But even if they succeed, she may have already revealed too much. We don't actually know how much she absorbed in Germany, however. She was informed of the overall plan as part of our scheme for using her, but, God knows, some blundering fool may have told her more."

"There will be violence to get her back?"

"If need be. Of course."

"I wonder," said Wilfred Koenig, a legal expert, "whether violence in America is in our interests. The lives involved are naturally unimportant, but it could antagonize at a critical time."

"Koenig," Haas replied patronizingly, "stick to your legal opinions, will you. There are more important things than popularity. We were never popular in the old days, but we were *very* effective. The Jew was most popular in 1945 when the stories about the camps came out. Popularity goes to the weak. Being despised is no shame if one is strong."

There were mutterings of total approval. Haas made a mental note to watch Koenig carefully for signs of softness. He then glanced at his watch. "Each of you," he announced, "will be given a sealed envelope with your orders. You will commit them to memory, then the papers will be burned. We will make a detailed inspection of the house and remove anything that might be of use to our opponents."

The phone rang. Haas looked toward it with eager anticipation. "That," he said, "is one of our people in New York. Our operation is underway."

II

BULLETIN
WASHINGTON, DEC. 3 (AP) THE FEDERAL AVIATION AGENCY ANNOUNCED TO-NIGHT THAT THE LADY WHO LANDED IN LOS ANGELES CLAIMING TO BE AME-LIA EARHART WAS AN UNEMPLOYED ACT-RESS ON A PUBLICITY STUNT.

Richard Sovern had arranged for the press announcement to keep reporters away from Earhart. It seemed to work. The press was already skeptical enough at the "impossible" story and most of those newspeople assigned to it now melted away.

Sovern rushed from the NOB meeting at Langley to Andrews Air Force Base, Maryland, where Earhart was being kept. She was housed in a furnished Quonset hut in a remote section of the base. Nearby was the hangar where the President's emergency plane was kept, an aircraft that would be used as a command post in case of nuclear war. When an Air Force officer told her about the plane she could comprehend little of what he was talking about. She had still not mastered concepts like "computer" or "transistor." Even nuclear war was an abstraction. The Nazis had not actually shown her pictures of a nuclear blast and she could only imagine it from the officer's description. She had not yet been told about Hiroshima or Nagasaki, nor did she know about intercontinental missiles.

Sovern carefully inspected the security arrangements for Earhart outside her hut. He saw the roving patrols with their guard dogs and the three jeeps with mounted, radar-controlled antiaircraft guns. He did ask that the number of armed men in the area be increased, to protect against a group of fanatical Nazis possibly trying to assault the Andrews gate. He also ordered two antitank guns to protect the hut against vehicles. Amelia Earhart would be the best-protected person in the United States.

"Don't think we're paranoid," he told her inside the chilly, cheaply decorated hut. "If a murderer is willing to exchange his life for the victim's, there's a good chance he will succeed. We're going to make sure that doesn't happen."

"Believe me, I approve," Earhart said with appreciation. "There's a lot I want to do and see now that I'm home. There are people I want to find, to be with again."

"I'm afraid that'll have to wait until this Hitler thing is resolved."

"Of course," Earhart agreed. "But after that . . ."

"Miss Earhart . . ."

"Please call me Amelia," Earhart said with a broad smile that showed that the personal touch delighted her. "I want you to."

Sovern, not the most informal person, felt somewhat awkward at calling a professional contact by a first name, yet he felt a remarkable familiarity with this courageous woman who had been a national idol during his youth.

"All right . . . Amelia," he said. But the informality came hard, and he wondered how long it would take

before he got used to it. "Try to understand that you
may be a target for some time. It's our responsibility
to protect you in much the same way that we'd protect
a former president. That doesn't mean you can't travel
once this thing is over. But we'd appreciate your ac-
cepting our security screen."

"Okay," Amelia Earhart said quietly.

"Now for the present, of course," Sovern continued,
"you will be with me. We'll be visiting the Soviet ambassador to get the Russian response to your revelation
on Adolf Hitler. Please do not allow him to interrogate you even in my presence. We can't always anticipate their motives. And should we be intercepted by
a reporter, please let me do all the talking. I hope you
don't mind this."

"Not really," Earhart replied. "Remember, my last
flight was an espionage mission. I understand all these
things."

Sovern looked around the hut with its few tiny windows and prefabricated metal walls. "Like the mansion?" he asked.

Earhart laughed. "It *is* a mansion compared to some
of the places I stayed during my flight around the
world. I feel like a VIP."

"I brought some things for you," Sovern said. He
reached into an attaché case and took out a raft of
photos, many of them browned at the edges from age,
some of them faded by the years. "You might like to
see these."

Sovern and Earhart sat down at an old, stained coffee
table. Earhart's eyes lit up as soon as she saw the first
pictures. "My God," she said, "where did you get
them?"

"They were in our file. The government collected
them after you disappeared."

Earhart looked at the first picture. None of the photos were captioned. "That's my sister Muriel when she was about eight," she said excitedly. "We were living on Quality Hill in Atchison."

She flipped to the next picture. "There's the house! I do wish I could see it again."

"You will," Sovern replied.

Earhart did not know it, but she was being tested. Despite his faith in her Sovern insisted on evaluating her constantly. He had asked Franklin Foreman to gather some old pictures from her past and was trying to determine whether she recognized the old people and places. He knew that any double trained or even biologically altered to appear as Amelia Earhart might have difficulty with all the details that the real Amelia would know.

She turned to the next picture. "That's the courthouse where Grandfather Otis was a judge. He was my mother's father." Suddenly, Sovern could see a reflective look in Earhart's eyes as she thought back to her family and ancestors. "He didn't care much for my father," she said. "He didn't think he was good enough for my mother. Grandfather Otis was a very rigid and successful man. He was a judge of the U.S. District Court. My father was a junior lawyer for the railroad. I've always felt that some of my father's alcohol problem came from grandfather's disapproval."

She flipped to the next picture. "Oh," she laughed, "those are the Indians in town. When you went to market they would lift the lids on your basket. I was terrified, but they were just being curious.

"And here's the St. Louis Fair of 1904. My father raised the money for us to go by settling a railroad dispute. Have you ever read the Sally Benson stories about life in St. Louis around that time?"

"No," Sovern replied with a slight laugh—his reading having been restricted to medical journals and politics —"but there was a movie based on them made while you were away."

"Really?"

"It was called *Meet Me in St. Louis* with Judy Garland."

"Who?"

"Judy Garland. She became one of our biggest film stars. She's gone now."

"Incredible," Earhart said. "I'm an entire generation behind. I don't even know the movie stars."

Suddenly the phone rang. "I'll get it," Sovern said, correctly assuming that anything this late at night must be for him. He picked up.

"Dick, this is the President." The voice was concerned, urgent.

"Yes, sir?"

"Listen, we just got a call on the White House hotline saying that unless Earhart was returned to the Reich Reborn within six hours, there'd be a tremendous disaster in Manhattan."

There was silence as Sovern absorbed the message. "How do we know it's genuine?" he asked.

"They said Amelia Earhart would have two small marks above her left elbow, where serums were regularly injected. That's how we'd know."

Sovern got off the phone for a moment. "Would you roll up your left sleeve?" he asked Earhart.

She seemed confused. "Is this about the injection points?" she asked.

"You don't have to bother," Sovern told her. He got back on the phone. "It's legitimate, sir," he told the President.

"Dick," the President said nervously, "this woman may be our greatest curse."

"No!" Sovern insisted. "She's our only *hope*. The Nazis are desperately afraid of what she might tell us."

"But the lives we'll lose," the President moaned.

"The loss is tragic," Sovern agreed. "But how many would be lost if Hitler actually returned? I'm afraid we'll have to think of this as a wartime situation."

"So what do you recommend?"

"Offer to negotiate."

"Negotiate what?"

"Anything. Stall for time. Ask them to clarify their demands. Maybe we can arrange some compromise."

"I don't know," the President said, "maybe we should just arrange to give Earhart back. I wonder whether she really is worth . . ."

"Mr. President," Sovern broke in, "we can't give up the potential source of information. You *know* that, sir. Let me set up a crisis center to handle this situation. Let's try to talk to the Nazis, reason with them if that's possible, make clear to them that their terror just increases our resolve to hold Earhart and knock them out. I'll take her with me. She might be able to identify a telephone voice or a speech style. I can't guarantee that anything will prevent a New York incident from happening, but it's better than debating."

"You'll take the responsibility for the operations of this center?" the President asked.

"Of course."

"Well then, go ahead."

III

Sovern and Earhart were whisked by a sealed Air Police van to the CRG building's underground garage, then taken upstairs in a private, guarded elevator.

The crisis center was a thirty- by forty-foot room with three rows of twelve seats each, arranged theater-style, each row higher than the one before. In front of every seat was a gray plastic console with telephones, briefing books, and note paper. The seats faced a wall-sized map of Manhattan, which was covered with plastic so that lines and markers could be drawn. A red circle already indicated FBI headquarters and another the CRG field office. There were other marks for police and fire centers.

A five-foot screen was off to the side, connected to an Advent Videobeam television projection system. This projected a TV picture onto the screen, allowing everyone to see closed-circuit reports from New York.

Amelia Earhart and Richard Sovern walked in quickly, Earhart drawing a few sharp glances from the CRG agents manning the consoles. The two took seats in the first row, Sovern in the chair reserved for the senior man. Franklin Foreman was on his right, tired from his frantic efforts at setting up the center and getting it staffed.

"Any further contact from the Nazis?" Sovern asked as he got settled.

"Negative," Foreman replied.

"How long till their deadline?"

"Five hours twenty-four minutes."

"What are New York authorities doing?"

"The mayor is standing by at City Hall and he's quietly alerted police and fire units. But in accordance with your instructions, New York has only been told that we have intelligence on a terrorist plot. We haven't even told the mayor yet that Nazis are involved."

Sovern turned to Earhart to explain. "The word 'Nazi,'" he said, "could create a panicky over-reaction up there. It's best not to use it until all the operations are set up and in place."

"I understand," Earhart replied.

"Now," Sovern went on, "all we can do is wait for them to make contact."

The Advent projector flashed on, showing an aerial shot of Manhattan from an FBI helicopter. The city looked magnificent, and Earhart leaned forward to get a better look.

"I wish I were there," Earhart whispered.

Willy Haas and members of the council watched as aides packed clothing and supplies that had been stored in the attic for this moment. Everything they would have to take on their mission to power in West Germany was there, including electric shavers that operated on two hundred twenty volts. They did not pack their uniforms or anything else that could betray their role. There was too much of a risk of luggage being lost or examined at some customs counter.

The squeaking and sliding of the bags provided a noisy backdrop to the tension that enveloped the farmhouse. Everyone knew that in five hours they'd have Earhart back . . . or a magnificent act of terror would be carried out. They wanted Earhart, but they loved the chance to prove their strength, to kill again. It was reason versus emotion.

Haas checked his watch and called an agent in

Texas. He instructed him, and the man in turn called the White House. No calls would be traceable to Haas himself.

A call from Texas went to the White House and was instantly transferred to Sovern.

The red URGENT light flashed next to Sovern's phone. He picked up.

"Yes, Sovern here."

"This is the Reich Reborn," the quiet, unassuming voice replied. "What is your answer?"

"We're not prepared to surrender Earhart," Sovern said, "but we'll negotiate on anything else. We urge you to exercise caution. Our security forces are efficient and will track you down if you hit us. We await your counter-proposal."

The Nazi hung up. To insure absolute security he drove five miles to another phone, then called Haas to report. Haas was not surprised at Sovern's reply. He had hardly expected the Americans to give up a major intelligence source. He immediately placed a call to one of his agents in Yonkers, New York, just north of Manhattan. "Move the missiles into the city," he ordered.

In the crisis center the red light on Sovern's phone lit up again.

"Sovern."

"You are speaking to the Reich Reborn," came a high-pitched, intense voice. "We will accept nothing but Amelia Earhart."

Sovern thought for a moment. "Then please extend your deadline so we can have consultations."

"We insist you reconsider on Earhart."

"We'll have consultations."

The caller hung up, once again making a trace impossible.

"Did you recognize the voice?" Sovern asked Earhart, who had been listening in.

"No, I've never heard it before," Earhart replied. She hadn't known the earlier voice either.

"I don't think they're bluffing," Sovern said. "Not after their murder of the West German chancellor." He turned to Foreman, who was on the phone with New York's police commissioner. "How're they doing up there?" Sovern asked.

"No sign of any unusual activity yet," Foreman reported.

"Damn," Sovern mumbled. He realized it would be impossible to search all but a fraction of Manhattan's buildings before the deadline.

He looked toward the Advent, which once again showed a helicopter view of Manhattan. For an instant his attention was caught by the Circle Line charter boat that steamed around Manhattan. He watched as it passed under the George Washington Bridge on its way back to berth to pick up its last group for the night.

It was 11:06 P.M. The deadline was four hours and eight minutes away.

CHAPTER 7

Elaine and Jack Merton had been married December 3, 1942, a day before Jack was sent to North Africa to serve with the U.S. Army. Now the Oldsmobile agency where Jack was senior salesman was throwing them a big anniversary party aboard the Circle Line charter boat *Peter Stuyvesant*. Sixty-eight people were waiting on Pier Eighty-six on West Forty-sixth Street to board the boat. The party would go until just after three A.M., when the *Stuyvesant* was scheduled to return to the pier.

Jack Merton was a bulbous, red-nosed man with rough, mottled skin who had made a reputation as one of the best and most reputable auto salesmen in the city. He was actually rather quiet, and as he waited for the *Stuyvesant*, dressed in a blue suit and red tie, he greeted his oldest friends with a warm smile but few words.

Elaine Merton, only five feet one, was the opposite— a bundle of dynamite. While her husband slowly made the rounds, she went through the crowd at top speed, cracking jokes and kissing cheeks. This will be the best night ever, she told herself. It's number forty. Who knows if there'll be a fifty?

The *Stuyvesant* came into view.

The Mertons weren't the only ones watching the tourist boat as it lumbered slowly down the Hudson River toward the old wooden pier. Friedrich Bunter had driven his 1978 Pontiac in from Yonkers and was now parked near the docks on West Fifty-eighth Street. In the back seat, covered with canvas, was a shoulder-launched missile system with a warhead packing as much power as a large artillery shell. It had been stolen from a U.S. Army arsenal in Philadelphia.

Bunter was sixty-three. He had served in the German Army toward the end of World War II, but had never seen combat. Tonight he would engage the enemy for the first time. He didn't know there was competition. Willy Haas had dispatched three other missile-carrying cars as well.

Three hours, forty-four minutes to deadline.

The crisis center was remarkably quiet. Sovern and Earhart, fortified with coffee, waited for the next contact.

At 12:41, with little more than two and a half hours to go, the red light on Sovern's phone flashed.

"This is the Reich Reborn," said the woman caller. "We reject your request to extend the deadline. Many will die."

"I appeal again for the deadline to be extended," Sovern said.

"Rejected."

"Then . . . what would happen to Earhart if she were returned?"

There was silence on the line.

"You will be contacted," the caller said and hung up.

Sovern felt a tinge of optimism. "They may bite," he told Earhart. "They may think we're weakening."

"But if you're not going to send me back, what good will that do?"

"It may buy time. If they finally do extend, it gives the police that much longer. It isn't much, but we count small blessings here."

Again the phone rang.

"Sovern."

It was still another voice. "We will not discuss what will happen to Earhart," the heavily German-accented caller said. "Release her or take responsibility for the consequences."

The caller hung up.

Transcripts of the calls were being fed to the President, waiting in the Oval Office. Now he urgently got on the line to Sovern.

"Dick, what do you think?"

"Sir," Sovern replied, "they're definitely going to hit, but we don't know where. There's no guarantee we're going to find out either."

"Dick, these people are crazy. We can lose hundreds of our people. Thousands maybe."

"Yes, sir."

"You accept that?"

"Of course not. But what's the alternative?"

There was a pause. "Dick," the President asked, "is she really that valuable?"

Sovern began to steam. "Yes, sir, she is. I can't guarantee what she'll produce, but it could be the key to solving this problem. We may take casualties tonight. But if the Nazi plan develops the way Earhart says, we'll take many more. Believe me I'm not being cold-blooded. Just realistic. I'm just as horrified as you are about what could happen up there."

"I know, Dick. I just hope you're right. . . ."

"Sir, I've given my advice," Sovern said softly. He looked apprehensively at Earhart, knowing the final decision on her disposition was not in his hands. "You, Mr. President," he continued, "will have to decide."

"If there's a change in policy," the President replied tersely, "I'll let you know." Then he hung up.

"We're nowhere," Sovern sighed to Earhart and Foreman. All three glanced at the Advent screen as the helicopter passed once more over lower Manhattan. The city was getting to sleep now, and they could actually see lights going out in the chic residential sections.

Sovern could sense by her sullen expression that Earhart was becoming increasingly depressed. "What's wrong?" he asked.

The flier took a deep, pained breath and let it out slowly. "Look," she said, "I pretty much figured out what the President was saying to you. I'm not sure I can be of much help. You have no right to condemn people to death just to keep me here. Let me be returned."

"No way," Sovern snapped.

"Why?"

"Because we need you. And your return wouldn't stop them from pulling something else. You're only one issue. Give in to terror once and you're forever at its mercy."

"What if the President decides otherwise?" Earhart asked.

"Then obviously . . ."

Sovern was cut off in mid-sentence by a sharp buzz on Foreman's console, a signal indicating a major development. Foreman grabbed his phone, listened, and reported to Sovern.

"Sir, New York reports a large, suspicious-looking cylinder has just been found just outside a patient wing at Bellevue Hospital. The bomb squad is check· ing. They're evacuating the wing."

The helicopter above Manhattan came in low over Bellevue, and those in the crisis center could see the patrol cars converging. It was logical, Sovern thought. Blasting a hospital was terror at its most unmerciful, its most potent. The emotional effect would be over· whelming.

All activity seemed to freeze as the New York Police Department's bomb squad appeared on the scene.

Sovern checked his watch. It was 1:18 A.M.

It would all be over in less than two hours. Maybe, he hoped, it was over now.

It took precisely twenty-eight minutes for the bomb squad to determine that the suspicious cylinder was an empty chemical container whose label had worn off. How it got to the Bellevue grounds was a mystery, but an unimportant one.

The surge of optimism melted at CRG headquarters. With an hour and a half remaining, only a sudden change in luck could help.

"Congratulations!"

The cheer could almost be heard on shore as Elaine and Jack Merton cut the huge white and blue anni· versary cake their friends wheeled into the main party room aboard the *Stuyvesant*.

"I don't know what to say," Jack Merton exclaimed as he whisked some topping from the cake with his index finger and sucked it. "Vanilla. That's all I'll say!"

"He's not a talker," Elaine Merton complained, "so I'll make the speech. You've all made Jack and me really happy tonight. I couldn't think of anything grander than to have all of you here with us. I don't know whose idea it was to have this party on a boat, but it was the greatest. Now we want all of you just to have a good time."

A band would've been too great an expense, but someone put a record on and the room was filled with nostalgic Glenn Miller music, the kind these people loved. Within seconds many of the guests were dancing a traditional fox trot, and the Mertons continued cutting their cake and giving out slices.

Friedrich Bunter heard the music from shore as the *Stuyvesant* passed his position once again. He returned to his car and began setting up the missile on the back seat. His instructions were to fire at precisely 3:14 A.M. if the boat was within range. Only a "cancel" order on a small walkie-talkie that Bunter had clipped to his belt could ruin the evening.

The one-hour mark passed. Sovern left his seat and began pacing through the crisis center. He still didn't know the target and the New York Police Department had turned up nothing. He knew what he would say if the Nazis called again, but the phone had been silent.

Then at 2:24 A.M. Sovern's phone rang. He rushed to it.

"Sovern."

"Have you reconsidered?" a young man's voice asked.

"We are examining our options," Sovern replied.

The man flew into a rage. "That was *not* the question! Have you reconsidered?"

"We are considering only the extent and time of our retaliation against you people," Sovern snapped. "We will make public the fact that neo-Nazis were behind this plot should you carry it out. There would be enormous public support for striking out against you."

"You are desperate," the caller said and hung up.

"Yes, we are," Sovern mumbled as he too hung up. "But only for now, buddy." He kept glancing at his watch. It finally came up to 2:45 A.M., less than half an hour from deadline. The President came on the line.

"Dick," the Chief Executive said, "I've thought about it all night."

Sovern instantly became apprehensive. He glanced quickly at Earhart.

"I've decided," the President continued, "that this is just what you said . . . a kind of war. I won't let Earhart go. We'll have to take what they dish out. I pray it isn't ghastly."

"So do I, sir," Sovern replied. His respect for the President grew a notch.

At three A.M., as Sovern continued to pace, Willy Haas gave instructions for the Nazis' final phone calls. Haas, showing his enormous capacity for calm under pressure, had changed into pajamas and was studiously casual about the murders he was prepared to order.

The Nazi caller reached Sovern at 3:03 A.M., eleven minutes to deadline.

"What is your final answer?" the female asked, her voice echoing through the line from Phoenix, Arizona.

Sovern thought briefly, then tried one last gamble. "We're reconsidering," he said. "This will take some time."

"We will get back," the caller said, hanging up and phoning Haas with the report.

Moments later Sovern received another call.

"We will not extend. You have had time to reconsider. Will you release her?"

It was 3:06.

"No," Sovern replied.

That was the end of the conversation.

At 3:09, five minutes from deadline, Sovern received a call from the State Department watch office. "Mr. Sovern," the watch officer practically shouted into his phone, "we just got an anonymous call saying the target is that charter boat going around Manhattan. The caller asked that the message be passed to you."

Sovern's eyes flashed toward the screen.

The boat was plainly visible. It was coming down the Hudson, passing Seventy-second Street.

Sovern could not hear the gaiety aboard. But he could see the people on deck having a ball.

"Get me New York!" he snapped. In a moment he was connected with the police inspector coordinating search efforts in Manhattan. "The target is that charter boat! You have four minutes. Alert the captain. There may be a bomb aboard!"

The police instantly contacted the *Stuyvesant*'s captain. Inexperienced at these things, he announced the alert to the passengers and ordered them to start searching.

The result was panic.

Screaming women; confused men.

Jack Merton tried to calm his friends. Elaine, the bouncy, together wife, became hysterical.

Crewmen started breaking out life jackets and rafts.

A radio alert went out for Coast Guard helicopters and cutters.

It was 3:13.

A few people on the *Stuyvesant* jumped overboard.

One man drowned immediately. Two others initially stayed afloat but soon disappeared.

Friedrich Bunter, hiding in the shadows, aimed the sight of his shoulder-carried missile. The sight was equipped with an infra-red device that made night seem like day. Once aimed, the missile would automatically seek out the target in the center of the crosshairs.

Fifteen seconds to deadline.

The crisis center was silent. Amelia Earhart, feeling a surge of guilt, stared at the screen.

The *Stuyvesant* turned sharply to starboard, hoping to make shore before the blast.

It was 3:14.

There was a brilliant flash as a single missile from Bunter's launcher sped toward the *Stuyvesant*.

A few seconds later it struck amidships. The blast cut the ship almost in two. Fires broke out and raged. The ancient steamer immediately began to careen.

The screams and moans reached both the New York and New Jersey shores.

Then a second missile was fired, this time by another of Haas's men. It struck the *Stuyvesant*'s bow, blowing it off.

Before people could get into jackets or rafts the boat capsized.

Jack and Elaine Merton grabbed each other as they went down, hitting the water the same time as the remains of their fortieth anniversary cake.

Only three people survived. . . .

Despite the flashes from the missile launchers Friedrich Bunter and his ally escaped easily. They simply dropped their weapons, abandoned their cars (which carried dummy registrations), and melted into the shadows.

* * *

Richard Sovern slowly picked up his phone and called the White House. "Mr. President," he said with a rare solemnity, "what can I say? We condemned those people to death and I will take full public responsibility. I urge you to maintain your resolve, sir. We must defeat these monsters as our predecessors did."

There was a long pause.

"Dick," the President said, his voice shaking from the terror that had descended, "I have more confidence in you than in anyone. Do what you have to."

Willy Haas disappeared momentarily into that mysterious chamber where the Chairman was housed. He emerged smiling with the visible satisfaction of a job well done.

"The Chairman is pleased," he told the other members of the council. "We have struck a blow against the enemy—a minor one compared to what will come—and have maintained the honor of the Reich. The Americans now know with whom they deal."

Richard Sovern drove Amelia Earhart back to her "home" at Andrews Air Force Base. Security cars with Secret Service agents surrounded his auto during the drive. Sovern decided to stay at a nearby barracks during the night rather than travel all the way back to Washington.

Hardly a word was exchanged between Sovern and Earhart once they left the crisis center. Nothing could be said or had to be. . . . Sovern mentioned that the National Transportation Safety Board would issue a statement pledging a full investigation of the harbor disaster in New York. No mention of the Nazis would be made despite his earlier threat to do so. He had decided, and the President had concurred, that it would be best not to focus public anger on the Nazis, possibly risking a heavy-handed Congressional probe while the delicate search for Adolf Hitler was just underway.

Sovern told Earhart to be ready to leave Andrews at eleven A.M. They would go directly to the Soviet Embassy.

The first round against Hitler had been lost in New York. The second was about to begin.

CHAPTER 8

Logan Airport, Boston

He was small, somewhat hunched, and wore frameless glasses and a well-trimmed Vandyke. His hair was long and gray and combed in a conventional manner with the part on the left. People watching him assumed he was in his mid-seventies, in fairly good health, and alert. He spoke only when spoken to and then in a soft, almost self-effacing manner. He never smiled.

His passport read Isadore Shapiro. Like the members of the Council of the Rebirth, the Chairman carried papers identifying him as an American Jew, naturalized, of European birth.

"Shalom," said the ticket attendant as he stepped slowly to the El Al counter and presented his ticket. The Chairman nodded but did not answer. Willy Haas stood behind him in the line, trying to look at ease, which he was not. He carried the Chairman's medicines in a small attaché case.

"I see you are with a travel group," the black-haired, twenty-seven-year-old woman behind the counter said.

Again the Chairman nodded.

"All right Mr. Shapiro, let me just check your reservation." She punched some keys on a small computer terminal and waited. Seemingly annoyed, she repeated the action. "There seems to be some confusion," she said.

The Chairman tensed. Haas's face broke into a frown and the other members of the council, standing in the same line, were momentarily agitated.

"What's the problem?" Haas asked sharply. "We've had our reservations for weeks. This is a very important trip to us . . . our first trip to Israel. We're widowers."

"Yes, yes," the attendant said, "but there is no listing for Mr. Shapiro. Did you book directly through us?"

"Through an agency," Haas said, barely concealing his contempt for these fumbling Jews.

The attendant tried a different computer program. "Ah," she finally said, "here it is. They had it spelled *Sch* . . . I'm so sorry."

"It's okay," Haas said. "We're all part of the same family."

The Chairman merely smiled.

"All right Mr. Shapiro, I see you preselected a window seat, and that is confirmed. Here is your boarding pass. Have a good flight to Tel Aviv."

The momentary crisis was over and the Chairman stepped away. The other members of the council were quickly cleared. Then they all went to the passenger lounge to wait for El Al flight eight-eighty to Tel Aviv, with stops in Paris and Rome.

As the Chairman sat in the lounge, Haas kept eyeing him carefully. He had not responded as well as Earhart had to being taken off the age-retarding machine. He fatigued more easily, his age lines growing deeper. He had to be constantly treated with special drugs, but they could only help his condition to a limited extent.

Willy Haas leaned over to whisper to him. "Chairman," he said, "I know how it bothers you to be among these creatures, these subhuman loudmouths on their way to Israel. But it is the most perfect cover. And someday we'll get this bunch, too, just like we got the others in the camps."

The Chairman smiled.

About twenty minutes later an accented voice came over the loudspeaker system: "Attention please. El Al flight eight-eighty to Tel Aviv is now ready to board at gate sixteen. Please have boarding passes ready. Visitors may *not* board the aircraft."

The nerve, Haas thought. One of *them* giving orders to us, to *him!*

There was the usual commotion and the smacking of good-bye kisses. Haas was revolted, especially when he heard Yiddish exchanged like in the old days before the Final Solution went into effect. If only they had been allowed another year, he mused, the operation would have been so much more thorough.

The Chairman and council boarded the Boeing 747 through an enclosed passageway. Haas knew what the Chairman was thinking as he stepped aboard. This was a Boeing, the company that gave the world the B-17 Flying Fortress, which ravaged Germany and destroyed her people. How ironic it was that a Boeing would take the leader of the reborn Reich on the first stage of his journey back.

The passengers got settled, the pilot received clear-

ance, and a few minutes later flight eight-eighty was
in the air, heading east across the Atlantic.

As Richard Sovern and Amelia Earhart prepared to
leave Andrews, scores of military intelligence officers
were already invading the National Archives and sift-
ing through the documents captured from the Nazis
at the end of World War II. Franklin Foreman set up
a research room in the basement of the building, giving each man a place at a long, wooden table. He instructed the group in what to look for—evidence of
medical experiments in age-retardation or hints of any
medical treatments given to Adolf Hitler himself.

There seemed something vaguely incongruous about
doing research on the Nazis in the same building that
housed the Declaration of Independence and the Constitution, and Foreman, who was rather sensitive to
tradition, felt as if he were soiling the air with his
work. But he pressed on with his usual efficiency,
organizing a system of spot-checking material. He knew
it would be impossible to go through everything before
January thirtieth. His job was complicated further by
Sovern's belief that the Nazis would almost certainly
advance their target date.

Sovern and Earhart sped to a huge gray mansion in
northwest Washington that was serving temporarily as
the Russian Embassy while the real one was being
remodeled and renovated. The house had twenty-two
rooms and had been used to quarter high-ranking officers during World War II. It was surrounded by a
massive stone wall, giving it, appropriately, a Kremlin-
like appearance. Security guards manned the front
gate and were posted along the wall. The Russians,
always security conscious, were especially so in a temporary building whose construction they had not su-

pervised. They knew there might be listening devices in the walls, floors, even in the pipes.

The security guards gaped as Richard Sovern and Amelia Earhart were driven through the gate. The sight, after all, was unprecedented—one of the leading espionage officers of the West entering the Soviet Embassy, not as an enemy but as a guest of the ambassador, greeted at the front door by the first secretary, and ushered inside with his unnamed woman associate.

The meeting had been arranged directly by the secretary of state. The matter was of extreme urgency, the secretary had said, and Richard Sovern had to see the ambassador at once. Soviet officials had thought that some new threat to peace had developed along Russia's long border with China and that the United States had detected it. Sovern's request for an audience with Ambassador Grechko had been instantly granted.

Yuri Grechko was a new-style Russian. He dressed in tailor-made suits from Saks Fifth Avenue, watched his weight, and jogged around the grounds each morning. He was as interested in American musical theater as in the Bolshoi Ballet and regularly hummed the score of *West Side Story*. He was the metropolitan, sophisticated Russian, far removed from the peasant gruffness of the Khrushchev era. He had even taken a course in American slang at Russia's USA Institute.

His office, though, was no reflection of the man. The Foreign Ministry insisted on proper proletarian simplicity—a simple wooden desk, small red throw rug, and rigid chair without rollers—and Grechko thought it politically unwise to change the decor, especially since some in the Embassy suspected him of liking America. His only contribution to the office was a Japanese stereo system, which the Embassy housekeeper kept stocked with Tchaikovsky records.

Well-built, forty-five, and prematurely gray, Grechko looked more like a country college dean than one of the world's most skillful negotiators.

Sovern and Earhart were already in his office when Grechko swept in, extending his hand. "Mr. Sovern," he said in perfect English, "welcome." He glanced at Earhart. "The secretary said you were bringing an associate. May I ask . . . ?"

"Mr. Ambassador," Sovern broke in, "would you forgive me if I delayed my introduction of the lady? You'll understand, I assure you."

The smile melted from Grechko's face. "This is very unusual," he said, "but as you wish." He saw the concern in Sovern's face. "There is obviously a problem," he said. "Please sit down."

"I'll be brief," Sovern said as he pulled up a simple visitor's chair. He glanced apprehensively at the stereo speakers, which were pouring out the second act of *Swan Lake*.

"Shall I lower it?" Grechko asked.

"No, make it louder," Sovern replied. "I don't want any leaks." He looked toward a door leading off the office. "Better still . . ." He gestured toward it.

Grechko understood. The three people in the office walked into the ambassador's private bathroom. Neither Grechko nor Sovern had to say a word. Both knew the old, tested method of foiling listening devices. Sovern turned the shower on full blast and Grechko let both faucets in the sink run. They stood close together, with Earhart, and talked.

"Mr. Ambassador," Sovern said, "it may seem strange to bring this up, but I came to discuss your army's capture of Hitler's bunker in 1945."

Grechko's bushy eyebrows popped up. "Yes, that is an unusual subject," he said.

"Your country," Sovern went on, "released data some years ago presumably proving that you found Hitler's body."

"Of course."

"That data, sir, has been called into question."

"This is so urgent?" Grechko asked. "Who cares what happened to the old kraut?"

"We do, sir, and I think you do too. Some American investigators believe Adolf Hitler may have survived the war."

Grechko shrugged and looked quickly at his watch.

"Look," he said, "these things come up all the time. The magazines always have something about Hitler escaping, or Bormann, or one of those boys. With the Orientals breathing down our necks, I can't see why this is a crisis."

"We have reason to believe," Sovern answered, "that Hitler may be alive today, in remarkably good health for a man his age because of German medical break-throughs, and may try to seize power in West Germany. The date may be January 30, 1983, the fiftieth anniversary of his becoming chancellor."

Grechko looked at Sovern as if the CRG director was slightly batty. "What is your evidence?" he asked condescendingly.

"We have none . . . directly. We have the opinion of a . . . highly qualified person."

"Who?"

"Mr. Ambassador, take a look at this lady. Does she look familiar?"

Grechko looked intently at Earhart, studying her every feature. "A charming lady," he said, "but there is no familiarity."

"Does the name Amelia Earhart strike you?"

"Of course."

"Meet her."

Grechko was expressionless. Being every inch the diplomat, he graciously shook Earhart's hand and bowed slightly. "It is a pleasure," he said with a touch of coldness, "but you must forgive me if I have questions. This episode is becoming more and more bizarre."

"Please believe me," Sovern pushed on, "this is the lady who landed in Los Angeles. Her identity has been confirmed, and I ask you to accept the word of my government on that. She was held by Nazi interests since 1937. She reports that Hitler is still alive. She received the same medical treatments he did and the effects are obvious."

Grechko was totally shaken, but refused to show it. He just kept looking at Earhart, not really believing Sovern's story, yet knowing the man's reputation for honesty. The idea that this was some kind of strange American trick entered his mind and lingered. He decided not to pursue the Earhart question further, assuming Sovern was well prepared to counter any objection.

"What do you want with the Soviet Union?" he asked snappishly.

"We'd like, sir, for your scientists to reexamine their data, to reconfirm it. No offense meant to your great scientists, but mistakes can be made and . . ."

Grechko put his hand up to stop Sovern. "You don't have to beat around the bush."

"All right, sir."

"I've been in the business awhile," Grechko said. "Frankly, this whole thing strikes me as ridiculous, especially since you give us nothing but the story of this very fine lady. You know, Mr. Sovern, you Americans sometimes get excitable. You love mysteries and you like to dredge up these old stories. We have Amelia Earhart and Adolf Hitler on the same day. It is very remarkable." He shrugged his shoulders. "But, if you wish, I will transmit your request to Moscow without comment."

"I'd appreciate that," Sovern replied. "But I wish, sir, that you'd regard it with some urgency. I can tell you that the boat disaster in New York Harbor was the work of the neo-Nazi Reich Reborn group. They demanded this lady back. There's *got* to be something to this."

"Mr. Sovern," Grechko said, "I am second to no one in my concern over the rebirth of fascism. We Russians suffered more than anyone in the war. But I'm sure you know that virtually every authority agrees that Hitler committed suicide in his bunker. Pardon me, but I can't get excited about a theory."

Sovern could not fail to notice Grechko's almost complete snubbing of Amelia Earhart.

The ambassador started turning off all the water in the bathroom. He noticed the sink had started to fill. "Poor plumbing," he said. "There is no workmanship anymore, even in the Soviet Union." He paused for a moment, then turned to Sovern and Earhart. "Look," he said, "I will ask that the Soviet government treat this with urgency. The situation in West Germany is too serious to have valuable people like you worrying about abstractions."

"Thank you, sir," Sovern said.

"As far as this charming lady," Grechko went on, with the barest smile, "I am pleased to have your company . . . whoever you are."

The three reentered Grechko's office.

"You have something else?" Grechko asked.

"No," Sovern replied, "that was the only reason for my visit."

"Good, then I will get the confirmation from Moscow. Please call me in forty-eight hours if you haven't heard from me first."

Sovern and Earhart left the Embassy and got into their car, which was waiting at the front door. As they did, Ambassador Grechko summoned the chief of his KGB unit, the man in charge of gathering intelligence on the United States. The two spoke quickly and urgently behind the closed door of the ambassador's office.

Sovern's driver sped downtown toward the National Archives, where the search of Nazi documents was underway. When the car was about three blocks from the Embassy, out of range of long-distance listening devices, Sovern turned to Earhart.

"What do you think?"

"He seemed pretty sure," Earhart replied, "although a diplomat would have to speak that way, right?"

"Right. He really didn't have any direct information, and I suspect Moscow will just confirm its earlier claims about Hitler's death. As for your role he didn't know what to make of it, and I can't blame him."

"At least he was gracious," Earhart said.

"More diplomacy. He'll report my claim about you to Moscow, and they'll tell him what more to say."

Suddenly Sovern became aware of a black car pulling up on his right. Inside were two Soviet security guards he recognized from minutes before. The Russian car lurched forward.

"What the hell is this?" Sovern asked, aware that the guards were staring at him.

The embassy car pulled ahead, then cut Sovern off.

"Jesus!" Sovern exclaimed. His driver jammed on the brakes, then went for a machine gun under the dash. Sovern pulled his pistol.

The two Russians jumped from their car.

Sovern pushed Earhart to the floor, then crouched behind the seat, his head above, ready to fire.

But the Russians were unarmed.

They simply waved their hands and smiled.

For a moment Sovern relaxed. The Russians approached his car and motioned for him to roll down his window. He did, holding his gun all the while.

"Do not be concerned," one Russian said. "We mean no harm, but we did not know how to make quickly the contact with your car receiver, so we chased you."

"What's the problem?" Sovern asked.

"Ambassador Grechko wishes you to return. He has further comments."

Sovern looked down at Earhart; the two exchanged quizzical glances. They knew the ambassador would not call them back, especially so abruptly, for something trivial.

Sovern and Earhart followed the Soviet car to the Embassy and were immediately ushered into Grechko's office. This time another man was there. Sovern instantly recognized him, and a chill went up his spine.

"Thank you for returning," Grechko said. Sovern thought he seemed nervous and perhaps intimidated by the man standing next to him. "Mr. Sovern," he continued, "I'm sure you recognize Anatol Suslov. You boys probably even know each other." He laughed tensely.

Of course Sovern knew that Suslov was the KGB's senior man in the United States. Thin, small, and physically unimpressive, he was known as one of the world's most brilliant spies.

Sovern nodded at Suslov, but did not extend his hand. "We haven't met," he said. "It's good to know you."

Suslov smiled broadly, taking pleasure in shaking people up.

At Grechko's insistence Sovern and Earhart sat. "Look," he said, "when you were here before there was some information that I withheld. It was necessary before consulting with Suslov. You will understand."

"Of course," Sovern said. He saw that Suslov kept staring curiously at Earhart.

"The ambassador has briefed me on what you reported," Suslov said in an intense, high-pitched voice. "Look, Adolf Hitler is dead. Quite dead. I myself have seen the documented evidence and I have already cabled Moscow to have that evidence sent here at once. You are a physician, Mr. Sovern, and you will soon have your doubts resolved."

Sovern immediately felt himself relax. There was a certain honor among intelligence men, and he had no evidence that it was being violated now. Hitler *was* dead, as he had always assumed. He looked over at Earhart, who had her eyes lowered, clearly in embarrassment. He saw that her pain ran deep. He left his chair and put his arm on her shoulders. "Look," he said quietly, "you did your best."

"What have I caused?" Earhart asked in visible agony.

"Madam," Suslov interrupted, "you must not despair about this. I do not know who or what you are, but I know you have been, as Americans say, 'set up'."

"What?" Sovern asked. "How do you know?"

Suslov walked to Grechko's desk and picked up a photograph he had brought from his own office. He handed it to Sovern. "Do you recognize this?"

Sovern studied the picture.

It was an aerial view of Willy Haas's farmhouse in Massachusetts.

"No," Sovern replied, "I've never seen it."

"This house is on Route forty-three in your Williamstown, Massachusetts. I believe there is a famous college there."

"Williams."

"Yes, of course. Our people have known for some time that this house is the center for some of the Reich Reborn people. Exactly how important this faction is, we do not know."

Sovern's eyes flashed with anger. "Why didn't you *tell* us? We could've moved on them."

Suslov shrugged. "My decision was otherwise. I have seen no evidence that Americans are particularly concerned about Nazis. Besides we have always believed there are Nazi sympathizers in the U.S. government who might . . . misuse information." Suslov smiled condescendingly.

Sovern remained angry, but restrained himself. He understood Suslov's conception about America and knew it was an honest, if wrongheaded, belief. "Go on," he said. "How was Miss Earhart set up?"

"We have been aware," Suslov continued, "that there is a man kept at this farmhouse. The Nazi types call him the Chairman. He apparently looks like Hitler and has been trained to talk and act like him. At least that is the conclusion of our analysts in Moscow. The Nazis have a story ready—should they ever return to Germany—that this so-called Hitler had special surgery or some medical treatment to retard his aging. Even some high-ranking fascists don't seem to know it's a fraud. They will try to install this puppet as a figurehead. It's an intelligent scheme, I think."

Sovern was silent. He glanced over at Earhart and saw her uneasiness at Suslov's revelations.

Earhart could imagine what Sovern was thinking. He might believe, she reasoned, that *she* was a fake, maybe even a Nazi agent trying to confuse the United States. No one could blame him for believing that, not after this devastating revelation by the Russians.

"How do you know about this Chairman?" Sovern asked.

"Look, this I cannot tell you. But we ourselves would've thought it was actually Hitler had we not had the evidence of his death. Your woman friend here was undoubtedly programmed to continue the myth into the highest reaches of your government. You were wise to check with us."

There was nothing Sovern could say. The Russians were far ahead in their knowledge of the Nazi movement.

"We will give you the address of this house," Suslov continued. "You can search it. A group of the Nazis left there today, probably for some meeting. We tried to follow, but our man lost track of them in traffic. They'll be back."

Sovern took a deep breath, then smiled sympathetically at Earhart before returning his attention to Suslov. "Thank you," he said. "I'm glad we share the same interest here. You've saved us a lot of worry . . . and sweat."

Suslov rendered a slight European bow. "At your service," he said.

Sovern and Earhart started out of the ambassador's office, Sovern carrying the picture. The ambassador slapped him on the back. "We'll have the Hitler evidence from Moscow by pouch tomorrow," he said. "Of course, I'll make a full report of this lady to keep our people up to date."

"Of course," Sovern said, somewhat humiliated by the Soviets' competence.

Sovern and Earhart left the Embassy. Their ride to the Archives was more leisurely now. The crisis was over. Sovern's attention would now be directed toward routine countering of the Nazi movement, although the violence in West Germany and America gave that a greater importance than before. He now began to piece together the puzzle of the missile attack on the *Stuyvesant* in New York Harbor. The Nazis, he reasoned, were trying to convince him of Earhart's genuineness and the accuracy of her Hitler story by taking extreme steps to get her back. It had worked. It had worked magnificently.

Sovern radioed ahead to the President, in code, the Soviet revelations. He also notified Foreman at the Archives and the members of the National Operations Board. Collectively, the security forces in Washington calmed down.

"I don't know how to ask your forgiveness," Earhart said as the car passed DuPont Circle and headed down Connecticut Avenue for the Federal Triangle, the main governmental center of the city.

"You're not the first person ever to be set up," Sovern assured her. "It happens to our people all the time. Frankly, I'm glad it turned out this way. You wouldn't actually want Hitler *alive*, would you?"

"Of course not."

"The Nazis may try some further terror tactics and link them to your name, but I think we can cope with it better now."

"What would you do?"

"Tell them what the Russians told us. Once they realize we know the score, it's going to throw them off."

"I guess," Earhart said with a resigned sigh, "you have no further use for me."

"Ridiculous! You did actually meet Nazis. You can still help us try to identify them. And we're going to go through that house in Massachusetts. There may be things there, documents or paraphernalia, that you've seen before. Once those Nazis return I'm going to interrogate them personally."

There was a period of silence as both Sovern and Earhart were lost in their own thoughts. Finally it was Earhart who revealed another aspect of her uneasiness. "Dick," she stammered, "you *do* believe the Russians, don't you?"

Sovern laughed, a cynical laugh. "Strange," he said, "how we were thinking the same thing. Yes, I believe them. Suslov's personal honor is at stake, and he's a vain man. There's no reason why they should lie about this. In fact, they're proud that they know more about the Nazis in America than we do."

"I guess so," Earhart said. "But I was so certain."

Sovern reached over and patted her on the shoulder. "When this is all over," he told her, "I'm sure you'll have a lot you'll want to do."

Earhart smiled ironically. "So you still believe I'm Amelia Earhart?"

"Sure," Sovern said. "That hasn't changed."

"There *is* a lot I plan to do once my identity is made public," Earhart revealed. "I want to go back and see people, see the places I knew when I was flying. By the way, do you know Buzz Aldrin?"

"Not personally. I know he was the second man on the moon. Same flight as Neil Armstrong."

"Aldrin's father serviced my plane at Teterboro Airport in New Jersey," Earhart said, "way back in the thirties. I want to meet Buzz. I want to tell him what a great guy his father was."

As Sovern and Earhart spoke, a Soviet code clerk sent a report of their visit to the Foreign Ministry in Moscow. After his transmission, the clerk excused himself for lunch. He left the Embassy, drove to a pay phone, and placed an urgent call to an apartment in Albany, New York, where Helmut and Greta—the two aides to the Council of Rebirth—maintained a clandestine communications center. He told them that the Americans now knew about the Williamstown house. The two had to return and make certain nothing revealing had been left there.

II

The National Archives is an imposing, pillared building on Pennsylvania Avenue, situated between the Capitol and the White House. It contains, in stonewalled rooms, the major papers of the Republic, the most important in bombproof vaults that can be lowered into the ground in the event of an enemy attack. The tourists filing through on this particular day had no idea of the drama being played out in the basement nor did they recognize the woman who walked by them on her way into the building.

Sovern and Earhart went immediately downstairs, where documents lined the tables at which Franklin Foreman's staff worked. Foreman greeted them with a smile. "Guess the Hitler business was a false alarm," he said, not realizing how humiliating the statement was to Earhart.

"These things happen," Sovern quickly responded, signaling Foreman with his eyes not to dwell on the idea that Earhart had been set up. "Anything here?" he asked, moving the conversation on.

"We've uncovered notations of experiments in hormone changes," Foreman replied, "and we're having medical people analyze them. But they don't appear to be related to age retardation. By the way, I've got a question on that."

"Shoot."

"If the Russians are telling the truth, doesn't that make you wonder why the Germans never tried the age-retarding device on Hitler?"

"Frank," Sovern replied, "drugs can have radically different effects on different people. It could be that the age-retarding treatment, especially in its earliest forms, didn't work on Hitler. Or maybe he was violently allergic to one of the ingredients. It could also be that he was afraid of it, especially after the assassination attempt against him in 1944. The issue now, though, is to track down the treatment and determine if the Nazis treated anyone else besides Miss Earhart. One of their key people could still be running around loose."

The phone on Foreman's desk rang. It was the President, wanting to speak with Sovern.

"Dick," the President said, "I'm pleased the Russians are sending us their documentation. Détente has its uses I guess. But look, I want you to check out that house in Williamstown right away. I want those responsible for the boat tragedy caught and punished. It bugs me that the Russians knew about the house and we didn't. Christ, it's embarrassing."

"Yes, sir."

"Well, I'm not blaming you, understand. I know it's an FBI flap. But you're the one who's got to straighten it out."

"I'll get up there, sir," Sovern said.

"Good, Dick. And by the way, I'm sure ol' Rudy Peddington is going to try to make you eat a bushel of crow on the Hitler business. I'll cut his tail on that. Don't worry."

They hung up.

"Frank," Sovern said to Foreman, "please accompany Miss Earhart and me to Massachusetts. Turn this operation over to a deputy until you get back."

"Of course," Foreman replied.

The simple act of leaving the Archives proved more complicated than Sovern had thought. On his way out he saw the familiar, unwelcome face of Hugo Lessing, puffing his cigar and smiling in the cynical, self-satisfied way that only Hugo Lessing could smile. Lessing was an investigative reporter for the Associated Press, a thorn in the side of official Washington for two decades, and a man of almost unprecedented slovenliness. In an age when journalists affected the elegance of a newfound prestige and professionalism, Lessing was a throwback to the image of reporter-as-untouchable. Rotund, with a five o'clock shadow, he always wore a rumpled suit—usually gray—and usually one that hadn't seen the inside of a cleaning establishment in months. Yet, Lessing also had a reputation for fairness, one of his few saving virtues.

When Sovern saw him he tried to head in another direction, gesturing for Foreman and Earhart to follow. But Lessing was quicker than he looked and stepped in front of them.

"Dick," the reporter said in his gruff smoker's voice, "what a coincidence seeing you here."

"Yes . . . incredible coincidence, isn't it, Hugo?"

"I was just refreshing myself on the Bill of Rights," Lessing continued. "It's very inspiring for we who labor for the public's right to know."

"I'm sure."

Foreman turned to Earhart. "We've got an appointment," he said and started moving the flier away.

"Oh, don't go," Lessing implored.

"They've got a schedule, Hugo," Sovern said. "My orders."

"Aren't you going to introduce me to the lady?" Lessing asked, although Earhart was almost out of earshot.

"She's a staff aide," Sovern said.

"Oh, really?"

"What do you mean by that?" Sovern asked, apprehensive over a menacing twinkle in Lessing's eye.

"Dick," Lessing continued, tobacco smoke drifting down to his grungy shirt collar, "that lady who landed in Los Angeles . . . the Aviation Agency says she was a hoax. Some actress they sent back home."

"So?"

"You know, we asked about her name, address, phone. They said they didn't have it or lost the papers or something like that."

"Hugo," Sovern said, "that's not my area."

"Wait," Lessing said. "After she landed I was one of the few guys who took it seriously. I did voice-prints on the TV statements she made and compared them with Amelia Earhart's."

"Oh, Christ."

"This is not all," Lessing went on, relishing every moment. "I know you were out in L.A. and flew with her. I have very good contacts at the airport out there."

"Wonderful."

"Suddenly Lessing moved closer to Sovern, enveloping him in smoke and putting his hand on his shoulder. "Dick," he said quietly, "I know what you two talked about up in the wild blue yonder."

Sovern was stunned. "How?"

"We bugged the plane."

"You . . . *what?*"

"As soon as I found out you were going up with her, I sent out the word. Our L.A. office managed to get a man inside the cockpit with some gadgets. Never trust airport security, Dick."

"Apparently not."

"All in a day's work," Lessing said.

Sovern looked Lessing squarely in the eye. "Hugo," he said, "I'm going to ask a favor."

"Don't print it," Lessing said.

"That's right."

"Look, Dick, I'm no fool. I'm not gonna do something that'll hurt the country. I won't use the story as long as you play fair with me."

"Which means?"

"Which means exclusives. When the thing finally breaks I want to be up front."

"You've got it," Sovern said, "as if you really left me an alternative." He smiled, the smile of an admirer. Although appalled at the news leak, Sovern nonetheless admired Lessing's aggressiveness. He only wished his own CRG people were as motivated.

"And I want interviews with her," Lessing continued. "Dick, she's the story of the decade."

"Sold," Sovern said.

"Those Nazis really had good medicine," the reporter went on, probing for more information.

"Yes, they did."

"What did Foreman come up with downstairs?"

"My, Hugo," Sovern said, "you're so eager today."

Lessing batted his eyelashes. "Why, Dick," he said with fake naïveté, "I'm just a little lamb in search of truth."

"That's beautiful, Hugo, really moving."

"Dick, let's cut the baloney. You believe what she said up there?"

"I think the Nazis are plotting something," Sovern replied, "but I don't know exactly what."

"She's helping?"

"She's trying. I don't know how much she actually knows."

"A plant maybe?"

"I'm pretty sure she's not. Look, Hugo, I've got to run . . ."

"Why? Williamstown is just a short hop."

"You want to give me the results of my last physical too?"

"If you like," Lessing replied, then coughed outrageously. "At least you passed yours."

"Hugo, we'll talk." Sovern started away.

"Hey, Dick, wait . . ."

Sovern stopped. "What is it?"

"You know what I'm gonna ask," Lessing said.

"I think I can guess. . . ."

"Dick, square with me. Is Adolf Hitler alive?"

Sovern laughed. "*That* we've already checked out with the Russians, Hugo. The answer is no. Definitely no."

"That's what I figured," Lessing said. "I didn't buy that either. You'd have to be crazy."

CHAPTER 9

It was nauseating, Willy Haas thought—these old men, some with beards, straining in their seats to get a better look when the pilot announced that the shoreline of Israel was ahead. Haas had always felt uneasy in America and Britain when he visited on Nazi business. But flying to London was an emotional holiday compared to the approach to Israel. He kept glancing at the Chairman—Mr. Shapiro to El Al—who tried to keep his eyes closed to avoid watching the religious zealots.

The plane made a normal landing at Ben Gurion Airport and taxied to a ramp. A few minutes later the Chairman set foot on Israeli soil for the first time. Haas saw the look of restrained terror on his face, as if he was being forced to drink some poison.

The Nazis divided into two groups, each taking a large taxi to Jerusalem. As they passed through the Jerusalem hills, they were amazed at how desolate the scenery was. The land of milk and honey was not pretty, certainly not like the mountains of the fatherland.

Haas rode with the Chairman. The Nazis said nothing as they traveled, something that amazed the Israeli driver, who was used to gregarious groups of Americans. At one point he looked into his rear-view mirror at the dour faces, then glanced back.

"Is the ride uncomfortable?" he asked.

Willy Haas instantly realized that the quiet was arousing suspicion. "No, no," he replied with almost too much enthusiasm. "It's a good ride. But this is our first time. It's very moving for us. We're widowers."

"Oh," the driver said with compassion. "I know what you mean. It's lonely without . . ."

"Yes."

"I came here a widower, too. My wife died in the camps."

A chill went up Haas's spine, and once again he saw the uneasiness, the contempt on the Chairman's face. "I'm very sorry," Haas said. "Some of us, we lost, too."

"I figured. Your accent, it's German. Yes?"

"German-Jewish!" Haas insisted.

"Of course. What else? Where? . . ."

"Köln."

"Köln?" the driver asked with a smile. "I knew people from Köln. Did you know the Friedmanns from the florists? Everyone knew them."

Haas hesitated. He wanted to play along, to seem like one of the old crowd, but he wondered whether the driver was an intelligence agent, feeding him a fake name to see if he'd respond.

"Maybe everyone knew them," he replied with a deep sigh. "Maybe I knew them. I don't remember. I blocked everything out. I don't like to talk about those days."

"Sure, sure," the driver said. "Sorry."

"It's okay."

"Your friend there seems so unhappy."

"Mr. Shapiro?" Haas asked. "He's not unhappy. He's looked forward to this for years. But he's tired. A sick man. Bad heart."

"Too bad," the driver said. "Make sure he takes it easy here. The sun is hot."

"His doctor told him."

In about an hour they arrived at the King David Hotel, the most famous in Israel. It had gained worldwide prominence in 1946 when a group of terrorists, fighting for an independent Jewish state, blew up one of its wings. The hotel at the time housed the British Mandatory Authority, which administered the area.

Haas and his group got out and waited on the sidewalk while the driver unloaded their baggage. Then the driver shook his passengers' hands. "I hope you have a good stay here," he said. He was especially warm to the Chairman. "Feel better." Then, the concentration camp number plainly showing on his left arm, he patted the Chairman on the back.

The Nazis entered the hotel, brushing past a German tourist group.

The first step once they moved in was for Haas to administer injections to the Chairman necessary to keep his delicate system free of infection. The Chairman immediately went to bed.

It was only about an hour later when Haas got a phone call from the main desk of the hotel. The attendant hold him there was a cable from America. Haas rushed downstairs, assuming the cable could only come from other Nazis. He rapidly opened the message in the ornate, paneled lobby of the King David. It read:

HOME HAS BEEN SOLD STOP WE ARE DO-
ING EVERYTHING POSSIBLE TO KEEP
SALE PRIVATE

It was code indicating that the Americans knew
about the Williamstown house, but that Nazi agents
would make certain nothing was discovered that could
reveal the Chairman's travel plans. Haas instantly
assumed that the information about the house had
come from Earhart, although in fact Earhart had not
known about it prior to meeting with the Soviets.

Haas sent back a reply:

CONFIRM SALE STOP KEEP ME INFORMED
OF ALL NEGOTIATIONS AND SNAGS

By prior agreement no Nazi business was discussed
in the hotel. The King David, often the sight of in-
trigue, might be bugged, Haas reasoned. When he returned upstairs, he summoned the other Nazis and
they went for a walk in the neighborhood, strolling
near the border that had divided the city when its
eastern section was under Arab rule. They carried
Minolta thirty-five-millimeter cameras, posing as tourists, frequently pointing out the sights.

The Nazis felt enveloped by the overwhelming presence of Jerusalem, which symbolized everything they
despised. They looked uneasily toward the ancient
wall surrounding the Old City and glanced toward the
sand-colored Church of the Assumption, where Mary,
according to tradition, ascended to heaven. They wondered when they would come to the Wailing Wall, not
realizing it was deep inside the Old City out of view of
the area surrounding the King David.

"The Americans know about Williamstown," Haas

told the group, "but I'm sure they don't know we're here, or we would have been intercepted. Besides, they get their information from Earhart and she escaped long before we made these plans. I see no immediate danger. We will meet with General Gottes as scheduled."

The next morning the group left the reddish, rectangular King David, dropping word that they were going to see the famous Chagall windows at the Hadassah Hospital. The Chairman was not with them. As the supreme leader he did not participate in tactical operations. He remained at the hotel, one member of the council with him.

Haas and his party boarded an ordinary public blue-and-white bus for the journey to the hospital, which was in a suburb of new Jerusalem. The bus was filled with men in shirtsleeves and women in plain cotton dresses, typical Israeli attire. There were a few Arab workers in traditional headdress, most going to a new construction project near the hospital.

Haas did not notice the two dark-skinned men in khaki pants and T-shirts who watched the bus carefully as it pulled away from the King David. They seemed especially interested in the passengers near the rear, including three members of the Council of Rebirth. After the bus left, they got into a green Fiat and drove away.

The bus, like many in Israel, was notoriously bumpy. It lurched to a stop at every other corner, taking on more and more passengers until the center aisle was full. There was no air conditioning, and the scent of sweating people was pronounced.

Haas looked out the window as the bus passed a square where the Davidka, a roughly made mortar, was on display. It had been instrumental in Israel's 1948 war of independence.

Haas was glancing at the weapon when suddenly there was a blinding flash of light.

The bus shook.

The roar of the blast was deafening.

Before anyone could realize it, the back of the bus was hurtling down the street. The entire rear half was in the air.

The bus turned on its side.

Women shrieked.

The wounded moaned.

Then, fire.

The gas tank went up.

Willy Haas, pinned under a seat, struggled to get free. His first response was rage. Someone had found them out! It was either the Americans or the Israelis. And they had planted the bomb to kill them!

Haas started choking on the dense black smoke. He felt the heat of the burning fuel as it leaked toward him.

He would die, he thought, in the Jews' land.

Then he felt the tight grip of a powerful hand as it grabbed his left arm and pulled. A crowbar appeared, wrenching the twisted seat from above him. An Israeli fireman pulled him strongly, violently, from the wreckage. He found himself lying on a sidewalk as an Israeli woman threw a shawl over him. "Thank you," he said weakly.

He turned his head to the left and saw firemen aiming foam hoses on the burning fuel. Bodies seemed everywhere. The moans still penetrated the air, but occasionally some moaning would cease as another victim died.

One thought shot through his mind: some council member, perhaps undergoing emergency surgery, might reveal something under anesthesia.

But what did it matter if they had been found out anyway?

Willy Haas assumed he would be arrested momentarily. He prepared a speech in his mind defending the glory of the Reich and pledging perpetual loyalty to its ideals.

So, he thought, he would die like Adolph Eichmann —at the hands of an Israeli firing squad.

But the arrest never came. Instead Haas began hearing onlookers—English-speaking tourists—using the words "Arab terrorists." A young man, punching one fist into the other, was shouting, "They must've come from Lebanon! From the PLO!"

Willy Haas, obsessed with his own mission, never considered that he was simply the victim of another episode in the Arab-Israeli conflict.

Within a few minutes he was sitting up. His injuries were superficial; his cuts and bruises were treated at the scene. He tried to stand. His legs were shaky, but he made it. Under ordinary circumstances a nurse or doctor would have stopped him, but they were too busy taking care of the seriously hurt. Haas began walking toward the wreck, gazing at bodies as he staggered along, trying to find the members of the council he had taken with him.

It wasn't long before he identified two. . . .

They were dead, their heads covered by cloths. They had been sitting in the rear of the bus where the bomb had been planted. It had long been a favorite practice of terrorists to position bombs under rear seats.

He found another council member untouched. Rolfe

Barlack, who was scheduled to be minister of finance in the new Nazi regime, had been wandering around looking for Haas.

The last man was a mess. Heinrich Wagner, the man the Chairman had picked to head the Education Ministry, was lying in the street, a leg practically blown off, deep punctures in his stomach, and severe burns around the head and neck. He was moaning, but drugs killed most of the pain. Haas approached a doctor working nearby.

"Sir," he asked, "that man over there is my friend. How bad?"

"Very bad. We're taking him in."

"In where?"

"Hadassah Hospital. A surgery team is waiting."

"He must have an operation?"

"One? He'll be lucky if he gets off with five."

Haas looked back at Wagner, realizing the security danger of putting this man in the hospital under the constant drugging that would be needed. Slowly, he walked back to Wagner, looking as anguished as he could, and knelt beside him.

"Jacob," he said, using Wagner's code name for the Israeli leg of the journey, "can you hear me?"

He got no response.

"It's going to be all right, Jacob. We'll take care of you." He took a handkerchief from his back pocket and started wiping Wagner's face. But carefully, using the handkerchief to shield his movements, he removed a small capsule from his camera case. He placed it inside the handkerchief and started wiping Wagner's mouth, letting the capsule drop inside. It dissolved quickly.

"We'll get the best doctors, Jacob," Haas intoned,

acting as if he wanted to cry. "From New York, from anywhere."

He heard Wagner choke. "Doctor!" he yelled. "This man needs help!"

A doctor rushed over. He made a quick examination, then placed his hand gently on Willy Haas's back. "It's all over," he said quietly.

Haas actually forced himself to cry. It wasn't all that difficult since Heinrich Wagner had been a boyhood friend in Germany. "Dirty Arabs," he mumbled. "Dirty Arabs."

Now only Haas and Rolfe Barlack remained. They, the council member left with the Chairman, and the Chairman himself, were the entire ruling body of the new order.

In the confusion Haas and Barlack slipped away. Despite their injuries they still were scheduled to meet the renowned General Gottes. They walked a few blocks and both bought some new clothes to change into. Haas still felt unsteady, and Barlack occasionally had to hold his arm, but he showed remarkable resolve for a man who had been near death a few minutes before.

"Barlack," Haas said as they walked to a bus stop, "I want you to handle the matter of the dead. Bury them here in Israel. Pretend it's a big religious thing. Learn some of the Jew prayers. We've said we're widowers, so no one will raise questions about wives coming. These people bury their corpses within twenty-four hours so we have an excuse about why no relatives are flying for the funerals."

"Good," Barlack replied. "Well thought out." Barlack was one of the more timid of the Nazi leaders, more a technician with funds than a pillar of strength.

He idolized Haas, who was only a year older, and believed Haas to be the Chairman's alter ego. He never questioned his judgment.

Bus schedules were disrupted by the terrorist bomb, and Haas worried that General Gottes would think the appointment had been cancelled. He hoped that Gottes had heard about the bombing.

The bus ride to Hadassah Hospital took about twenty minutes. There was still an enormous commotion around the emergency entrance as victims from the attack were brought in, many by helicopter. Relatives and friends, many grief-stricken, huddled in small groups waiting for familiar faces, covered or not.

General Sigmund Ludwig Gottes was a Nazi legend. An armor lieutenant during World War II, he single-handedly accounted for thirty-three American and British tanks during the Battle of the Bulge and was personally commended by Adolf Hitler. At the end of the war he fought his way through Allied lines and hid in the Black Forest for three years, making contact with a number of other loyalists who would not abandon the Nazi cause. He was revered by Willy Haas and the neo-Nazis because, unlike others, Gottes stayed in Germany and refused to escape to Latin America. He forged identity papers, grew a beard, shaved his head completely, and got work as a carpenter in Bavaria, at one point constructing executive offices for the Bavarian Motor Works. No one ever suspected his identity, and Allied records still listed him as missing, presumed dead.

The Chairman assigned Gottes the rank of general in 1976 and ordered him to command the military phase of the new Nazi takeover. Still working at carpentry, Gottes spent every evening formulating plans and cultivating sympathetic contacts in the German Army.

Ramrod straight, not a wrinkle in his face, Gottes waited at the hospital's bus stop for his reunion with Willy Haas. His straightness was only partly related to military bearing. Gottes stood only five-four and tried to compensate with perfect posture. His shrill, high-pitched voice did not help his self-assurance. A military genius but a social failure . . . he had never married.

Haas's bus stopped and he and Barlack got off. They saw Gottes wearing, as usual, his sunglasses. By prearrangement there was no warm or unusual greeting. That might attract attention.

"We were delayed," were Haas's first words. "Maybe you heard."

"I heard," snapped Gottes with military correctness. "Casualties?"

Haas lowered his head. "We lost three of the best," he replied.

Gottes showed no emotion. "This is unfortunate," he said, "but such is war. Sometimes the shells fall in the wrong places. I'm sure you agree there must be no interruption."

"Of course," Haas assented. "The Chairman would never hear of it."

The men walked along the road, leaving the commotion of the hospital behind them. No one suspected what they were up to. No one suspected who they were. They walked into a large field, which Haas and Gottes always thought provided the best cover. There was no place for someone watching them to hide. They reached a grassy spot and sat down. Again, by prearrangement, Gottes had brought some sandwiches in his briefcase, giving the impression that this was a simple picnic lunch. He packed roast beef, his own favorite, not terribly concerned about the others' tastes. Although Haas was technically Gottes's superior, Gottes had contempt for all politicians—except the Chairman. He felt himself to be irreplaceable and treated Haas, at best, as an equal.

"So," Gottes said as the three sat down and spread out some napkins, "we must accelerate. This is a wise decision. Besides, I always thought the January thirtieth date was childish. Pure sentiment. It's something Goebbels would have thought up."

"How soon can you be ready?" Haas asked, somewhat intimidated by Gottes.

"Ready? We are always ready. We can actually execute a return to power in ten days."

"You aren't exaggerating? It's such a convenient number?"

"I am not exaggerating. Ten days."

"Then we make it ten days," Haas said. "We take power December fifteenth."

"Barring weather problems," Gottes pointed out.

"Explain."

"The only thing that can stop us," Gottes said, "is snow. It stopped the Americans at Bastogne. We can learn from it."

"So," Haas said, "we watch the weather as well as the calendar."

"Correct."

"Your plans, General?"

For the next hour and a half Gottes presented the outline of the plan to retake Germany. Of course, much of it had been discussed and approved by the Chairman before. But these were the final details, the military tactics. Gottes handed Haas a number of encoded notes for study before December fifteenth. When

the discussion was over, the three walked casually back
to the bus stop for a ride into Jerusalem.

"Tell me, General," Haas asked, "you have been in
Germany far more than I have. Are you absolutely
certain that the people will respond?"

For the first time that day Sigmund Gottes smiled.
"Certain? I am more than certain. You should see what
is happening in the homeland now. People literally
cry out for a strong leader."

"*Our* leader?"

"Of course. Even the young. It's amazing. They look
for books by the Chairman, articles, anything. A li-
brarian told me that the microfilm copies of newspapers from the great days are practically worn out.
Our people want to relive those days."

"Do they understand the risks?"

"Of course. They know the Russians will panic when
the Chairman takes power, but they realize the Americans will prevent the Bolsheviks from moving. After
all, America is much more concerned about commu-
nism than about us. The only reason the Americans
fought against us in the war is because Churchill and
the Jews led them into it. Many Americans like us,
even admire us. They never hated us the way they
hated the Japanese, even during the fighting. They
even let some of our people with war records come to
America after 1945. We have many followers in America today. Look at all the commotion that magnificent
group of National Socialists caused in Chicago. You
remember, don't you? They wanted to march through
one of the Jew towns in the suburbs. I wish it had happened. You would have seen how strong we are there."

"I'm not so sure the current American government
admires us," Haas snapped.

"This we can handle," Gottes assured him. "And if

we should have to meet the American Army, this can be handled too."

With full confidence the three rode back to Jerusalem for a reunion with the Chairman and the burial of their comrades. Gottes, ostensibly on vacation, would then fly back to Germany. The Chairman and the others would stay in Israel until three days before the takeover, when Gottes would become the key figure, the focal point of years of dreaming and planning.

"The Chairman has decided on a codeword for the operation," Haas told Gottes as the general was leaving the King David. "It is . . . HARRIS."

Gottes raised his eyebrows, then laughed. "The Chairman retains his wonderful sense of the ironic." He knew the significance of the name. Sir Arthur Travers Harris had been chief of the Royal Air Force's Bomber Command during World War II and the leading architect of the night saturation bombing of Germany.

The coming days would bring a remarkable revenge.

CHAPTER 10

Williamstown, Massachusetts

"That's it," the FBI agent said.

He sat behind the wheel of his 1976 Chevrolet Nova, with Sovern, Earhart, and Foreman in the back seat. They were parked about a quarter mile from Haas's farmhouse, camouflaged somewhat by trees and bushes.

"You have no doubt?" Sovern asked.

"None. We checked phone records and found a strange pattern of outgoing and incoming calls, all to or from pay phones, the night the tour boat went down."

"Traffic?" Sovern asked.

"There are two young people in there, one male, one female. I'd say they're in their twenties. Every now and then the girl goes out to the Grand Union, but that's all. Their car is rented from Avis . . . legitimately."

"You do a garbage check?"

"Of course. We had a man posing as a sanitation worker pick up their garbage and go through it. There was nothing there."

"We'll have to go in," Sovern said.

"Break in?"

"Is the place ever empty?"

"No."

"So a break-in is academic anyway unless we want to wait around for both of them to go to the movies. We haven't got that kind of time. How complete is your stakeout?"

"I've got eight men in the area," the agent replied. "You see that guy over there?" He pointed to a man in coveralls at the top of a telephone pole, ostensibly working on the cables. "And the guy over in the field looking like a surveyor is ours. The rest are either hidden or in a light plane that comes over at irregular intervals."

"Communications?"

"They all have walkie-talkies in pockets, but we wouldn't want to use them until we absolutely have to."

Sovern understood that walkie-talkie signals were easily intercepted.

"How you want to work it?" the agent asked.

"Foreman and I go in," Sovern replied. "I want five men backing us up from concealed positions. No massing of strength. I don't want to create a panic in there."

"We'll stay cool," the agent assured him. Sovern hoped so. His confidence in the FBI was limited.

"I have a warrant," Sovern continued, "and we'll do a full search. Take the lady far away. There's a chance of stray bullets."

"We'll drive to Williamstown and wait for your call."

Within a few minutes another agent pulled up in

a second car, which Sovern and Foreman prepared to take.

"Good luck, Dick," Amelia Earhart said.

"Thank you, Amelia," Sovern replied warmly.

The time was 1:36 P.M. Sovern set the time of entry into the farmhouse at 1:50. He and Foreman drove slowly toward the house as Earhart was sped away. Sovern honked twice as he passed the agent on the telephone pole. It was a signal for the man to come down and assume a rear position as Sovern and Foreman entered the house. Other agents discreetly moved toward the house, using shrubbery as cover. The day was crisp and cold, about thirty degrees, but dry. The sky was clear, the sun bright.

At 1:46 Sovern drove past the farmhouse, looking it over, watching for any suspicious activity. He saw none. He circled back and pulled into the driveway.

Sovern and Foreman got out and walked toward the gray, wooden front steps. There was no sign of life inside.

They were on the second step when, suddenly, the front door swung open.

"Watch out!" Sovern shouted.

He and Foreman dove for cover as a shotgun blast cut through the late fall air.

Sovern heard a moan. He rolled in the bushes, drawing his pistol.

In a few seconds the farmyard was blazing with gunfire as the FBI agents opened up, three with pistols, two with submachine guns.

Sovern lay prone, trying to find a position from which he could shoot. He crawled a few feet and now was able to see Foreman. His assistant, for whom he had a genuine affection, was dead, a gaping hole in his chest. "Oh my God," Sovern groaned softly.

The gunfire continued. Sovern saw two FBI men with submachine guns charge forward, seeking closer cover behind thick trees. Still, shotgun and pistol blasts poured intermittently from the farmhouse. Sovern deduced from the sound pattern that two people were firing. He decided to make a move. Edging close to the house, he crawled around to the rear. When he reached the back, he slowly got up, pistol in hand. He wanted to look in one of the windows, but had to avoid getting hit by FBI bullets passing through the house. He quickly ran to the side, where he was in view of an agent. Using hand signals he gestured his intentions.

Within seconds FBI fire was directed to the second story, allowing Sovern a clear field. He peeked through one window and saw two figures barricaded behind furniture, firing through the shattered panes in the living room. Every few seconds they changed position, running or crawling from room to room to confuse the agents.

Sovern had a clear shot, but he wanted these people alive. He moved swiftly to the back door. When the young man started crawling to a new location, Sovern burst in, taking cover behind a refrigerator.

"Hold it!" he shouted.

Helmut Pflug, startled, did not hold it. Instead he spun on the floor and fired, darting to his feet and charging Sovern.

Sovern fired twice.

Pflug was dead before he hit the floor.

Immediately Greta Berndt turned toward Sovern, fear etched in her face. But she still held her pistol.

"All right, put it down!" Sovern ordered.

Greta hesitated. Her gun, though, was not pointed

at Sovern. Now a quizzical look came over her, as if she couldn't believe what was happening.

"Put it down!" Sovern ordered again.

Instead Greta casually pointed the gun at her right temple. "I will not be taken," she said. Then she fired.

For a moment Sovern couldn't believe what he had just seen. Doctor or not, he couldn't accept suicide and had never witnessed it before. He just stood there, staring. The silencing of Greta's and Helmut's guns had resulted in a corresponding lifting of FBI fire, and for a time all was silent.

Sovern knew that if he opened the front door and tried to wave an all clear, he might, in the first second, be mistaken for one of the Nazis and killed. So he walked to the rear door and shouted.

"This is Sovern! I'm coming around with my hands raised!"

He did, giving the agents plenty of time to identify him. "They're both dead in there," he announced, then ran to his fallen aide.

Sovern looked down at his aide, a tear forming at the side of one eye. Why, he asked himself, had they assumed the Nazis would open the door without resistance? The cost of the assumption was obvious.

Sovern took off his jacket and covered Foreman's face. Then he and the FBI men entered the house and inspected the bodies of the Nazis, searching for identification and for information on the Reich Reborn. At Sovern's order an agent radioed for Earhart to be brought back. He also stationed two agents outside to watch for any Reich Reborn associates who might happen by.

"Call the phone company," Sovern ordered. "Find out if these two made any calls in the last ten minutes. They could've called for help."

The check was made. The phone hadn't been used.

Sovern and the agents quickly went through the house looking for any radio transmitting equipment that the Nazis could have used to send an SOS during the battle. There was none.

Earhart arrived fifteen minutes later. She saw the covered body outside, and an agent told her who it was. She rushed inside and found Sovern on the second floor.

It was not in Amelia Earhart's character to create a scene in the face of tragedy. She had always had a low regard for those who drew more attention to themselves than to the dead or injured. When she saw Sovern she simply walked up to him, compassion in her eyes, and placed both hands on his arms. "I'm so sorry," she said. "He was a very decent man."

Sovern lowered his eyes. Earhart was unaware of the exact circumstances of the death, but she sensed what Sovern was going through. The CRG director had seen too many men die.

"I lost a number of my flying friends," Earhart said softly. "I think I know how you feel."

She had said exactly the right thing, and eased Sovern's pain slightly. "Have you found anything?" she asked.

"Not a thing. Those people did a thorough job of sanitizing this place, that is, they removed anything that could've caused a breach of security."

"I know," Earhart said. "I used to be in the trade."

For the first time since Foreman's death Sovern attempted a slight smile. "Slipped my mind," he admitted.

They searched a bedroom that looked like any bedroom in any farmhouse. One of the FBI agents trailed after them, dusting for fingerprints. Another one took photographs of all the rooms, then started taking close-up "macro" shots—some from as little as an inch away —of virtually every object. A small detail, the agents knew, might give a hint of where an object was made or bought or whether it came from a particular region. They meticulously labeled each photographic frame.

Sovern and Earhart went from room to room, also taking notes. They found a writing pad in a second bedroom and took it for evidence. Nothing was on it, but Sovern knew that pencil impressions sometimes penetrated many sheets down.

"Is there anything in this room or in any other," Sovern asked Earhart, "that is even vaguely familiar to you?"

"Not so far," Earhart said.

"Don't only consider large objects," Sovern emphasized. "I doubt if they'd bring furniture from Germany. I mean little things. Pens. Cigarette lighters. Look for the personal things that some flunky might have left here."

Amelia Earhart looked, but there was nothing.

They went downstairs and continued the search. Now the FBI men were taking pictures of everything, and the flashes punctuated every few seconds of the examination.

Finally Sovern came upon the small room with the steel door and the gate outside. "What the hell is this?" he asked.

An FBI agent came up to him. "We figure they might've had a vault in there," he said. "Sometimes people in the crime families have weird things like that."

The gate was unlocked and the steel door was open.

Sovern entered the room. It had no windows and had been stripped almost bare. Only an air conditioner remained, unplugged.

"Strange," Sovern said to the agent. "If they had a vault, why didn't they put it in the basement?"

The agent shrugged.

"And why does a vault need an air conditioner?"

"Well," the agent said, "maybe they had things in there that had to be kept at a certain temperature, like photographic films or some chemicals."

It was a possibility, Sovern realized.

Earhart appeared in the hallway and examined the gate and steel door. They meant nothing to her. Then she entered the room.

Sovern saw the sudden terror in her eyes.

"What's wrong?" he asked urgently.

"Smell it."

"What?"

"That smell. Don't you sense it?"

True, Sovern thought, there was a subtle pungency in the room that wasn't present in the rest of the house. He hadn't thought anything of it.

"That's one of the chemicals used in the age-retarding process," Earhart explained. "I *do* remember it. I can't remember exactly at what point it was used or why, but it was there. One of the labs had this same smell, except it was stronger. The chemical was reddish brown, almost like rust."

"Are you certain?"

Earhart paused. "I'm pretty sure. That part of my memory is holding up. Maybe I'm more than pretty sure."

"Could you be confusing it with some other chemical? Is it possible you smelled the same thing somewhere else?"

"I . . . really don't think so. You're a doctor. Have you ever smelled the same thing before?"

Sovern took a few deep breaths and tried to think back all the way to medical school. "No," he replied tersely.

"He was here," Earhart said almost mystically. "Adolf Hitler was here."

"Come on, we've ruled that out," Sovern admonished her. "But it *is* possible that they've preserved someone else." He thought for a moment. "Maybe it was someone who bore a resemblance to Hitler, maybe even a relative."

"The Russians were probably right, then," Earhart responded. "There *is* a chairman, or whatever they call him."

"I'll ask the Archives to keep watch for any notes on Hitler look-alikes in those documents," Sovern said. "After all, the British had a double for Field Marshal Montgomery. The Nazis may have dreamed up the same thing for Hitler, then put the man on their age device."

Earhart continued to glance around the bare room, captivated by the scent. "It's incredible," she said, "that this preservation was going on in the United States, right in a small college town."

"I'm not so sure it's incredible," Sovern replied ironically. "Who would expect to find them here? Our security services really can't sweep beyond a few major cities and defense installations. I've always had the impression most of the really important espionage is based in small towns."

They continued searching, but the only suspicious item they found was a small pile of ashes in the fireplace. "I assume they burned papers before they left," Sovern told the flier.

They had been there more than two hours when Sovern felt he was reaching the point of diminishing returns. "They obviously rehearsed the art of leaving," he said to Earhart wryly. "But if they went somewhere distant, they had to make travel arrangements. Most people do that by phone."

"The phone records," Earhart reminded Sovern, "didn't show any outgoing calls to travel agencies."

"No, they wouldn't use the phones here. But they might have used pay phones in town."

He ordered the records of pay phones in the Williamstown area checked. Then he and Earhart agreed to reexamine the entire house, going over every item one by one. It was during this reexamination that Earhart noticed, under the oblique light of a wall fixture, something curious in the kitchen. In the yellow paint next to the phone there was an impression—18½—apparently left when someone wrote with ball-point pen on a piece of paper held up to the wall, a normal procedure when speaking on the phone. The number "18½" seemed unusual. "Look at this," Earhart said, pointing out the impression to Sovern.

Sovern looked and shrugged. The number was odd to him, too. "It couldn't be a price," he said. "It's not written that way. Obviously it was something someone *said* on the phone, something that was received here and written down."

"A measurement?" Earhart wondered.

"*One* measurement?" Sovern responded. "Usually they come in sets."

"True."

"Maybe weight," Sovern said. "What would weigh eighteen and a half pounds or ounces . . . a figure that they would have to get from the outside and which was important?"

"A camera?" Earhart theorized. "Or an instrument?"
The guesses, she knew, were wild.

While he was wondering, Sovern was notified by an
FBI agent that phone records of area pay phones
showed no calls to travel agents, bus, or rail lines. It
was logical. People made those arrangements from
home. The Nazis, Sovern deduced, had their travel
plans taken care of on the outside and either phoned
or mailed to them in code by confederates.

"Time," Sovern mumbled.

"What?" Earhart asked.

"The eighteen and one half could refer to time. It
could be eighteen and one half hours. The length of
a terror operation could've been the issue. Or it
could've been the length of a trip."

"That's logical," Earhart said.

"What is?"

"The length of a trip. It would be the kind of thing
they'd want to know just before leaving."

"That's right."

"Maybe," the flier went on, "they wouldn't call out
to travel agencies or the like, but they left this number,
say, with an airline, for last-minute cancellations."

"Possible," Sovern said. "It's also possible that some
flunky did that without authorization."

Neither Sovern nor Earhart had particular confidence in their deduction. It was a wild guess, after all,
one of many that day. But Sovern instructed an FBI
agent to start checking all travel organizations, transport lines, and ticket offices in the region to see if any
had a record of calling the farmhouse. The agent re-
cruited additional manpower from the Boston FBI
office to handle the job.

Sovern and Earhart soon finished their second sweep

of the house, discouraged at having come up with nothing clear or dramatic.

"Our best hope," Sovern concluded, "is that the Nazis call in. We have tracers on the line that can fix the source of a call without the phone being answered here."

"And of course it *can't* be answered here," Earhart said, referring to Greta and Helmut's deaths. "What if they call from a pay phone in the middle of nowhere and get suspicious when no one answers?"

"In that case our raid will have had the effect of alerting them. There's always a risk in these operations of doing more harm than good. We've got to accept that risk. It's part of the game."

"Are we going back to Washington?" Earhart asked.

"As soon as we finish here."

"I think we should start in the Archives," Earhart went on. She paused and looked around. "Maybe these were just second-level Nazis here anyway."

"With that chairman in the other room?" Sovern asked. "No, these were major leaguers."

"At any rate, I'm anxious to get back to the Archives, Dick. They *had* to make some record of those experiments."

"Why don't we grab a bite and fly back on an Air Force jet," Sovern suggested. "We can start going over documents in the morning."

"Fine."

There was food in the refrigerator, but Sovern refused to touch it and wouldn't let Earhart or the agents eat it either. There was a chance the Nazis had left one or two things poisoned in case the house was invaded. So an agent drove into town and brought back sandwiches. Dinner, on the floor of Willy Haas's

living room, was served at 6:30 P.M. One agent remained on watch in a car outside.

It was 6:51 when Sovern heard the crackling of
static on the watchman's car receiver. Then he heard
a blurred voice deliver a message. A few moments later
the agent rushed in the front door. "Mr. Sovern," he
said, "we just got a call via Albany. Please contact
Ambassador Grechko at once. Extremely urgent, sir."

"Did they indicate subject?" Sovern asked.

"No, sir. Grechko wouldn't say."

Baffled, Sovern went to the phone in the kitchen
and placed a call to the Soviet Embassy. But he
quickly hung up.

"What's wrong?" Earhart said.

"I don't want to call from here," Sovern replied.
"There might be listening devices in the wall or
hooked into the phone wires where we can't see them."
He took Earhart and an FBI agent and drove into
Williamstown, where crowds of Williams students were
scouring the stores for Christmas presents. Sovern went
into a coffee shop and squeezed into a phone booth.
He knew the number of the Soviet Embassy and asked
the Williamstown operator to dial it.

Yuri Grechko, his tie knot lowered beneath his
collar, his collar button open, beads of sweat on his
worried forehead, paced his office while Anatol Suslov
slumped in a chair, his face equally lined with concern.

"Where is he?" Grechko asked angrily. "These
Americans are never around when you need them."

"I'm glad Sovern isn't around too often," Suslov
replied cynically.

"I wish he was working for us," Grechko said. He
glanced at his watch again. "This is such a humilia-

tion. Prestige is important in America. This will do nothing for ours."

"Or our nerves," Suslov said. "We will have many sleepless nights."

The phone rang. Grechko snapped it up. "Grechko," he said sharply.

"Mr. Ambassador, this is Richard Sovern."

"I thank you for calling. I don't know whether I'm glad to hear from you or not. This is not going to be pleasant."

"What's wrong?"

Grechko slumped down in his desk chair. He whisked a piece of paper from his large green blotter and flipped on his reading glasses. "I have an official statement," he said.

Sovern tensed. He didn't like the nervous, clipped tone that he heard from the other end. This was not the Grechko he knew. "Go ahead," he said.

"This comes directly from the Foreign Minister," Grechko said. "I quote:

THE SOVIET GOVERNMENT IS IN RE-CEIPT OF THE REQUEST BY THE UNITED STATES GOVERNMENT FOR CONFIRMA-TION OF THE DEATH OF ADOLF HITLER, CHANCELLOR OF THE DEFEATED FAS-CIST GERMAN REGIME. THE SOVIET GOV-ERNMENT WISHES TO COOPERATE IN EVERY WAY WITH THIS REQUEST. HOW-EVER, THE UNITED STATES MUST REC-OGNIZE THAT DURING THE DISCREDIT-ED COUNTERREVOLUTIONARY YEARS OF THE STALIN RULING CLIQUE MANY STATEMENTS AND CLAIMS WERE MADE

FOR THE PERSONAL GLORIFICATION OF STALIN HIMSELF. THESE STATEMENTS . . ."

"Just a second!" Sovern said. His face was turning white. He could feel his heart begin to pound. "What are you saying?" he asked tensely.

For a few moments, Grechko didn't reply. "Let me finish," he finally said.

"Go on," Sovern agreed.

"THESE STATEMENTS WERE OFTEN FALSE. IN 1945 THE STALINIST ELEMENT ANNOUNCED THAT SOVIET TROOPS HAD FOUND THE BODY OF ADOLF HITLER. SOME YEARS LATER THESE CIRCLES RELEASED SO-CALLED MEDICAL EVIDENCE TO SUPPORT THE CLAIM . . ."

Grechko paused to catch his breath. Sovern now gripped his phone tightly, his body taut, his mind sensing an impending catastrophe.

"THE CLAIM WAS A LIE. THE BODY OF HITLER WAS NEVER FOUND."

"For Chrissake," Sovern moaned.

"There is more," Grechko revealed.

"I don't need more."

"Apparently," Grechko pressed on, wanting to disclose everything in the Foreign Ministry note, "they falsified the medical evidence by using data found in Hitler's doctor's files. Believe me, Sovern, I didn't know about this until Moscow sent this note. I swear to you . . ."

"I know," Sovern said. He had a high opinion of Grechko's integrity. "So what you're saying is that Hitler might well be alive."

"One can assume anything," Grechko admitted.

"Does your government have a revised opinion about this Chairman?"

"The people doing the surveillance," Grechko replied, "were proceeding on the assumption that Hitler was dead. They weren't aware of the . . . deception. They now withdraw their description of the Chairman as a fraud. *They* don't know. But *you* have the woman."

"Are you prepared to believe that she's Amelia Earhart?"

"Sovern," Ambassador Grechko said with a deep sigh, "I am prepared to believe that the moon is made of green cheese."

"We'll keep you informed," Sovern promised. The conversation ended. Richard Sovern looked through the fingerprint-covered glass of the phone booth at Amelia Earhart. He did not have to give her a full explanation. She had already guessed from his expressions and the few words of his phone talk she could make out. He opened the booth.

"You've been vindicated," he said.

They drove quickly back to the farmhouse. The mood in the car was grim, somber. The Russians had dropped a bombshell, but had furnished no information on how to defuse it. Sovern was no further along in his pursuit of the Nazis than before he phoned Grechko. Only now the original urgency of his mission was restored. Through his mind ran the spectre of a violent Russian reaction if he failed.

Sovern and Earhart entered the farmhouse and in-

stinctively went back to the little room with the steel
door and iron gate.

"So he *was* here," Sovern said, looking around.
"That man was in this room where we stand."

"Just a second," Earhart said, playing devil's ad-
vocate. "The Russians only said they didn't find him.
They didn't say he was alive."

"He's alive," Sovern said bluntly. "Their admission
removed the one piece of evidence to the contrary.
Your story and all the other things that have happened
make me positive."

"According to the Russians," Earhart said, "we must
have missed him by a few days."

"Where, logically, would they have taken him?" Sovern asked. "Back to Germany maybe? Once they knew
you landed they certainly accelerated their plans for
taking over. They're not going to wait around until
January thirtieth."

"So we'll have to center our efforts in Germany,"
Earhart said.

"Based on what? We really know nothing." Once
again that number eighteen and one-half passed
through his mind. "It doesn't take eighteen and one-
half hours to get to Germany," he said, almost to himself.

"So?"

"What *could* that number mean?" He paused and
argued it through in his mind. "Maybe he isn't in
Germany. Maybe that's too dangerous."

"Where then?"

"Almost anywhere. If they had a base in the United
States, why not other countries?" Sovern called for an
FBI agent and asked that travel time from area airports be checked to see if there was an eighteen-and-
one-half-hour flight to any point. He also ordered a

chemical analysis of the small room, hoping to trace the drug that produced the scent, the drug that Adolf Hitler needed.

"Chip the paint off," he ordered an agent. "Send samples to the FBI lab, my CRG lab, and the Bethesda Naval Hospital. Also cut out some floor boards and do the same." He looked around and up. "Take a cloth and unscrew the light bulb. Fumes flow upward and stick to glass. I want to know what that drug is. Anywhere they take Hitler, he's going to need it. Unless they have a lifetime supply that means they'll be buying chemicals." He turned to Earhart. "Do you recall what that drug was used for?"

"No," Earhart replied. "But it was used all the time."

Sovern turned back to the agent. "Alert every pharmacology and toxicology department in the country that's cleared to work with CRG. I want that drug identified and reproduced."

Sovern and Earhart left the farmhouse and raced by car to the Albany Airport. On the way, though, they were intercepted by a message from the White House, ordering them to divert to a nearby Air National Guard base. There two Air Force F-111 fighter-bombers waited. Each one had room for a pilot and passenger, so Sovern flew in one plane, Earhart in the other. The order for the special flights came directly from the President. Informed of the Soviet revelation, he wanted Sovern back in Washington as quickly as possible.

Sovern and Earhart landed at Andrews Air Force Base, Maryland. A heavy downpour and winds made a helicopter flight to the White House risky, so Sovern was whisked to the White House by car while Earhart returned to her quarters for a much needed rest.

Sovern couldn't see him, but standing just outside the Andrews gate, soaking wet but keeping his eyes on everything, was the man who seemed plugged into the world—Hugo Lessing.

CHAPTER 11

The National Operations Board met in emergency session in the White House at two A.M. The session was informal, held in the Oval Office, and the President appeared in red-striped pajamas. His desk as usual was cluttered. He never allowed anyone to straighten it up.

"Well, it's a new ball game," the President said. "We've got sweat. Anybody got suggestions?"

Rudolph Peddington, sitting properly in a straight-backed chair, waved a pencil.

"Rudy?" the President nodded.

"Mr. President," Peddington declared, "I know we're all shocked at what the Russians have said, and we obviously have to go on the assumption that Hitler is alive, but I'd like to know just what we're doing about it."

The President turned to Sovern. "Dick?"

Sovern was surprised and annoyed by the question. "Rudy," he said, "I think you *know* what we've been doing. You know about our contacts with the Russians, our work at the Archives. You know about the search at Williamstown."

"Ineffective!" Peddington snapped. "We've got a crisis, Dick!"

"I'm glad you finally agree!" Sovern shot back.

"Now don't call me a Johnny-come-lately! I have always been concerned about the Nazis. But what've you done? You handled that thing in New York and got a boat blown up. You ask the Russians some questions and they lead you around by the nose before coming clean. You set up a basement full of librarians at the Archives and haven't come up with anything. You went up to that farmhouse and got your assistant killed."

"Rudy, control yourself!" the President barked.

"Oh come on, Mr. President," Peddington insisted, "it's the talk of the community." Community, everyone knew, was government slang for the intelligence services.

Sovern remained calm, although he was far from an unemotional man. "Mr. President," he broke in, "I ask that we hear Mr. Peddington out."

The President was surprised. "Dick," he said, "you'll never make a politician."

"Mr. President," Sovern answered, "I don't intend to become one. I'd like to hear what Rudy has to say."

The President shrugged and nodded to Peddington.

Peddington glanced around the room, sensing some shock at the intensity of his assault. "I certainly didn't mean anything personal," he assured the room. "I have the greatest respect for Dick Sovern. But like everyone else here I've got to think of the country first. The fact is, Dick, that the results of your effort have been pretty meager. Your office has worldwide resources, yet they haven't even been used."

"May I reply?" Sovern asked.

"Certainly," the President said.

"Everyone in this room can judge what has occurred so far. I don't feel a need to defend anything I've done. It isn't for me to say. But an operation like this is not going to succeed in a matter of hours."

"Would you like to arrange a time schedule with Adolf Hitler?" Peddington asked, a smug, victorious lawyer's smile bending his lips.

Sovern ignored the question. "The Nazis had years to prepare Hitler's security. We have weeks, if that, to break it."

"True," boomed Chester LeVan, who, though no intellect, thought Sovern was getting a raw deal.

"And you haven't dented it a bit," Peddington charged.

"Leads are being pursued," Sovern replied. "I can't guarantee a quick result."

"I can," Peddington said.

Everyone was stunned. The claim had come out of the blue.

"Explain that boasting," the President insisted.

"Mr. President, my CIA is the proper agency to handle this problem. Dick's is too small and specialized. This isn't some little executive mission, it's the biggest thing since the war. I recommend that Miss Earhart be turned over to us at once and that my deputy director of operations be put in overall charge of the search for Hitler, under my control of course. Now, Dick can certainly advise. I welcome it."

Sovern turned toward the President. "Sir, that is entirely your decision."

The President turned around in his chair and looked out the window. "It seems to me," he said, "that Miss Earhart asked to talk to Dick Sovern when she came in."

"Sir," Peddington insisted, "that was a first contact. It was like seeing the family doctor before going to a specialist."

"Well put," the President agreed. "Rudy, I'll take your request under advisement. For now I don't think it would make sense to change horses. Dick, you continue."

"Thank you, sir. I appreciate the confidence you've shown in me."

Peddington simply lowered his eyes and made some notes on a yellow pad, already thinking of ways to obtain what he had just been denied.

"Dick," the President asked, "what's your next step?"

"Our next step," Sovern said, realizing how minor it sounded, "is to continue with our crash examination of the Archives documents. We're also having our agents in Germany question known Nazi sympathizers. West German agents are doing the same thing. I'm not optimistic that they'll find out anything significant. The plan to put Hitler in power is probably known only by a few people in the hierarchy. What we need is some hint of major activity within the German Nazi movement, the kind of thing that would immediately precede an attempt to seize power."

"Like?" Chester LeVan asked.

"Like an intense propaganda campaign in a particular city, or highly concentrated terror. We might even find a sudden increase in AWOLs from the West German Army."

"Why's that?" the President inquired.

"Because the Nazis would certainly recruit some of

their shock troops from the current army. They can't defend their new regime with old men."

"If these signs pop up, what do we do?" the President wanted to know.

"Very often," Sovern replied, "an opponent spills a good part of his plan during the preparations. The Nazis, after all, actually had the details of the Normandy invasion in 1944 but didn't believe them. Admiral Nimitz deduced the Japanese attack on Midway in 1942 by studying their operations up to that point. If the signs come, we've got to comb every one, looking for the hints that give us the overall blueprint."

"Sounds pretty vague to me," Peddington said.

"It *is* vague," Sovern snapped, "until it happens."

"What if it doesn't?" Peddington asked. "What if their security is so good that we don't learn anything about them."

"Then we're in trouble," Sovern concluded.

"I think that's where I came in," Peddington said. Sovern seethed, realizing he'd been outfoxed by Peddington's verbal gymnastics.

"I've worked a lot with military types," LeVan broke in. "I know there's a big element of luck in all of this. What Dick says seems pretty right. I mean, even in running a corporation you aren't sure every minute where you're going or what the competition is doing. If you did you'd be God."

Sovern hadn't expected much help from LeVan and he was grateful for the defense secretary's support. He had never realized it, but LeVan had an obsession with fairness. Although he was known for treating people somewhat roughly, LeVan always observed definite limits, never dropping personal insults or degrading a man in front of others. His bullheaded manner, though, disguised his good side.

The door swung open and one of Sovern's CRG
aides who had been assigned to the White House
entered. He went quickly to Sovern's side, whispered
urgently in his ear, and handed him a handwritten
message.

"Are you *sure*?" Sovern asked the man in a loud
whisper.

"Positive," was the reply.

Sovern glanced at the note as the aide was leaving.
"Mr. President," he said, "I can't be sure if this is
significant, but we found the number eighteen and
one-half on a wall at Williamstown. One possible explanation was that it was the length of time an an-
ticipated trip might take. We now find out that there
is an eighteen-and-one-half-hour flight from Logan
Airport in Boston."

"Where to?" the President asked.

"Tel Aviv, sir."

The President laughed. "Tel Aviv? The Nazis?"

"It would be the perfect cover," Sovern reminded
him.

"Yes, but you're just guessing about what that eighteen and one-half meant," Peddington said.

"I'll admit that," Sovern replied. "But this is in-
triguing. When our people discovered the possible
Tel Aviv angle, they started checking the airlines that
fly there. We should know soon whether any of them
had contact with the farmhouse."

"Fair enough," the President said.

"In the event there *has* been contact," Sovern said,
"we'll try to track down these people in Israel."

"How much time do you think we have?" LeVan
asked.

"There's no way of knowing. Certainly there's *some*
time. When Earhart landed three days ago the Nazis

had almost two months to go until their great day. Even if they accelerated, there's still some required preparation."

Sovern had no way of knowing that he had precisely ten days to stop the Nazi takeover.

A few minutes later the President's red emergency phone rang. He quickly picked it up. "This is the President," he said. He listened, then looked toward Sovern. "It's for you, Dick. Grechko on the line." He clicked on the amplifier so everyone could hear the conversation.

Sovern rushed to the phone. There was a series of clicks as Grechko was connected. "Sovern," he asked, "are you there?"

"Yes, Mr. Ambassador."

"It's very grim, isn't it?" Grechko went on.

"Well . . . it's serious, Mr. Ambassador. What can I do for you?"

"Find him," Grechko answered.

"We're trying."

"Look, Sovern, that's not enough. I have just spoken with my premier. The Soviet government is deeply worried."

"I can understand that, considering your history with the Germans," Sovern said.

"We don't know whether to have confidence in you or not," Grechko continued. "We must take steps."

A slight surge of fright shot through the CRG director. "What do you mean?" he asked.

"What if you fail?" Grechko went on. "The Soviet government and people cannot allow the monster to return. We would have to take . . . certain actions."

"Mr. Ambassador, would you be more specific."

"Important actions," Grechko replied. "Actions with profound significance."

"I see." Sovern could cut through the diplomatic jargon and realized that Grechko was hinting at, but did not want to directly threaten, military force. "We urge restraint," he replied to the ambassador. "Sir, we're not sure just how strong the Nazis will be if they surface. Their entire threat could fizzle. Even if Hitler is alive, and returned, the Germans could easily dismiss him as a fraud. If they *did* accept that he was Adolf Hitler, they might well turn against him, even laugh him into oblivion . . . or arrest and try him."

"You don't know the Germans," Grechko said philosophically.

"*No* one really knows what's in their minds," Sovern replied. "That's why we think rashness on the part of your government or ours will accomplish nothing."

"We are being as restrained as our national interest requires," Grechko said. "But we will not be deterred."

"I'm sure you realize," Sovern responded, the President nodding his approval, "that the United States will protect its interests as well."

"We shall talk," Grechko said. "I wish you success." Then he hung up.

Sovern returned his receiver. "Not very warm, was he?"

"What do you think they'll do?" the President asked.

"They're probably already doing it," Sovern replied. He picked up the internal White House phone and asked for the latest satellite photography from central Europe. The response confirmed his hunch. "Mr. President," he reported, "the Russians are beginning to move troops into East Germany. Those already there are deploying along the West German border."

"For Chrissakes!" the President exclaimed. "Do you think they'll run?"

"I don't think they're looking for a pretext to invade the West," Sovern replied. "I think they're genuinely concerned about the Nazis. It's a red flag to them. They may panic."

The President turned to LeVan. "Chester, I want you to beef up our European command. Alert the Eighty-second Airborne. I want them ready to go in an hour if they have to."

"Yes, sir," LeVan snapped.

"And make sure the Navy has all its carriers at sea."

Peddington seemed pained. "What the hell is wrong?" the President asked.

"Mr. President," Peddington replied, "how do we explain this to our NATO allies?"

"Maybe we have to tell them the truth," the President said.

"No!" Sovern objected. "The whole thing would become public in minutes. You'd have panic all over the place. Why don't we simply tell NATO that we're responding to the Soviets' own buildup."

"What explanation do we give for *their* action?" Peddington asked.

"We don't have to give any explanation. We're just responding. We're always accused of sitting around until the Russians do something, then reacting. So we'll do it again. It's true to form, I'm afraid."

Sovern's cynicism was rare, but the President enjoyed it. "That's good thinking," he said. "Let's do that."

The meeting broke and Sovern prepared to rush back to Andrews. On his way out, however, he once again found himself face to face with the unsightly and unwelcome figure of Hugo Lessing, reporter. Lessing was still drenched from the earlier storm. It didn't seem to bother him; he was obsessed with the story.

"Hugo," Sovern said, glancing at his watch, "it's three in the morning, and you're soaked. You should be home in bed."

"Always the brushoff," Lessing said in his needling way. "The chief goose-stepper himself is out there and you expect me to go nighty-night."

"You know about that, too?" Sovern asked resignedly. "You should write a horoscope column, Hugo."

"You want the future?" the reporter asked. "I can give it to you."

"Oh?" Sovern could see by the intensity on Lessing's face that something urgent had come up.

"That's right," Lessing said. "For instance, why don't you contact a ticket agent named Diana at El Al Israel Airlines in Boston?"

Sovern tensed. "Why?"

"Dick, we know what's going on," Lessing said forcefully, holding back a cough. "We can check these airlines too, and we have shortcuts. That girl called the farmhouse in Williamstown, Dick. And she was confirming a reservation for seven Jewish widowers who wanted to make the pilgrimage. You don't think seven Jewish widowers lived on the farm, do you Dick?"

This was one of those rare cases where the press was giving the government information. Sovern felt somewhat humiliated, but Lessing's tip confirmed the missing piece of the eighteen-and-one-half-hour puzzle.

"Hugo," he said sardonically, "I've always wanted to see Jerusalem."

CHAPTER 12

"They know about us," Willy Haas said to the two surviving council members as he crumpled the heavily coded cable he had just received from Massachusetts. The Chairman was sleeping in his own room. He would be spared the truth until later.

"There was gunfire at the farmhouse. One of our people observed it from a nearby field," Haas went on. "We don't know what happened to Greta and Helmut, so we assume they were captured and were tortured into revealing where we are."

"Maybe they resisted," Rolfe Barlack said.

"The young don't resist," Haas shot back with a certain contempt. "It's a different generation. They do what makes them comfortable."

"*Our* people?" Barlack asked.

"They are untested. It's one thing to run minor operations and help the council. It's quite another to resist torture. This Sovern was seen around the farmhouse. He's very effective."

"So what do we do now?" Barlack asked.

"We get out. Fast. We've had too much bad news today."

The other bad news was another cable, now just ashes in the bathroom sink, from Haas's ally in the Soviet Embassy in Washington. It alerted Haas to Moscow's admission that Hitler's body was never found. Haas knew that Sovern's sense of urgency would be at the maximum. The CRG director, Hass deduced, would assume he was chasing Hitler himself.

"Aren't we trapped?" Barlack asked. "The Americans will alert the authorities here. Willy, these Jews will be fanatics about us."

"We are *not* trapped!" Haas insisted. "Sovern may know the names we traveled under and that we came in a group. But I have other passports. If we each leave separately, we can slip by. We also must divert attention and provide a welcome for Sovern should he come looking for us."

"How do you plan to do that?"

"You watch," Haas said.

Haas ordered the others to pack their bags quickly while he wrote out some cables for transmission to America. As usual the messages sounded innocent enough, but were written in a highly sophisticated code that Haas had designed.

The Chairman was awakened, told the news, and flew into a rage. But he agreed with Willy Haas's plan for countering the new threat.

The group checked out, explaining that the loss of their comrades in the bombing made the stay in Jerusalem emotionally difficult. But Haas made sure to drop comments to bellboys and cashiers that they would go next to Haifa and then north to the Galilee, where they would plant trees in memory of their friends. Everyone on the hotel staff understood and tried to make their departure as easy as possible. They were especially helpful toward the Chairman, who seemed tired and a little unstable.

They took a cab to the Jerusalem railroad station, which was close to the King David. Along the way Haas made sure to tell the driver that the group would stay at the Dan Carmel Hotel in Haifa.

"Nice place," the driver said. "I have relatives in America. They go there. But it's expensive. I don't think we Israelis could afford it."

"Maybe someday," Haas assured him.

"Not driving cabs," the man said.

As they approached the station, though, the driver suddenly pulled over to the side.

"What's wrong?" Haas asked.

The driver didn't respond. Instead he reached into his glove compartment and pulled out a timetable. "I *knew* you were making a mistake," he said. "Someone gave you wrong information."

"What do you mean?"

"There's no train to Haifa for six hours. Why go to the station? I take you back to the hotel."

"No!" Haas snapped. "We want to go to the station."

Willy Haas had underestimated the obsession with security in Israel. Irrational behavior was immediately suspect, and he could now see the driver's eyes examining him, the Chairman, and the two others. "What are you looking at?" he asked.

"Nothing," the driver replied. "I'll take you to the station."

Haas now realized his blunder. "On second thought," he said, "maybe you have a point. You know, we lost good friends in that bombing and we were in a hurry to get out of here. We didn't check the schedules."

"Back to the hotel?" the driver asked.

"No. We want no memories. How much would you charge us to drive around the hills for an hour. Then we'll go and have something to eat."

The driver shut off his meter. "Ten American dollars," he said.

"It's a deal."

The others were baffled by Haas's maneuvers. They knew that the railroad station was simply a dropping off point and that the plan had been for each to take a separate taxi from the station, heading for different airlines at Ben Gurion Airport. True, the driver's knowledge of timetables was a problem, but what was Haas up to?

They found out within eight minutes.

As soon as the driver left the populated section of Jerusalem and entered the hills surrounding the city, Haas started to cough. "Pull over," he ordered the driver. "I don't feel well."

The driver pulled to the side of the road. Quickly Haas took a tiny syringe from his pocket, leaned over the front seat, and jabbed it into the driver's neck. "Hey!" the man screamed. A quizzical look crossed his face before he slumped over.

"That is the price one pays for being too helpful," Haas said. "This was a necessary action. If he had been questioned he would've told about the timetable. The Americans would become suspicious and realize we're not going to Haifa."

The Chairman, desperately tired in the back seat, still gazed at Haas approvingly.

Haas moved into the front seat, pushed the driver to the floor, and drove the cab along the road, dropping the two council members near bus stops. Carrying their luggage, they took buses back to Jerusalem, then hailed separate cabs to the airport. Haas parked the cab in a desolate area, wiped it free of fingerprints, then he and the Chairman waited on a nearby road for a taxi, telling the driver they had been visiting nearby and got lost trying to find a bus stop. They, too, drove to the airport.

Using new passports which certified them as Austrian, the Nazis went separate ways, agreeing to reassemble at the next staging area once they were sure Richard Sovern was off their necks. Rolfe Barlack flew to Paris, the other council member to Madrid. Haas and the Chairman flew to Athens.

As they left Israel, another group of Nazis were flying in. Their arrival was ordered as a response to one of the urgent cables Willy Haas had sent after learning of the farmhouse gunfight. The new group was composed of four commandos. They were determined that if Richard Sovern and Amelia Earhart came to Israel, it would be their last stop.

The first thing Willy Haas did when he checked into the King's Palace Hotel in Constitution Square, Athens, was to phone General Gottes in West Germany. He told Gottes what had happened.

"You must assume the worst," Gottes announced.

"I already have," Haas conceded.

"No you haven't. You have assumed only that the first shipment may be spoiled." Gottes meant that the flight to Israel had been detected. "You must assume that the entire order may be cancelled." Operation Harris, Gottes feared, might be destroyed.

"What do you recommend?" Haas asked.

"We must once again move up the day of the mer-

ger. It's unlikely the competition will be too successful
if we move quickly."

"What day?"

"Three days earlier."

"Will you be prepared?"

"My sales staff is always prepared. They all want
to get rich."

"Does the rest of the marketing plan stay the
same?" Haas asked.

"Precisely. Only the date is changed."

"Agreed," Haas said.

The conversation ended. The date for the Nazi
takeover of Germany and the return of Adolf Hitler
had been advanced to December twelfth.

It was December sixth.

II

Richard Sovern and Amelia Earhart roared off the
Andrews runway in an Air Force C-135 transport,
headed for an Israeli military field somewhere in the
Negev Desert. The transport had been carefully selected and flown in from the Boeing plant in Seattle.
It had been built for surveillance and was equipped
to receive television satellite transmission as well as
wirephotos and coded messages.

Sovern had learned a great deal since his remarkable conversation with Hugo Lessing outside the
White House. Once he knew that El Al was involved
it was comparatively easy to check the seven tickets
that had been sold to the Jewish widowers who had
listed the farmhouse number as the one the airline
should call in case the plane was delayed. Sovern now

knew the Nazis' cover names, including that of Shapiro. He had radioed ahead and found out that the
group had indeed landed in Israel, had been booked
at the King David Hotel in Jerusalem, had lost three
of its number in a terrorist attack, and had abruptly
left for Haifa.

A CRG agent had made inquiries in Haifa and had
learned that the surviving four Nazis had registered
at the Dan Carmel Hotel. Sovern didn't know it, but
the registrations were fakes. The four who registered
were older Nazis who had been hurriedly ordered to
Israel, along with the commandos, by Willy Haas to
act as stand-ins for those who had just fled. The role
of these "dummies" was to confirm that the trail led
to Haifa and to lure Sovern and Earhart there, where
the Nazi commando group was ready and waiting.

Everything Willy Haas had planned was working.
Richard Sovern was sure he was on the brink of a
great capture, perhaps the greatest capture of the century.

The decision to take Amelia Earhart on the flight
to Israel was an easy one for Sovern. First, he thought,
she could provide on-the-spot answers to his questions
if the Nazis were encountered or if any new information came out on the new Nazi threat. Second, he
wanted to keep watch on her physical condition, especially any signs of further deterioration. Since he knew
nothing of the age-retarding system and its effects, he
could not know if—or when—Earhart might become
seriously ill or even die. And third, Sovern did not
relish the idea of Earhart remaining in Washington
where the vultures opposing him on the NOB might
be able to influence her.

Besides, Earhart *wanted* to go. She felt a sense of
being needed, of being a contributor to history. "I

wonder," she said to Sovern as they flew at thirty-five thousand feet, "which ones were killed in the terror bombing. I wonder if they were famous from the old Nazi era."

"The Israeli authorities are exhuming the bodies at our request. We'll know soon enough."

"You don't think one of them could have been . . . ?"

"Hitler? Not a chance. They wouldn't be traveling with him on a bus. No, I think I know which one Hitler is. Hitler is Isadore Shapiro."

"How do you figure that?"

"The El Al agent remembered Shapiro of all the members of that group. He was the only quiet one among them. I'm certain that Hitler tries not to speak or to risk recognition of any kind."

"Sounds logical," Earhart said.

They sat in a compartment with two seats on opposite sides of a brown Formica working table. The seats were fore and aft, and Sovern rode backwards. Aside from surveillance equipment the plane carried some CRG technicians and a group of bodyguards for Amelia Earhart.

Sovern kept glancing at his watch, wishing the flight time would pass quickly. Yet, he knew that the trip would be filled with work and possibly surprises. The exhumation report from Israel, which would provide at least an initial idea of whether the three Nazis killed in the blast were known, was due shortly. The labs in Washington that were analyzing the samples from the Chairman's room in Williamstown had reported that they, too, would have something to say in a matter of hours. And the people at the Archives were assembling documents that Amelia would be able to examine through television.

But there was a lull. Sovern remembered one of the

elements of military training: relax or sleep whenever you can. He leaned back in his chair, sipping a Bloody Mary, occasionally following another plane as it passed in the distance. Earhart closed her eyes a few times, but found it impossible to doze. The level of tension, of anticipation, was too high.

"The last time I flew the Atlantic was in the thirties," she told Sovern.

"And you predicted regular transatlantic air service, didn't you?" Sovern asked.

"Sure did. Do you know when that service began?"

"The late thirties sometime. Am I right?"

"It began the week I disappeared. Pan Am started it with their old flying boats, but I don't think my disappearance was the most reassuring publicity they could have had." She laughed, and once again Sovern saw the magnetic smile that always photographed so well. "It's strange," she went on. "I once made a speech and said that I wanted to fly the Atlantic as a passenger aboard a scheduled airliner. Well, I'm flying the Atlantic. But what a strange reason I have."

Out of the blue Sovern asked something he had always wondered about. "What was your husband like? Oh, maybe I shouldn't ask."

"That's all right," Amelia said. "I like discussing my real life before I became a lab specimen. Well," she continued with a shrug, "George Palmer Putnam was not a man of his time, I'm afraid. He was tough, a promoter, always had public image on his mind. He was more a corporate type than anything else. He would have fit in fine with the big conglomerates the world has right now. Back then people resented him."

"Did you?"

"Oh, I don't know. When I married him I made

him pledge that I could get out of it if I wished. He didn't object, which wasn't in his nature. I appreciated him for that. He was always good to me and he never seemed to resent my success. I know, people said he used me. Maybe he did. But I never really felt used."

"It's hard to think of Amelia Earhart being used," Sovern said.

"I tried to watch for it. People wanted me to endorse things and I did some of that. But I think I've always been my own woman."

"When did your husband die? I've forgotten."

"It was 1950. He had remarried. I do want to visit G.P.'s grave."

"You know," Sovern said, "he spared no effort to find you, even after he remarried. The government never told him the truth for security reasons, and he made a number of trips to the Pacific."

Earhart didn't respond to that. She had mixed emotions about the government deceit, her husband's remarriage, and his death. "G.P.," she said, trying to lighten the subject, "would've had a wonderful time with television and all these new technologies."

"Why do you say that?"

"Well, he was imaginative and he wasn't afraid of technical things like my flying. He would have taken something like cable television or these home video recorders and stood the industry on its ear."

"It's amazing that you know about those things," Sovern said.

"After my escape I spent some time in libraries reading every magazine I could find. I learned quite a bit, although I'm still not fully caught up with technology. You'd be surprised how quickly a person learns about gadgets, though. It's easy. It's much harder to absorb the mood of a period, the feeling, or the way people think."

Sovern could see a certain somberness in Earhart's eyes as she made that statement, as if the mood of the early nineteen eighties pained her. He didn't want to depress her by pursuing it.

"I try to watch the television programs," Earhart continued, "and I've seen some movies. I can't say that I've enjoyed them. They seem emotionally empty compared to the ones in my era. Movies in those days were so human. There were real stories, and you could hum the music. Maybe it was the depression. Hollywood had to entertain."

"Maybe you know," Sovern told her, "that after you were reported lost in 1937, Hollywood made a movie about a woman pilot flying over the Pacific. They didn't use your name, but everyone knew who they were talking about."

Earhart smiled. "I didn't realize that. Who played me?"

"Rosalind Russell."

"I don't recall her."

"I think she became famous after you were lost. The story had her on a spy mission. She crashed into the sea."

"Not too far off," Earhart said.

A steward appeared at the door to the compartment, handing Sovern a sealed brown envelope.

"What's this?" Sovern asked.

"Cable from Moscow to Washington, sir. The President ordered it shown to you."

"Thanks."

Sovern broke the seal and read the cable inside:

SOVIET GOVERNMENT PREPARING NEC-
ESSARY MILITARY ACTION TO DEAL
WITH SITUATION IN GERMANY. IN
EVENT OF NAZI RETURN TO POWER
WILL MOVE AT ONCE. WE REQUEST U.S.
NOT TO RESIST SUCH ACTION. RESIS-
TANCE WOULD BE INTERPRETED AS
HOSTILITY TO SOVIET UNION AND OUR
JOINT CAUSE DURING WW II. NO NU-
CLEAR WEAPONS WILL BE USED.

"The nerve of these guys," Sovern mumbled angrily as he finished. He alerted the radio room and within seconds was connected with the President.

"Sir," he said, "I've just seen Moscow's latest friendship card."

"Some people here think they're bluffing," the President said. "State is convinced they're just testing our defenses."

"Would you like to take a chance on that?" Sovern asked.

"Not really," the President conceded.

"We have to proceed on the assumption that they're seeing that red flag we talked about. I recommend you move the Eighty-second Airborne to West Germany immediately."

"I was thinking of doing that."

"Quickly, Mr. President. Leave them no doubt that we would resist any move."

"Good point. I want to send their premier a good, stiff note."

"I wouldn't do that."

"Why, Dick?"

"The actions are sufficient right now. They're definite and unmistakable. A note could be misinterpreted no matter how we phrased it."

"True."

The conversation ended. The United States and Soviet Union were now moving toward a confrontation based on the Russians' pathological fear of a Nazi resurgence.

The activity aboard Sovern's plane picked up. A few minutes after the Presidential call Sovern was informed that the exhumations in Israel were complete and that one of the bodies had been identified as a minor Nazi war criminal. In addition, fingerprints on all three exhumed bodies matched prints that had been radiophotoed from the United States—prints found in the farmhouse at Williamstown.

Sovern and Earhart were called to a forward communications room. There a television receiver had been turned on. Sovern was put in touch with the CRG lab; Doctor F.D. Ingersoll, CRG's chief chemist, was waiting. Ingersoll could only hear Sovern, but Sovern could see Ingersoll in full color.

Ingersoll was one of the CRG elite, a man in whom Sovern had complete confidence. It was Ingersoll who had traced and identified the poison used to kill an American ambassador to Sierra Leone when all forensic pathologists had given up. It was Ingersoll who had detected changes in the Soviet agricultural program by analyzing blood samples taken from American diplomats in Moscow. He was about thirty-five, wore thick corrective lenses, and was disgracefully bushy-haired. He stood and walked crouched over from years of studying in the wrong kinds of chairs.

"Ingo," Sovern said to him, "I guess this is about those paint samples from Williamstown."

"Correct you are, Dick," Ingersoll said in his youthful voice, tinged with a Virginia accent.

"What've you got?"

"Some goodies, I think. We haven't been able to break down the paint entirely, but there is a definite chemical coating here. I'm convinced it has a lecithin base."

Sovern's medical mind began to work. "That seems logical for age-retardation," he said.

"That's what we were thinking," Ingersoll agreed. "Lecithin, of course, can be used to counter the tendency of cholesterol to clot the arteries."

"Anything else?"

"There are some traces of basic aspirin, and I'm sure you know about the research into that as an anticoagulant. And there's some vitamin D extract, which may have had something to do with bone preservation. We can't be sure on that. We're positive, though, on one thing: the chemical coating is still fairly damp, which means the Nazis were using these drugs recently. Yet, it shows rapid molecular breakdown."

"What does that tell you?"

"That the drug has a short usable life. I'd compare it to ampicillin, which lasts only ten days, even if it's refrigerated. If we're right, the Nazis will have to get new chemical supplies wherever they are."

"Lecithin?"

"Lecithin and maybe the aspirin too—unless they're carrying the stuff with them."

"Ingo, you're brilliant, as always," Sovern said.

"At your service," Ingersoll replied with a mock, deep bow.

"Keep working. Tell me if you come up with anything else."

"Will do. Have a good flight."

The TV screen went dark. Sovern turned to Earhart. "Do you recall the word 'lecithin' ever being used?"

Earhart thought a moment. "No . . . but I can't be sure. I don't remember it."

"Do you recall any ingredient they gave you that looked like little tan granules?"

Earhart's eyes lit up. "And tasted like nuts?"

"Precisely."

"I remember—it was last year. I had some of that. There was a barrel of it. It was in a supply room."

Sovern smiled with satisfaction. "That's it. It's lecithin, a soybean extract. Some people eat it these days because they think it prevents heart disease. There may be some basis for the belief. The Nazis apparently thought so. It may not be difficult to trace if they buy it in quantity. It's a lot easier to trace than common aspirin, that's for sure."

Sovern's idea was to use possible lecithin purchases to zero in on the Chairman's whereabouts. He immediately contacted the Food and Drug Administration, which put its own communications network into operation, contacting drug supply houses and individual drug dealers in the United States. The FDA contacted foreign agencies, emphasizing Israel and West Germany, asking that lecithin sales be traced. Of course, Sovern could not reveal the reason for this sudden interest in lecithin, so drug authorities were told that it was simply an urgent "police matter."

Realizing that Hitler—if he existed—was being treated with drugs, Sovern began to wonder whether Earhart should be getting some medication also, perhaps to slow the deterioration of her arteries. But what medication? Since he knew nothing of the age-retarding process, Sovern understood that any drug he prescribed might prove catastrophic. He would simply be guessing. He recalled the admonition to physicians contained in the Hippocratic Oath—to do no harm. Earhart, he quickly decided, would be given no drugs.

It was only forty-five minutes before the first piece of information came back in reply to his inquiries. A drugstore in Williamstown reported that a man with a mild European accent had bought six tins of R&G lecithin, at $6.49 a tin, each month for the previous three years. The man had explained that he was a heart patient who used it to thin out his cholesterol intake. Yes, Sovern was told, the man gave his address as the farmhouse.

Sovern asked that Jerusalem and Haifa drugstores be checked immediately. Again an affirmative reply came back, this one from Jerusalem. A man with a German accent had bought lecithin and had given his address as the King David. Sovern assumed that both druggists recalled the sales because lecithin, although carried by many drugstores, was a specialized item.

The check in Haifa, though, revealed nothing positive. Sovern simply calculated that the Nazis had a sufficient supply. He did not suspect that the Nazis registered at the Dan Carmel were fronts.

The main point, in Sovern's mind, was that the trail of lecithin purchases seemed to lead to Israel. It confirmed that the Nazis were there.

The lecithin discovery was the last major development during Sovern and Earhart's flight. Their plane passed over Paris, then Rome and Athens, and began its approach run to the airfield in Israel. Sovern made a last inquiry to Washington, asking about progress at the National Archives. He was told that scraps of documents had been found that *might* be related to an age-retarding experiment, but that the staff was not yet ready to make a definite conclusion. It would take,

Sovern was told, another twenty-four hours before any report was ready.

III

Wilhelm Brandt loved Adolf Hitler. When he was a student at a Berlin cooks' school he had plastered his dormitory room with pictures of Hitler and the insignia of Nazi military units. His views became such an embarrassment that the school had sent him packing back to his family in Bonn.

Brandt was now twenty-three. He had been expelled from school at nineteen. His parents, both respected schoolteachers, had refused to take him back, having barely put up with his pro-Nazi fanaticism when he was a teenager. So Wilhelm found an admitted Nazi sympathizer who had served in the SS, and he put the young zealot in contact with Willy Haas. Wilhelm Brandt was trained as a commando and had assassinated eight public officials in West Germany. He was known for his marksmanship and dedication.

When Haas needed a man to head a commando team in Israel, he called on Brandt. The murder of Richard Sovern and Amelia Earhart required the best.

Brandt knew he could not carry weapons into Israel because of the tight airport security. That was no problem since the Nazis had established a working relationship with a small band of right wing Palestinian terrorists in East Jerusalem. When Brandt flew into Israel from Munich he simply picked up four pistols and two grenade launchers from a Palestinian comrade, whom he then proceeded to dispatch with a single pistol-butt blow on the head. Good security,

Brandt was convinced, transcended personal friendships.

Now Wilhelm Brandt sat back in a rocker in his fourth-class Haifa hotel room, cleaning and adjusting the pistol he would use to accomplish his assignment. It was an American-made Smith & Wesson, with its barrel shortened so it could easily be concealed. The blinds were drawn, and the room faced the inner wall of another building, but Brandt had still insisted on rearranging the furniture so he would not have to sit in direct line with the window. Security. He also had a chair jammed up against the door. More security.

Brandt looked his part. His eyes were intense and ever-searching, his bearing quick and alert. He was medium-size, and although somewhat thin was in superb physical condition. His reddish brown hair was styled in an old-fashioned crew cut. He always wore a freshly pressed suit and spotless underwear. If he was killed, he reasoned, and his identity discovered, he wanted the Nazis to appear clean and neat.

The three commandos he brought with him were all in separate hotels. They had not been seen together since their arrival. All of them had studied file photographs of Richard Sovern and Amelia Earhart at an underground Nazi intelligence center before leaving for Israel. They had watched movies of Sovern delivering speeches and had carefully studied his voice. They did not know when he would arrive or where. But they knew the trail would lead him to the Dan Carmel Hotel in Haifa. One of the commandos was always within sight of the hotel's entrance. He carried a tiny walkie-talkie that could send out a beep if Sovern and Earhart showed up. The signal sounded in a small, almost invisible sensor attached behind the ear and could be heard by no one but the commandos who wore it.

Brandt was obsessed with acquiring information about every assignment. He had studied maps of Haifa on the flight from Germany. He had even read a brief history of the city and its conquerors. In his first hour in Haifa he quickly scouted sniper sights. But he still wanted to know more. He finished working on the gun, placed it in a holster concealed under his trousers, and walked down to the street. He carried a Leica camera over the shoulder and had a tourist book stuffed in his right jacket pocket, making him look like any eager visitor. Then, feigning confusion, he sat down next to a young Israeli man. He always chose men for these conversations, believing from experience that they were less suspicious than women.

"Do you speak English?" he asked.

"Yes," the man replied. "But not perfectly."

"Neither do I," Brandt said, exuding charm. "I'm so confused. I'm at the Dan Carmel and naturally, being in Israel, I'm interested in the religious shrines nearby. Are there any within walking distance?"

"Jewish?" the man asked.

"They don't have to be."

"Well, you know, Haifa is the world headquarters of the Bahai Church. Have you heard of it?"

"No. Is it one of those cults?"

"I don't know," the young man said. "I think so. But they have a kind of shrine right on Mount Carmel, down the mountain from the hotel."

Brandt knew the hotel was the highest point on the mountain and that killing Sovern and Earhart there presented a problem, since any escape route could easily be observed. But it was the only place Sovern was sure to come. The shrine interested him. Religious houses made excellent hiding places both before and after an operation since most security types never expect assassins to hang out there.

"Can you get there from the Dan Carmel?" Brandt asked.

"Oh yes."

"Quickly? I hate long walks."

"Sure. A couple of minutes. I've taken friends myself."

"And they let anyone in?"

"Yes, although they sometimes don't like pictures, depending on what's going on."

"Oh, I understand. Is it usually crowded? At times you can't get into these places."

"There are always people there, but it isn't jammed."

"Thank you. You've been most helpful."

The Israeli just smiled.

Wilhelm Brandt took a cab to the circular, pillared Bahai Shrine on Mount Carmel. Above him loomed the modern, uninteresting lines of the Dan Carmel Hotel. He studied the shrine, looking for logical places to melt into the background. Then he timed the walk to the hotel and back. He walked slowly, casually, as anyone would when planning an inconspicuous escape.

His operation would be over in less than fifteen hours.

CHAPTER 13

Sovern and Earhart flew into an Israeli base just south of Beersheba, in central Israel. Just before getting off the plane, Sovern was handed a cable from the CRG office in Washington:

> MUNICH STATION REPORTS BUSLOAD OF 26 AMERICAN TOURISTS FOUND ON COUNTRY ROAD OUTSIDE MUNICH. ALL SHOT TO DEATH. COPY OF MEIN KAMPF AND SMALL NAZI FLAG FOUND AT SITE. PHONE CALL TO US EMBASSY BONN WARNED AMERICANS WOULD BE SPECIAL TARGETS BECAUSE OF YOUR EFFORTS.

And a second cable arrived from the Defense Intelligence Agency:

> SATELLITE PHOTOGRAPHY SHOWS SO-VIETS MOVING ROCKET LAUNCHERS

AND ARMOR IN LARGE QUANTITY TO THE GERMAN FRONT. AMMUNITION AND FOOD STOCKPILED, APPARENTLY IN BELIEF YOUR EFFORTS WILL FAIL.

The pressures were building from all sides. The United States was in trouble no matter what Sovern did.

Sovern and Earhart were met by Israel security officials and Lance Herrin, the chief of the CRG office in Cyprus, who flew to Israel to head the anti-Nazi search. Herrin was blond and handsome and insisted on wearing large sunglasses no matter what the weather. No intellectual, he was still one of the best tacticians in the CRG organization. He was twenty-nine.

Herrin immediately took Sovern and Earhart to a hangar used for servicing American-built F-15 Eagle fighters. Herrin had with him a map of Haifa, a floor plan of the Dan Carmel Hotel, and photographs of the four Nazis. He put the materials on a work table.

"These people are in adjoining rooms at the fourth floor front of the hotel," Herrin explained.

"What do they overlook?" Sovern asked.

"Haifa Bay. It's a very nice view," Herrin said in his correct, official manner.

"Is there a direct line of sight from the ground into the rooms?"

"Not really. You'd have to be standing pretty far down Mount Carmel to get a shot far into the room. It's a terrible upward angle."

"What has their procedure been like?"

"Strange. Three of the four always stay in the rooms. The fourth goes out for anything they need, like shaving supplies."

"How'd you get the pictures?"

"We sent an Israeli security man up posing as room service. The camera was in the tie clasp."

"Do they show any signs of running an operation?" Sovern asked.

"None. We have the room bugged, but they just talk about their old homes in Germany and how much they hate Israel. Stuff like that."

"Well, they're just being careful," Sovern pointed out. "Any phone calls?"

"Not one. We get the feeling they're here for a while. If there's any action being planned, it's somewhere else."

"Any indication of medicines being used?"

"We haven't been able to check. When they call for room service they get together in one room. We thought of sending in someone dressed as a maid while they were having dinner. She could check for medicines in the other rooms—but it's too risky. If one of them went back and caught her snooping, we'd be blown."

Sovern looked carefully at the photographs, most of which were blurred. Taken at moments of opportunity, they did not, in most cases, show the full face.

"Which one is Adolf Hitler?" Sovern asked bluntly.

"We don't know," Herrin replied. "Frankly, none of them look like him."

"They could've done plastic surgery for some reason," Sovern said, "or there could be makeup and wigs involved. Maybe even elevator shoes."

"Are we going to take them?" Herrin asked with obvious relish in his eyes.

"I don't know," Sovern replied. "We can either take them now and end the thing or let them continue and hopefully lead us to the whole Reich Reborn structure."

"I think we should end it now," Earhart broke in. "I've been with these people. They're utterly vicious and you can't take the risk of letting them through the net."

"She's got a point," Herrin said.

"I'd still like to know about the other Nazis," Sovern countered. "Even after this top leadership has been neutralized, even when Hitler himself is in our custody, there will be Nazi activity. It might even get worse. The leadership becomes a set of martyrs."

"Who decides?" Earhart asked.

"The President."

They all returned to the plane to put through a direct call to the White House. In moments the President was on the line. Sovern outlined the situation and the alternatives. "Mr. President," he said, "there are advantages to either plan—taking them now or following them around."

"Now," the President said.

"Why, sir?"

" 'Cause of the Russians. That's my main sweat right now. I want them to know we've nailed Hitler. We can mop up the rest later. This is the head of the snake."

Sovern was still deeply concerned about the remaining Nazi infrastructure. "But sir," he said, "why don't we give the Russians a detailed view of what's happening. I'd be more than happy to have one of their representatives on my team."

The President pondered. "Nope," he said.

"What's the objection?"

"Objection is that I can't let it come out that I've let Russians work with Americans on an intelligence project. No matter what alibi I give, it looks bad. The hawks and the military types'll crawl all over me."

Sovern realized that the President's position, tinged as it was with political acumen, was unshakeable. "All right, sir," he said, "we'll try to take Hitler alive."

"I don't care what you do," the President said. "Just get him."

Sovern, Earhart, and Herrin immediately boarded an Israeli Army helicopter for the flight to Haifa. Herrin had already assembled fifteen CRG agents in the city, so Sovern had all the manpower he needed for the operation. Although he felt seizing Hitler now was premature, his enthusiasm for the prospect grew as the helicopter flew north over the barren Judean Hills. This would be the high point of his career, of course, even more dramatic and historically significant than his first meeting with Amelia Earhart. The capture of Adolf Hitler would clearly rank with one of the great international coups of the ages. When made public it would create a major bombshell. There would be press conferences, Sovern mused, and books. Maybe a movie. He felt vaguely uncomfortable at the prospect. What would it do to him? What effect would it have on his growing feeling toward Amelia?

During the flight, Sovern, Herrin, and Earhart conferred on their approach. Sovern asked Earhart to study the poor-grade pictures carefully. "Is there anyone there who is even similar to anyone you saw in Germany?" he asked.

"No," she replied quickly.

"Is there any physical characteristic on any of them that reminds you of Adolf Hitler?"

"Again, no."

The answers in no way discouraged Sovern. The pictures were too poor to allow for valid judgments.

"We have to assume," Sovern told Herrin, "that

there's a whole net of security guards at the hotel to protect these boys."

"No doubt," Herrin said. "They've probably installed sound sensors in the carpeting outside the rooms to keep track of movements. There are some foreigners registered on the floor and we're assuming they're connected."

"We'll have to go up with enough men to seal off those other rooms immediately and block the elevators and staircases." Sovern studied the floor map of the hotel and pointed to several sites. "We'll have men here, here, and here."

"One problem," Herrin said.

"What's that?"

"We don't know if the Nazis have a suicide plan for use in case of capture. We could do everything right and find them munching cyanide when we go in."

Sovern shrugged. "Lance, that's something we'll have to accept. I'd like to bring Hitler back alive if only so doctors could study him, but you heard what the President said. The order is to end this thing now."

"There's something else," Herrin continued. "They've got to have an escape plan."

"I was thinking the same thing."

"But we can't figure what it is. The only route out of those rooms is down the hall. The fourth floor is too high to go out the windows."

"Strange," Sovern said. "I would have thought they would have been on either the highest or lowest floors. Then they could either use the windows or go up to the roof."

"Look," Herrin said, "maybe we're thinking too much like American security types. The Nazis were always overconfident, right to the end. Maybe they think there's zero chance of being detected, so they're lax on security. They may even think that too much security could be noticeable."

Sovern stared out of the helicopter at a group of Bedouins below tending their sheep. He was lost in thought, fully confident of Herrin's ability yet worried over the seeming contradictions in the surveillance data. Something had been bothering him on the flight over, yet he repressed it until he could have a full consultation with Herrin.

"Lance," he said, a somewhat pained expression in his eyes, "the top Nazis must certainly know by now about the raid in Williamstown."

"I'd imagine so."

"You said they received no phone calls. How do they communicate with their people?"

"We don't know. We've done electronic sweeps of the hotel but haven't detected any strange radio signals. Our theory is that the one man who leaves the hotel communicates in some way, although we haven't actually seen him do it. Remember, Dick, these people have always been scientifically sophisticated. They may have new devices."

Sovern did not immediately respond. He was more concerned with working out his own thoughts. "If they know about Williamstown," he said, "they must've considered the possibility that we'd discover their destination."

"Possible," Herrin said. "But from the report you wired to me I'd say they had that pretty well hidden."

"They'd *consider* it though!" Sovern snapped, feeling frustration at the uncertainty.

"What are you saying, Dick?"

"Maybe they left Israel."

"What?"

"Maybe these are decoys."

"No way," Herrin said.

"How do you know?"

"They've done what they said they'd do in Jerusalem. They've come to Haifa."

"That's no problem. These could be new people flown in."

"It's theoretically possible," Herrin conceded, "but if the others tried to leave we would have detected them."

"I wonder," Sovern said. "People elude security nets."

Herrin smiled. "Okay," he said, "you want the *real* proof?"

"Of course."

"Dick, we showed these pictures to the hotel clerks in Jerusalem. Of course, most of them couldn't give us anything definite, but two identified these men as the ones who were there."

"They were sure?"

"They were sure."

That satisfied Sovern, who now leaned back in the uncomfortable helicopter seat and continued thinking out the operation. Perhaps it was the fatigue or the tension, but both he and Herrin had overlooked a basic investigative point—the tendency of witnesses to think they recognize faces. Willy Haas had dispatched decoys to Haifa who bore some resemblance to the four senior Nazis, and had ordered them to alter their appearance to strengthen the resemblance. The clerks at the King David in Jerusalem were simply trying to be helpful to authorities.

Richard Sovern was twenty minutes away from Haifa. Four Nazi decoys waited to deceive him.

Wilhelm Brandt waited to kill him.

II

As Sovern approached Haifa, Willy Haas and the Chairman boarded an Olympic Airways Caravelle for the flight across the Mediterranean to Rome. They traveled as two tourists. Once in Rome they cabbed into the city and boarded a train for Florence, the main staging area for Operation Harris. There were four days to go, and Sovern seemed safely detained.

Rolfe Barlack and the fourth surviving member of the council also headed for Florence, dreaming of the time in ninety-six hours when they would leave for the triumphant entry into Munich, leaders of the new order.

Like Jerusalem, Florence was the perfect cover city for a gang of monsters. A city of art, serene, seemingly oblivious to the outside world, Florence was the most civilized of urban centers, ravaged in its history far more by the flooding of the Arno River than by war. It was the last place one would look for the remnant of the Nazi leadership, the last place one would suspect as the jumping off place for new Nazi conquest.

The Chairman, Willy Haas, and the other two council members met at the Hotel de la Ville, a few blocks from the Santa Trinita Bridge. As in Jerusalem the group had adjoining rooms. This time they faced other buildings in the rear. Haas had chosen the hotel after arriving in Florence and therefore knew that it could not have been bugged. He spoke freely as the group assembled, the Chairman resting comfortably in an oversized easy chair.

"We had a close call in Athens," Haas said. "I could not buy lecithin at any of the drug stores, and our Chairman almost had a seizure. I had to go to one of the local hospitals. This must not happen here.

Barlack, I want you to make certain we have an advance supply this afternoon. But don't use the hospital. We'll be staying here three days and I don't want any records. Go to another city if you have to, even as far away as Rome, but get the chemical."

"Absolutely," Barlack said.

"I spoke with Gottes by phone from Athens. The Americans are preoccupied with the Russians at this point. They're sending more troops to reinforce their line, and British units are expected shortly. They're all spending much more time guarding against the Russians than in looking for us. The only troops they have in Munich are the ones on leave.

"Sovern is on his wild goose chase. I will decide within half an hour exactly how I want that end of it to work. There are several alternatives for dealing with him.

"Now," Haas concluded with a smile that contorted his wrinkle-lined old face, "I have something magnificent." He walked to a suitcase that he had not been carrying on the flight from Athens or even on the train ride up to Florence. It had been passed to him at the Florence station.

He opened it and reached inside. Then, one by one, he carefully took out four perfectly made Nazi uniforms—brown with red and black armbands, filled with insignia and decorations. The gold on them glistened. The creases in the pants were heavily starched and almost knife-edge thin. The jackets were packed and stretched on cardboard to maintain their shape.

The Chairman and others gazed at the uniforms as if they were religious garments. They had not seen the Nazi insignia on clothing for more than a generation.

"My God," Rolfe Barlack said, a tear plainly evident

in his eye, "I have never seen anything so beautiful."

The Chairman smiled broadly and nodded his approval.

"They are not to be worn until the last moment," Haas said. "They are from the old period. This one, of course, is our Chairman's."

The council members, with the exception of the Chairman, stepped up to feel the uniforms, to admire the insignia.

"By order of the Chairman," Haas went on, "each of you will be entitled to wear the Iron Cross on the day of triumph, in recognition of your service. The crosses are still encased."

The two members clicked their heels and bowed to the Chairman.

Haas repacked the uniforms. "I know that seeing them inspired you," he said. "I know they make us all realize how close the time is. I can hear the crowds. I can feel the emotion."

Haas ended the meeting and walked downstairs to the desk where he inquired about train service from Florence and a number of other points. Although arrangements and plans had been made, he wanted to study all possibilities once again. He took a batch of timetables from a wooden rack.

Then he phoned Haifa.

III

Richard Sovern and Amelia Earhart landed at a small Israeli Army base outside Haifa. They and Lance Herrin drove into the city by cab to set up headquarters at a hotel near Mount Carmel. But

Earhart was immediately taken by CRG agents to a second, heavily guarded location for her own safety. This was Sovern's operation.

Herrin learned from his observers that three of the four senior Nazis were in their hotel rooms as usual, while the fourth was out buying some newspapers and having a snack at an outdoor café. This fourth man was Heinrich Kimmel, a low-level courier in the Nazi underground, who, despite his sixty-one years, had never made much political progress in the movement. But he was intensely loyal and expected his reward once the Nazis took power.

Kimmel, like many of the other couriers, had been trained in a skill that Willy Haas believed was crucial to good communications—lip reading. Unknown to the CRG agents watching him, it was this skill that allowed Haas to communicate with the decoys in Haifa. Haas's phone contact was a Nazi agent staying at a rooming house. He gave the agent instructions in voice code, and the agent then waited for Kimmel to come to the outdoor café. The agent carried a small transistor radio and tuned it to an Israeli rock music station. Then he appeared to mouth the words to the songs. Actually he was giving instructions to Kimmel, who sat two tables away. The agents watching Kimmel never suspected.

Heinrich Kimmel left the café and returned to the Dan Carmel, where he wrote Haas's instructions in detail on hotel stationery and had the other three decoys study it. After they memorized the plan, the stationery was dissolved by chemical and flushed away. Looks of resignation crossed the faces of the four decoys. They understood the reasons for Haas's plan, yet the lack of glory in it left them dissatisfied.

Once Sovern knew that all four Nazis were in their

rooms, he decided to move. He continued to be sensitive to the probability that the Reich Reborn movement had accelerated its schedule and that the Nazis might therefore leave Haifa at any moment. He ordered all CRG agents in the city to converge as discreetly as possible on the Dan Carmel and prepare to cover the seizure of the Nazi leaders.

As Richard Sovern gave instructions, Wilhelm Brandt waited in his room, his pistol oiled and loaded. Then, at precisely 1:06 P.M., for the first time since he arrived in Haifa, he heard the beep on his walkie-talkie. His body tensed as he sat in his chair. For a moment he simply looked down and stared at the instrument clipped to his belt under his jacket.

There were three beeps in all.

Richard Sovern had been sighted.

Wilhelm Brandt was to take up his position. He cleared his mind of anything but the mission ahead. Mentally he was ready for the role of assassin.

Sovern had been sighted by one of Brandt's men driving in the vicinity of the Dan Carmel, being briefed by Lance Herrin on the layout and traffic pattern of the area. Sovern liked, whenever possible, to get the physical feel of an area of operation. In the case of Haifa he was particularly interested in the eighty-six-degree heat, which he had never experienced in December. He had decided to dress in sports clothes and had bought an Israeli golfer's hat with sweatband. He knew what a drop of sweat in the eye could do in the midst of a gun battle.

Wilhelm Brandt walked quickly to Mount Carmel and sat down on a bench opposite the Dan Carmel hotel. His pistol was strapped to his right leg underneath his khaki pants. He too wore a hat with sweatband for the same reason Sovern did. He also wore sunglasses with reflective, silver-coated lenses. No one could see the movement of his eyes.

Sovern picked 1:30 as the time he would enter the Dan Carmel. He assumed Nazi security men were in the area and decided to enter through a garden in the rear. That was no problem for Wilhelm Brandt. His men had every line of sight covered.

Herrin's CRG agents began filtering into the hotel. Some, dressed as bellhops and janitors, drifted up to the fourth floor. They were surprised to learn that virtually everyone on the fourth floor was out, except the Nazis. This meant there were *probably* no security people to contend with up there. Who knew how many Nazi agents were in position to get to the fourth floor quickly?

Herrin gave Sovern an automatic pistol that had been serviced and adjusted. Sovern once more studied the floor plan of the hotel. He checked his watch. It was 1:18.

At 1:25 Sovern pulled around to the rear of the Dan Carmel. He, Herrin, and two other agents got out of their car, a 1975 Mercedes. Other CRG agents were nearby, watching for any sign of their Nazi counterparts.

Brandt's man spotted Sovern, and once again Brandt got a beeped message. Quickly, but nonchalantly, he walked to a garden at the side of the Dan Carmel. He could see the rear of the hotel and, at 1:27, saw Richard Sovern. Brandt walked to an unoccupied patio which had a good, low wall. It was ideal for shooting.

Richard Sovern and Lance Herrin started walking toward the hotel's rear entrance.

Wilhelm Brandt glanced around, memorizing the escape route he planned to take.

It was 1:29.

Sovern looked up toward the fourth floor. Brandt removed the pistol from his leg holster and caressed it under his jacket.

Then suddenly, unexpectedly, Brandt received five sharp beeps on his walkie-talkie. He was stunned, disheartened, angered. It was the "don't shoot—operation off" signal, to be given only by highest authority.

Brandt couldn't understand, but his obedience was total. Crushed, he returned the pistol to its holster and watched as Richard Sovern entered the hotel. He hoped that the "hold" was only tentative, that whoever ordered him not to shoot simply wanted the operation carried out when Sovern *left* the hotel.

Richard Sovern entered the Dan Carmel. He started up a rear stairway to the fourth floor. He would not take an elevator. The risk of an elevator being sabotaged or of being trapped inside when a hand grenade was tossed in was too great.

Sovern reached the fourth floor with Herrin right behind. Twelve other agents now converged, some appearing to be tourists, others hotel workers.

Through arrangements with the hotel, Herrin and three other agents carried room keys to the Nazis' rooms. In unison they stepped up to the doors. Then every agent in the hall drew his pistol. The first objective was to shoot out any chain that might be keeping a door closed.

Sovern was right behind Herrin at the first door. At Sovern's nod four keys were quickly inserted in four locks and the handles turned. Agents pushed open the doors.

All four were chained.

Bullets fired from silencer-equipped pistols burst those chains.

The agents rushed in and hit the floor in case of counterfire.

There was none. In each room was an aging Nazi who looked shocked at what had happened. Two of the four were standing when the agents barged in. The other two were in easy chairs, one in pajamas.

Richard Sovern charged into the room occupied by Heinrich Kimmel. Kimmel, standing, maintained his calm but showed anger.

"What is this?" he asked. "Is there some terrorist problem?"

"No, there's a Nazi problem," Sovern replied. For the first time since entering the case he showed his identification. "Would you please tell me who you are?"

"My name is Heinrich Kimmel," came the answer. "What of it?"

"Are you sympathetic with the Nazi cause?" Sovern asked.

"I'm an American citizen," Kimmel protested. "I don't have to answer."

"You're not being charged with a crime," Sovern said.

"Still, I don't like this. Why are you here?"

"We believe you're affiliated with the senior leadership of a Nazi organization known as Reich Reborn."

"And of course you have proof."

"Of course," Sovern assured him.

"And if you are right?"

Sovern was stunned at Kimmel's nonchalance, his failure to resist the charge. "If we're right," he said, "you may have to answer some very serious questions, including some right here in Israel. These people don't consider it courteous to plan Nazi movements from their soil."

"I'll send a note of apology," Kimmel said sarcastically. Then he spat on the blue carpet.

"And we don't consider it courteous," Sovern continued, "to blow up river boats or kill American tourists or murder German officials."

"I'm shocked that you would think that of us," Kimmel said. He maintained the cool demeanor that Haas had ordered.

"All right," Sovern said, "let's all have a party in the same room." He motioned for Kimmel to come with him.

"Is this legally required?" Kimmel asked.

"I would suggest it . . . *strongly*," Sovern said.

"Very well."

They walked into the hall, then into the room of another Nazi. Sovern ordered the remaining prisoners to be brought. None of them had offered the slightest resistance. Sovern examined each of them, studying facial features, eye color, and general demeanor. It was incredible, he thought, but one of these nondescript men might be the greatest human monster in history.

"You are all prisoners of the United States," he told the assembled Nazis. Not one of them batted an eyelash. "Do any of you object?"

Again not a word, in accordance with Haas's plan.

"All right," Sovern said, "which one of you is . . . the leader?"

"I can speak for the group," Kimmel answered.

"That's not what I meant. You *know* who I'm looking for."

Suddenly, Kimmel began to smile, and then the others assumed expressions of resignation.

"What's the giggling about?" Sovern asked Kimmel.

Kimmel took a deep breath, let the smile melt

from his face, and slapped his hands together as if in-dicating that the act was over. "Look, Mr. Sovern," he said, "there's no point in us carrying on a glib charade. We always knew this was a possibility and we agreed to behave with the dignity becoming National Social-ists."

"Congratulations," Sovern said. "I'll commend you to Dale Carnegie."

"Please don't ridicule me," Kimmel said. "We have fought for something we believe in. For we four it is over; for others, the fight goes on."

"You do not deny, then, that you are senior mem-bers of the Reich Reborn leadership?"

"Of course not. It would be like Goebbels denying who he was."

"All right," Sovern asked bluntly, "which one of you is Adolf Hitler?"

The question stunned the other CRG agents, none of whom had been let in on the ultimate purpose of the capture. But the four Nazis remained stoic.

"May I have an answer?" Sovern asked, anger in his voice. "Frankly, none of you looks the part."

Kimmel stepped forward. "Uh, Mr. Sovern," he said, "information is valuable, no?"

"What does that mean?"

"We have families, responsibilities. We would ap-preciate some . . ."

"Consideration?" Sovern asked.

"It is given to common thieves," Kimmel said.

"That's up to the legal authorities," Sovern snapped. "But cooperation is always considered." His reply com-mitted him to nothing. "And *lack* of cooperation is also considered."

"Very well," Kimmel said, "that is the best we could hope for. Mr. Sovern, Adolf Hitler is quite dead."

Sovern's mouth dropped. "What are you saying?"

"He died in 1945 by his own hand, in the bunker, exactly as everyone thinks. But the body was buried, not found by the Russians. Yes, we tried to establish the idea that he was alive and ready to return to power in Germany, even going so far as to drop hints to hostile intelligence services."

Sovern was totally disoriented. He couldn't believe what he was hearing. All this distance for a quartet of pathetic Nazi executives? All this effort for a phantom? He felt enraged, but suspicious as well.

"We have evidence to the contrary," he said curtly.

"Evidence?" Kimmel asked. "What evidence? A house in your Massachusetts?"

"Among other things."

"And a so-called Chairman," Kimmel said with a smile.

"What about him?" Sovern asked.

"I thought you would tell *me*. The house in Massachusetts is where we came from. The Chairman was a nonexistent person. It is all simply a diversionary tactic."

"There were chemical smells in that house," Sovern said. "We have an expert who knew those chemicals."

"The woman flier, I presume," Kimmel retorted.

"Yes."

Sovern looked cynically at Kimmel. The Nazi had all the answers, all the explanations.

"The so-called Chairman's room was set up in such a manner as to be identifiable as the place of certain age-retarding experiments, should knowledge of such experiments become known. It worked magnificently, don't you think? You came to Israel expecting to find a man who perished a generation ago, sad to say. And we do appreciate Miss Earhart's help in all this."

"Appreciate?"

"The lady, like her male counterpart Charles Lindbergh, developed quite an admiration for Germany. Oh, she's not disloyal to the United States, but she wants you to see the light. She has performed her diversionary tactic well."

An emptiness grew within Richard Sovern. He could not believe that Amelia Earhart was, as Rudolph Peddington had once suggested, an agent of the other side. But it *was* possible as he himself had admitted. Had he become so hopelessly intrigued by the lady flier that he had lost objectivity? If so, he realized, he had done immense damage and surely ended his own CRG career. Almost numbed by what Kimmel was saying, he tried to resist it.

"Miss Earhart," he said, "has been medically treated. The treatment has worked. It's logical that others in Germany were similarly treated."

"Of course," Kimmel said, "but that proves nothing."

"Hitler would have been a likely choice."

"Yes, but you cannot prolong the life of a dead man. As I said . . ."

"He wasn't dead when these age experiments began. They began during the war."

"Quite wrong," Kimmel said. "In fact, they began in 1947 in our secret headquarters. Miss Earhart had been instructed to tell you otherwise."

Sovern now exchanged apprehensive glances with Lance Herrin. Kimmel had thrown him. "What if I don't believe you?" he asked the Nazi.

"That's your problem," Kimmel replied haughtily. "Frankly, I hope you don't. Then you'll waste more time."

"For die-hard Nazis you certainly have confessed easily," Sovern charged.

"Again, we are appealing to your sense of fair play."

"How do I know you aren't decoys?"

Kimmel fell silent. Although the question was an obvious one, he hadn't prepared for it. He thought quickly as he broke out in a combination smile and smirk, a device for gaining time. "You don't," he finally answered. "We can't prove that we're not."

"Did you live in Williamstown?"

"Yes."

"Are you known to the people there?"

"Storekeepers, yes."

"We'll have them identify you. Did you go to Jerusalem?"

"Yes, and stayed at the King David," Kimmel volunteered. "Unfortunately, three of my comrades were killed in one of these terrorist attacks. You can have the hotel people look at my lovely face if you wish."

Sovern was bothered by Kimmel's volunteering. It appeared too genuine, too real. Experience had shown him that people who volunteer are usually telling the truth.

"Where are the other members of your leadership?" Sovern asked.

"I don't know."

"What do you mean, you don't know?"

"Mr. Sovern, surely you're familiar with the 'need to know' concept. As in your secret services we're not told anything we don't absolutely have to know. Although we have responsibilities, we are never sure where other senior comrades are."

"Is there one leader?"

"No, there is a rotating presidency of our movement. It prevents the cult of personality."

"Who is president now?"

"I don't know."

"How *can't* you know?"

"It is a strict movement."

Sovern sensed it was time to end the questioning. Kimmel was becoming increasingly vague, and a more vigorous interrogation by teams of questioners was called for. He only felt the absolute urge to ask two more.

"By the way, who else *was* preserved in those medical experiments?"

"Some of our senior officers," Kimmel said. "The experiments were rarely successful. Many subjects died."

"All right," Sovern concluded, "when will your people attempt to take power? January thirtieth?"

Kimmel smiled. "I don't know," he said.

Sovern, Herrin, and the other agents took the four Nazis into custody and left the Dan Carmel. Outside Wilhelm Brandt waited. His frustration grew as his receiver stayed silent. Enraged at the change in orders, he watched as his target got into a car and drove away. He learned later that Haas decided it was too big a risk to dispose of Sovern, better to convincingly lead him astray by letting him think he captured the Führer.

Richard Sovern had survived. His mission, it might have appeared to an observer, had been accomplished.

But he had his doubts, and he was right to have them.

His ordeal was just beginning. . . .

CHAPTER 14

UNITED STATES GOVERNMENT IS
PLEASED TO INFORM SOVIET GOVERN-
MENT OF CAPTURE OF SENIOR NAZI OF-
FICIALS IN HAIFA. INFORMATION OB-
TAINED AS RESULT OF CAPTURE INDI-
CATES RUMOR THAT ADOLF HITLER
WAS STILL ALIVE IS FALSE—RESULT OF
NAZI MISINFORMATION PROGRAMS.

Sovern was livid.

The President had sent the reassuring message on the
hotline without fully consulting him. It was an overly
optimistic, somewhat misleading note, Sovern realized,
and not justified by the circumstances. How senior
were the Nazis? The United States really didn't know.
The "information" on Hitler was simply a claim with
no proof to back it up. Sovern was dismayed that his
advisory to the President on the events at the Dan
Carmel would be so misused.

Sovern paced in his headquarters in Haifa, waiting

for his call to the President to go through. It was only four hours after the capture and he had not yet had a chance to talk with or confront Amelia Earhart. His main concern now was establishing the truth of what Kimmel had said, and minimizing the damage that the exaggerated note to Russia might do.

The call to the President would be conducted over an open phone line. Both men knew, as the Haifa operator made the connection, that they would have to be extremely discreet in the words they used.

The link was made.

"Sir," Sovern said, "this is Dick."

"Go ahead, Dick," the President responded from the Oval Office. Unknown to Sovern, Rudolph Peddington was beside the Chief Executive.

"Sir," Sovern continued, "our people here gave me a copy of that note you sent out to the caviar people . . ."

"Yes?"

"I think we may have gone a bit far, sir."

"What makes you think that?"

"The people who gave us this information," Sovern explained, "are not of proven reliability."

"Well, that's a decision I've had to make myself," the President went on. "It's important to reassure the caviar people. Getting them upset creates problems for me."

Sovern was growing angrier by the minute. Once again, the President seemed to be making decisions based on his political convenience. Of course a crisis with Russia could have unpleasant consequences. But Sovern understood, as the President chose not to, that deceiving the Russians could have worse consequences later on.

"I understand your situation," Sovern said, "but I

think we may be making it worse. The caviar people will get very upset if this turns out wrong."

"I'll take care of that when it happens," the President said, annoyance creeping into his voice. "Don't be such a worry wart."

"But, sir," Sovern pushed on, "the man we've been concerned with . . . he may actually still be . . . available."

"I don't think so," the President announced, "and neither does Rudy."

Rudy. Sovern should have known that Peddington, never a fan of the Hitler search, had done his work while he had the President's ear to himself.

"I want you to finish up there and come back," the President said. "There are things we've got to do here."

"Sir, I think there's business in Germany . . ."

"Home first," the President snapped, and it was evident to Sovern that he had been torpedoed and the President would not change his mind.

The conversation ended on that note. The President had attempted to solve the problem by announcing it had been solved. He had often told his cronies that most government crises could be ended by simply announcing they were over.

It was not long after his call to Washington that Sovern received a CRG advisory from the London station, which was coordinating much of the anti-Nazi intelligence activity in Europe:

INFORMED THAT MALE WITH GERMAN ACCENT PURCHASED UNUSUAL QUAN-TITY OF LECITHIN AT ATHENS HOSPI-TAL. MALE GAVE ADDRESS THAT

TURNED OUT FALSE. NO FURTHER IN-
FORMATION.

The report fascinated Sovern and frightened him,
for it suggested the possibility that the Chairman, if
indeed he existed, was eluding him. The false address
was not surprising, but certainly discouraging. There
would be no chance to track down the Athens connection. An any rate, Sovern reasoned, the Nazis—if it
were they who bought the lecithin—were probably in
another city by now.

Fascination and fright were now mixed with a resignation rare for the CRG director. At any other time
he would have seized the Athens report and flown right
to Greece to look for even a shred of evidence. Now,
with the President's new attitude, he wondered whether it was all worth it. The uncertainty over Earhart
didn't help.

Sovern's mood wasn't helped either by a cable from
Ambassador Grechko, transmitted through the United
States Embassy in Tel Aviv:

CONGRATULATIONS ON YOUR EXPLOIT.
SOVIET UNION AND PEOPLE WILL LONG
REMEMBER YOUR SUCCESSFUL EFFORTS
IN DESTROYING HEAD OF SNAKE. THIS
IS IMPORTANT DAY IN MARCH OF DÉ-
TENTE.

Sovern knew how humiliated the Russians had been
when they had to admit that Hitler might be alive. He
wondered if he and his country faced similar humiliation if the President's Pollyanna message to Moscow
turned out to be wrong.

Before returning home Sovern had some remaining chores in Israel. First part of the staff of the King David Hotel was flown to Haifa to identify the four Nazi captives. As in any lineup each staff member was taken into a room where one of the Nazis stood next to entirely innocent men. He made his identification, then went into another room, then another and another, until he had tried to identify all four as the men who had stayed in the King David just days before.

The results of the lineups stunned Sovern. Not a single staff member could identify a single Nazi. It was perfectly apparent that the Haifa group was not the same as the Jerusalem group.

But then the embassy in Jerusalem received an anonymous call, claiming to be from someone "inside" the King David. The caller charged that the staff members taken to Haifa had been contacted and threatened if they identified the right people.

Sovern confronted each of the staff members with the contents of the call. Two admitted they had been threatened. Sovern knew that the lineup therefore meant nothing. People who feared for their lives were simply not going to make an accurate identification.

Willy Haas had ordered the telephone threats as part of his effort to confuse and disorient the Americans, an effort that was succeeding splendidly. Haas didn't require a scheme that would work for an eternity. A few days were all that was necessary.

Sovern, thoroughly exhausted, fell asleep. When he awoke it was December 10th. Willy Haas had forty-eight hours to go.

Sovern drove to the small Israeli Army encampment outside Haifa where Amelia Earhart was being kept.

The flier was in the living room of a cottage where the base commander normally lived. Outside three Israeli soldiers stood guard, one of them sitting in a jeep with a mounted machine gun.

Earhart, despite making a number of inquiries during her stay, had been told nothing about the events in Haifa. She had simply been informed that Richard Sovern would give her all the details. When she saw him approaching through a window she rushed immediately to the door. Knowing Sovern, she expected triumph. She smiled broadly as he entered, not realizing how strange her smile now looked to the man she trusted so much.

"Well?" she asked.

"We got all four," he replied tersely with no expression at all. "He wasn't among them."

"Oh," Earhart replied. The smile melted away. She saw there was more on Sovern's mind than the failure to capture Adolf Hitler.

"They claim he died in 1945," he went on, "and that the rest was a hoax the way the Russians said."

Earhart sighed. "Do you believe them?" she asked.

"I don't know what to believe," Sovern replied, glancing around the room at the oil colors of Israeli street scenes. "I want to believe *you*."

Earhart's heart skipped a beat. She sensed something was coming.

"They told me," Sovern went on, "that you're a plant." He looked toward her, again expressionless, and saw her retain her perfect poise. There was no anger, no hysteria.

"That is not correct," she said simply.

"They claim you've done your job well."

"Not for *them*," Earhart answered. There was still no rancor.

Sovern slumped down in an oversized easy chair with a number of badly worn areas. "I'm sure you realize," he said, "that this is going to complicate things. There are people in Washington who haven't exactly been rooting for you. They'll insist on some kind of investigation, maybe even cutting you off. I opposed a lie detector test for you before because I didn't know if the physical changes produced by the treatment would affect the outcome. Others may insist on that test now."

"I'm prepared," Earhart volunteered.

"Don't jump," Sovern said. "You could fail. That could be devastating."

Earhart went to a window and gazed out over the sandy plains. "It's very strange to suddenly be accused of being a Nazi sympathizer in this particular country."

"Oh, I'm not accusing . . ."

"I know. *They* are. I know it's all part of some diversion, but I can understand if others doubt me. I kind of expected it."

"I won't abandon you," Sovern said resolutely. "I'm enough of a judge of character to . . ."

"Abandon me," Earhart responded. Sovern was flabbergasted. "I'm now a liability. There's nothing more I can do. I'll just throw a cloud over your efforts."

"Rejected," Sovern snapped. "There's a *lot* more you can do, especially in the Archives."

"But everything I say will be suspect."

"That's not unusual in this business." Ironically, Sovern was drawing strength from this episode, becoming more and more determined to get at the truth of the four Nazis in Haifa and the strange testimony they had given.

"I appreciate your loyalty," Earhart said. Then she

walked over to Sovern and looked him straight in the eye. "But maybe you'd better reconsider."

"I've just reconsidered," Sovern said. "We'll be flying back to the States tomorrow . . . together."

II

Sovern and Earhart returned to Washington aboard an Air Force transport. In the rear of the same plane, handcuffed to their seats, were the four Nazi prisoners. They had given no information of consequence. However, lie detector tests, for whatever they were worth, awaited them in Washington.

The atmosphere aboard the plane sizzled with tension. Lance Herrin and several other CRG agents objected privately to Earhart's sitting next to their chief. Although they also realized the four Nazis might have been decoys and that their story on Earhart might have been misinformation, they thought the boss was taking an unnecessary personal and security risk. Sovern sensed their displeasure but stood firm.

Sovern's obsession during the flight was trying to determine if his capture in Haifa had produced any effect on Nazi operations in Germany itself. He got on the phone to Charles McEvoy, his heavily set, Texas-accented station chief in Munich, who was prepared with a report.

"We're sensing a step-up in Nazi activities," McEvoy said. "There has been an increase in radio transmissions, coded of course, from clandestine transmitters. In addition the leading anti-Nazi newspapers in both Munich and Bonn had their presses blown up last night."

"Any military activity?"

"None directly, but some West German military units reported a sudden increase in stolen equipment. We've always believed that's the kind of thing that might precede a coup."

"Is there anything to indicate a sudden loss of top leaders, like confusion or units operating at crossed purposes?"

"No, sir," McEvoy said. "Our Nazi watchers say that things appear very stable in the movement."

"Are we any closer," Sovern asked, "to knowing who their top planners inside Germany are?"

"No, I'm sorry to say. That remains a mystery."

"Keep me posted," Sovern ordered.

"Yes, sir."

The conversation ended as the plane headed out over Gibraltar, then across the Atlantic for the flight to America. McEvoy's comments troubled Sovern. The Nazis had a long history of failure in developing leadership below the top levels. General Eisenhower observed in his *Crusade in Europe* that German units would fall apart if they lost their senior officers, but that Allied soldiers would obey even their corporals. Sovern knew that if the four Nazis arrested in Haifa were critical to the fascist leadership, the movement would be showing signs of confusion. It was not.

"We're falling into a trap," he said quietly to Earhart. "I can feel it closing around me. We're flying in the wrong direction. We should be going to Germany."

"Tell the President," Earhart said.

"I'm afraid the President hears other voices," Sovern replied. "This is another potential public relations crisis to be managed."

The flight became uneventful. There was no news

from Munich, and the only advisories from Washington said that the Russians were delighted with American efforts. Some Russian troops were being withdrawn from the German front, and the President had cancelled the alert status of the Eighty-second Airborne Division.

CRG agents continued interrogating the Nazi captives in the rear of the plane, but they still produced no new information. For a time Sovern went back and questioned each of the four, and although each claimed to want to be helpful in exchange for favors, none of them was. Sovern deduced that they were either masters of doubletalk, trained to reveal things selectively, or simply decoys, as he had suspected, who really knew little. He spoke with Kurt Krueger, a fifty-seven-year-old, about the structure of the Nazi organization:

"What position do you hold?"

"I'm a captain of administration," the stocky Krueger replied.

"What does that mean?"

"I manage things."

"Like what?"

"Like anything they give me."

"What have you managed?"

"Operations of various types."

"What types?"

"Logistics. Reconnaissance."

"Look," Sovern said, "I want specifics. What reconnaissance operations have you run?"

"I ran operations in Germany."

"Specifics!"

"I sent a group of men to an American Army base near Bremen once."

"What were you looking for?"

"We were interested in the morale. The morale of the enemy is important."

"How did you determine the morale?"

"We counted the jokes they told."

"The jokes?"

"A lot of jokes, good morale; few jokes, poor morale."

It seemed utterly pointless. Sovern simply went back to his seat and went through the routine diplomatic cables that had been sent to the plane and awaited his attention. Most dealt with minor matters in Asia.

Then, as the plane was about halfway across the Atlantic, a sudden commotion arose in the rear. Sovern and Earhart heard scuffling, then shouting, then "Stop him, Goddamnit! Get it out of his mouth!"

Sovern bolted from his seat and charged back to the section where the prisoners were kept. He saw an Air Force nurse on her knees, pounding the chest of a man so hard the sound reverberated off the cabin walls.

The man was Heinrich Kimmel. Blood was pouring from his mouth.

"What the hell happened?" Sovern demanded.

"Cyanide capsule," a crewman explained. "We don't know where he kept it. It was glass. He just crushed it in his mouth."

The nurse tried to revive Kimmel, but it was no use. The leader of the Nazi group, potentially Sovern's most important captive, was dead.

The plane touched down at Andrews Air Force Base in cold, windy weather, the temperature hovering around twenty degrees. The skies were dark and desolate; snow was threatening to fall.

As Sovern looked out the plane he saw a startling sight. On the apron was the presidential limousine, a red carpet extended to the boarding stairs. When the engines were finally turned off, the limousine's rear right door swung open and the Chief got out. He was all smiles and hadn't even bothered to wear a coat. He strode to the carpet and waited for Sovern to come down.

Earhart saw too. "Look," she said strongly, "I'm not walking down with you. It would cause a blow-up."

This was one case where Sovern agreed. Yet he was annoyed by the President's pretense of good will, knowing it wasn't genuine. The President hadn't come to express appreciation for Sovern's triumph; he had come to make any further resistance to his optimistic message to Moscow impossible. This Chief Executive thought he was a master of human psychology and felt that a presidential backslap had a way of muting criticism. The President, Sovern knew, was trying to put him into his pocket.

Sovern stepped out of the cabin and walked down the ramp. He could literally count the gold teeth in the President's grinning mouth.

"Dick, welcome home," the Chief said, grasping Sovern's hand tightly and gripping his left shoulder. "You've done a fine job, a *fine* job!"

"Thank you, sir," Sovern replied poker-faced. "Of course there's more . . ."

"You relax," the President said. "This is *your* day. Now you come with me."

Sovern got into the limousine, which whisked the pair away to the White House.

"Sir," Sovern said as they were passing through the Andrews gates, "I want to be sure Earhart is well treated."

"No problem," the President said. "We're not going to take what those Nazis said about her at face value. Why, they might just be trying to discredit her. I do think, though, that we'll have to be just a little careful, if you know what I mean."

"Of course. But I'd like to ask that she still be housed at Andrews."

"I can't see why not. We'll talk about that at the next NOB meeting."

Sovern had dinner with the President at the White House. The President went out of his way to discuss anything but the Nazi situation, despite a few gentle attempts by Sovern to bring it up. There was an NOB meeting scheduled for later that evening, the President said, and there would be ample time to discuss the Nazis then.

"We've got to concentrate more on Korea," the President kept saying. "Dick, I'm sure the North is going to invade. All our intelligence reports point to it."

"I don't necessarily agree, sir," Sovern retorted.

"Well, you look at them again when things aren't so hectic. You'll see what I mean. Now when you get the chance, I want you to go out there as my envoy and see what our real capabilities are."

Sovern did not respond.

"The Asians think we've pulled out on them, Dick," the President continued. "I think they're all gonna cozy up to China or Russia unless we show some backbone. What do you say on that?"

"I'd have to consider it, sir."

"Off the cuff."

"I'd say you should invite the prime minister of Japan and some other leaders to the White House to get a firsthand appraisal," Sovern suggested, simply going through the motions of responding to the President.

"Good thought," the President said. Sovern was becoming increasingly apprehensive over his warmth and generosity.

"Uh, sir," Sovern finally said, "it seems to me that my major value right now is with the Earhart case."

"I think we're on top of that," the President said with a smile.

"Of course, sir. But it goes beyond the Nazi thing. I'm sure you have reports of Earhart showing some signs of physical deterioration. I think it's important that I continue monitoring her on that score rather than devote my time to Asia. With my medical background . . ."

"Sure, sure," the President responded graciously. "I take everything into consideration. You can be sure of that, Dick. Believe me. We've always worked well together."

"Yes, we have," Sovern replied with less than complete candor.

The President met with his secretary of commerce after dinner, leaving Sovern to stroll around the dampish White House grounds. Most of the staff had gone home, as had the press corps, but one man remained, leaning against his old blue Pontiac in the parking lot. Sovern saw him and tried to turn away, but as usual Hugo Lessing was not easily shunted aside.

"A man in your position needs a friend," Lessing said, as he quickly walked toward Sovern. The provocative nature of his remark was not missed.

"Hello, Hugo," Sovern said with resignation. "You welcome all the dinner guests these days?"

"Some."

"Those in *my* position?"

"Just performing a public service, Dick. A reporter can sometimes help a man forget his troubles, like where his next paycheck is coming from."

A chill shot through Sovern. "It's that bad, ay?"

"Well, you didn't think this personal tribute by the clown-in-chief was the prelude to a promotion, did you?"

"Not really, but I didn't think they were flushing me down the tubes."

"Oh, not down, Dick. They've actually got big plans for you."

"Yeah. Envoy to a Korean rice paddy."

"Oh, did he talk about that? I doubt if it'll come off. That just whets your appetite."

"I'm really starving. Okay, Hugo," Sovern asked, "what'd they leak to you?"

"Dick, you're going to be the President's right-hand man. You're on top, Dick." Lessing heaved a massive cough that turned his face red and shook some of the tobacco from his coat.

It was, in a way, a cruel revelation. Being right-hand man to the President would place Sovern somewhere below the valet. The President had four "special assistants," all former high officials he had decided to dump but whose public reputations made dismissal impossible. They had offices across the street from the White House and wrote background papers on subjects like the future of American participation in world's fairs.

If Hugo Lessing was right, and he usually was, Richard Sovern's career was over.

CHAPTER 15

Florence, Italy

Willy Haas was ecstatic.

Everything had worked.

The Americans had plainly been thrown off by the Haifa decoys, and even Haas hadn't expected the enthusiasm with which the President of the United States would greet the "revelation" that Hitler was indeed long dead. Haas had toyed with the idea of killing Sovern and had deployed Wilhelm Brandt for that purpose. But he then decided at the last minute that an assassination would possibly enrage the United States Government. Letting Sovern live and try to fight his way out of the confusion wrought by Haifa was far more effective and allowed Haas the breathing time he needed.

While it was still December eleventh in Washington, it was the early hours of December twelfth in Florence. Only hours remained before Operation Harris would begin. Only hours remained before the untested Nazi movement would try to create a new German government with the man known only as "the Chairman" at its head. Willy Haas, who prided himself on possessing the detached coolness of the Prussian, felt an enormous swell of excitement. It was 1933 once again. Although the others slept, he remained awake, waiting for a coded cable from Munich. As he waited, he reviewed a dispatch given to him earlier in the day. It had been written by General Gottes and carried by courier to Florence:

THE SITUATION IN THE FATHER- LAND AS OF DECEMBER ELEVENTH.

The government is not worthy of the name. Krueler's selection as acting chancellor has been greeted by disappointment and derision. Our people have been instrumental in arranging for the general strike now under way in Munich. Everywhere the people and press call out for strong leadership. The massing of Soviet troops on the borders has been one of our greatest assets. People are learning where bomb shelter locations are, and a few are even practicing with weapons. They do not trust the United States, believing it to be weak and indecisive. There is an undercurrent of talk about the days of Der Führer when Germany could take care of itself.

The army seems increasingly restless, not believing the current government can handle the Soviet threat and the internal discontent. Some terrorist incidents by local Communists, unpunished, have added to this feeling. I note with pleasure that there is also restlessness among the police, some of it stimulated by our own agitators.

We have succeeded in defacing churches and beating a number of ministers to increase the calls of the clergy for strong government. On the other hand our allies in the press and television are regularly blaming the Bolsheviks for the most extreme of the terrorism.

With the proper use of shock action as the hour approaches, with the proper use of crowd control, with the proper exploitation of the national malaise, our movement can succeed and the Chairman can be installed by popular will over the heads of the so-called elected authority. We are convinced that most elements of the army and police will either side with us or stay neutral.

Our task is not easy, but our determination is great, our preparations complete. In their hearts the people are with us. That and the Chairman are our greatest weapons.

The future belongs to us!

In a way, Haas mused, Earhart's escape and her subsequent landing in America may have been to the good. The situation in Germany seemed riper now than ever. If he had waited until January thirtieth, as originally planned, the new chancellor might have been able to consolidate his power and perhaps make critical changes in the army and police. And the United States might have decided to act more decisively, perhaps introducing a new, if illegal, occupation force into Germany. The Nazi god, Haas told himself, surely worked in strange ways.

Only one thing worried Haas. He had read in the international *Herald-Tribune* that a snowfall was possible in southern Germany that night. Snow could present serious difficulties. Haas periodically checked a Venice station, which he was able to get in Florence, for the southern Europe forecasts.

* * *

Rolfe Barlack awakened, and he and Haas smoked a cigarette. Barlack kept looking at his watch, noting that it was 2:10 A.M. Operation Harris would begin in less than six hours.

"I feel I am at the dawn of history," he told Haas. "This is 1933."

"Even better," Haas said. "This time we avoid mistakes. No more trusting incompetent generals and scientists. We will promote only the best. Our agents are already penetrating the atomic installations in France and Britain, and advanced weapons labs in America. We will have the *means* to maintain power."

"I don't want to pry into security affairs," Barlack said, "but how many people do you plan . . . ?"

"To exterminate?"

"I was going to say, to neutralize."

"Use the right word, Barlack. Exterminate is a word of honor. We exterminate vermin, don't we? And germs? Extermination is one of mankind's greatest contributions to the natural order. The Chairman believes that we will have to exterminate between one hundred and two hundred thousand immediately, mostly leftists, intellectuals, and professors. There might be more later, especially in the civil service. There must be no sabotage of our programs."

"Of course not," Barlack agreed.

The call came from the desk. A cable had arrived marked "emergency." Haas knew it was from Gottes. Not wanting to wait for the sluggish room service, he rushed downstairs and picked it up himself, opening the seal as he rode up again by elevator. Reentering the room, with an eager Barlack waiting, he glanced over the lengthy message and decoded it. A beaming, full smile came to his face as he saw confirmed the

extent of Nazi penetration of West German centers
of power.

FROM MUNICH HEADQUARTERS:
1800 HOURS DEC 11—THREE TANK COM-
PANIES WITH COMMANDERS LOYAL TO
US BROKE OFF FROM SECOND ARMORED
DIVISION AND HEADED TOWARD MU-
NICH FOR SO-CALLED MANEUVERS. OR-
DERS ARRANGED BY OUR PEOPLE. UNITS
WILL HOLD CENTER OF CITY.

1915 HOURS DEC 11—TWO MAIN BRIDGES
FROM U.S. SEVENTH ARMY ENCAMPMENT
TOWARD MUNICH REGION BLOWN UP.
POLICE UNITS ROUNDED UP LOCAL
LEFTISTS, BUT OUR PEOPLE WERE RE-
SPONSIBLE. U.S. FORCES WOULD NOW
HAVE GREAT DIFFICULTY GETTING TO
MUNICH TO COUNTER OUR TAKEOVER
IN REASONABLE TIME PERIOD.

2005 HOURS DEC 11—EXPLOSIVE CHARGES
SUCCESSFULLY PLACED AT RADIO AND
TELEVISION ANTENNAS OF STATIONS
MOST HOSTILE TO US. CHARGES ALSO
PLACED IN PRESS ROOMS OF LEFTIST
NEWSPAPERS.

2130 HOURS DEC 11—THREE MILLION
COPIES OF PAMPHLET ANNOUNCING
CHAIRMAN'S ARRIVAL TAKEN BY TRUCK
FROM UNDERGROUND PRESSES TO GA-
RAGE IN MUNICH AND LOCKED UNDER
GUARD. DISTRIBUTION TEAMS ALERTED
AT THEIR HOMES.

2200 HOURS DEC 11—THIRD INFANTRY BATTALION SECOND DIVISION ORDERED TO MUNICH AREA AS A RESULT OF OUR FORGED ORDERS.

2207 HOURS DEC 11—CHIEF OF CIA STATION MUNICH ELECTROCUTED IN HIS HOME BY TV RECEIVER RIGGED BY OUR PEOPLE.

2320 HOURS DEC 11—FOUR HUNDRED THOUSAND LOAVES OF BREAD, READY FOR DISTRIBUTION TO THE UNEMPLOYED, AGED AND ECONOMICALLY OPPRESSED, TAKEN BY TRUCK TO MUNICH.

2400 HOURS DEC 11—BY PREARRANGEMENT WITH YOU CODEWORD FOR OPERATION HARRIS NOW CHANGED TO MULBERRY.

"Mulberry," like "Operation Harris," was ironically named. It was the name given to the artificial docks used by the Allies in the Normandy invasion on D-Day.

"Glorious," Willy Haas said as he handed the cable to Barlack. "Read it and get some sleep, Rolfe. Tomorrow your name will be flashed around the world."

II

The National Operations Board met at the White House at eleven P.M. Some of the actions that General Gottes noted in his cable to Willy Haas had already been reported to the members. Sovern was deeply concerned and Chester LeVan was at least mildly upset. The others felt that these activities were simply a continuation of neo-Nazi petulance over the loss of Amelia Earhart, or the work of leftist terrorists. Prophetically, Sovern sensed that the mood of the board was like that of its predecessors before Pearl Harbor. All the vital signs were being ignored once again.

The meeting was convened, as usual, in the Oval Office. This time, however, the President sat informally among the members, lounging in an easy chair. He was dressed in a blue sports shirt and plaid pants and clearly felt that an enormous burden had been lifted from his back.

"Meeting will come to order," he said, displaying a rare attention to formality. "I think before we begin we owe Dick Sovern a tremendous thanks. I've already told him privately how much the nation appreciates what he's done. I know you all share my views. The Nazi threat isn't over, but it's been seriously weakened and the main cause for concern has been eliminated."

Sovern sat expressionless, watching and listening to the grand illusion unfolding.

"Mr. President . . ."

"Rudy?"

"I want to underscore what you just said. Dick as usual has done a fine job. As for Amelia Earhart, I can just say that I'm glad we're finally being sensible about her. After all these years God only knows what's in her mind."

It was Peddington's patronizing comment that brought rage to Richard Sovern. Controlling his anger, he simply broke in without being recognized.

"Mr. President," he said firmly, "I appreciate the kind compliments but I wonder if we shouldn't keep open the chance—just the chance—that Hitler is alive."

"Why?" Peddington asked. "Your captives in Haifa . . ."

"Why don't we admit the obvious?" Sovern asked. "They could've been lying."

"Have you given them detector tests?" Peddington asked.

"You know how I feel about their accuracy," Sovern said.

"I suggest you're being too conservative," Peddington added, "especially about your accomplishment here. Dick, there never was a shred of evidence to suggest that Hitler was alive. And there was never a shred of evidence to suggest that Earhart was a genuine escapee from the Nazis. The fact is that everything those Nazis told you in Haifa was logical, and nothing you believed up to then was."

"Makes sense," the President said.

"Besides," Peddington pushed on, "when we went with the Hitler thing you *saw* the Russian reaction. We almost had World War III out there, Dick. Since the Haifa thing, though, they've pulled back. Much better this way."

"The Russian thing," the President agreed. "That was the big problem."

"All right," Sovern countered, "what happens if, in theory, Hitler is alive?"

"Then we tell the Russians we were wrong and then go to town on Adolf," Peddington replied. "But we certainly don't announce in advance that we're not a hundred percent convinced about this. Jesus, Dick, grow up. This isn't a fifth grade civics course."

As usual Peddington was persuasive. Sovern looked around the room and saw not one supportive face. Only LeVan kept glancing at the bulletins from Germany. "There's a lot of activity in West Germany," Sovern said. "I don't like it. I especially don't like those bridges being blown up near our forces. They'd have a hell of a time moving."

"The Reds did that," Peddington said bluntly.

"How do we know?"

"The German police told us."

"You sure of them?"

"They're not absolutely reliable," Peddington conceded, "but we have no reason to doubt them in this case."

"Why would Communists blow up bridges that would make it difficult for our forces to counter a Nazi move in Munich?"

"Maybe," Peddington said, "some of the local Reds thought we would be on the Nazi side and wanted to keep our forces in place."

"Logical," the President agreed. "The Reds always think we're a truckload of fascists." He smiled at his own phraseology.

"Just a second," Chester LeVan interrupted. He turned his powerful frame in an oversized chair, obviously agitated by what was going on. "Now I'm no alarmist, y'all know that. But we're painting pretty faces on everything. Okay, I agree that the Hitler thing may have been far out. Sure I'd put money on the idea that Hitler died in '45. But there *is* a Nazi movement and things *are* happening in Germany. We're gettin' too relaxed. Even without Hitler, what's to prevent these clowns from putting in a *new* Hitler, maybe a guy who understands how to use TV?"

It was the most logical statement made, and Sovern nodded his appreciation to LeVan. LeVan, always careful about identifying with a man being lynched, did not directly respond but simply looked down at his papers.

"All right," the President said, "we have division here, but we're going to fight those Nazis. Dick, you've worn yourself out on this thing, and I want you here for a special assignment. Rudy, take overall charge of anti-Nazi efforts."

That was it, the diplomatic easing out of Richard Sovern. He could not remain silent. "Mr. President . . ."

"Now, Dick," the President admonished, "please don't volunteer. A man should not overdo it."

"I'm *not* overdoing it!" Sovern snapped, showing his first real anger. "I'd like to continue in charge. I know exactly what's being done."

"And we don't?" Peddington asked.

"I'm not criticizing the CIA," Sovern said. "But I don't understand the shift, that's all."

"I'll lay it right on the line," the President said. "Dick, you're identified with the Hitler thing, especially as far as the Russians are concerned. The shift is symbolic. Foreign policy reasons."

"There's something else," Peddington broke in, clearly echoing the arguments he had presented privately to the President. "During one of our previous discussions of command structure you pointed out that Miss Earhart had asked for *you* and no one else. I would respectfully suggest, Dick, that this is no longer a consideration."

"In fact," the President chimed in, "I think you'd be exactly the man to stay with Earhart and find out what she's really about. Learn about the physical deterioration she's having, just like you said."

"Is that my presidential mission?" Sovern asked.

"Can you think of a more important one?"

"Frankly yes, sir."

"But you mentioned this deterioration when we spoke. You emphasized it. I'm letting you stay here rather than go immediately to Asia *just* so you can study this woman. Dick, I'm surprised. I thought . . ."

"I understand, sir," Sovern responded. "Perhaps I didn't make myself clear. Miss Earhart's physical problems are very important to me. They should be important to *all* of us. But studying Amelia Earhart doesn't preclude me from pursuing the Nazi threat."

The President raised his hand to stop Sovern and looked sternly at him. "Dick," he said, "break the Earhart mystery."

"What rank do I have?" Sovern asked sardonically. "Minister of mysteries?"

"CRG director," the President said, not cracking a smile. He was, as always, a superb politician. He knew that firing Sovern would create an internal convulsion in his administration. So Sovern would keep his job, but with none of the responsibilities that went with it.

"If I'm assigned exclusively to Earhart," Sovern pointed out, refusing to be shelved so easily, "I won't be able to run the shop."

There was a sudden silence in the room as truth finally met political conniving. The President at first said nothing, simply staring at Sovern, as if confirming the situation.

Sovern looked around. There were no allies. "I'd like to consider the assignment," he said.

"Fair enough," the President said. "But I don't want to lose you, Dick." The statement was genuine. The President truly valued Sovern but had been convinced by Peddington that he was simply the wrong man in the slot at the moment.

"Give me till morning," Sovern asked.

"Agreed."

The meeting ended on a somber, indecisive note. No one had ever recalled personal matters being discussed before the full NOB.

Alone, Richard Sovern walked the long corridors of the White House to his waiting car outside. It was a few minutes before midnight, a few minutes before the start of Operation Mulberry half a world away. Once again he was confronted by Hugo Lessing, who seemed to wear a genuinely compassionate expression.

"Remember Winston Churchill," Lessing intoned, quoting the plaque in the floor of Westminster Abbey. Sovern instantly understood the reference. Churchill, too, had been ignored when he warned of the Nazis.

"I remember," Sovern said with not a little sarcasm. "But Churchill had years to get his warning across. I've got days."

"They wouldn't listen to anything in there?" Lessing asked.

"They all want to believe happy thoughts. And Peddington, well . . ."

"Say it."

"No, I don't go in for that stuff." Sovern had a long reputation for never engaging in personal disputes. He didn't want to lose it now.

"Our bureau in West Germany says things are getting sticky there," Lessing explained. "This new chancellor looks like a wet fish."

Sovern clasped his hands together in frustration. "But what do the *people* think?" he asked rhetorically. "They're the key to it all."

"That's the scary part, from where I sit anyway," Lessing replied. "Our bureau says that whenever the lefties get blamed for something, their headquarters get firebombed. If some Nazi group beats the mush out of somebody, nothing happens. I tell you, Dick, no matter what anyone says, a lot of those people want the Nazis back—on general principles. It's the way they are, the way they think. The schools covered up the truth about Hitler."

"And we're treating it as a routine CIA matter," Sovern said. "We make the same mistake over and over. I guess it's true: every generation has to learn its lessons from scratch. History makes no impression."

Without a further word Sovern got into a waiting car and asked to be driven to Amelia Earhart's temporary residence at Andrews. He quickly realized that the car had no radio receiver. "We'd better get another car," he told the driver. "I can't get radio messages from my people in here."

"I was told to take *this* car, sir," the driver replied. "This one and no other."

"Where'd the order come from?"

"The White House, sir."

The humiliation had blossomed. Now Richard Sovern, ostensibly still the CRG director, had been stripped of his source of information, the one essential he needed to maintain even the semblance of office.

William Katz

III

It was eight A.M. in Florence, a cool, beautiful day, with a mellow sun rising over the Arno.

Willy Haas, the Chairman, and the others left the de la Ville by taxi after paying their bill and leaving tips large enough to make eternal friends of their hosts. They went back to the Florence railway station, marked for travelers by the vertical FIRENZE painted on a nearby smokestack. Other travelers were waiting on the platform for the train from Rome which would take them northwest to Milan. Among the travelers were eighteen Nazi security guards dressed in ordinary clothes and carrying cameras and tennis racquets to blend in with the others. Haas made only the slightest eye contact with the leader of the group. There was to be no hint that so many people were traveling together for the same purpose.

The Rome train arrived. Suitcases were lifted aboard. Haas kept the case with the Nazi uniforms in his compartment, not daring to entrust it to baggage handlers. The uniforms were now packed in false bottoms, in the event the cases were opened by customs inspectors.

The train began moving north toward Milan. With each mile the sense of anticipation among the Nazis grew, and Haas could see a new liveliness, a new determination in the eyes of the Chairman.

A half hour from Florence, Haas gathered the Chairman, Barlack, and the other remaining member of the council in his compartment. The last man was Gustav Hoffmann, a mechanical engineer of sixty-three who had designed pontoon bridges for the German Army during World War II. Now he was a technical adviser to Haas, a man who spoke little but who performed his job through diagrams, memos, and charts. He calculated the technical capability of each of the Reich Reborn units, chose weapons, and designed bombs and grenades for terror operations. It was Hoffmann, a gaunt little man, who had designed the charges used to blow the bridges outside Munich.

Once the four men were inside the compartment, with its wood panels and curtains, Haas closed and locked the door. The men sat on the cushioned benches common to European trains, two riding forward, the other two backward. Outside the lush, green Italian countryside, spotted with reddish brown buildings, rushed by.

"The Chairman is of course aware of what I am about to say," Haas began. Everyone noticed there was a new stridency to his voice, a sense of command and urgency. "The needs of security have prevented us from disclosing out entire plan for the first day. Now you will know. You *must* know to understand what is happening.

"Each of you realizes that all actions are taken in the name of the Reich and for the good of Germany's children. However, sacrifices must be made to insure our success. The German nation has always been willing to sacrifice. Even our young have been willing."

The Chairman smiled. He well remembered the German teenagers who fought to the last at the end of World War II.

"In a short time we will be in Milan. We will be taken by small plane to an airstrip outside Munich. We will then enter the city by train and start the new National Socialist revolution. Some will laugh, but you will see. Throngs will gather at the railroad station in Munich to greet the Chairman. He will immediately make an appeal to the armed forces to join him, and I have no doubt what the result will be. He will then proclaim his peaceful intentions toward all nations. You may ask, 'How can you be sure, Herr Haas?' And I will tell you that in my heart I am sure.

"The people are psychologically prepared for a return to the old order. But there must be one last push, one outrage by our opponents in Germany to make them demand the Chairman, to make a hard core among them yearn for him, scream for his very presence. That outrage must be painful. We must arrange for it. It will be painful for us, too, but the future of Germany hangs in the balance.

"As we approach the Fatherland, our comrades will engage in many acts to smooth our entry. Some will be routine military seizures of communications lines, police stations, transportation depots, and the like. But the outrage will be different."

Haas looked around, hoping that Barlack and Hoffmann would accept emotionally what he was about to say.

"There are, as you know, child-care centers in our great cities for mothers who work. Just before we enter Munich, eight of these centers will be destroyed by firebomb." He lowered his eyes. "There is no doubt that hundreds of Germany's children will sacrifice themselves for the Chairman in these actions. It may even be thousands. Evidence will be left at the scene of some blasts linking them to the Bolsheviks. Our friends on the television will echo this charge. There will be overwhelming grief throughout Germany and it will quickly turn to anguish and anger. The Bundestag will meet immediately in Bonn, but it too will be exterminated by firebomb at the moment the gavel falls. There will be no descriptions strong enough to describe the feelings in the hearts of our people.

"Then leaflets will appear announcing the Chairman's return to save Germany from these outrages. Broadcasting stations will interrupt programs. Flags will suddenly appear on poles—the flags of the Reich. Then, only minutes before our arrival, the people of Munich will be told to come to the station. We will appear. It will be greater than 1933."

Haas leaned back. The Chairman smiled. Both Barlack and Hoffmann nodded their approval. "This is a plan," Barlack pronounced, "that bears the indelible mark of the brilliance of the Chairman."

"Of course," Haas said. "The Chairman decides everything."

In fact Haas had designed the plan. Although the Chairman's mind was still strong, he was showing signs of the inevitable deterioration that would befall anyone being weaned off the age-retarding device. True, he still received regular chemical injections—those with the lecithin base—to help maintain the retardation, but there were moments of mental lapse, extreme fatigue, occasional loss of some memory, and a general slowing down. And the Chairman's appearance was showing subtle change. The lines of 1945 were beginning to appear more prominently and to deepen. The brown skin patches common to aging were becoming more pronounced. And new gray hairs were evident.

Haas couldn't know it, but Richard Sovern was seeing milder versions of these changes in Amelia Earhart and still assuming that the Nazi leader's deterioration was much greater than hers. He was, however, expanding his notion as to *why* it was greater. He had earlier theorized that it was simply because the Chairman was older than Earhart and in worse shape when his treatments began. Now he reasoned that his *mental* state would have to be a factor—the stress of leadership, the pain of defeat, the shame of being reduced to a man on the run, the need to plan a return to power. The mental punishment, Sovern deduced, would have the same effect on the Nazi chief as on any other man, a wearing down of the body. Sovern was guessing that the Nazis were under pressure to make their move quickly . . . before their exalted leader deteriorated too drastically or even died.

"The train into Munich," Barlack asked, "will have non-German passengers?"

"Oh yes," Haas replied. "We must maintain the cover till the last moment. But they can be dealt with. Sacrifices must be made by all." He smiled broadly.

The train arrived at a small railroad station with an open platform. Most of those waiting to board were local sales people who often visited Milan's industrial plants. Others were workers going on vacation in the north.

A Nazi courier entered the train and went quickly to Haas's compartment. He carried a cable from General Gottes, received at a small Nazi radio set-up in a local house:

MULBERRY IS IN READINESS. LIGHT SNOW FALLING, BUT NOT INTERRUPTING OUR OPERATIONS. TRUCKS CARRYING INCENDIARY DEVICES NOW PARKED IN VICINITY OF CHILD-CARE CENTERS. CENTERS UNUSUALLY FULL BECAUSE OF WEATHER. ESTIMATE ALMOST TWO THOUSAND CHILDREN WILL FALL FOR GERMANY.

GOTTES

CHAPTER 16

Washington, D.C.

A dejected Richard Sovern arrived at Andrews Air
Force Base and was driven to the restricted area where
Earhart stayed. To enter the area he had to get out of
his car, be fingerprinted, present an I.D. card, and be
recognized by an officer who had seen him previously.
Then he was taken by Air Force jeep to Earhart's
Quonset hut.

Earhart awaited him anxiously, knowing that the
session at the White House could not have been
pleasant. As Sovern walked up the flagstone path she
saw his grim, tired expression. She opened the door
and let him in.

"Hi," he said sardonically, "meet your new social
escort. What'll it be tonight, a movie or a race to the
top of the Washington Monument?"

Sovern explained in detail what had happened at
the White House. "It didn't have anything to do with
you," he assured her. "It's all political."

"I'm afraid your support of me *did* damage your
credibility," Earhart said.

"I was doing my job. You were part of it. I don't regret a thing," Sovern responded. He found it strange that he was confiding in Earhart like this. After all, she *could* have been a Nazi spy just as Kimmel had charged in Haifa. But he could not accept that she was, and although it was unprofessional to trust instinct alone, he was doing it. Sovern believed he had gone through enough in his career to be able to sniff out who was for him and who against. Earhart, his innards told him, was on his side.

"Did anyone insist on my taking a lie-detector test?" she asked.

"It never came up."

"I say again, I'm ready. I'm ready to do *anything* that could help you."

"It's a strange thing," Sovern said, glancing at the photos of bombers on the wall, "but the only thing that will help would be a major Nazi move in Germany. God only knows, it's a horrible way to be helped."

"If they've reduced you like this," Earhart asked, "why don't you resign?"

"I'm thinking of it. I didn't accept the assignment to probe your inner soul. I'm only supposed to be thinking it over. Of course, this whole thing is completely ridiculous. It's small men doing small things. If I resign, though, I lose my contact with the government."

"Do something else," Earhart urged. "You're a physician. You're not likely to be out of a job."

"I still think," Sovern explained, "you might be right about the Hitler thing. This Haifa business never overwhelmed me. The problem is that I haven't got a shred of proof, and these guys at the White

House know it. I don't even have *access* to the proof anymore."

Sovern slumped in a couch, showing a rare anger. The behavior of the government in a time of potential crisis enraged him. But he had read enough history to know that pettiness was the rule, not the exception, in the governments of the world.

"You can use some coffee," Earhart said.

"Yes, thanks," Sovern replied quietly.

As Earhart brewed the coffee in a Norelco coffee-maker, Willy Haas was being told by a conductor that the train to Milan was on time. Haas informed the Chairman, who had begun to feel weak again and was lying down. Haas planned to inject him with more of the lecithin-based formula within the hour.

Richard Sovern sipped the coffee, not saying a word. He welcomed the respite from the constant conversation and confrontation he had experienced all night. But as he gazed over at Earhart he noticed that the skin on her hands was developing new age spots. He wondered if he could use this observation to deduce what was happening to anyone else who might be going through the same thing . . . like a supreme Nazi leader. He realized he could only guess that the man was showing increasing signs of age, was perhaps frightened by them, and that these signs were a source of frustration and concern to those around him.

Sovern was right. Deep in the recesses of Willy Haas's mind there was the recurring fear that Adolf Hitler might collapse, or die, just before the moment of Germany's liberation.

The phone rang sharply. Sovern thought it odd that Amelia would be getting calls. She picked it up.

"He's right here," she said.

Of course, Sovern mused, it was for him, and it was probably more trouble. Maybe some other prerogative of office was being cancelled. He went to the phone.

"Yes?"

"Dick, this is Chester LeVan."

"Yes, Ches?"

"Dick, you're gettin' the mighty shaft."

"Understatement of the year, Ches."

"It's not right, but, you know, there was nothing I could say to the Chief."

"Oh, I understand."

"But I don't like this business of cuttin' off your flow of information. I'm tellin' you, off the record of course, that you'll be hearing from me. You'll know what's goin' on, Dick."

Sovern was flabbergasted. Chester LeVan had never been known to extend himself, especially when there was political risk. Then Sovern glanced down at the phone.

"Chester, you're fantastic, but maybe we'd better not talk . . ."

"Oh, don't worry," LeVan said. "This is a secure line. That hut we put Earhart in is set up for it."

Sovern knew, of course, that a secure line—with cables that probably ran deep underground—could not be tapped. The fact that it was a secure line explained why LeVan sounded so distant and echoed.

"Ches," Sovern asked, "do you think I'm exaggerating the Nazi thing?"

"Christ, no," LeVan said. "But I don't think that's the political point to watch. There's no way this President is gonna wake up unless the Nazis write their intentions on a blackboard in front of him. It's the nature of the man. Sure, if Hitler showed up he'd have to open his eyes, but short of that it'll take a big bang."

"I have to admit," Sovern said, "that I thought I was in better with him."

"You don't know him," LeVan came back. "He has no professional loyalties, only personal ones. If you came to him and said you're broke he'd whip out his checkbook. But then he'd fire you because he didn't want a debtor in his administration. Simple as that."

Sovern had rarely spoken with Chester LeVan in any but the most official circumstances, and he found himself impressed with LeVan's sensitivities. It was something he hadn't expected of him. "Ches," he said, "maybe *I'm* the one who's had his eyes closed."

"Yup, no doubt about it," LeVan said. "You leave your political flanks open, Dick, but don't sweat it. You're a better man than any of us."

"Thanks, Ches. I'm beginning to wonder though."

"Don't wonder and don't think. It's dangerous to think too much around here."

"Apparently."

"I've just gotten the latest from the Defense Intelligence Agency. There's been some hot stuff goin' on over in Hun-land. We've gotten word of some German generals getting shot and a few others disappearing. Course all of this is being blamed on the Communists, but we have our doubts. The Nazis would want to mess up the high military command and confuse things just before tryin' to take over."

"Right," Sovern said.

"There's also been a blast at the phone company in Munich. The phones in central Munich are out, and it's hell getting in contact down there."

"The police?"

"They say they're workin' on it. Big deal."

"Ches, is there any unusual traffic entering the country?"

"Not that we know of. Of course, all their people might be inside."

"Still, maybe they should seal off the border."

"I'll bring it up to the German military attaché here. But I know them, Dick. They'll never do it. It insults their God-almighty pride. They just keep on using the same security procedures year after year. As long as they were German-developed and German-refined, that's all that counts. You know the story."

"Anything else, Ches?"

"Just some foul weather. They've got snow drifting into south Germany. Our units report trouble moving. The planes are grounded."

"Sounds like the Battle of the Bulge," Sovern said.

"Dick, I'll keep you informed," LeVan went on. "What are your plans?"

"Well," Sovern replied with a sigh, "*if* I stay on, I'll have to stay with Miss Earhart." He glanced at her and smiled. "That's my assignment. Of course, I'm not going to deny that it fascinates me. There are these medical questions, you know." He stayed intentionally vague, not wanting to embarrass or hurt Amelia.

"I understand," LeVan replied.

"In addition," Sovern said with exaggerated cheeriness laced with sarcasm, "I may plan an entire schedule of Washington historical tours."

"Dick, don't quit," LeVan advised. "I think you may be back in the saddle pretty soon."

"Why?"

"Because you may be proven right. Then the Chief'll wave his magic wand and, poof, you'll be on top."

"Well, maybe," Sovern said, still despondent.

"We'll talk."

"Ches, I can't thank you enough."

"Don't try. Maybe you can do a favor for me some day."

"Any time."

The conversation ended, and at least Richard Sovern knew he had an ally.

II

Willy Haas's train was an hour from Milan. He was constantly receiving coded messages regarding the situation in West Germany. Communications experts from the Reich Reborn had stationed personnel at intervals along the track. These men were equipped with small walkie-talkies. They were given information by couriers, who, in turn, had received it on strong radios in nearby towns. As the train came near, the men along the track sent their data in radio code and Haas's men aboard the train received it. One message from Gottes said that there was no change in the disposition of NATO forces and that the moment was approaching with total surprise.

Haas handed the message to the Chairman, who smiled. Although the Chairman was weakening somewhat, Haas could now see a positive sign, which he attributed to the nearness of "the moment." The Chairman, making on obvious effort, sat up straight, seemingly determined to affect the posture of the supreme leader, to recapture his look of steel.

A few minutes later, though, there was a sharp knock at the wooden door of the compartment. "It is

Herrmann Schmidt," announced the voice from outside.

Haas opened and Schmidt entered, clicking his heels
and bowing toward the Chairman. "Sir, beg the intrusion," he said. He turned toward Haas. "One of
the conductors is an Italian security man."

Haas did not panic. "How do you know?"

"We have his picture on file. One of my men recognized him."

Haas leaned back to ponder the problem brought
by Schmidt, the thirty-five-year-old director of the security detail. Schmidt was small but well-built. He
was famous throughout the movement for his intellect
and his eye for detail. He had been an instructor in
political science at the Free University of Berlin before
deciding that the future lay with the Nazis. His father
had been with the SS and Schmidt had been raised on
stories of the glorious era.

"Is there evidence that he's here for us?" Haas asked.

"No," Schmidt replied, "but he certainly wouldn't
leak it."

"Of course, it would be logical for security agents
to travel the trains," Haas mused. "The Red terrorists
use the trains for their operations."

"According to our records," Schmidt said, "this man
does not deal with Communist threats. He's a specialist in right-wing operations."

Haas raised his eyebrows. "Is he being watched?"

"Yes, we always have a man near him. But he could
be carrying some type of transmitting device that can
be used secretly. He could tap on it in code, for ex-
ample, by putting his hand in his pocket."

"If the Italians were on to us," Haas asked,
"wouldn't they have acted by now? It hardly seems
likely that they would wait."

"They might simply want to learn about our operating methods before moving in," Schmidt said. He marveled at how cool Haas was when presented with a potentially explosive problem.

Haas looked up at Schmidt, a glisten in his eye. "I want you to force this individual into a compartment and search him. Then question him . . . vigorously. Tell him his life will depend on the accuracy of his answers." Haas paused. "Better yet, when you capture him, call me. I will ask the questions. It will be my privilege to get the truth out of this fellow. It's a fine art, you know."

Schmidt left the compartment. Only then did Haas's face show the concern he truly felt. No, he said to himself, this could not be. Not after coming so far. Not a few hours from final victory. He glanced over to the Chairman. "Don't worry," Haas said. "It's probably nothing. These security people are common."

Herrmann Schmidt passed the word to his security team to bring the suspect conductor in. There were many empty compartments on the train, and Herrmann chose one near the end of the car, where the wheel noise would keep an interrogation very private. It took no great skill for a Reich Reborn security man to follow the conductor, jab a finger in his back, and inform him in fluent Italian that he would be taking some time off from the job for a social visit to an empty passenger compartment. A few minutes later Haas was called in.

The conductor was medium-height and poker-faced, a professional counter-espionage agent who looked somewhat older than his forty-five years. He had always lived his life aware of the possibility of death in the service and he seemed remarkably resigned and stoic as Willy Haas confronted him. He was sitting on a passen-

242 William Katz

ger bench smoking a cigarette, two Reich Reborn men sitting opposite him, one with a pointed pistol. He looked Haas up and down, then looked out the window, as if in contempt at his captors.

"So," Haas said in English, "my associates tell me you work for the Italian government. Is it true?"

One of the Reich men immediately translated into Italian.

"There is no need," the Italian said. "I speak English as well as six other languages. Whichever one you choose to use will be fine with me." He blew some smoke in Haas's direction.

"You are brave," Willy Haas said, trying some reverse psychology. "We admire brave men. You know at one time we were allies."

"Our mistake," the Italian said.

"Perhaps," Haas laughed. "However, had it not been for traitors, we both might be leaders of powerful nations today."

"I am happy to be a civil servant," the Italian responded, still not breaking his dour expression, accented by eyes that seemed too close to each other. "Now, if you will tell me what you want, I would be grateful. I have tickets to collect."

"Why are you on the train?" Haas asked.

"As I just said, to collect tickets."

"In your government capacity," Haas said sternly.

"The government protects its citizens."

Haas motioned to one of his men, who grabbed the Italian's wrist and pressed down severely on the main blood vessel. The Italian winced, clamped his teeth together, but did not make a sound.

"I am not interested in evasive answers," Haas said. "I am a busy man."

"The government assigns security men to the trains

to watch for international travel by terrorists," the
Italian said matter-of-factly.

"What kind of terrorists?"

"All kinds."

"You're getting cute again. What kind are *you* assigned to?"

"Right-wing groups. We have them in Italy."

"Only Italian groups?"

"Yes."

"Do you know who we are?"

"Yes."

Haas was stunned. "Who?"

"Very rude Germans."

Again the Reich man applied severe pressure to the
Italian's wrist. And again the man refused to cry out.

"We can go further," Haas assured him.

"Look," the Italian said, "there is nothing I can tell
you. I'm here to watch for some well-known Italian
terrorists who slip in and out of Switzerland. They
often use this train. Frankly, I don't know who you are
and I don't care."

Haas turned to his agents. "Go through him."

The agents began searching the Italian, emptying
his pockets, feeling the lining of his jacket, examining
his shoes for hollowness in the heels. Besides his service
pistol, which was strapped to his right leg, they found
nothing. There was no transmitter.

"How do you communicate?" Haas asked.

The Italian shrugged. "I make reports," he replied.
"How else?"

"You have no radio equipment aboard the train?"

"No. Of course there's a radio in the cab in case of
an emergency. But everyone knows that."

"Obviously," Haas said. "Is there anyone in particular on this train you're watching?"

"Yes," the man said.

"Who?"

"Do you want his name?"

Haas was surprised. "Yes." He saw the Italian gesturing to speak. "Are you actually going to tell me his name?"

"Why not?"

"Is this the way you Italians run your security service?"

"Look," the Italian said, "this is low-level stuff. My instructions are to cooperate if captured except for revealing methods and the names of our secret agents. Besides, you're not my territory and you have nothing to do with the groups I'm interested in."

"How do you know this?" Haas asked.

"I know my people like my mother. I know their methods and style, and the methods and style of their allies in other countries. You're not like them. Your style is more like the old Nazis, and I assume you're one of these Nazi groups running around loose and worried about every security man you see. You must learn to calm down."

Haas was flabbergasted, but tried not to show it. The Italian was a thorough professional, absolutely unflappable, and seemingly indifferent to his fate. . . . His cool analysis of Haas's approach was utterly remarkable.

"Who is the man you are watching?" Haas asked.

"His name is Antonio Bocca," the Italian replied. "He is in car two, seat B thirteen. He is about five-eleven, wears khaki pants, a dark red polo shirt, and has a large mustache. His age is twenty-one. He has a wound on the left side of his neck from a knife slash that almost took his life, poor fellow. A thousand Hail Marys for him."

"Is he in his seat now?" Haas asked.

"Probably. He sleeps a lot."

Haas turned to one of his men. "I want that man here."

"I wouldn't," the Italian said. "He's carrying explosives under his jacket. They all are. If you try to take him, everything goes bang."

Haas hesitated. He wanted the man brought to the compartment to question him, to try to check the Italian agent's story. Haas also had a plan for disposing of the two men together, making it look like a fatal confrontation between agent and prey, something that would draw suspicion away from anyone else on the train. But he understood the phenomenon of the suicidal terrorist and he realized that an explosion aboard would stop the train.

Haas, though, did not rise to the top of the Nazi movement by being uncreative. He immediately worked out a plan of attack. "Wait here," he advised the others. He left the compartment and went to the second car, where he quickly located Antonio Bocca. Bocca was dozing, but not quite asleep. The seat beside him was taken, but the one behind was not. Haas slipped into it, leaned forward, and whispered.

"Bocca."

Bocca instantly reached under his jacket. "Don't worry," Haas whispered. "I am *one* of you. There is a conductor on this train who's a security agent. He's been sent to cut you down."

Haas proceeded to describe the Italian in perfect detail. "You watch yourself," he advised Bocca. "When he comes into this car, that will be it. We cannot help you because we are on a mission. If you doubt me, you look for the bulge under the conductor's right pants leg. That gun is for you, Bocca."

Without waiting for a reply, Haas slipped out of his seat and disappeared into another car, returning to the interrogation compartment where the Italian and the two Reich Reborn men waited.

"I'm having difficulty spotting Bocca," Haas told the agent. "You will help me. I want you to go to the second car, walk to where this man is sitting, then turn around. He'd better match your description." Haas turned to one of his men. "Empty his gun and give it to him."

The man was baffled by the order, but re-strapped the gun under the Italian's right pants leg.

"We'll be behind you," Haas said, "so I advise against heroics."

"I'm not the type," the Italian replied.

They left the compartment, headed for the second car. The Italian entered first. "Go," Haas told him. The man started down the aisle. Haas could see Bocca now. He was turned to the left, his eyes watchful. He had taken the tip seriously.

The Italian moved further down. Bocca's eyes moved to the gun bulging under the agent's pants. Suddenly, he jumped up, whipping out an automatic pistol.

"Everyone down!" Haas shouted as Bocca fired off eight shots.

The Italian dropped without a word.

Panic-stricken, Bocca charged up the aisle, passengers screaming around him. He reached the area between cars and jumped, rolling down an embankment.

Haas jumped to his feet. "Did you see what that man did?" he screamed. "Murderers! They're all murderers!" He rushed to the Italian's side and pretended to give aid. He had disposed of the man in brilliant style and he knew that the mere death of a conductor in the age of modern terrorism might delay the train for a few minutes at a stop—for removal of the body— but that was all.

Haas returned to his compartment and reported to the Chairman. "It is not difficult," he told him, "to predict the reactions of these terrorists. This man Bocca was like all the others. Give him a chance to shoot and he shoots. It was all very easy."

Of course, Haas could not be sure the Italian was telling the truth. It was possible that he had been aboard not to watch Bocca, but to watch the Nazis. It was also possible there were other agents on the train. Haas ordered his security staff to be especially vigilant, but there was no sign of further trouble from anyone aboard.

Some time later the train stopped, the body was removed, and Haas was questioned by local police. Witnesses lavished praise on him for shouting his warning, and that was the end of the episode.

The train started once more.

III

Sovern slept at Earhart's residence that night, too exhausted to go home. He stretched out on a dusty sofa in what passed for the Quonset hut's living room, where he and Earhart had talked things over. Earhart slept in the bedroom.

It was around three A.M. when the phone next to the sofa rang. Sovern awakened, used to middle-of-the-night interruptions, and grabbed the receiver.

"Sovern."

"Christ," said Chester LeVan's voice, "of all the dumb things . . ."

"Ches, is that you?"

"Who else, the tooth fairy?"

"What's wrong?"

"What's wrong? I'll tell you what's wrong. I call your place and get no answer. I begin to wonder whether anything's happened to you. I check the police. They have nothing. Then I think, Jesus, maybe he was dumb enough to stay with Earhart. So I call. You were dumb enough."

"What's up?"

"Dick, our people have been going over those guys you got in Haifa. They gave them lie-detector tests tonight, stress analyzer screenings, the works. They flunked everything."

There was a silence. Sovern realized he had his first opening. "This may be the best news I've had all year," he said sardonically. "But Ches, what specifically were they asked?"

"Okay," LeVan said, "here it is. They asked all of them whether they were senior leaders. They said yes. The machines belched. They asked them whether Hitler was alive. They said no. More belching. They asked them whether they were decoys. They said no. And this time the machine had a gastritis attack!"

"That's enough," Sovern said, a slight smile coming to his face. "Has the President been told?"

"The President is nighty-night. He doesn't respond well when disturbed."

"Or any other time," Sovern said.

"I won't comment on that," LeVan replied. "But Peddington knows."

"What does he say?"

"He says we should proceed with caution. He quoted you on the unreliability of these machines."

"The man remembers everything," Sovern observed. "But when a group fails those tests on the same questions, we've got a case."

"There's something else," LeVan said. "The FBI showed mug shots of those clowns to a lot of people in Williamstown tonight. Nobody knew 'em. And the Nazis couldn't supply the name of a single store up there."

"All right, they're frauds," Sovern replied, now sitting up, his mind clear. "How do we convince the President?"

LeVan muttered a few angry curses, then settled down. "I don't know," he said. "He's obsessed with the Russians right now and it'll take something big to convince him. But I'll talk to the man, Dick. I can't do anything more."

"Do I assume," Sovern asked, "that Earhart is now in the clear?"

"You can assume it," LeVan replied, "but I wouldn't show it. For your own sake, be careful. By the way, some anti-Nazi newspapers in West Germany had their presses blown. No one is claiming responsibility, but assessing blame won't tax your imagination too much."

"Understood," Sovern said.

"I'll get back to you," LeVan promised. "Now get some sleep. Tomorrow is gonna be hot."

IV

The train was approaching Milan without incident. Willy Haas began assuming that the conductor was precisely who he said he was and had described his assignment honestly. Haas almost felt sorry for him, but restrained his emotions. He did wonder, though, what had happened to Bocca when he jumped from the train. He had visions of him limping around on a broken leg, believing he had just escaped from a trap and feeling grateful to his unknown benefactor, the venerable Herr Haas.

Haas drew the shades and snapped on the light in the compartment. It was time to give the Chairman an injection of the lecithin-based drug that would maintain the stability of the age-retarding chemicals already in his body. This was not a drug that Amelia Earhart needed because her treatment had been started at a much earlier age.

Haas administered the serum with an ordinary syringe, injecting it into the Chairman's left arm. The Chairman was used to the daily routine and hardly moved as the needle went in. Haas rubbed the wound with alcohol and that was that.

"Soon, Chairman," Haas said, "we will begin modifying your appearance for the return."

The Chairman nodded his pleasure. He knew that his Vandyke would be shaved, his hair cut in the style of the great era, and a small mustache put in place to complete the picture. Every detail of his prior appearance had been studied from photographs to assure absolute accuracy, even down to the precise length of each sideburn in his last public appearances.

Suddenly, Willy Haas heard a commotion in the car. There was rapid talking among his men. He wondered whether something had gone wrong. Had another security agent been discovered? Immediately, he took a small bag from an overhead rack; in its false bottom were four pistols. Haas held the bag on the seat.

A few seconds later a sharp rap came on the door. "Schmidt!" the voice said with urgency.

Haas threw the door open. "What's going on?" he asked excitedly.

"A message from Gottes," Schmidt replied. "We just received it. He thrust it into Haas's hands.

> VERY HEAVY SNOW BEGINNING TO BLAN-
> KET MUNICH AREA. TANKS AND TRUCKS
> ENCOUNTERING DIFFICULTY. TRAFFIC
> TIED UP. CANNOT CONTINUE OPERA-
> TION. MUST DELAY.
>
>   GOTTES

Haas crumbled the message; his face turned red.

"We can stay in Milan," Schmidt said.

"We arranged for ordinary commercial transportation to the airfield in Milan," Haas replied disgustedly, "to make us look like routine travelers. Questions will be asked about our cancelling. Of course, we can claim that one of us has taken sick. Yes, that will be it. Only we four of the council will remain behind. The rest of you proceed as if nothing has happened. That will help maintain the cover."

"You will stay in Italy?" Schmidt asked.

"I don't know yet, but I doubt Italy. One never knows if we left a trail here. We will stay outside Germany until the weather clears. It won't be more than a few days, I'm sure. We'll be in contact. Good luck."

Haas tried to sound cool, but the disappointment was crushing.

CHAPTER 17

"The President doesn't give a damn," Chester LeVan told Sovern by phone the next morning at the same time that Willy Haas, the Chairman, and the two other council members huddled at Milan's Malpenza Airport for a flight to London. "He doesn't care whether the Nazis failed their lie tests—says those things aren't any good anyway."

"What if *I* talked to him?" Sovern asked.

"You'd get the same answer and a 'mind your own business.' Besides, the President has one powerful item on his side. All that action in West Germany has suddenly stopped. Absolutely ceased. We thought something was about to happen, and it hasn't."

"Maybe it's the time-honored lull before the storm," Sovern theorized.

"I don't think the Nazis can afford lulls," LeVan said. "People plotting coups don't start blowing things up, then suddenly stop."

"Except when going ahead entails greater risks,"

Sovern cautioned. "Did anything odd happen in West Germany?"

"No."

"You mentioned weather."

"They did have some bad weather. Still having it. But that wouldn't affect short-range operations."

"It might affect people coming from the outside, though, and it could affect something spectacular that required clear highways."

"True."

"If they were trying to pull something off, then they'll try again," Sovern emphasized. "I don't know when, but it's got to happen."

"*If* they were trying to pull something off," LeVan replied.

"The Russians?" Sovern asked.

"The latest is that they've expressed pleasure over the reduction of violence in Germany. Right now they're pretty relaxed on their side of the line."

"Has anyone been in touch with Ambassador Grechko?"

"State has. But they're talkin' arms control."

Sovern rubbed his aching eyes. Earhart, sitting opposite him, was trying to follow the conversation. "I'm going to the Archives with Amelia," Sovern said, "to see what they've come up with."

"Good idea," LeVan agreed. "If anything comes up, I'll get it to you."

LeVan hung up. Sovern looked directly into Earhart's eyes. "I'm more sure than ever that you're telling the truth," he said with conviction. "You're not going to disappoint me, are you, Amelia?"

Earhart smiled. "No," she said quietly.

II

Sovern personally drove Earhart to the Archives, with security cars traveling in front and behind. Rudolph Peddington, however, was keeping close tabs on the two of them. The driver of the first car had gotten his job through a friend of Peddington's, and he was reporting to him every move Sovern and Earhart made.

Tom Larner greeted Sovern in the Archives basement. Larner, a civilian deputy director of the Defense Intelligence Agency, had been put in charge of the documents project after Foreman's death. He was relatively insulated from the political machinations at the White House and was prepared to extend every courtesy to Sovern and Earhart. Besides, the Defense Intelligence Agency reported to Chester LeVan.

Larner was a six-foot-six former basketball center for the University of Michigan and had a thin, almost gaunt frame. They called him "Lincoln" or "Abe," and in high school he was routinely asked to deliver the annual reading of the Gettysburg Address. He wore frameless glasses and looked his forty-eight years.

"We don't know what we have," Larner said. "Any optimistic stuff you were told may not stand up. We followed the few leads we thought would take us to age-retarding, but none did."

"Was it mentioned in any paper?" Sovern asked.

"Not directly in the ones we've gone through. But we've still got hundreds of thousands to cover, and Lord knows when we'll finish."

"How *close* did any document come to age retardation?" Earhart asked, recalling related experiments in Germany.

"Quite a few dealt with related things like blood-cell

aging, senility, and muscle deterioration. So we held them aside, as well as pictures of some scientists who worked in those areas."

"Did you find anything on construction of equipment for research in those subjects?" Earhart continued.

"Yes, but it was very specific," Larner replied. "No equipment diagram described an age-retarding device. But have a look at the blueprints. Some of these gadgets might have been used in *conjunction* with age stopping."

The three started toward piles of documents that had been kept separate. "Tom," Sovern asked, "were there any papers on Hitler's medical state?"

"Yes. We have specialists' reports, dental records, stuff like that. We know pretty much what the doctors were concerned with, but aging wasn't among them. They weren't worried about the age of a generally healthy man in his fifties."

While Earhart sifted through the papers trying to find anything recognizable, Sovern took Larner aside out of range of her hearing.

"Tom," he asked, "is there anything in this stuff about Earhart?"

"Yes," Larner replied, "but I didn't want to bring it up with her around."

"What is it?"

"Well, there are references to a woman flier. Earhart's name is never used, but there can be no doubt who it is."

"What do they say?"

"That she was a prize of the Führer's, someone whose health had to be maintained at any cost. There was a notation that, and I'm quoting, the frontiers of German medicine would be open to her."

"That may be the age thing," Sovern said with evident but controlled satisfaction.

"May well be," Larner agreed.

"Anything *else* to support that?" Sovern inquired.

"No, I'm afraid not. At least not yet. But we're looking. There *was* a paper, though, that said Hitler had big plans for her . . . regardless of the war's outcome."

"Tom," Sovern asked, with obvious strain, "is there any suggestion that she was loyal to Hitler?"

"You'd have to have the wisdom of Solomon to decide that," Larner replied quietly. "Everything the Nazis wrote was so full of propaganda and Heil Hitlers that you never know what was true."

"What are you driving at?"

"Some documents referred to Earhart's German heritage and how much it meant to her. They reported she understood the yearnings of the German people to serve their Führer."

"That could mean anything," Sovern said. "She could have nodded once during a propaganda lecture."

"Sure," Larner replied, "but there are some documents open to interpretation."

"Is she *quoted*?"

"Once. It was an appeal for the world to side with Hitler in his invasion of Russia. But we checked the wording. The person who wrote it clearly wasn't an English-speaking American."

"I don't want unsubstantiated stuff used against her," Sovern insisted.

"I understand," Larner replied, "but Rudolph Peddington is requesting reports."

"You sending them?"

"I only send mine to Secretary LeVan. But there

are CIA people working here. What Peddington wants, Peddington gets."

Sovern knew precisely what Peddington would do. He wouldn't insist that the documents were accurate—he was much too smart for that—but would simply state that they cast "grave doubt" on Earhart and should be probed. Like any first-rate lawyer, Peddington was a master at casting doubt.

Sovern and Larner returned to Earhart, who was deeply involved in her documents.

"Anything?" Sovern asked.

"Some of these things bring back memories," the flier replied. "I recall this research being discussed, but that wasn't unusual."

"Remember," Sovern said, "our objective is to find any hint of what these Nazis planned to do after the war, anything that would lead us to Reich Reborn."

A few moments later Earhart came upon a glossy five-by-seven photo, brittle with age, showing two scientists in a chemistry lab. Sovern noticed her concentrating on it.

"Something there?" he asked.

"The picture is so faded," Earhart answered, "but that man on the right . . ." She strained to make out the image.

Larner gave Earhart a heavy magnifier with a built-in light to study the mystery picture.

"There was a chemistry professor," she went on. "He was always around during the age experiments. I can't be sure this is him. It *looks* like him. But my memory is so . . ."

"Do you recall his name, an initial?" Sovern asked urgently.

"I never knew his actual name. But I *think* . . .

they called him . . . Professor." She saw there was no name on the photo's back.

"We could try to trace that," Larner said. "The file it came from has a lot of names and other pictures. It's possible we can cross-reference."

"Do it in ten minutes," Sovern said with a smile.

"Five," Larner replied.

One of Larner's aides walked up to him quickly. "Phone, sir," he said. "The White House."

Larner went to a nearby desk and picked up the phone with a flashing light. He listened intently, then returned, stone-faced, to Sovern and Earhart. "Uh, Mr. Sovern, could I have a word with you?" he asked.

Once they stepped away, Larner spoke quietly. "That was Elmer Rose. We've gotten an order from the President to bar you and Miss Earhart from the Archives. I'm sorry."

Sovern refused to lose his dignity at this new set-back. He walked resolutely back to Earhart. "We have to go," he told her tersely.

"Of course," she replied, understanding fully. She had learned to read between the lines in Washington.

"Tom," Sovern said to Larner in parting, "I'd appreciate it—a personal favor—if you'd track down the name of that chemist. It's more important than any of us, if you know what I mean."

"I'll order the research under my own name," Larner responded. "Of course, I'd . . ."

"Don't worry," Sovern broke in. "No one will know." He led Earhart out.

"We have been officially excommunicated," Sovern said to the flier. "The President of the United States believes that the Nazi threat has taken care of itself, with the grace of God and the blessing of Rudolph

Peddington. And I'm sure by now he's convinced you are a conspirator of the lowest sort and waiting to seize power in the United States."

Earhart laughed, but it was a forced laugh, for she knew how critical things had become.

"It's tragic," Sovern said, "that more people will die before they realize how wrong they are. But they won't admit it even then. Peddington'll find some flunky in the CIA European division and sack him for poor analysis."

They reached their car. "Sir," the driver said, "we just got a radio message from the White House. You're ordered to remove Miss Earhart from Washington."

III

For Willy Haas and the Chairman it was the ultimate irony. They had flown to London to wait out the European snowstorm and had checked into the Europa Hotel in the Mayfair section. During World War II, Haas learned from a plaque on the wall, the building attached to the Europa had been General Eisenhower's headquarters. And around the corner, with its oversized eagle sculpted to the roof, was the American Embassy.

Haas and the Chairman felt wonderful about the geography. "Chairman," Haas said as they took a brief stroll through Grosvenor Square, "our hotel would make a wonderful embassy for us."

The Chairman nodded his agreement. They walked toward Claridges a few blocks away, the most elegant and famous of the London hotels, where the Chairman had once hoped he would be greeted by a beaten

British government. The Chairman, having received a massive injection of the lecithin-based age-retardant, walked slowly but securely. He looked better than he had looked in days, but realized that another bout with fatigue would probably occur soon. He wanted to see as much as possible before that happened.

So although there was work to be done back at the Europa—planning the next attempt at a coup—he insisted on extending his stroll. He was becoming enthralled with the city he had failed to conquer during the Battle of Britain in 1940. Haas was concerned over the supreme leader's physical state, but saw he could not be dissuaded. He hailed a large, black taxi cab and told the driver to go to Whitehall, the center of the British government, on the banks of the Thames.

There was one building the Chairman wanted particularly to see—the reddish brown, windowless hulk near Whitehall that was Winston Churchill's bunker during the war. It was from here that Churchill planned strategy, addressed the British people, and spoke by phone with President Roosevelt. Haas and the Chairman toured the structure with a group of Canadians, and the Chairman was able to sit in the tiny room where Churchill made his trans-Atlantic calls. He saw the maps of the Normandy invasion and the large reconnaissance photographs of bomb damage in downtown Berlin.

"*That* will never happen again," Haas muttered under his breath. He then studied maps depicting the defenses of London during the buzz-bomb attacks of 1944. The map showed locations and anti-aircraft guns and spotters. "One atomic bomb," Haas again muttered, "and all would have been different." Hatred welled up inside him—hatred of the Jewish atomic scientists who, in his twisted mind, had deserted Germany during the 1930's.

Haas and the Chairman then took a cab ride around Victoria Embankment, bordering the Thames. Their cab driver this time, like many in London, was a thoroughly knowledgeable and thoroughly talkative chap who liked to give his passengers more than just a ride. He was in his late sixties, but spoke with the vigor of a teenager.

"Your first time in London, sir?" he asked Haas.

"No, I've been here before."

The driver detected the German accent and stiffened somewhat. "From the Continent?" he asked with a slight chill.

"No, we're Americans. We were born in . . . Austria, but we left many years ago . . . before the war, of course."

"That's good. I like the ones who left. You showed real courage against Hitler."

"He was a madman," Haas said. "He destroyed everything."

"Sure did. You look over there, sir. Y'see that big brown building?"

"Yes," Haas replied.

"Y'see part of it is missing. That's bomb damage from the Blitz. Some of that stuff still hasn't been repaired. Maybe it's better, don't you think?"

"Yes, I do," Haas said. "It reminds people of what the Nazis did." He would have smiled at the Chairman, but he was afraid of being seen in the driver's rearview mirror.

"Your quiet friend, his first time in London?" the driver asked.

"Yes. He doesn't talk much, but he loves it. Has a breathing problem."

"Oh, sorry to hear that," the driver said. "There's Guy's Hospital on the other side of the river. The Heinies knocked out part of that, too."

"Animals," Haas responded.

"We may have 'em again, I'm afraid," the driver continued. "You look at what's happenin' in Germany today. All they do is beat each other up. They can't solve any of their problems without a dictator."

"That's one of the reasons we left," Haas said with a sigh. "Hitler had just taken over Austria. Who wanted to live that way?"

"You think we'll have to fight 'em again?"

"No, I don't think so. It can never happen again that way. Never."

"I hope you're right."

Haas could stomach the driver no longer and asked to be let off near Tower Bridge, which, he said, he wanted to inspect on foot. But moments after he and the Chairman got out he hailed another cab and the two went back to the Europa.

The Chairman lay down on a bed to rest, having overdone it with his brief tour of the enemy camp. Haas met briefly with his senior intelligence man in London, who was assigned to maintain communications with General Gottes. Gottes had sent only one message since the Chairman's arrival in London:

OUR UNITS RETURNING TO ORIGINAL POSITIONS. PAMPHLETS AND PROPAGANDA MATERIALS HIDDEN. BOMBS PLANTED ARE BEING REMOVED WHEREVER POSSIBLE. ANTICIPATE CLEAR WEATHER CONDITIONS IN FORTY-EIGHT HOURS.

Haas made his plans for the new attempt to take place December 15th. That gave the Nazis three days to prepare.

It was just before dinner that Haas heard a knock at the door. The Chairman opened one eye but immediately closed it again. Haas assumed it was either Barlack or Gustav Hoffmann. He went to the door.

"Yes?"

"Sir, would you open please? It's Scotland Yard."

A sharp chill ran up Haas's spine. But not wanting to increase any suspicions, he quickly opened. "What is it?" he asked. "Is something wrong?"

"Not really, sir," the man from the Yard replied, quickly glancing around the room. He was Inspector Michael Hanson, a weather-beaten man of forty-five who specialized in international terrorism. "We just wanted to ask you some questions about the incident on the train."

"What train?" Haas asked, checking himself before becoming too defensive.

"The Milan train, sir."

"How did you know I was on that?"

"Oh, sir, don't be at all worried," Hanson said, his bushy mustache bobbing as he spoke. "As you know, there was an unfortunate murder aboard the Milan run. The report said that there had been some witnesses and that the best one had gotten off at Milan station and told a conductor there was some illness in his party. The Italian police tried to find him— that's you, sir—and traced you to the airport and a flight to London."

"Well done!" Haas said with a smile.

"Now sir, there's no suspicion here, but we did want some further information on the attack."

"I'll help in any way I can," Haas said, realizing that there was probably no danger.

"Oh, by the way," Hanson continued, "your sick friend, is that him?"

"Yes," Haas replied, "but he's feeling better now."

"A little odd that you should fly to London with a sick man, ay?" Hanson asked.

The tension returned to Willy Haas. He had slipped up on the alibi.

"He's sick off and on and we wanted to be near an English-speaking doctor," Haas replied, quickly and nonchalantly. "We had only been planning to spend a little time outside England, so we simply decided to cancel all the rest.

"I see," Hanson said, jotting notes in a little dog-eared pad. "Can we get him some medical attention?"

"No, he's all right."

"It's hard for me to believe that he was bad enough to cancel the rest of your stay, yet, here he is, not even needing a doctor."

Haas leaned secretly toward Hanson. "You don't understand," he whispered, "the man is a little eccentric, but very rich. Many of us depend upon him for our livings and we have to do what he says."

That hit home. "Oh," Hanson said. "I understand fully."

"It's unfortunate," Haas whispered, "but true."

"Now," Hanson went on, "as I understand it, you witnessed the shooting."

"Yes," Haas replied, "but why is Scotland Yard interested in something that happened in Italy?"

"We believe," Hanson answered, "that a terrorist group with a unit in London may have been involved."

"Ah," Haas said, "now I follow. Well, I saw this

tragic murder first hand. The conductor was walking down the aisle of the passenger car . . ."

"Your car, sir?"

"No."

"What were you doing in this other car?"

"Stretching my legs, taking a walk. It's fun to walk through a train and just observe the passengers."

"Yes, sir. And you say the conductor . . ."

"He was just walking down the aisle. Suddenly this man jumped up from his seat, pulled out a pistol, and aimed. I shouted something—I don't recall what it was —and people started diving for cover. Then this man fired . . . many, many times. The conductor just fell."

"There seems to be some confusion on just what happened next, sir."

"From what I saw," Haas replied, "the man ran up the aisle to the section between the cars. Then someone shouted, 'He jumped!' I personally went to the conductor."

"Did the murderer have any confederates?"

"Not that I saw."

"Did the conductor say anything before he passed on?"

"No, I think he was very dead when I got to him. The man had no chance."

"Did you know this conductor?"

"No."

"Are you certain?"

"Of course I'm certain."

"At least two passengers, sir, have said that you and several other men escorted the conductor into a compartment minutes before his death."

Haas hesitated, then smiled. "It's true," he finally conceded. "We . . . uh . . . had a little card game. Look, I didn't want to embarrass the man's memory."

"That's all right, sir. Perfectly common practice."
Hanson closed his little pad.

"Is that all?" Haas asked.

"For now, certainly," Hanson answered. "But we may want to speak with you again, sir. Will you be staying at the Europa?"

"Oh yes."

"For how long?"

"Oh, at least two nights."

"And where to after that, sir?"

Haas hesitated. "Well, we haven't made definite plans. There is so much we want to see."

"The Christmas season is approaching, sir. I'd make reservations if I were you."

"Yes, we'd better."

"Well, let me give you my card," Hanson said. "When you move on, I'd appreciate having your itinerary. It might help our investigation."

"I'd be happy to cooperate," Haas told the detective. He took the card.

When Hanson left, Haas wondered whether there wasn't more to the visit than appeared. He fought the tendency to become paranoid, to wonder about every person who looked his way. He privately cursed the weather in Europe, which had forced him to sweat out still more hours before the triumphant entry. Then, almost routinely, he picked up a copy of the *Manchester Guardian* which he had gotten at the desk and rechecked the weather forecast for the Continent. Yes, clearing was expected as Gottes had said.

There were still no definite plans for the new takeover attempt. Gottes's activities would remain essentially the same, Haas knew, but the Chairman's entry into Germany would have to be different for security reasons. In fact, Haas now preferred that

GHOSTFLIGHT 267

Munich not even be entered from another German city. The Chairman, who had gained prominence in Munich, where the Nazi party was born, had remarked that it would be glorious if it could be the first city in Germany where he would set foot on the day of renewal. Haas carefully studied maps and decided that Paris would be an ideal jumping off point. The Chairman was sure to like that. Paris was the sight of his proudest, most magnificent triumph. It symbolized the Reich at its grandest.

CHAPTER 18

New York City

The full order from the White House directed Sovern to take Earhart on a nostalgic trip through her old haunts. It was, Sovern knew, a convenient way of getting them both out of Washington, away from the chance to influence contacts in the government. The President had further ordered Sovern to investigate the chance that Earhart was disloyal to the United States, citing, as expected, the raw documents uncovered in the Archives.

Accordingly Sovern and Earhart flew to New York, where Amelia had attended Columbia as a pre-medical student after World War I. The city was the closest logical point to Washington from which Sovern could get back quickly if called, as he fully expected to be.

The two checked into the St. Regis, one of the fashionable hotels in town and one that did not receive an overwhelming mass of conventioneers. Sovern and Earhart craved *some* privacy.

Their rooms adjoined with a door between them.

Each was tastefully decorated with traditional furniture and looked out on chic New York shops. As a concession to the possibility that the Nazis might try to kill Earhart—for whatever reason—the President had authorized the detachment of Secret Service men to cover the hotel. Three checked into rooms on Earhart's floor and the rest posed as visitors or simply strolled outside. The outside agents were changed regularly so hotel personnel wouldn't become suspicious.

Sovern's first problem in exile was to maintain communications with Chester LeVan. Calling from the hotel room was out of the question because his opponents in the government probably had the line tapped. Yet his use of pay phones would arouse Secret Service suspicion. So he phoned an old friend in New York, Leonard Marshall, who had formerly served as deputy assistant director of CRG. Marshall was now a professor of economics at New York University and remained fiercely loyal to Sovern.

Sovern requested that Marshall visit him in the hotel. Marshall, a short, stocky man who waddled rather than walked, obliged. The two exchanged the usual greetings then sat around a coffee table. Sovern assumed the room was bugged by Rudolph Peddington's CIA, so while engaging in chit chat, he wrote notes to Marshall.

"Len," Sovern said, "you've got to tell me all about the research you're doing. Are you still in East European studies?"

"Yes, that's right," Marshall replied in his tediously slow style, "I'm writing a book on the 1968 revolt in Czechoslovakia." He looked down and saw Sovern writing a quick note. He was experienced enough not to ask about it.

"Good subject," Sovern said. But he wrote:

IN OFFICIAL JAM. MAY BE TAPPED AND
BUGGED. WILL YOU HELP? NO PHYSICAL
RISK.

Marshall nodded that he would.

"It's taken me two years to do all the work," Marshall said. "Research is impossible over there. You never know when you're talking to a KGB man."

"They're the ones who smile a lot and use American slang," Sovern said with a laugh. He wrote:

CHES LEVAN FEEDING ME CRITICAL
INFO. PLEASE CALL HIM AT HOME IN
WASHINGTON 202-382-5731. HE'LL FILL
YOU IN. WOULD YOU COME HERE WITH
ANYTHING HE HAS?

Again Marshall nodded affirmatively, but there was a baffled expression on his face. He gestured as if to ask, "What's happened to you?"

"I think I've got a good manuscript," Marshall said as Sovern wrote. "It'll be published by Harvard University Press and then bought by university libraries. It takes a pretty hard line on what the Communist government did there, so I guess some of the ideologues on our faculties won't be talking to me for a time."

Sovern's note:

BEING FROZEN OUT FOR UNDUE HON-
ESTY ABOUT NAZI THREAT. IT'S SWEET
DREAMS AND KIND THOUGHTS IN WASH-
INGTON THESE DAYS. PEDDINGTON
USING SITUATION TO MOVE UP.

Leonard Marshall nodded his understanding. He had seen similar situations during his own Washington years. After spending a reasonable amount of time with Sovern, he left. Sovern knew he could depend fully on Marshall. He was the kind who did everything with an enthusiasm that belied his plodding manner.

It was ironic, but Richard Sovern and Amelia Earhart had been forced into sightseeing at about the same time as Willy Haas and the Chairman. Whereas for Haas it was a temporary diversion to be followed by glory, for Sovern it was a trip through nowhere that could burn up valuable days, even weeks, while events in Germany plowed ahead.

The next day Sovern took Earhart to Columbia. Several Secret Service agents rode in the cab behind Sovern's as it traveled from the elegance of midtown to the seediness of the once-magnificent Columbia neighborhood at One-hundred-sixteenth Street and Broadway.

"My God," Earhart said as the cab got further and further north, "what happened to this place?"

Sovern explained how the middle-class population had moved out as minorities, often ill-prepared for urban life, moved in. He recalled Amelia Earhart's reputation for fighting bigotry long before it was fashionable and wondered what her reaction would be to the plight of the underclass in her old neighborhood.

She had no reaction. The sight of slums where spotless neighborhoods had been was simply too overwhelming.

"What's it like at night around here?" she asked.

"You don't go out at night," Sovern replied.

"When I was at Columbia we went anywhere at night." She shook her head sadly. "How did people allow this to happen?"

Sovern did not respond. He had no stomach for extended discussion of urban politics, of conservative rigidities, and liberal simplicities.

They arrived at Columbia and got out. "Now *this* place," Earhart said, "hasn't changed all that much, although there are some new buildings." She walked quickly to the middle of the huge quadrangle, with its stone halls. Then she turned left, looking toward the domed Low Library. "I used to sit in its lap," she said. A devilish look came to her face.

"Now wait a second," Sovern protested. "Somehow I don't think that would become a returned national heroine."

"I guess you're right," Earhart replied. Besides, she understood that Sovern's trip to Columbia was simply a way of passing time, of carrying out a mechanical make-work assignment. Despite their affection for each other, the overall situation was critical and tense. It was hardly the time for sentimental pranks.

"Would you care to visit the top of the library?" she asked quietly. "I used to go there often just to think."

"Sure," Sovern said.

As they walked up the long, wide steps of Low Library and entered, Earhart recalled her days as a pre-med student after World War I. Her interest in medicine had been stimulated by working as a nurse in a Canadian military hospital. She remembered, too, how her studies were interrupted by urgent calls from her parents in California. Their marriage was breaking up, and they wanted Amelia home as a buffer between them. She recalled how she went, how destiny took her to the small, dusty airfields of the West and into history.

Sovern and Earhart climbed to the top of the library dome and looked out over Morningside Heights. Earhart pointed toward One-hundred-third Street.

"Remember George Gershwin?" she asked.

"I don't remember him, but I know of him," Sovern replied.

"He used to live over there, on One-hundred-third. I always felt a connection with him because his death came the same week as my disappearance. We were the same age, both of us born in 1898. They never told me in Germany what he died of."

"It was a brain tumor," Sovern said. "They operated, but it was in a part of the brain that couldn't be touched."

Sovern could see in Earhart's face the memory of her early years as she gazed pensively across the Hudson River toward the Jersey shore.

"We used to go hiking on the Palisades," she said. "I wonder if I could find some of the people I went with."

"If they're still . . ."

"You can say it. If they're still alive. I accept my actual age. It doesn't bother me. The only thing that bothers me is . . ."

"Now *you* say it," Sovern insisted gently.

"What bothers me is the way people live these days. Life in my time was more genteel, slower-paced, even for an adventurer like me. Everyone now seems in such a hurry even if they have nothing in particular to do. I don't want to criticize," Earhart continued, "but I think people in the thirties were more genuine. People today seem so conscious of their . . . I think the word they like to use is image."

"That's the word. But your husband, George Putnam, he was a PR man. Didn't he concern himself with *your* image?"

"Yes, but I was a public personality, and even with that he didn't go around taking polls every ten minutes. All right, I'm being overly sensitive."

"No, go ahead . . ."

"If I could choose a time to live," Earhart went on, "I'd choose my natural time."

Sovern thought about it for a few moments, then smiled sardonically. "Let me tell you a little secret," he said. "I think I'd have preferred the thirties too, but I could've done without the depression."

"Of course," Earhart replied. "But I get the feeling," she continued, looking around the neighborhood, "that there's a different kind of depression today, a depression of the spirit."

Sovern knew the point was well taken.

The two walked down from the dome, talking about the architecture of the building and hearing their voices echo off the stone walls. Richard Sovern wondered what news might come from Chester LeVan that evening, when he expected a visit from Leonard Marshall. As he and Earhart passed a newsstand, his eyes swept the headlines. They said nothing of importance. Germany wasn't even mentioned. The big news was a possible sanitation strike in New York and the fear that any settlement would raise the already high taxes. "Strikes," Sovern mumbled, "are one of the great local institutions."

Earhart wanted to go next to Carnegie Hall, where she had often heard Walter Damrosch conduct the

New York Symphony Society. During the drive to
Fifty-seventh Street Sovern told her how the Hall had
almost been demolished, but had been saved and declared a national landmark. It did not appear much
different from the days when Amelia Earhart sat upstairs, enduring the smell of garlic from the less-af-
fluent concertgoers.

While in the car Sovern took a handful of photographs from his inside jacket pocket. It was, after all,
part of his assignment to continue to check Earhart's
authenticity, and this was still the best way.

"More pictures," he told her.

As before, her eyes sparkled. She had become obsessed with re-living her past.

Sovern flipped to the first picture. "Do you recognize
this?" he asked.

Earhart smiled. "That's Sam Chapman. He was a
boarder in my parents' house. I used to go out with
him, and a lot of people thought we'd get married.
You know, we used to go to meetings of the IWW together."

"The Industrial Workers of the World," Sovern
said. "Many still think that all the people who attended their meetings were Communists."

"Well, some were," Earhart replied, "but we weren't.
They used to call the members Wobblies. We'd sit
around and listen to a lot of revolutionary talk, then
go home and forget it."

Sovern flipped the picture.

"Bill Kinner!" Earhart exclaimed. "He was a family
friend who manufactured the Kinner Canary, a pretty
fine airplane. My parents and sister chipped in to buy
me one for my twenty-fourth birthday."

Next picture.

"That's Neta Snook, my flying teacher. She was a

real woman pioneer. I didn't have the money for the lessons, so I worked at the Los Angeles phone company."

Sovern turned to still another photo.

"Oh my goodness, that's Rogers Field in California. I was almost killed there. During a 1922 air show I put the plane into a tailspin while in the clouds. I didn't realize how low I was and almost didn't pull out of the dive in time."

"How did you feel after that?" Sovern asked.

"I stayed cool, but I felt stupid," Earhart replied.

They arrived at Carnegie Hall and Earhart looked over the posters adorning the outside.

"I see the Philadelphia Orchestra will be here tonight and tomorrow. Could we go?"

Sovern wanted to be back in his room for Leonard Marshall, yet did not want to restrict Earhart. He could not, though, consider letting her go accompanied only by the Secret Service. He felt personally responsible.

"Let's see how the evening turns out," he responded evasively.

Earhart toured the inside of the hall, going up to the balcony and pretending she was back in the nineteen thirties. "I remember one Boston Symphony concert," she said. "They played Tchaikovsky's Sixth Symphony and the audience applauded for fifteen minutes. I'd never heard anything like it. When I made my first trans-Atlantic flight I got a tremendous reception in England, and it reminded me of that Carnegie Hall ovation."

Sovern marveled at how utterly civilized Earhart was. She was so unlike the rough image of the adventurer or the rigid, militant image of the early feminists. But, he kept asking himself, how long would

she live? What convulsion might occur now that she
was no longer under Nazi treatment and was showing
some signs, however slight, of deterioration. Sovern
had frightful visions of her suddenly dying or of the
age mechanism going mad and turning her old and
decrepit within a month.

They returned to the St. Regis, where Sovern waited
for Leonard Marshall, realizing he'd only come if
LeVan had something to report. Amelia discreetly suggested that they put off plans for a concert to a more
suitable time, and Sovern agreed. He hoped, though,
to be able to take her the next night.

Marshall showed up at 8:35, carrying a message
from LeVan. He slipped it to Sovern during a seemingly casual conversation.

NO UNUSUAL ACTIVITY IN GERMANY.
SMALL-SCALE STREET FIGHTS AND PET-
TY TERROR BETWEEN LEFT AND RIGHT
CONTINUES, BUT NO SIGN OF TAKEOVER
ATTEMPT. WILL KEEP YOU POSTED.

A few minutes after Marshall left, the phone rang.
Sovern assumed it was something official.

It was not.

"Dick? Hugo Lessing."

"Hugo, I'm a retired man," Sovern replied.

"I know, like Frank Sinatra."

"Nobody banished *him,* Hugo."

"Dick, the betting in the newsroom is you'll be back
pretty soon."

"Oh? Well if you've got a secret, Hugo, I hope you
keep it." Sovern was referring to the chance that the
phone was tapped, and Lessing got the message.

"You know I don't believe that it pays to advertise," the reporter said.

"Why'd you call, Hugo?"

"Just to be friendly, Dick. I'm concerned about you. A lot of people down here care about what happens to the original Mr. Clean of the spook trade. In fact, we were writing some background on you today and felt bad going through all that old stuff in the files— press releases, pictures, dispatches, negatives with names. . . ."

That was it. *That,* Sovern knew, was why Lessing had called. He had been plugged into the work being done at the Archives and knew that the picture Amelia thought familiar had been identified.

"I appreciate your sentiments," Sovern said, "and I think I understand them. Old pictures can have an impact."

"At any rate," Lessing concluded, "that's why I called, and now I've got to get to work. Look, if there's something I can do . . ."

"You're a pal, Hugo. If there is, I'll let you know."

The conversation ended. Sovern knew Hugo Lessing wouldn't have wasted a call unless the identification represented some kind of breakthrough. And even that wouldn't mean a thing unless the man in the photo were still alive.

But, if he was, how could Sovern contact him? Cut off from official support, he realized there was nothing he could do until events in Germany vindicated him, and he was called back to service.

II

Willy Haas had seen the black-and-white newsfilm in 1940—the Führer standing in full uniform before the Eiffel Tower doing a little jig, literally dancing for joy at the seizure of Paris. The film, shown around the world, had become a symbol of Nazi "invincibility."

Now the Chairman stood before the Tower once more. Of course, he would not risk attracting attention by dancing around, but Haas had not seen him so animated since the War. His eyes glistened. There was a spring to his walk that belied his age and condition, and it was becoming apparent that he would be able to lead the takeover with much of his old charisma.

Gottes had just reported that roads were clear and that Mulberry was back on the track. Everything would be precisely the same as in the aborted attempt except that the Chairman would approach Munich from Paris.

The stay in the French capital was overwhelmingly sentimental. In 1940 the Chairman had taken a dawn ride through the nearly deserted streets of Paris, receiving the frightened salutes of French policemen and demonstrating that he could ride in an open car through the conquered city without fear. And so, on the morning of December 14, 1982, twenty-four hours before the moment he would leave for his new triumph, the Chairman, accompanied by Haas, once again took the dawn ride. It all looked the same, for the outline of Paris never really seems to change. The gendarmes still walked their beats. The fruit vendors prepared for the new day. A few book and magazine stalls began to open.

Haas drove the rented car along the weaving streets,

trying to follow the route of Hitler's famous drive. He stopped at one address in particular to point out the Paris headquarters of Richard Sovern's CRG. The Chairman and Haas knew that inside the white-stoned building the American agents planning to destroy Reich Reborn had barely one day to succeed.

Haas and the Chairman returned to their hotel, an obscure second-class establishment. There a messenger delivered a bulletin from Reich Reborn operatives in Washington stating that Richard Sovern appeared to have been removed from his post.

Haas was delighted. Immediately, he examined a list of those who might take Sovern's place in the anti-Nazi operations of the U.S. Government. He quickly arrived at the name of Rudolph Peddington and just as quickly ridiculed it. Peddington, he knew, had an excellent reputation, but was given to extremely conservative approaches. Neither he nor anyone else on the list had Sovern's grasp of modern Nazism. No one could act quickly enough to stop Reich Reborn.

The train to Munich was leaving at six the next morning.

III

Amelia Earhart got her wish when Sovern reserved tickets for the Philadelphia Orchestra concert the night of December fourteenth. The program, consisting of Beethoven's Third Symphony, the Eroica; the Tchaikovsky Violin Concerto, with Isaac Stern as soloist; and a series of Schubert songs, would be the first live music Amelia had heard in more than a generation.

Before leaving for Carnegie Hall, Sovern received
another visit from Leonard Marshall. He carried word
from LeVan that there had been an increase in clandestine, coded radio traffic throughout West Germany.
The increase was following the same pattern of several
days before when, unknown to Washington, the coup
attempt had been underway. In addition, a small unit
of West German tanks had been detected on a road
leading to Munich. When a British officer reported
the unscheduled movement to the West German Army,
it was found out that the tanks had improperly drawn
orders. An investigation, LeVan reported, was in progress.

Unfortunately, LeVan was unaware that the investigation was headed by a German colonel loyal to the
Reich Reborn.

To Richard Sovern, the reports meant that something was in the wind. He did not, though, want suddenly to cancel plans for the concert, an action that
might cause the Secret Service to take a closer look at
Marshall's visits. Besides, there wasn't much he could
do in a hotel room. He did write a note to LeVan for
Marshall to transmit by phone, urging that American
troops be positioned near West German cities so that
a coup attempt would not catch them off guard. Sovern
also made sure that Marshall knew where he'd be that
evening.

The night was cold and damp, typical of New York
in mid-December. The crowds outside Carnegie Hall
ranged from the wealthy patrons of the New York
arts establishment to college students from Columbia,
NYU, and neighboring schools, who, like the Amelia
Earhart of earlier days, would sit in the balcony to
save money. As usual there were a number of sidewalk violinists and guitarists who lined the row of

billboards between Carnegie Hall and the Russian
Tea Room, playing their hearts out for the contributions from the crowd.

The Secret Service had already gone through the
hall, and agents were sprinkled throughout the knots
of people waiting outside. Sovern and Earhart arrived
in what appeared to be an ordinary yellow cab, but it
was driven by an agent. They went immediately inside
and were shown to their seats, which were on the aisle
in the orchestra. Earhart wore glasses supplied by the
Secret Service, their lenses nothing more than optical
glass, as a means of preventing recognition.

And yet one woman to the right of Amelia kept
staring at her. Sovern wondered whether the aging
music lover was seeing a face she had seen before, perhaps from news photos of the twenties or thirties. But
the woman soon looked away.

The concert, with Eugene Ormandy conducting, began promptly at 8:30, the maestro getting his usual
enthusiastic ovation. Earhart's applause was particularly vigorous. She recalled Ormandy from the thirties,
when he was conductor of the Minneapolis Symphony.
When the applause died down, he raised his baton,
and the mellow sound of the Philadelphia's string
section meshed with the superb acoustics of Carnegie
Hall to produce music of rare elegance.

It was during Isaac Stern's rendition of the Tchaikovsky concerto that Sovern became aware of sudden
activity in the rear of the hall. Instinctively, he reached
for the pistol in his shoulder holster and looked back.
Three Secret Service men were engaged in animated
conversation to the chagrin of those seated in the rear,
who shushed them with enormous vigor.

Then an agent walked down the aisle and knelt beside Sovern.

"Sir, phone call. The White House."

Sovern moved quickly to the office and grabbed the phone from the startled manager.

"This is Sovern," he said.

There were a few clicks on the line as the operator made a connection.

"Dick, this is the President," came the familiar voice. "You get down here. Fast."

Sovern was elated, yet stunned. "What's the problem, sir?"

"You're right and Peddington's wrong. That's the problem," the President replied. "I get the feeling that's *always* the problem."

"What's happened?"

"It's an open line, Dick, but what's goin' on over there is incredible. Now I just sent a plane to La-Guardia to pick up you and your lady friend. See me tonight please."

"Yes, sir."

Sovern felt like the proverbial new man, the resurrected intelligence expert. He recalled how Churchill had been brought out of the political wilderness at the beginning of World War II to lead England through the Nazi assault. While hardly comparing himself to Churchill, he enjoyed the thought.

He rushed back into the hall, and suddenly the nightmarish thought hit him that a coup might already be underway, that perhaps Adolf Hitler had reappeared. The vision of being too late haunted him; the idea that the events, whatever they were, might trigger a massive Russian response gnawed at his mind.

He reached Earhart, bent down, and whispered. "Sorry, but we've got to go. The President."

He must have been excited, for even his whispers

were overheard and three people turned sharply at the mention of the President.

Earhart instantly forgot the music and left her seat. Moments later they were outside. The Secret Service had already alerted the police. It was only two or three minutes before a squad car pulled up, followed quickly by another. Sovern and Earhart got into the first car with an agent, other agents following.

Sirens wailed as the cars sped through the city, soon picking up a motorcycle escort. Sovern leaned forward to the cop driving his car. "Anything big happening tonight?" he asked.

"Murder on East Sixty-second," the cop answered.

"I mean in the world," Sovern said.

"Nothing much."

"Nothing in Germany?"

The cop shrugged. "There was somethin' on the radio earlier about some tank accident, or some shootin' by mistake or somethin'. I don't know."

"American tanks? German tanks?"

"Both," the cop replied.

CHAPTER 19

Paris

The phone rang next to Willy Haas's bed.

He turned uncomfortably, still largely asleep, and mumbled something. The Chairman, in the next bed, did not stir.

Haas finally realized it was the phone and grabbed the receiver. "Yes, what is it?" he asked, annoyed at the intrusion.

There was static, then, in broken English, an operator cut in. "Is this Mr. Gabriel?" she asked. It was Haas's code name in France.

"Yes," Haas replied, his annoyance turning to concern.

"Munich calling," the operator said. "Go ahead, please."

"Mr. Gabriel," came a distant voice at the other end. It was Gottes.

"Yes," Haas replied tensely.

"This is Mr. Ehrlich."

"Yes, Ehrlich. Why do you call at this hour?"

"There is a serious illness in our party which may

be catching, Mr. Gabriel. You'd better stay in Paris."

"I'm so sorry," Haas replied, trying to control his anger and frustration. "Who is sick? And how badly?"

"You don't know him, but we will cable more information. Right now I must get off. People here are so concerned."

"Of course. I understand. Thank you for calling."

Haas slammed down the phone and looked over at the Chairman sleeping serenely. How, he wondered, would he tell him that once more the operation was in jeopardy? Could the man's constitution stand another disappointment?

Gottes sounded far more worried than he did when snow cancelled the first attempt, Haas realized. What was it *this* time?

There was a security breach. That was the *only* explanation . . . and the most serious one. Automatically, Haas's mind started reviewing the names of possible defectors and double agents who might have betrayed the Reich Reborn. Looking for traitors had always been a favorite Nazi activity.

A few minutes later Haas heard a rap at the door. Fright shot through him, as it did any time a visitor appeared.

Haas rushed to the door. "Mulberry," whispered the messenger, and Haas felt as relieved as the situation allowed. The man was hardly inside before Haas grabbed the envelope he was removing from his coat pocket. The coded note made the situation clear:

ONE OF OUR TANK UNITS CHALLENGED FOR IDENTIFICATION BY US ARMY AR- MORED PATROL IN OUTSKIRTS MUNICH. COMMANDER PANICKED AND OPENED

FIRE. BATTLE FOLLOWED. UNIT LARGE-
LY DESTROYED. MANY CAPTURED.

Haas threw the note violently to the floor. "Stupid
morons! Amateurs! What does he mean, 'panicked'?
What kind of Germans are these?"

He regained control, realizing his outburst in itself
was a security breach, and began to assess his position.
Clearly the movement had been severely compromised
on the most important day of its existence. Now, every
NATO unit would be on the alert, every security
agency would have its men out in force, watching,
waiting. When news of the damage spread through
Reich Reborn, there was the chance of defections by
those who'd believe the cause was lost. Some might
give information to the authorities to avoid prosecution. True, only a few at the top knew of the Chairman's existence, but others knew tactical plans.

Haas would have to await further reports from
Gottes to make a full assessment. In the meantime he
felt obligated to awaken the Chairman. After sending
the messenger away, he walked slowly to the leader's
bed and began shaking him mildly. It took fully four
minutes before the leader of the Third Reich was
completely conscious.

"Chairman," Haas said calmly, "we have suffered a
setback. One of our units has been discovered." He
went on to give all the details he knew, then watched
the Chairman's face fill with anger. But both men
were determined to go on, to counter this catastrophe
as well.

A messenger arriving twenty-five minutes later
brought another cable from Gottes confirming Haas's
initial fears:

NATO ARMOR AND INFANTRY UNITS
TAKING UP POSITIONS AROUND MAJOR
CITIES. SOURCES IN WEST GERMAN IN-
TELLIGENCE REPORT NATO BELIEVES
COUP ATTEMPT IN WORKS. MOST RR
PRISONERS TAKEN BY AMERICANS HAVE
REMAINED LOYAL, BUT ONE MAN DIS-
CLOSED LOCATION OF ONE MAIN WEAP-
ONS DEPOT. AS RESULT HAVE LOST
ABOUT TWENTY PERCENT OF ARMS AND
AMMUNITION.

Haas understood the critical nature of the situation.
Yet, an audacious, seemingly reckless thought entered
his mind: the possibility of launching a quick, clandestine attempt to seize power within a week. He
knew the less imaginative in the Reich Reborn would
scoff, but the Chairman would understand the possibilities. NATO, Haas reasoned, would conclude that the
Reich Reborn had been severely disrupted by the
tank debacle near Munich and that the movement
would cancel any imminent plans for action. In a few
days NATO troops would be returned to regular bases
lest their alert status worry the Russians and attract
too many probing reporters. NATO's anti-Nazi defenses, raised to high pitch and then lowered, would be
at their psychologically weakest. It would be a good
time to strike.

Haas took pencil and paper in hand. The odds were
long, but his will was overwhelming.

II

"There is no doubt that a coup was attempted," Chester LeVan told the National Operations Board. Actually, the report from S-2—Intelligence Section—of the U.S. Seventh Army in Germany had said that an attempted power grab "possibly" was underway when the Reich Reborn tanks were intercepted near Munich. LeVan had upgraded the "possibly" to "probably" when the report was disseminated within the Pentagon, and upgraded it further before the Board to strengthen Richard Sovern's position.

It was one A.M. The board was meeting in the Oval Office. The dampness that Sovern had experienced in New York had found its way to Washington in the form of a violent rainstorm. The clattering of the drops on the bulletproof windows heightened the already tense atmosphere that pervaded the meeting.

Aside from the "rehabilitated" Richard Sovern, it was Rudolph Peddington who was the center of speculation. He had underestimated the Nazi threat, and how he handled himself would be a key to his future in the administration.

"Our interrogations of the prisoners," LeVan continued, "show they are part of a vast network trained for military operations in West Germany. They apparently were never told the objective of the mission they were on when intercepted. To me the idea of tanks moving toward Munich, where Nazism was founded, has only one meaning."

"That's why I brought Dick Sovern back," the President interjected. "When a man's proven right, he's valuable."

"It depends on what you mean by 'right,' Mr. President," Peddington broke in. "We were all concerned about the Nazis, but it was Dick's emphasis on Hitler that threw us off."

"Explain your point, Rudy," the President demanded.

"We put our resources into the search for a ghost. That's how I explain it, and I think I've got the proof. They just attempted a coup over there without a public word about the Führer coming back. They'd certainly prepare the German people."

"Why?" Sovern asked. "If you were German, how much preparation would you need for the return of Adolf Hitler?"

"There'd be fanfare."

"Maybe we cut them off before it came," Sovern retorted. "Or maybe something happened to Hitler. We know that Earhart is showing some physical deterioration. Maybe Hitler is in a bad way and could only be a figurehead, if that. Maybe he can't be seen in public. Maybe he's half dead. We've got to find out."

"Good God, Dick," Peddington pressed, "are we still going to chase after this Hitler thing?"

"I certainly hope so."

"On the basis of *what*?"

"On the basis of Amelia Earhart's story."

"Nothing has turned up to substantiate it."

"I disagree."

"You *have* something?" the President asked, startled.

"Not directly, sir, but there is one significant factor here. Amelia Earhart said a coup would be attempted on January 30, 1983. Clearly the Nazis wanted to accelerate that date once she defected. The fact remains that a coup is being attempted around the time she said it would happen. We must accept that *other* information she provided might also be accurate."

"I see the point," the President said.

"Speculation," Peddington barked. "This kind of thing would never be accepted in a courtroom."

"No one's on trial," Sovern reminded him.

"But the method of proof is the same. I think we're being set up. I think we were set up in Williamstown, by those people in Haifa, maybe by Earhart. *Her* loyalty is still a question mark, you know."

"We're not showing her the blueprints for the cruise missile," Sovern answered.

Peddington smiled. "There's stuff in the Archives on her, isn't there?"

Sovern stiffened. "Raw data," he snapped back, refusing to weaken. "It's the work of Nazi propagandists. You want to run the government according to that?"

The intensity of Sovern's attack shocked the room. Even the President remained still, surprised that anyone would take on Peddington so strongly.

"It still troubles me," Peddington replied. "It's an old technique for an agent to give the enemy accurate information to gain his confidence, then feed him one massive lie to throw him off. How do we know that isn't the case with Earhart?"

"We don't," Sovern replied strongly. "We evaluate her information as we do anyone else's. Frankly, I resent your throwing up roadblock after roadblock."

Peddington turned red. "I am doing my duty."

"Then assist me in carrying out a *thorough* investigation."

"Assist *you*? Why, I thought . . ."

"Cut it out!" the President suddenly snapped. "I've had enough of this bickering. Dick, you use Earhart any way you wish and Rudy, if you don't like it, quit!"

"I'm sorry, Mr. President," Peddington reacted, "but I was just trying . . ."

"You try too damn hard! We'll use Earhart for all she's worth. Christ, she isn't the only thing we're depending on. We've got all our security services going and half of NATO on alert. Dick, what are you planning?"

"Mr. President, there have been some discoveries at the Archives. I'd like to take Earhart over."

"Whenever you wish."

"Now."

"In the middle of the night?"

"The clock hasn't stopped in Germany, sir."

III

Tom Larner, director of the Archives project, was awakened and driven to the Archives to prepare materials for Sovern and Earhart. The two arrived at the building in a White House limousine at 2:06 A.M.

As Sovern was about to get out of the car, the two-way radio crackled. The receiver, which could handle code, began getting a message from the Oval Office.

"What's coming over?" Sovern asked the driver, who operated the decoder.

"It's from the Russian ambassador via the White House," the driver replied.

Sovern realized the Russians hadn't been heard from since the new action occurred in Germany. The driver handed him the message:

SOVIET UNION EXPRESSES CONCERN AND DISMAY AT ARMOR BATTLE OUTSIDE MUNICH AND MASSIVE MOVEMENT OF NATO TROOPS THROUGHOUT WEST

GERMANY. MOVEMENTS ARE EITHER
NATO PROVOCATION OR ADMISSION
THAT FASCIST ANTI-SOVIET POWERS IN
WEST GERMANY HAVE BECOME UNCON-
TROLLED. WE REGARD THESE DEVELOP-
MENTS AS THREAT TO SOVIET PEOPLES
TO WHICH WE WILL RESPOND.

"Not pretty," Sovern said to himself, realizing that
war in Europe could come through a massive Soviet
miscalculation. "Ask the White House how the President responded," he ordered the driver.

A few moments later the car receiver printed out a
copy of the President's reply to Moscow:

URGING RESTRAINT. WE ARE DOING ALL
WE CAN TO QUIET GERMAN SITUATION.

Sovern was troubled by the brevity of the message
and its lack of explanation. The Soviets, he reasoned,
might see it as evasive. He got on the White House
phone and was immediately connected with the President, who was still at work on the German situation.

"Sir," he said, "I've looked over the Russian-Ameri-
can exchange and I think we should contact them
again."

"What about?" the President asked.

"I think we should tell them precisely what happened near Munich and give them an hour-by-hour
account of our troop movements. I know it creates security problems, but it's the only thing that will calm
them down."

"You may be right," the President responded.

"I'll go even further," Sovern said. "Offer to let
Soviet observers watch the NATO units in the alert."

"That's a fantastic idea," the President replied.

"Thank you, sir."

"But I reject it. Congress'd destroy me. Letting Russians spy on American units . . ."

"But that wouldn't be the case, sir."

"Tell that to the cavalry of Capitol Hill," the President replied. "Look, Dick, I know you must think it's small to think of political survival, but a president always has to think of that. He can't lead effectively if he doesn't survive politically. I'll give Moscow an account of what we're doing and make sure Ambassador Grechko here is kept fully informed. I can't do more."

"All right, sir."

Sovern's respect for the President went up a notch. At least the man had a coherent view of how to maneuver, although Sovern wished he'd take greater risks.

Sovern and Earhart got out of the car, immediately feeling the needle-like slap of the rainstorm. They rushed inside the Archives, where Tom Larner was unlocking safes containing the highly classified results of the anti-Nazi search.

"Tom," Sovern said as he entered, the water dripping from his hair and clothing, "I understand you traced the picture Miss Earhart thought she recognized."

"How did you know?" Larner asked.

"Mental telepathy."

"Well, the brain waves were accurate. In addition we tried to identify everyone else in the picture, in case they were needed."

Larner took the picture from the safe and showed it to Earhart. "The man you recognized," he said, "is Doctor Frederic Van Ep. He was a leading endocrinologist in Hitler's medical program. He's still alive, although retired, and lives in a small house outside Stuttgart."

"Does his name mean anything to you?" Sovern asked Earhart.

"I'm thinking," Earhart replied. "I do vaguely recall the name Van Ep being used, but it could have been in reference to another man or an unrelated project."

"We'll contact the good doctor," Sovern said, taking the picture and placing it in a separate file. "An endocrinologist studies the growth system, which would be important in any age-retarding work.

"Why don't we look at some other pictures," Larner suggested. Sovern and Earhart agreed, impressed with Larner's thoroughness.

Earhart studied pictures through the early hours of the morning. It was just before seven A.M. when she discovered another face she thought she recognized. Forty minutes later still another came to light. Identification was available in each case, but Earhart couldn't recall the names. Sovern took each photo and placed it in his special file. He also began considering for the first time the possibility of hypnotizing Amelia to help her remember things that had been blotted out.

As Earhart continued searching, Sovern went to a far corner of the basement and placed a call to Doctor Steven Sieverts, chief of CRG's psychiatric branch. Sieverts, at sixty-four, was the oldest employee of CRG. He had served in the Office of Strategic Services during World War II and in various medical intelligence posts since. A somewhat frail-looking man, he spoke in a gravel-filled voice made worse by an ailment of the vocal cords.

"Steve," Sovern said after the usual courtesies, "what

do you think of the idea of hypnotizing Earhart?"

Sieverts, half-dressed and preparing for work, mulled the question for about half a minute. "I don't know," he replied cautiously. "You made the point earlier in this case that her medical alterations may make routine procedures unworkable."

"All right," Sovern countered, "if it doesn't work, it doesn't work. But it *might*."

"True, but be careful. Hypnosis, as you know, can have side effects. We don't know what changes the Nazis made in Earhart's brain chemistry. We can put her under, but . . ."

"You might not be able to bring her out of it."

"Precisely."

"How would you assess the odds?"

"There are no odds. Earhart is a special case. And you also have to consider the chance of a temporary disorder."

"Like?"

"We might fail to bring her out immediately, and a delay of several days could be critical to you. Or we could bring her partially out. There might be disorientation, even a change in personality. It's hard to speculate with a medical first."

Sovern pondered what Sieverts had told him. He had a hellish vision of Amelia Earhart dying in hypnosis, a vision complicated by his feeling of responsibility for her. He couldn't let her take that risk.

"Maybe I'll pass for now," he told his old friend. "Is there any other procedure you could recommend, Steve?"

"You could use drugs," Sieverts remarked, "but you've got the same risk, maybe greater. The only thing I can think of is suggestion."

Suggestion, Sovern knew, meant that if Amelia

could hear recordings of voices she heard during her confinement in Nazi Germany, it might bring back other memories. But the problem, he realized, was that no one, including Earhart, could be sure which voices she had heard. And the time it would take to find recordings would be prohibitive. Sovern tentatively gave up the idea of trying to probe Earhart's mind.

Sovern and Earhart left the Archives for Andrews Air Force Base. Once there, Sovern called CRG in Munich and ordered his men both to determine Doctor Van Ep's whereabouts at the moment and to track down the others that Earhart picked out in the Archives pictures. Then he pondered two alternatives: Should he let the CRG people in Germany interrogate these men, or should he and Earhart fly over to do it? His objective, of course, was to extract any information these scientists had on the possible age-retarding treatment of Adolf Hitler. They might be more willing to reveal what they knew, Sovern reasoned, if they were confronted by Amelia Earhart. And talking with them might stimulate Amelia's own recall of crucial information.

Earhart was preparing to catch up on some sleep. Sovern knocked at her door. She opened, dressed in a simple red housecoat.

"Would you be willing to go to Germany to question those scientists?" Sovern asked her. "There might be risk."

A surge of excitement shot through Earhart. She finally felt needed, a full partner. "I'll take the risk," she replied. "I *want* to go. But where will *you* be?"

"With you," Sovern replied.

Earhart smiled. "Just tell me when," she said.

IV

As December sixteenth approached, Haas's predictions started to prove accurate. It appeared to NATO analysts that the coup attempt had passed into history, so NATO troops began returning to their bases. Although Sovern had urged a much longer alert, European governments believed a more relaxed posture would reassure the Russians.

The Chairman, Willy Haas, Rolfe Barlack, and Gustav Hoffmann met in a tense, expectant atmosphere. "It is the next few days . . . or maybe never," Haas declared, reviewing charts of the Reich Reborn forces that remained after the Munich tank debacle. "They now know something of our operation and they're bound to find out more. Maybe they'll locate other ammunition depots or our communications network. They might even break our code. There is no other way but to strike immediately."

The nods of heads showed acceptance, but everyone realized the enormous risks.

"What does Gottes say?" Barlack asked.

"Gottes agrees."

"Can he do it?"

"He says morale is actually higher than before. Our people are determined to erase the blot. And I remind you what happens when spirited fighters are not used."

"What date?" Hoffmann asked.

"I propose December eighteenth, a week before Christmas, two days from now."

The group agreed. Haas outlined a new plan of attack that would use only a third the number of people as the first plan. He was trying to find every way to reduce the chance of detection. As he proceeded, confidence began to build. There was something about a battle plan that rekindled visions of glory . . . that rebuilt the dreams of the Reich.

Zero hour was less than forty-eight hours away.

CHAPTER 20

Stuttgart, West Germany

Doctor Frederic Van Ep had lived alone in a two-bed-room bungalow in a Stuttgart suburb since his wife died three years before. Although retired, he still gave an occasional lecture to parents' groups and treated bruises for neighborhood children. His record as a researcher under the Nazis was well-known, although he wasn't regarded as a "Nazi" doctor. A postwar investigation had cleared him of any role in the medical atrocities of the concentration camps. That probe, of course, had not revealed his connection with the age experiments, and Van Ep himself, separated from the project near the end of the war, did not know how they had turned out.

Sovern had ordered CRG not to forewarn the elderly doctor that he would be questioned. He wasn't sure whether Van Ep would cooperate and he didn't want to provide him with any chance to flee or con-coct stories.

And so Sovern and Earhart, riding in a bulletproof car, were driven into Stuttgart by a CRG agent. Surveillance had shown Van Ep was at home, reading in his living room. Two other cars, filled with CRG and West German agents, traveled behind Sovern and Earhart for the pair's protection. Although Sovern knew German, a translator came along should Van Ep require him.

An agent and the translator went to Van Ep's door and rang the bell. A few moments later the white-haired, slightly stooped physician answered. Sovern and Earhart, waiting in their car, watched the animated conversation that followed. They knew the agent was telling Van Ep that his name had come up in an investigation of past medical research. The West German government was cooperating with the United States in the probe and his recollections were needed. If he willingly helped, he would be immune from any prosecution.

Apprehensive, Van Ep invited the party in. He had been told that Americans were in the car outside, and he waved for them to come too.

Sovern and Earhart, under the watchful eyes of agents parked nearby, walked up the flagstone path to the bungalow. Sovern was particularly interested in Van Ep's facial expressions as Amelia Earhart got closer. The CRG director saw that the old man was gazing at Earhart, the gaze becoming quizzical when she started up the stairs. He still hadn't been told her name.

The translator was about to introduce Van Ep to Richard Sovern, but it was obvious that the doctor was entranced by the vision of this mystery woman in his midst. He kept staring at her as the translator began talking, describing Sovern's role in the United States government.

"You don't have to!" Van Ep suddenly told the

translator. "I speak perfect English." He continued his stare at Earhart, now looking her up and down much as Richard Sovern had done the first time they met. Suddenly his lips began to quiver. He stepped closer to her.

"You," he said softly. "It *is* you?"

There could be no doubt what he meant. "Yes," Earhart replied.

"Say again," Van Ep ordered, as if speaking to a patient.

"Yes," Earhart repeated.

"The voice," Van Ep said, "it has hardly changed. I don't believe it. I *don't* believe it." Then he finally rushed over and touched Amelia Earhart on the shoulders. He gazed down at her left arm. Amelia sensed he was looking for final proof. She raised the sleeve and exposed the two puncture marks.

"My God, my God!" Van Ep exclaimed. "Never did I think I would see you again. You are a miracle."

He then looked suspiciously at Richard Sovern. "*She* is why you're here, isn't she?"

"Partly."

Van Ep started walking slowly backward, extending his arms out as if defending himself. "I did nothing wrong, absolutely nothing. I was simply and innocently engaged in humanistic medical experimentation. You can see before you the magnificent result, although I do not take credit. Here the famous flier, preserved for another generation. What is wrong with that?"

"Doctor Van Ep," Sovern replied, "you are not on trial, sir. I assure you."

"You have not come to take me to America?"

"Of course not."

"Then why do you bring the flier?"

"Because we wanted to see if you would recognize her, and she you. I think we've answered our question."

"This is the only reason you brought her?"

"There are others."

It was clear from Van Ep's expression that he was not yet satisfied by Sovern's assurances. Suddenly his face seemed to freeze. He looked at Earhart, then back at Sovern. "There are many things happening in Germany today," he said. "Many strange things." He began to look saddened and distant. "Yes, that is why you're here. You want to know about the things that are happening. You want to know about the other . . . person."

"Exactly," Sovern replied.

Van Ep turned around and walked slowly to a favorite, well-worn easy chair. He sat down, the pain of arthritis clearly evident in his mannerisms. He heaved a sigh as he finally got settled. "There is little I can tell you," he said. "They talked about many ideas for preserving the Führer in case Germany was betrayed. The procedure they used on Earhart was the one they chose. But then, I'm sorry to say, I left the project. . . ."

"Why?"

"Who knows why? One day they said leave. One did not question. My work was good."

"Did you hear any reports of the age-retarding work on Hitler?" Sovern asked.

"Yes, although no one was supposed to talk. But I had students, you know, and some of them were young doctors with the project. One of them told me the treatment given to the Führer was working well, though not as well as with the flier. Of course, the Führer was much older and he was fatigued by this time."

"Was there any specific problem you recall?"

"They never told me details. That far they would not go."

"You heard nothing after the war?"

"Nothing."

"Doctor Van Ep, do you believe that Adolf Hitler is alive today?"

Van Ep hesitated and ran his hand through his still-full shock of gray hair. "In medicine," he said, "it is very difficult to predict, especially in an experiment. I look at this great woman pilot, so healthy, her voice practically unchanged, and I know that Hitler was the *second* person. Any mistakes they made with the flier they had a chance to correct. I know also that Hitler would have received the most complete attention from the doctors. Of course, as with any organism, Hitler could have developed a fatal disease. But if not . . ." He paused and looked around the room, his eyes growing wide with excitement. "If not, Hitler is still alive."

For Richard Sovern this was a watershed moment. For the first time someone beside Amelia Earhart had confirmed the success of the age-retardation experiments. "Doctor," Sovern asked, "Miss Earhart reported that the Nazis planned to return Hitler to power. Did you ever hear of that?"

"Of course. That was why he was preserved. But those discussions were so long ago."

"Was there a date mentioned . . . even then?"

"This I do not recall."

"Doctor Van Ep, let me ask you a direct question. Are you partial to any of these neo-Nazi groups?"

Van Ep shrugged and seemed to smirk. "Look," he replied, "I was never partial to the original Nazis. I worked for them, yes, but they were the only government we had. I don't care for these new fellows either."

"Will you help us track down Adolf Hitler?"

Van Ep's expression turned to a knowing smile, the smile of a man who had learned much about human nature. "If I say no," he replied, "my reputation is doomed. I might even be held responsible if this Führer comes back. On the other hand, if I say yes, someone among the new Nazis will find out."

"Not necessarily."

"Oh, I've seen," Van Ep insisted, waving his hand. "They *always* find out. I would unquestionably be killed or, at the very least, made an outcast."

"By whom?"

"My good man, don't be so naive. Hitler is the subject of fond memories here."

"In this neighborhood?"

"In this house. Even my wife, rest her, was one of them."

"I understand your concerns," Sovern said, "and we would do everything possible to shield you, doctor. I pledge that to you. So I ask again, would you help us?"

"I'm an old man," Van Ep replied, "and I value my reputation among decent men more than among these new Nazis and certainly more than the little time remaining to me. I will help."

"Thank you," Sovern said graciously. "Now, sir, do you recall the names of any doctors who worked on the age project?"

"Yes, but they're all dead."

"All?"

"Some died in the war, the rest from old age."

"Is it possible there were others you don't recall? If we showed you pictures taken during the war, do you think you'd remember?"

"It is possible, but why do this?"

"If these doctors are alive," Sovern explained, "they could lead us to Hitler."

"I have the feeling," Van Ep observed, "that you underestimate Nazi ability at suppressing evidence, but I will go along."

Sovern took the Archives pictures from a briefcase and showed them to Van Ep. Van Ep studied them carefully, his serious expression never changing.

"These faces I have not seen," the doctor said, turning the photos back to Sovern.

"You're certain?"

"Certain."

"Do the names Martin Studer or Joseph Benz mean anything to you?" Sovern asked. They were the other scientists Amelia had recognized in the Archives pictures.

Van Ep thought for a moment. "No, they do not," he replied.

Sovern was discouraged by Van Ep's answers, but pushed on. "Doctor," he asked, "do you recall any chemicals or drugs that the process required, drugs that Hitler might need today?"

"This came after my separation from the project. I would not know this."

"Is there anything else you know that might be of help to us?" Sovern asked.

Again Van Ep shrugged. Sovern observed the deep age lines etched in his face. "I don't think so," he replied, and Sovern instinctively believed him.

The CRG group prepared to leave. Sovern ordered two agents to guard Van Ep's house for the immediate future and convinced the doctor to let a third man live with him for a time, pretending to be a relative. He also asked Van Ep to continue searching his memory and to report anything he recalled about the age experiments, however trivial it might seem.

Knowing he had hardly left the starting gate in a race that might be over in hours, Sovern had no choice but to proceed to his next target, Doctor Martin Studer, a retired physiologist living in Cologne.

II

It was December seventeenth.

One day remained before Willy Haas's go-for-broke attempt to put the Nazis back in power. Haas, the Chairman, and the others left their hotel, heading by rented car for the French-German border, where they would board the Munich train. Haas had ruled out boarding at the Paris station, where, he assumed, security would be tight. As before, a contingent of twenty Reich Reborn agents was protecting the Chairman. They rode in nearby autos, blending in with the traffic.

The ride through the French countryside brought back memories of the war, pleasant and unpleasant. "I recall how our tanks rolled across this landscape in 1940," Haas reminisced. "The world thought the French would crush us, but they melted like butter."

Haas could see by the glint in the Chairman's eye that he too was remembering the glorious days before the tide turned against the Reich.

The Nazis arrived at the railroad junction near the border undetected. The plan was to stay at the local

motel overnight and board the train in the morning.
Haas checked his watch. It was 12:14 P.M. on a chilly,
dry day. In twenty-one hours the train would leave for
Munich; in twenty-four hours it would arrive tri-
umphantly.

Once inside the motel the group received a messenger carrying word from General Gottes:

REGROUPING RAPIDLY. OPPOSITION
FORCES CONTINUE TO RELAX. SMALL
TEAM OF PEOPLE POSING AS POLLSTERS
HAS ASKED GERMANS THEIR RESPONSE
IF CHAIRMAN COULD ACTUALLY BE
BROUGHT BACK. ENOUGH WERE EC-
STATIC TO GIVE US CONFIDENCE.

Haas was grudgingly impressed by Gottes's coolness
and sense of public relations. Once again the air was
filled with the earlier, simpler optimism, and the
Chairman was in remarkable spirits. Lunch, brought
to Haas's room and had by all four Nazis, was a
spiritual event. It would be, after all, the last lunch
before Germany.

Willy Haas finished dessert at 2:41. In less than
twenty-two hours it would all be over.

Then at 4:10 he received another message from
Gottes, notifying him that Richard Sovern was in
Germany, but that Gottes would handle it.

Although reassured by Gottes, Haas was still concerned by the development. Why would Sovern be in
Germany except to intercept a new coup attempt?
Later, though, Gottes reported that Sovern and Earhart were both in West Germany interviewing doctors
who had worked for the Third Reich. There was no
indication that they had scored any breakthroughs,

and it appeared, Gottes said, that they were way off the track. Haas was relieved.

It was an incredible irony, Haas thought as he lay back in his bed, that the Reich would regain power with Amelia Earhart back in Germany.

And Richard Sovern?

The nemesis of the neo-Nazis would be the first man executed by direct order of the Chairman.

III

CRG and West German intelligence had reported that Doctor Martin Studer spent most of his time in his Cologne apartment working on his stamp collection. His wife was usually with him, as was a grown, unmarried daughter who lived with the family. Studer had enjoyed a distinguished reputation as a physiologist, specializing in cell research. After World War II he had taught at German universities and had often visited the United States on lecture tours.

Sovern and his staff used the same procedures in approaching Studer as they had for Van Ep, arriving at his apartment unannounced. Their latest surveillance report, received only hours before, had stated that Studer and his family were at home and had received visitors during the day.

An agent and the translator walked up to the second-floor apartment and rang the bell.

There was no answer.

Repeated rings brought the same result. The agent and translator walked back downstairs and reported to Sovern. It was odd, Sovern thought, that there should be no answer when the surveillance report specifically placed the Studers at home. He left his car and accompanied the agent back upstairs. They rang the doorbell repeatedly with no response. There was only silence in the apartment.

Sovern ordered three more agents upstairs and, together, they broke in the door.

Martin Studer lay in the hallway, his throat slit.

His wife and daughter lay together on a living-room couch, their throats slit also.

There was no sign of a struggle. The Studers' visitors for the day had obviously included skilled killers.

A note had been left, written on the living room wall in spilled blood:

You cannot stop us, Sovern, so why try?

Sovern raced downstairs to the CRG car with Amelia inside. "Get her out of here!" he ordered an agent. "Take her to a nuclear weapons depot." These depots had the best security in Germany.

The agent looked confused.

"Don't wonder about the reason," Sovern barked. "Just do it!"

Then he had another agent contact the surveillance team watching Joseph Benz, the next man on Earhart's list. The team reported that Benz and his family were at home and that they, too, had received visitors.

"Take them into protective custody!" Sovern ordered. He waited at his car for confirmation that his order had been carried out.

A few minutes later the report came back: Benz and his wife had been found dead in their dining room. A note had been scrawled in blood on the wall. Its words were familiar.

His resolve unshaken by the setbacks, Richard Sovern was driven to the nuclear weapons depot where Earhart had been taken.

The depot was made up of an underground storage cell which was entered through an artificial hill built on top. The hill prevented bomb damage to the nuclear weapons stored below. The entire facility was surrounded by barbed wire and was patrolled constantly by troops, jeeps, and guard dogs. There was no other building for at least five miles.

Sovern had to be disarmed before entering. The greatest fear in the depot was of someone going berserk with a gun or using it in an attempt to steal a nuclear device.

Sovern set up a temporary command post near the communications room, which was equipped to receive all NATO codes. He was not there long before a message came from Washington. It was terse and meant largely for the depot's crew:

SOVIET ALERT

Instantly, Sovern called Chester LeVan, who was already at the National Military Command Center in the Pentagon. LeVan, in shirtsleeves, was going over the latest advisories from Europe when Sovern's call came through.

"Ches, what's happening?"

"Everything," LeVan replied. "We just got word from Moscow to the effect that the Russians have gotten all shaken up over the military activity in Germany in the last few days and the arrival of you and the lady. They think the Nazi threat has grown once more and are taking what they call reasonable precautions.

"The reasonable precautions," LeVan explained, "consist of moving two hundred thousand troops toward the East German border with West Germany and keeping ten percent of their combat planes in this sector in the air. We've also picked up substantially increased submarine activity out of the Baltic. At this point the President has come completely clean with them on everything we're doing just as you advised. And, Dick, he gave them all we now know about the Hitler business. He figured if Hitler did come back, the Russians might think we'd been deceiving them. He called Ambassador Grechko, cancelled our previous advisory that Adolf was definitely gone, and told him we're investigating further."

"What was Grechko's reaction?"

"They're still scrapin' him off the ceiling. He's called four times warning that all hell would break loose in Germany if we didn't solve this problem and, Christ almighty, I think he means it. Hold on."

A military aide handed LeVan another message. He read it, then got back on the phone. "Get this one," he told Sovern. "It's from Ten Downing Street. The British prime minister says her intelligence people report evacuation of some population centers in East Germany in anticipation of military action."

"They've never done that before," Sovern observed.

"And the Russians have never closed their U.N. mission in New York before, which is what they've just done. The President thinks they may be using the Hitler thing as an excuse for some massive action they've planned all along."

"Possible, but I don't think so," Sovern replied.

"The Russians have always been paranoid about a new Nazi rise to power."

"We were alerted to the murders of those doctors," LeVan continued. "You have any other leads?"

"Negative. We may have to wait for the Nazis to move. It's a hell of a fix to be in, but we haven't anything else, only a confirmation from Van Ep that they did plan to preserve Hitler. I'm having my people go through the files of the doctors who were murdered, but I'm not optimistic."

"The President's on my other phone, Dick. I'll keep you posted."

The conversation ended. Sovern was about to go to Earhart when he received an advisory from CRG, Washington, that something may have turned up in Paris. He waited as a code clerk in a small, plasterboard room with a single fluorescent light decoded the message:

DRUGGIST IN PARIS REPORTS SALE OF UNUSUAL QUANTITY OF LECITHIN TO GERMAN-SPEAKING MALE TWO DAYS AGO. STILL CHECKING, BUT NO SUCCESS IN TRACKING BUYER.

This was a break, Sovern assumed, but without the identity of the buyer it was a break that would evaporate. "If anything comes in on this," he told the code clerk, "let me know instantly, even if I'm asleep."

He went to Earhart, who was being kept in the office of the U.S. Army captain who headed base security. For extra protection two MPs with machine guns stood outside the office.

Sovern briefed Earhart on all that had happened. "The Nazis obviously knew we were heading for those doctors," he said, "which means they probably know everything else we're doing. I'm surprised they didn't try to kill us, but maybe the security kept them away. If the Paris thing materializes, that'll determine our next step. But we're not exactly soaring."

"I guess the work I did in the Archives won't amount to anything," Earhart remarked.

"Don't say that," Sovern replied. "You led us to Van Ep, and at least we have confirmation of the experiments. He may yet come up with more. I'd still be sitting at my desk in Washington reading reports if it weren't for you."

Earhart smiled. She needed the boost in morale. "Will you insist that I stay here?" she asked.

"Depends on the dangers," Sovern replied.

"I want to be with you."

"Well, *I* want you to be with me, too, but your safety comes first."

While they were talking, Sovern received another message from CRG in Washington reporting that CRG in Paris had traced four German-speaking Americans registered in a hotel in the vicinity of the druggist. They had checked out that morning, and the hotel maid had detected a medicinal smell in one room.

Sovern studied the note carefully, growing more and more fascinated. "We may have them," he told Earhart, though knowing that detecting them and having them were entirely different. He immediately flashed a bulletin to Washington ordering that fingerprints in the Paris rooms be checked against those taken from the Williamstown farmhouse and the homes where the two German doctors were murdered. He also ordered paint samples scraped from the Paris room and examined for residue of drug fumes. Then, realizing his manpower in CRG was becoming stretched, he got back on the phone with LeVan.

"Ches," he said, "have you seen the CRG advisories?"

"Right, I have," LeVan replied. "Looks like there's meat here. What do you think?"

"I think Paris might be their jumping off point for Germany. But remember Haifa. These could be decoys too."

"I'm remembering."

"Look, I'm understaffed. I need troops."

"You've got 'em. I'll order all my MP units in Europe to put themselves at your disposal. And the Army's Criminal Investigation Department will be available. The French are cooperating fully for a change and are sending military units in civilian dress into Paris to try to keep the whole city under observation. They think these Germans may be planning some terrorism."

"Very possible. Paris would be a symbolic target for any Nazi group, considering the past."

"Of course," LeVan continued, "those German types checked out of the Paris hotel this morning. If they flew out of France, we're out of luck."

"I have a hunch they're not flying," Sovern said. "Airports still have the tightest security, and after their flap a few days ago they'll be especially careful. Make sure to put people at border crossings."

"Will do," LeVan responded.

They both hung up. Rarely had Sovern had the kind of cooperation he'd received from Chester LeVan. It was obvious that LeVan, despite his reputation as a tough, cold businessman, was the kind who could rise above petty competition at a time of crisis.

Sovern realized the difficulties LeVan would have,

though, in setting up maximum security throughout Europe. The kind of dragnet required to stop four German-speaking Americans was enormous. Undoubtedly, he reasoned, they would change passports at every stop. He was right. Willy Haas had a full supply of passports from a variety of nations.

And, Sovern conjectured, the group might even separate.

It was already seven P.M. in Munich.

In seventeen hours the Chairman would step off the train in full Nazi regalia.

The depot mess hall served Sovern and Earhart an overcooked Swiss steak, which neither digested particularly well. Then at just after eight the bad news started pouring in. The litany of gloom was recorded on a coded teletype ticker in the communications room, where a bored Army specialist fourth class with only two weeks to go in the service had taken over from the regular code clerk.

From CRG Paris:

HOTEL PERSONNEL HAVE GIVEN GENERAL DESCRIPTIONS OF FOUR GERMAN-ACCENTED AMERICANS REPORTED EARLIER. NO DISTINGUISHING CHARACTERISTICS NOTED.

From Chester LeVan:

SECURITY FORCES IN FRANCE AND GERMANY HAVE NOTED NO UNUSUAL GROUPS OR PERSONS TRAVELING. BUT MUCH OF OUR SECURITY AT PRESENT IS PAPER THIN, AND DEPENDENT ON LOCAL, INEXPERIENCED PERSONNEL.

From CRG Stuttgart:

> DOCTOR VAN EP STILL CLAIMS TO RE-
> CALL NOTHING OF VALUE AND IS BE-
> COMING SOMEWHAT UNCOOPERATIVE,
> OBVIOUSLY TIRING OF HIS INVOLVE-
> MENT WITH US.

There was no progress at all, Sovern realized. The
Paris lead was not materializing, and he really had no
realistic plan for a next step. A bulletin from the Defense Intelligence Agency just after 9:30 was curious:

> ARMY INTELLIGENCE MUNICH REPORTS
> UNIDENTIFIED INDIVIDUALS TAKING
> POLL ON POPULARITY OF ADOLF HITLER
> AS LEADER IF BY MIRACLE HE RE-
> TURNED. TRYING TO TRACK DOWN
> SOURCE OF POLL.

It could be anything, Sovern knew. Polls about Hitler were constantly taken, and the fact that pollsters
asked about his possible return could be coincidence.
It was a logical, if hypothetical, question.

Sovern decided that he and Earhart would stay at
the depot for the night. He got to bed early to make
up for lost sleep; there was nothing further he could
do at the moment.

But at 11:13 Sovern received an urgent message
from CRG in Washington confirming that the people
in the Paris hotel had been identified as those who
occupied the farmhouse in Massachusetts. A photo
sketch accompanied the message—the man identified
was Willy Haas.

The description given in Paris by hotel clerks, combined with information supplied by shopkeepers in Williamstown, was enough for a CRG artist to make a detailed sketch. This was then fed into a computer-like device made by Minolta of Japan, which turned it into something that looked like a photograph, giving the viewer a highly realistic image.

It was 11:15—only thirteen hours were left. Not far away at the French-German border, Sovern's opponents slept soundly.

CHAPTER 21

URGENT/PRIORITY URGENT FROM CRG MUNICH: PAMPHLETS APPEARING ON STREET ANNOUNCING RETURN OF ADOLF HITLER.

Sovern was shaken awake by an Army lieutenant who had been chief watch officer in the communications room. The time was 6:48 A.M.

Sovern darted out of bed, his heart pounding, his pulse racing, his head dizzy yet clear enough to understand that this was the Nazis' D-Day. Everything up to now suddenly didn't matter. All theories were trivial, all speculation completely insignificant. Only questions ran through Sovern's mind: When will the attempt at a power grab come? Where? What forces will the Nazis have? Is their attempt the product of a mad illusion, a farce that will collapse instantly?

He threw on slacks and a sweater and went to awaken Amelia Earhart. In a way he was relieved. The fruitless search for Adolf Hitler and his comrades was

over. Now there would be a direct confrontation somewhere in Germany.

Even before reaching Earhart's tiny room—which
under normal circumstances was usually occupied by
an Army major—Sovern was intercepted by still another message, this time transmitted by the Defense
Intelligence Agency office in Bonn. Like the one of just
minutes before, it had the unmistakable ring of crisis:

> *URGENT/PRIORITY* URGENT FROM DIA
> BONN: INTELLIGENCE SOURCES BERLIN
> INDICATE SOVIETS DETECT PAMPHLET
> DISTRIBUTION RE HITLER. TWO SOVIET
> DIVISIONS MOVING TOWARD BORDER.
> THREE AIR SQUADRONS RELOCATED IN
> EAST GERMANY. FORTY PERCENT OF
> PLANES NOW KEPT IN AIR AT ALL TIMES.

One miscalculation, Sovern realized, and a generation of peace in Europe could be shattered.

He knocked vigorously on Earhart's door, awaken-
ing her. He quickly gave her a rundown. "Could it be
a hoax?" she asked. Sovern was surprised by the
question. After all it was she who had given the message that Adolf Hitler's return to power was being
planned.

"No," Sovern replied tersely. Of course, he couldn't
actually know. But it was not the time for Peddington-
like speculation. He looked deeply into Earhart's eyes
and saw the glint of recognition. Her prediction was
bearing out. But *her* vindication might mean the
world's catastrophe.

Munich was the center. That was clear from all the
activity there. Or was it the center? Sovern once more

realized the activity in Munich could be a decoy. But the city's history as a center for Nazism convinced him that Adolf Hitler wanted to make his move on emotionally satisfying territory. He wondered, though, why the coup wasn't staged in Bonn, the capital of West Germany. He alerted Chester LeVan to move troops into Bonn just in case.

Sovern and Earhart grabbed some milk and rolls for breakfast, then boarded an Army helicopter for the flight to Munich, where Sovern wanted to set up his headquarters. The helicopter was an armored "gunship," designed to repel any attack from the ground.

Once off the ground, though, Sovern realized he might be making a critical, perhaps fatal mistake involving Amelia. "Look," he said over the din of the chopping blades, "things are going to get hot today. Even with all our Seventh Army troops in the Munich region, we can't guarantee your security. I'm ordering that you be flown back to Washington."

"No," Earhart replied firmly.

"You have no choice. You're here on official business. You don't have a regular passport."

Earhart smiled. "I led you into this."

"You don't understand," Sovern said. "I'm responsible for you. Number one you're a national heroine. Number two you're medically important. Number three there's frankly nothing for you to do."

"What if I recognize a voice or a face?" Earhart asked, recalling Sovern's earlier description of her potential value. "What if that puts you onto something? What if it's critically important?"

Sovern could not disagree. There was a moral choice between risking Earhart's life or freedom and risking the chance that he might miss something by her absence. Only *he* could make that choice. Despite Earhart's resistance, he could force her out of the country if he had to.

"If something happens to me," Earhart pushed on, "it would be fitting—I'm living on borrowed time anyway."

Sovern could see her determination. "All right," he said, "tentatively I'll let you stay. But I want you to promise me that you'll be evacuated if I think the situation is becoming too dangerous."

"All right," Earhart replied, realizing it was the best compromise she could hope for.

While still flying, Sovern received another advisory from CRG Munich, announcing that the traffic lights had gone out all over the city. The power supply had been sabotaged. Mass confusion had resulted.

Sovern knew that the goal of the sabotage was the draining of manpower from the German police forces. Within a few minutes he learned that the traffic control systems had gone out in three other German cities.

But it was just before landing in Munich that Richard Sovern received an advisory that told him just how shrewd, how capable, his opposition really was: Bread and milk were being distributed at several centers in four German cities, while police were tied up in traffic problems. At present the food was being distributed largely to those who needed it. The people handing out food were openly identifying themselves as soldiers in the army of Reich Reborn. The distribution could not be stopped without provoking a serious disturbance.

The helicopter came down on the roof of the U.S. Consulate in Munich. Sovern and Earhart could see the massive traffic jams all around. And a few blocks

away they could see crowds grabbing for the free food
being handed out. They were descending into chaos,
citizens of a democratic country that might not be
democratic by sundown.

II

The Chairman boarded the Munich train at the
French-German border. Haas and the others followed.

No one stopped them; no one was even suspicious.
Although the French border police had received an
alert for four German-speaking Americans, the descriptions had gotten misplaced in a communications
foul-up and the Nazis simply melted into the crowd,
many of whom spoke German anyway. No advisory on
the Germans had been sent to the hotel. The Minolta
photo sketch, which would surely create problems for
Willy Haas, had been sent by wire from the United
States, but was only available in large cities. The train
crew, used to alerts for criminals and drug smugglers,
largely ignored these episodes. It was dangerous to get
involved.

The train pulled out at 9:05 A.M. As always the four
top Nazis of Reich Reborn were surrounded by security guards posing as businessmen or workers. And
as always the Chairman traveled in a compartment
with Haas, Barlack, and Hoffmann. The diesel locomotive slipped smoothly away, gathering speed and
reaching fifty miles an hour as the train crossed the
border into the green lowlands of Germany.

"We are in the Fatherland," Willy Haas said. The
Chairman looked out, a mist in his eyes, and Barlack
and Hoffmann strained to see every inch of the scenery

passing by. They were all transfixed, like immigrants to America seeing the Statue of Liberty for the first time. Willy Haas stopped staring just long enough to glance at the suitcases on the overhead rack, cases containing the uniforms that the leadership would soon wear. Then he turned back to the countryside, watching a few farmers in the fields. "Nothing has really changed," he said. "It has the same beauty as the old days, except now these people will get a leader worthy of them."

In the next compartment Herrmann Schmidt, once again the director of the security detail, as he had been on the Italian train just days before, also stared out the window. Schmidt felt lucky. There had been no interruption whatever in the plan, and he was finally back in Germany again. He knew that the pamphlet distribution that was starting throughout Germany and the sudden giving out of food by the Reich Reborn people would attract Allied security forces, already alerted by the traffic signal failures. Schmidt realized that the most intense challenge to security would come as the train approached Munich, especially after the violent operations that Reich Reborn would soon carry out. Like Willy Haas, he too glanced at overhead racks. But his suitcases contained submachine guns as well as explosives, should any opposition require a higher level of violence.

The train was close enough to Munich for Willy Haas to speak directly with General Gottes through an intricate communications hookup that garbled each man's voice and decoded it at the other end. The system was common to great powers, but it had never been adapted for such mobile, portable use. Haas simply used a walkie-talkie in his compartment, which was attached to the "garble box." The box in turn activated a small transmitter/receiver. Along the track at five-mile intervals Reich Reborn men posing as railroad inspectors and maintenance workers carried booster transmitters, usually in the backs of cars, to carry the signal.

"Gottes," Haas asked as ten A.M. approached, "what is the status?"

"It could not be better," Gottes reported. He was still in ordinary coveralls and shirt in the basement of a garage in suburban Munich not far from Dachau. "The government's security apparatus seems inept in the face of our threat. They're confused. They don't know where we will strike or with what."

"The pamphlets?" Haas asked.

"Interesting," Gottes replied. "As you know, they say that the Chairman is returning to power through the quality of German science, and that proof would soon come. Most people read it utterly intrigued. Only a few laugh."

"But are they *working*?"

"Of course they are. The objective of the pamphlets was to arouse excitement and interest. The statement at the bottom that the Chairman would seize power today is the only subject of conversation in the streets. But wait for the broadcasts, Haas. Wait until they hear . . . the voice."

Haas smiled. "Where are your troops, Gottes?"

"Most are already in Munich. Of course, this time they wear civilian clothes and carry weapons in salesman's cases. There will be no mishaps."

"Tanks? Armored vehicles?" Haas inquired.

"They will come in at the last minute, in response, the story will go, to the child center bombings."

"And they . . . ?"

"They are set."

For the first time Haas felt a choking sensation as the bombings of the child-care centers were brought up. It was so close now, no more than an hour away. Even Willy Haas, the hardened Nazi, had visions of children playing with blocks, painting pictures, singing songs, their parents at work. But he quickly got over such sentimental rubbish. These children would die for the Reich, just as their ancestors did in the bombing raids during the war. There was no difference. Service was service.

"Gottes . . . the car?"

"Ready."

"Good luck, Gottes. Remember, everything depends on the reaction of the German people. With their help Germany will be saved. Without it we will meet in jail tonight.

III

Richard Sovern and Amelia Earhart were taken by bulletproof German police car to a modern, two-story office building in downtown Munich. It was, according to the name outside, the headquarters of Revis International, a marketing consultant firm. Actually, it was the Munich headquarters of the Central Intelligence Agency. Its communications room, which was equipped to receive the most secret of American codes, was shared by CRG.

Sovern and Earhart went to a twenty by twenty-five-foot operations room on the second floor. Its center was entirely taken up by a table whose top consisted of an aerial photograph of Munich. The picture itself was some twelve by eighteen. Key points like the police station, railway depot, airport, and municipal hall were pointed out by white labels.

Spencer Bettel, director of CRG for Munich, met Sovern at the door. Bettel was forty-three, stooped, with the rugged, narrow features of a Midwestern farmer. He was wearing his standard uniform of rumpled white-on-white shirt, blue tie, and gray patterned suit. Bettel spoke in the ratty-tat manner more appropriate to an urban detective of the nineteen thirties than the Harvard Law graduate and student of classical archeology that he was. He had never been known to lose his temper or his demeanor, which is why Richard Sovern had put him in charge of one of the most difficult CRG offices in the world.

"All right," Bettel said as Sovern entered, practically ignoring Amelia Earhart, "here it is: There's a hell of a lot of confusion, and the new chancellor in Bonn doesn't seem to know how to handle it. But the police are still pretty much together—except for the neo-Nazi infiltrators among them."

"How many?" Sovern asked.

"Who the hell knows? We've never been able to get an accurate count. More important, if this is D-Day, then the Nazis have forces inside the city dressed as civilians. That would be the smart thing.

"Seventh Army is sending troops and tanks, but how much good will they do? If old Adolf starts struttin' in here and has protection, we may have to kill German civilians to get to him. That would be a mighty help to his cause."

"What's the latest on the Russians?" Sovern asked.

Bettel glanced up at a huge wall map of Europe. "Dick," he replied, "I think they're shrewd. If something happens they're ready for a limited thrust into

West Germany. Our troops will be all over trying to keep domestic order."

Sovern looked at Bettel intently. "Spence, where do you think Hitler is?"

"Inside the city," Bettel replied. "He wouldn't risk coming in from the outside on the day itself. He'd know we'd be watching transportation links."

There was a bank of wall phones at one end of the room, each phone a different color depending on its function. Suddenly, a light flashed above the red phone at the end, and it buzzed with each flash. All fifteen CRG agents in the room, manning various desks, fell silent. The phone was the direct connection to the President.

Bettel answered, then turned the phone over to Sovern. All eyes in the room were on him.

"Yes, sir," Sovern said.

"Dick," the President replied, "this has got to be the worst day we've ever had."

"I won't dispute that."

"Before we get to plans and excuses, let me be the one to give you some more good news. You remember that car that Hitler used to drive, that big open Mercedes?"

"Yes."

"You know it's been in the United States. Been sold to private collectors since 1945."

"Yes, I remember that."

"It's missing."

"What do you mean . . . missing?"

"Dick, what *could* I mean? The guy who owns it lives in Muncie, Indiana. About two weeks ago he reported it'd been stolen. The cops thought it was a local prank. They finally notified FBI. It's gonna turn up in Munich, Dick. Mark me."

"Sir, I don't doubt it."

"Second we finally got that photo sketch over to Europe. The clerks at that Paris hotel said that was one of the guys. Now follow this. There's a little hotel on the French-German border near a railroad station. A cop from Germany was staying there last night, then went back home. He saw this picture on the wirephoto machine in his headquarters. He could swear the guy was there."

"Have the hotel employees seen it?"

"Not yet. We're gettin' it to 'em."

"I'll have all trains checked that went through there," Sovern said.

But it was already ten A.M. Only two hours remained. . . .

Sovern glanced toward the other end of the room, where a commotion broke out as a message came across the teletype. "Turn it on," someone said. "Turn it on."

Bettel rushed over to Sovern. "They just attacked two TV stations and one radio outlet. There was West German security there, but it melted away. Half the security guards joined the Nazis. They're broadcasting, Dick!"

Sovern could hear clicking and popping on the public address system as CRG engineers piped in a local broadcast that was about to go on the air.

"Mr. President," Sovern asked, "did you hear what was just said to me?"

"I did."

"All right, sir. I'm having them establish a radio hook-up through the consulate direct to the White House, if possible."

But the broadcast began. "Too late," Sovern said. "I'll just hold the phone up to the speaker."

Sovern held the phone close to one of the loud-speakers. The broadcast, of course, was in German. Sovern knew the language, as did Earhart from her years in captivity. The President did not, so Sovern translated over the phone as the announcer began to the strains of "Deutschland, Deutschland über alles," the anthem of the Nazi period.

CITIZENS OF GERMANY: TODAY IS THE DAY OF OUR REBIRTH, OUR DELIVERANCE FROM WEAKNESS AND EXPLOITATION AT THE HANDS OF THE BOLSHEVIKS AND THE JEW BUSINESSMEN. TODAY THE GLORY OF 1933 WILL RETURN.

TODAY THE REICH REBORN, SPIRITUAL EXTENSION OF NATIONAL SOCIALISM, WILL TAKE COMMAND OF GERMANY AND RESTORE OUR NATION.

TODAY THE VERMIN AND CRIMINALS WILL BE SWEPT FROM OUR STREETS, THE CHILDREN OF GERMANY WILL BE PROUD, ORDER WILL BE RESTORED, THE GOVERNMENT SHALL HAVE THE RESPECT OF OUR MAGNIFICENT PEOPLE. GERMANY WILL BREATHE AGAIN.

TODAY, OUR GREAT LEADER WILL RE-EMERGE FROM THE ASHES OF 1945. HE WILL RETURN DESPITE THE TREACHERY OF TRAITORS AND INCOMPETENTS.

OUR FÜHRER, ADOLF HITLER, DID NOT DIE IN HIS BUNKER AS LIARS AND ZIONISTS HAVE TOLD YOU OVER THE YEARS. UNABLE TO CAPTURE HIM, FEARFUL OF THE LOVE THE GERMAN PEOPLE HAVE FOR HIM, THEY HAVE DECEIVED

YOU INTO THINKING HE WAS DEAD.

THE FÜHRER IS IN GERMANY.

YOU WILL SEE HIM AND HEAR HIM TODAY.

HIS YOUTHFULNESS, HIS PASSION FOR THE FATHERLAND, HAVE BEEN PRESERVED BY THE MIRACLES OF NATIONAL SOCIALIST MEDICAL SCIENCE, PERFECTED BY OUR BRILLIANT PHYSICIANS.

THE TIME IS APPROACHING.

PEOPLE OF MUNICH, TAKE TO THE STREETS.

PEOPLE OF GERMANY, MARCH TO YOUR CITY HALLS AND GOVERNMENT BUILDINGS.

IN HOURS, YOU WILL BE LIBERATED.

KEEP YOUR RADIOS ON. YOU WILL BE INSTRUCTED. YOU WILL HEAR THE VOICE OF THE FÜHRER.

It was unreal, Sovern thought, something out of Orson Welles's Mercury Theater of the 1930's, whose broadcast about men from Mars landing in America frightened the entire nation. Would people take this seriously? Was Germany rejoicing? Or laughing?

"Dick, Dick," the President shouted through his phone line, "what do you think?"

"Mr. President, I don't know what to think," Sovern replied. "But I doubt that they'd bother to broadcast that if it were a hoax."

"What action are you taking at those radio stations?"

Sovern turned to Spencer Bettel, repeating the question.

"We're organizing a force to re-take them," Bettel

reported in his clipped manner. "But they've got people in there with automatic weapons and dear Lord
knows what else."

"What force are you using?" Sovern inquired.

"West German Army."

Sovern got back on the phone. "Mr. President, I'm
asking your authorization to use American troops
where I see fit."

"Big order, Dick," the President replied.

"Sir, we can't trust the German Army in this. They
may be infiltrated up and down. And after that broadcast . . ."

"I see what you mean. Let me check with LeVan."

Sovern held while the Chief Executive contacted
Chester LeVan at the Pentagon.

"Okay," the President said, getting back on the line.
"Ches has looked over the situation and he thinks it's
a good idea. But I want you to keep it to three thousand troops. Nothing comes out of the NATO line,
not with the Russians acting up."

"Fine, sir. I understand."

The conversation ended. Sovern ordered all trains,
planes, cars, buses, and trucks entering Germany or
approaching Munich to be stopped and searched. Once
again the order was too big for the forces available to
him. He would have liked all searches to be carried
out by non-German troops, but there simply weren't
enough. So German police, many from small towns,
were pressed into service.

The door to the operations center opened and a
West German general in full regalia strode in, accompanied by three aides. Spencer Bettel, acting through
defense officials of the West German government in
Bonn, had requested that Germany name a high military official to command the German elements in any

anti-Nazi moves. General Kurt Hindemann, a senior member of the general staff, a former commander of armored divisions and a veteran, as an enlisted man, of the Battle of the Bulge in World War II, was selected. He enjoyed the full confidence of the United States government, which believed him to be passionately anti-Nazi.

Hindemann was the rarity, a smiling, informal German who had a wry sense of humor and collected books of jokes, as well as histories of military strategy. He had a doctorate in mathematics and had devised critical elements in the computers used by the modern West German Army. He was best known to the German public, though, as having lost two teeth when assaulted in 1973 by a leftist terrorist gang while strolling near his country home in Bavaria. The teeth, having become symbolic, had not been replaced.

Hindemann knew Sovern and immediately approached him. "So Dick," he said in his flawless English, "you've come to Germany to meet Der Führer. Shall I arrange dinner?"

"Not tonight, Kurt," Sovern replied with a wry smile, "it's my night for bowling."

"So sorry," Hindemann reacted. Then his smile melted away. "Look," he said, "you'll forgive me for sounding down, but we've got trouble out there."

"Don't we know it," Sovern said. He glanced over to the corner toward Amelia Earhart. Hindemann was unaware of Earhart's identity, and Sovern made no attempt to introduce him. There was no time for long explanations. "You've seen the reports from Paris?" Sovern asked.

"Of course."

"What do you make of them?"

"Exactly what you do. They could've been in Paris

but maybe not. We're carrying out your request to search all vehicles to the extent possible. We have the photo sketch. But if it blows today, then the time factor is impossible." He handed a copy of the photo sketch to Sovern, who had not seen it. It was a remarkable likeness of Willy Haas, with the face looking only slightly heavier than it actually was. Sovern placed the photo on a table.

"I'm afraid," Sovern said, looking over the huge aerial picture of Munich, "that all our efforts will be concentrated after Hitler's presence is actually announced. That's what we should shoot for. For all we know he's already in the city and thoroughly protected."

"I know the German," Hindemann said with a touch of sadness. "If Hitler comes back and he wants Hitler, he will have him. All your troops and tanks will not be able to control the crowds."

"And the Army?" Sovern asked.

Hindemann glanced each way toward the insignia of rank on each shoulder. "Probable mass defections," he said. "Most units would become nonfunctional, at least for internal security."

"And for external use?"

"That's another story. If the Russians move on a new Nazi regime—and they will—the army will fight like hell . . . especially for a strong leader."

"And considering the position that would put us in," Sovern said, "we'd practically be forced to go along with Hitler to stop the Russians—exactly the reverse of World War II."

"You may be certain," Hindemann answered, "that the new Nazis have thought of that."

"In addition to inspecting vehicles and getting forces

in Munich," Sovern said, "I think we should start broadcasting our *own* stuff to the people."

"You mean denials that Hitler is coming?"

"Yes."

"Forget it. The damage is done. The kind of German who will believe that broadcast we just heard will just have his belief strengthened by a denial. Besides, I have a feeling all stations will be off the air soon . . . blown transmitters. . . . The Nazis will want to control all information themselves."

Hindemann was right. Even as he spoke, radio transmitters were being sabotaged.

Sovern didn't notice Earhart walking over and picking up the photo sketch he had left on a table. She studied it intently, looking at it from different angles. Then, urgently, she walked up behind Sovern and tapped him on the shoulder. He turned.

Sovern saw the look of excitement in Amelia's eye. He looked down and saw her holding the picture.

"I think I know this man," she said.

Hindemann appeared confused, Sovern exultant.

"His name is . . . Hess, or Haas. He used to come around the lab during the war. I think he had something to do with security, but I can't be sure. If I remember right, people thought he was very bright, a good leader."

"Are you certain?" Sovern asked.

Earhart looked at the picture again. "I know it's only an artist's sketch made to look like a picture," she said. "I could be wrong, with my memory problems. But I've seen that face."

Sovern knew there was one technique that might make Earhart absolutely positive. There was a way of altering the photo sketch by computer to make the subject appear as he would have looked years before. It could only be done at the National Security Agency at Fort Meade, Maryland, and Sovern immediately cabled an urgent request for a computer picture to be made and wirephotoed. Then, hurriedly, he told Hindemann who Earhart was.

Hindemann was flabbergasted. But he was also reflective . . . and realistic. "Now," he said, gazing intently at the flier, "I believe that Hitler is with us."

Suddenly, there was a flash of light outside, followed by a deafening, resounding blast. The operations room shook so severely that the electricity went out. Plaster fell from the walls. Two CRG men were cut as glass flew in from shattered windows.

Within seconds emergency generators took over.

The street below was a mass of panic. All that could be heard was screaming followed by wailing sirens.

In the operations center everyone froze. The front had moved closer, the danger was near. Was it an attempt to get the center, whose very location was a secret?

Sovern assumed so.

For a minute.

"Oh my God!" Bettel moaned as he received a panicked call from the local police precinct. He rushed to Sovern. "Dick, you won't believe," he said. "They've blown up a child-care center." Tears welled up in the normally cool Bettel's eyes. "There were hundreds of kids in there, Dick."

Then from the street below, Richard Sovern and Amelia Earhart could hear people running through the crowds shouting about the blast. Moments later a Nazi-controlled radio station delivered the word: the Communists did it.

CHAPTER 22

SQUADRON OF SOVIET MIG-28s HAS OVER-
FLOWN PARTS OF WEST GERMANY AS
WARNING OVER IMMINENT TRIUMPH
OF OUR MOVEMENT.

Willy Haas beamed as he read the message from
one of his commanders.

Everything was working perfectly.

The train raced toward Munich and the expected
triumph of Reich Reborn. The first attack on a
child-care center, while it unnerved Haas, was having
its intended effects. A senior officer radioed excitedly
that crowds were surging through Munich demanding
death to Red terrorists and insisting that the government show some backbone. The radio broadcast announcing the coming of the Führer had been effective.
People were clustering at street corners as they had
when the first pamphlets announcing Hitler's return
were distributed. The senior officer's report, while
overly romantic, told the story: People were going

around smiling. Grown men and women ran to neighbor after neighbor with the good news. Some appeared
in the street with World War II uniforms. A few pictures of the Chairman were being taped to windows.
Already bands of youths had marched through neighborhoods smashing shops run by leftists. Radio stations were picking up the spirit and playing long-
banned records from the Nazi era. The swastika was
appearing without authorization at flagpoles, often re-
placing the current flag. It was being saluted!

Gottes, Haas knew, was about to order the destruction of another child center.

It was 11:05 A.M.

Then, without warning, the train began to slow. It
wasn't near a station or crossing, and Haas assumed
there was another train up ahead that was holding up
traffic. It angered him. Nothing should be allowed to
slow the progress of the Chairman.

But Haas saw a sight that scared him, almost panicked him. There were West German police vehicles
parked near the track, with uniformed officers milling
around, obviously waiting for the train to stop. Willy
Haas jumped to his feet, ready to dash to Herrmann
Schmidt's compartment. But as he went to open his
door, Schmidt was already knocking. The security
chief entered.

"They are going to board," he said tersely. "They're
holding what appears to be a picture. I recommend
we stay absolutely cool and display no weapons. We
have all our papers."

Haas slowly returned to his seat, seeing the wisdom
in Schmidt's advice. He watched as policemen approached the train and boarded several cars ahead.
What, he wondered, was in that picture, if it *was* a
picture? "Don't worry," he told the Chairman, "I'm

sure they're inspecting every train. We have nothing to hide."

Schmidt left to see what precisely was going on.

Half a minute later he was back, throwing Haas's door open furiously. "It's a picture of *you!*" he announced.

Haas froze. The Chairman's eyes flashed with anger and frustration.

Haas shot up. "I'll hide in the baggage car," he said. He tried to dash past Schmidt, who stopped him. "Sir, they're already in the baggage car. They're coming in *here*." The despair in Schmidt's voice was evident.

"Seize the train," Haas quietly ordered.

Schmidt turned to leave.

Suddenly, a policeman in brown uniform appeared at the door. The officer glanced down at his picture, then at Haas. The man's eyes widened with the look of discovery.

But before he could do a thing, Schmidt grabbed him around the neck. The eyes of discovery bulged, then froze. Willy Haas finished the job with a thrust of his pistol butt to the man's right temple.

Schmidt deposited the policeman on the seat, then dashed down the corridor, instructing his agents. His brilliance in his job, his German efficiency, quickly proved themselves. Two Reich Reborn men moved swiftly to the diesel locomotive and dispatched the crew with silencer-equipped pistols. Then another group of agents dashed from the train at several points, machine-gunning the policemen who waited outside. The police aboard the train were trapped and quickly eliminated by strangulation, gunshot, or knife.

But passengers panicked and several had to be killed to silence the others. Reich Reborn agents now stood with guns at the front of each car, warning against rebellion and announcing the true purpose of the ride into Munich. Willy Haas himself appeared in each car, telling passengers they were taking a journey into history, that the National Socialist regime was about to return, that Germany's magnetic leader from the "great era" was aboard and was well.

The French passengers sat listening in fright, not quite believing Haas's words. But most of the Germans were transfixed. They sat rigidly, with perfect discipline, some not wanting to hear, others feeling a link with the past they had rarely felt before, believing they were destined to be on this particular train.

"You will tell your grandchildren about this," Haas said as he passed from car to car. "You will tell them how you were present at the making of the new Germany."

It was 11:21.

Munich was forty minutes away.

A few Reich Reborn agents stayed behind to dispose of the dead policemen at the side of the track and disperse their vehicles to avoid suspicion. Two Reich Reborn men trained in railroad operations took over in the cab and started the train, quickly reaching fifty-five miles an hour.

It was now simply a race to enter the city before anyone discovered what had happened aboard the train. Herrmann Schmidt had ordered the men who stayed behind to contact his people in the West German police and find out how to answer radio inquiries correctly.

Thirty-six minutes to Munich.

Willy Haas returned to his compartment. The final preparations began. He took out a small barber kit, then summoned a member of the Reich Reborn security force, a barber by profession. The man shaved off the Chairman's beard, then trimmed his hair, restoring the hairline that became famous around the world between 1933 and 1945. He darkened its color and then brushed the hair sharply across the forehead, spraying it so it would remain.

Then the barber took a small artificial mustache that he had fashioned himself from photographs and affixed it with glue beneath the Chairman's nose. He took out a small mirror to show the Chairman the result. It was perfect. The Chairman actually looked better than he had looked in those last days in 1945. He smiled, then altered his facial expressions to show, in succession, strength, kindness, anger, determination. Although fatigued, he still had that incredible magnetism. Even Willy Haas felt the excitement in the compartment.

Haas took down the suitcases and unpacked the uniforms. No step was more moving than this. For the first time since the war these top Nazi leaders would wear their insignia for the world to see. First Haas assisted the Chairman as he undressed and carefully donned the brown uniform, the red armband, the military-style hat.

Haas felt a glow around the man. All concealment had vanished; all pretense evaporated. There was one last step now to be taken, one last symbolic act that would complete the transformation of the man who would lead Germany once again. The polite title—Chairman—used for years so that more provocative words would not accidentally slip out in public conversation, had to dissolve into history, to become a mere footnote to Operation Mulberry.

"Mein Führer," Willy Haas said, and the leader of

the Third Reich could see the tears well up in his operations director's eyes. He placed his hand on Haas's shoulder.

"We do this for all Germany," the Führer declared. "It is our destiny to serve our people."

Willy Haas rose from his seat. He clicked his heels together and thrust out his right arm.

"Heil Hitler!" he said. It felt good. It felt right.

Twenty-one minutes to Munich.

II

The mood in the CRG Munich center was desperate.

Below in the streets anger grew. The death of children had galvanized hotheaded Germans, just as the burning of the Reichstag had done in 1933. Although two radio and three television stations had been recaptured from Reich Reborn forces, four TV stations throughout West Germany were still in Nazi hands. "Adolf Hitler is returning" was the message sent into German homes.

And now the people waited—in squares, on sidewalks, in town centers. They talked. Many ridiculed; others did not.

Amelia Earhart had received the revised photo sketch of Willy Haas, showing him as he might have looked during World War II. Yes, Earhart told Sovern, that looked like him. Willy Haas was in their midst. But where? And where was Hitler? To those questions the combined forces of Richard Sovern, General Hindemann, and NATO still had no answers.

The Führer's train was eighteen minutes away.

BULLETIN
CHILD-CARE CENTER HAS BEEN FIRE-
BOMBED IN COLOGNE. AT LEAST THREE
HUNDRED FIFTY CHILDREN BELIEVED
KILLED.

The news spread through West Germany. "The
Communists did it!" was the line hawked by the Reich
Reborn agents and provocateurs. Germany was becoming a fantasy world, a sea of lies and deceptions,
just as in 1933. Deep in his gut Sovern feared that
these people had learned nothing since then, that they
would react just as their fathers and grandfathers had.

The reports of vehicle checks and airport inspections poured in, all negative. Sovern was skeptical
about many of the reports, believing that the combination of neo-Nazi infiltration of security forces and
the hurried inspections made it possible for Willy
Haas and his party to slip by easily.

One report, though, attracted Sovern's attention. A
train approaching Munich from France was to have
been stopped and inspected. The inspection team was
then to go to a local bus depot and conduct another
inspection. The team reported that it had found nothing aboard the train. But it never arrived at the bus
depot.

"Find out why!" Sovern ordered.

An urgent radio message went out: "Report to
depot."

But the Reich Reborn agents who had seized the
police vehicles that received the call did not know the
orders of the men they had killed. They dared not ask
for clarification, for that would reveal who they were.
So they pretended radio interference and constantly
asked for repetition of messages.

Still, their failure to report to the bus depot was highly suspicious. Sovern ordered a U.S. Army helicopter to find them by homing in on their radios.

He also ordered the Munich train stopped.

Adolf Hitler was fifteen minutes from the city.

General Hindemann, through the West German Transport Ministry, ordered a message sent to the cab of the Munich train:

HALT AT ONCE. TROUBLE ON THE TRACK.

Within a minute Hindemann learned and told Sovern that the message had not been acknowledged.

Trouble with the police radios.

Trouble with the train radios.

The evidence began to mount.

"I want helicopter gunships," Sovern ordered, "and two companies of troops. Fast."

The Munich train had to be stopped. It was fourteen minutes away.

Sovern prepared to leave the center to lead the helicopters in. Hindemann would be with him. The troops would be all Americans, parts of MP companies brought into Munich to try to maintain order.

Earhart began following Sovern out. "Oh no," Sovern said, "you stay here."

"I think I have a right to come," Earhart replied. "I'm the only one in this room who can *positively* identify Willy Haas."

She was right, as usual. But this time there was sure to be trouble—gunfire, resistance.

"I might be dead in a week anyway," Earhart continued. Sovern looked into her intense eyes and realized that her proper place was in the final confrontation with Adolf Hitler. Even if the worst happened to her, she would still possess a final contentment that he could not refuse.

"Stay on the helicopter deck!" he ordered her. "It's armored."

She remained silent and followed him out. Within three minutes an American Seventh Army helicopter, bristling with air-to-ground rockets and machine guns, landed on the roof. Sovern, Earhart, and Hindemann got in. The craft took off and Earhart immediately saw other helicopters hovering near the outskirts of the city, ready to follow Sovern's lead.

But Adolf Hitler was nine minutes away. . . .

BULLETIN
CHILD-CARE CENTER HAS BEEN DE-
STROYED BY BLAST NEAR CENTER OF
HAMBURG.

Another bulletin came seconds later. The army helicopter sent out to locate the errant police detail reported seeing two German police cars near the railroad line, driven by men in civilian clothes. The helicopter flew on to the site where the police had been ordered to board the Munich train. The co-pilot reported seeing puddles of blood on the ground—the spot where Herrmann Schmidt's men had massacred the police.

"Fly directly along the rail line!" Sovern ordered his pilot. "We'll intercept the train head on."

Eight minutes . . .

In the streets of Munich loudspeaker trucks suddenly started calling the masses to the railroad station. "A MAJOR EVENT IN THE FATHERLAND'S HISTORY IS ABOUT TO TAKE PLACE," the speakers shouted. "GATHER AT THE RAILROAD

STATION. YOU WILL TELL YOUR GRAND-
CHILDREN YOU WERE THERE!"

Sovern ordered American forces to converge on the
station to break up any rally. West German units and
police under General Hindemann started converging
as well. But it became quickly apparent that any effort
to prevent a mass meeting would be in vain. Reich
Reborn loyalists, carried in sealed trucks, started pouring into the terminal area, armed with automatic
weapons and anti-tank guns, all stolen from NATO
arsenals. They quickly herded crowds of fascinated—
or cheering—Germans toward the end of the rail line.
There was no way any opposing forces could move in
without killing thousands.

Sovern looked down as his helicopter passed over
the terminal on its way out of Munich.

"Get snipers on nearby buildings," he ordered
through his air-to-ground radio link, which hooked
him in to the CRG operations center. "Start throwing
up roadblocks around the area. Use parked cars, anything!"

"We can use tear gas to disperse the crowd," Hindemann said.

"You'd have mad panic," Sovern responded. "The
Reich Reborn people would make sure of that, then
blame us. Things would just get worse."

"If Hitler is on the train," Hindemann went on, "I
don't think *anything* could be worse."

Sovern did not answer. He feared that any mob violence, even without Hitler, could erode the authority
of the German government and provoke the Soviet
Union. Even as he flew toward a confrontation with
Willy Haas's commandeered train he was told by radio
that Soviet troops were massing on the Czechoslo-
vakian frontier with Bavaria and could cross in a mat-

ter of minutes. He swept the sky, seeing the vapor trails of NATO jets as they patrolled near the Eastern border, watching for the MIGs that were coming across as warnings against a neo-Nazi move.

"The train must be stopped," he told Hindemann tersely.

Six minutes . . .

At the railroad station, protected by the surging crowd and groups of armed guards, Reich Reborn loyalists hurriedly put up a prefabricated platform with microphones. Then, as the crowd gave out a deafening roar, they raised the swastika over the station.

Pictures of Adolf Hitler appeared on the outsides of buildings.

Five minutes . . .

III

"Helicopters heading this way!"

Herrmann Schmidt sounded worried, anxious as he delivered the blunt message to Willy Haas, now dressed in his full Nazi regalia.

"Whose?" Haas asked.

"American."

"It might be unrelated."

"I would not assume *anything* is unrelated at this point," Schmidt argued.

"Have the engineer increase speed," Haas ordered.

"Impossible. We are too close to the station."

"Are there many?"

"At least six helicopters so far. There are others in the distance."

Adolf Hitler looked up from the speech he was studying, the speech of greetings to his German people. The look in his blazing, magnetic eyes was fierce, not unlike the look Germany saw before the attack on Britain in 1940. "They will not stop us!" he declared. "Our forces will destroy them. That is my order."

Haas turned sharply, almost contemptuously to Schmidt. "You have your orders!" he snapped.

Schmidt clicked his heels, rendered the Nazi salute and left. He had twenty-three men on the train, plus small pockets of fighters along the tracks leading to Munich. Three of his men on the train carried shoulder-launched surface-to-air missiles in suitcases. The missiles were now unpacked, and the men stationed on the landings between cars.

Four minutes . . .

Willy Haas looked out the window and saw the first two helicopters in the distance as the train went around a curve. He also saw a sign—DACHAU—a suburb of Munich, the site of the first concentration camp. There were more houses now as the train passed through the suburbs, racing for the station. Haas, using a small walkie-talkie, was in communication with Schmidt and the cab. The small speaker crackled as the engineer came on.

"They are ordering us to halt," the engineer reported.

"Ignore them!" Haas ordered.

Suddenly there was a flash from one of the helicopters. An air-to-ground rocket blazed downward, striking the ground about fifty yards to the right of the onrushing train.

"They fired a warning shot!" the engineer yelled.

"Keep moving!" Haas demanded.

But now Haas's face broke out in a sweat. Beside him Adolf Hitler stopped studying his script.

"Where are the troops?" Hitler demanded to know.

"They're coming, Führer," Haas replied. "We have them along the tracks."

Three minutes.

A helicopter streaked in overhead, its crew trying to get a close look at the train. A Reich Reborn man standing between the cars mounted his shoulder launcher and fired. A missile, trailing flame and white smoke, shot upward.

The helicopter veered, but not soon enough.

The warhead exploded amidst the rotor blades, severing one, twisting another.

The copter went into a violent spin, hurtling to earth.

It crashed near the speeding train, shooting off flaming fuel and splinters of steel against windows, killing three passengers.

The other helicopters veered away.

"They're running!" Haas shouted.

The sign outside read MUNICH.

The station was two minutes thirty seconds away.

IV

"Christ!" Sovern yelled as he watched his lead helicopter go down. "That's the train, dammit!"

"We can blow it up!" Hindemann declared.

"I want him alive!"

Still far out of range of Reich Reborn's shoulder-launched missiles, Sovern ordered his pilot to swing around ahead of the train and fire his entire load of rockets at the track.

The pilot complied. The gunship shook violently as it veered and gathered speed, far outdistancing the Munich train. The pilot unleashed rocket after rocket, watching his payload streak toward the main Munich line.

Some of the rockets exploded on either side of the track. But six hit the rail, blasting steel and wood into the sky.

Sovern could see the sparks shooting from the wheels of the Munich train's diesel as the engineer jammed on his brakes, trying to stop before reaching the crater that had been his track.

"Land!" Sovern ordered. "Have all gunships land!"

There were now twelve helicopters in all and they began floating to earth. A few strayed too close to the train, drawing more shoulder-launched missiles. But the gunships managed to evade the missiles and none was shot down.

The train came to a complete stop only sixty yards before the break in the track. Sovern could see passengers coming through windows and running away, apparently freed by Nazi guards who now had more important things to do than watch them.

The helicopters started landing. Sovern's came down not far from a water tower with MUNICH written across it in huge yellow letters. He dashed from the copter, followed by General Hindemann and Amelia Earhart. Sovern immediately dispatched two soldiers to protect Earhart, to keep her down and out of the line of fire.

The American force organized into infantry squads and started approaching the train. Some of the men carried bazookas—anti-tank weapons—that could be used to blast into the train if need be.

Suddenly, machine gun fire started bursting from some of the cars. Three American soldiers were immediately hit and fell. The others dove to the ground, then crawled for cover.

Sovern and Earhart dropped behind a hedgerow, out of sight of the Nazi gunners.

"I want him alive!" Sovern repeated through his walkie-talkie to the commander of the American force.

Crawling through weeds and over gravel not far from a dead-end suburban street of small cottages, the Americans inched forward. Infantry riflemen covered the advance with fire from AR-16's directed at the tops of the cars. They were under strict orders not to kill unless absolutely necessary. "Take Hitler alive" had now become the mission, although the identity of the man the troops were to seize was known only to their senior commanders.

The crackling of fire echoed off distant hills and buildings. Then two men in Nazi uniforms jumped from the train and started charging the American troops, throwing hand grenades as they ran. They were cut down quickly. Sovern assumed they had acted without orders, drunk on the glory of attacking the enemy.

Richard Sovern was now within one hundred twenty yards of the train. There was no doubt that he had deduced the right target. His heart pounded and his head throbbed with the excitement of the action. For a flash he thought of Rudolph Peddington in Washington, the man who had assured the President of the United States that Amelia Earhart's story had been a hoax.

It would all be over soon. The gunfire from the train became more intense. The advance slowed. But there were limits to how much ammunition the Nazis could carry.

V

Willy Haas and the Chairman crouched in the aisle. The compartment was no longer safe.

"How bad is it? How bad is it?" Haas shouted through his walkie-talkie.

"The track is gone," the engineer reported back.

"Can it be fixed?"

"It is *gone*. Kaput!"

"Can you get around it?"

"There is one rail line. We would have to go backward, then be switched to another track near Dachau."

"Do this! Do this!" Haas ordered. His voice reflected the increasing realization that this was more than a close call. Each thirty seconds brought new reports of the advancing Americans. Haas hardly needed reports. He heard the bullets tearing into the top of the train.

"It is like the bunker that everyone thought I died in," Adolf Hitler lamented. "Just like the bunker." Then he fell silent and, incredibly, began studying his speech of greetings to the German people once more.

The train lurched as the engineer applied power and started moving backward. The Dachau switching center was four miles behind. A quick run could get the train onto another track. It was a long shot, for the Americans had their helicopters. There was one ace Willy Haas hoped could still be played, though—the Reich Reborn troops rushing to help.

Those troops were converging in trucks, buses, even private cars. But they weren't even getting near the train. American and British units were intercepting them on highways and roads, and Haas's saving force was quickly becoming a phantom.

The train gathered speed. But then Haas heard two deafening thuds behind. The train shook wildly. Haas could hear "Stop, stop!" through his walkie-talkie.

The train ground to a halt.

"What happened?" Haas demanded.

"Bazooka shells!" the reply came from a Reich Reborn man stationed at the rear. "They blew the track behind us!"

Now they were trapped. The tracks both front and rear were gone. "Beat them off!" Haas ordered. "Hurl yourselves against them!"

"Are our troops here?" Adolf Hitler asked.

"Momentarily," Haas assured him. "We will beat them off and go into Munich by motorcade. He radioed ahead to Gottes's headquarters:

AMERICANS WILL BE PUSHED BACK WITH HELP OF ARRIVING REICH RE-BORN TROOPS. SEND MERCEDES TO MEET US. WE WILL GO IN BY CAR. SET UP RALLY AT MAIN SQUARE.

Haas realized he had to maintain a brave front and drive forward, like his Nazi heroes in the last battle for Berlin, hoping to work himself out of the enemy trap.

"They are sixty yards away!" he heard through the walkie-talkie.

"Grenade launchers!" Haas ordered.

Within seconds, the Reich Reborn security force

attached grenade launchers to their rifles and started firing at the American force, destroying part of the advancing front line.

Haas could not understand why the Americans were not using their anti-tank weapons against the train. Adolf Hitler had the same thought. "They want to take me alive," he finally said, answering Haas's question. "They want to put me in a glass booth like Eichmann." Haas knew he was referring to Adolph Eichmann, tried in Israel and kept in a glass booth during the trial to prevent assassination.

"Get out the green boxes," Hitler ordered in a quiet, dispassionate voice.

Haas looked at him and realized that Hitler was fully aware of the situation. But Haas also realized the implication for himself in Hitler's order. "Our forces are coming, Führer," he replied. "They may be able . . ."

"The green boxes!" Hitler said sternly.

"Yes, mein Führer!"

Haas gave the order to Herrmann Schmidt. Gloom and despair crossed Schmidt's face as he received it, but he carried out the command without question.

Then Adolf Hitler rose to his feet and stood erect. "We will not be on our knees," he said.

Willy Haas stood, as did all the others crouching in the corridor to avoid fire.

"Turn on the radio!" Hitler ordered.

Willy Haas picked up a black portable radio made by Braun of West Germany. He turned it on, tuning to a station he knew was under Reich Reborn control.

It was the perfect moment. The station was playing "Deutschland, Deutschland über alles," using the lyrics of the Nazi period. Adolf Hitler began singing

along, his voice strong and clear. The others joined
. . . "Germany over all . . ."

The song was interrupted.

"They are coming!" a voice crackled through Haas's
walkie-talkie. "Our people are coming!"

The Reich Reborn lookout excitedly reported the
appearance of two truckloads of troops in the distance. But then there was the clap of explosions and
automatic-weapons fire. He hesitated. "They are
gone," he reported. "They are destroyed."

Haas and the Führer looked at each other. The
emotions ran high, but neither man so much as
blinked.

"Mein Führer," Willy Haas said, "you are the leader
of all Germany, and history will so honor you."

He rendered the Nazi salute.

Adolf Hitler returned it.

VI

"Resistance is falling off," Sovern heard through his
walkie-talkie, as he, Hindemann, Amelia Earhart and
the two soldiers watching Amelia crouched behind
some concrete piping. It was clear that the Nazis were
running out of ammunition, and most of their security
force was dead.

"Tear gas!" Sovern ordered.

The firing continued, but about forty-five seconds
later the front line of American troops fired a volley
of tear-gas cannisters at all sections of the train.

Now Sovern realized his responsibility as leader of
the American force. If there was to be a final charge,
he had to be at its head.

"Keep her back!" he ordered the American soldiers protecting Amelia. Although she tried to resist, they prevented her from following him.

Sovern began crawling forward, finally reaching the infantry captain now only fifty yards from the train.

Despite the tear gas, no one was coming out.

Sovern gave his nod.

The entire front line, supported by withering machine-gun fire from the rear, started moving forward.

One by one, the Nazi gunners inside were knocked out, some by gunfire, others by tear gas.

Sovern was forty yards away. He saw movement inside the cars. In moments, he was sure, he would come face to face with Adolf Hitler.

But then, as he and the Americans were within thirty-five yards, there was a blinding, sizzling flash from one of the cars. The car blew apart with a roar unequalled by anything Richard Sovern had ever heard. Metal and upholstery and human blood shot outward. Sovern dove for cover behind a railroad shed, itself buckling under the blast.

Another explosion.

And another.

All within the same car.

Bits of the green boxes that had held the explosives streaked overhead and floated to Earth.

Then silence.

Sovern looked out as columns of dust and smoke rose. Where a railroad car had stood there was nothing.

Richard Sovern knew what had happened: Adolf Hitler had committed suicide, just as in the fable of the bunker. . . .

Now, all resistance from the remaining Nazis ceased. Sovern led the troops forward, and they seized the train with no difficulty. The reason for the ease of the capture became instantly apparent: The Nazis who survived the earlier attacks had taken cyanide pills as their orders required. It was a point of honor that no one would survive the Führer.

Army medics moved in to help those passengers injured in the blast. The surrounding cars had been blown off the track and scores were badly hurt or dead.

Earhart rejoined Sovern. As she approached him, he placed his arm around her, and she placed hers around him. They stood silently, looking at the wreckage of Adolf Hitler's last refuge. The dust and ashes made their eyes water, and anyone passing might have thought they were crying.

"You warned us," Sovern finally said. "You made it possible for us to save the world from Adolf Hitler. You are the heroine here."

But Amelia simply gazed around the carnage, at the innocent victims who lay near the track, at the American soldiers who had fallen. It was not the moment to accept compliments and she said nothing.

Ordnance experts went through the wreckage of Hitler's car, making sure there were no live explosives. Then, when they gave the all-clear, Sovern and Earhart walked forward to get a personal look at the wreckage the Führer had left as his legacy.

"I would have liked to have taken him alive," Sovern said poignantly, "but there is justice in this. He died knowing he had failed twice and that his dream was over."

Earhart, still stunned by the magnitude of what she had just witnessed, did not react at first. Then, slowly, she began to feel a restrained pride. Yes, she had inspired the final battle against Adolf Hitler, fought, ironically, in the shadows of the Dachau she knew well. Her last mission, interrupted in 1937, had been completed, and she had made her contribution to history.

She and Sovern walked amidst the rubble, looking at the fragments of steel, glass, and cloth. The people in the Führer's car had been blown to dust.

Suddenly, Sovern saw a ragged, brown object resting near the remains of a wheel. He walked quickly to pick it up. He saw that it was a section of a military hat, and still pinned to it, charred and twisted, was part of the insignia of the Führer of Germany.

Sovern brought the remnant to Amelia Earhart. She took it, feeling each part as if it was the physical confirmation of her journey's end. Then she dropped it in the ashes.

They walked away.

EPILOGUE

Richard Sovern and Amelia Earhart flew back to Washington aboard Air Force One, which had been sent by the President of the United States. Sovern was more relaxed and optimistic than he had been in weeks. The destruction of Adolf Hitler had broken the back of Reich Reborn, and with that the threat both to West Germany and to the peace of Europe had dissolved.

Sovern's position was stronger than ever. There were even rumors that Chester LeVan wanted to leave government, and that Sovern would succeed him as Secretary of Defense. On the flight home with Earhart, though, he wanted to talk only of other things, of the chance she would now have to get to know her country again, of his willingness to help her locate old friends and relatives who had survived the years.

And yet, Sovern noticed a change in Amelia's personality as they flew back. She fell silent for long stretches, preferring to look out the window at the endless ocean below. She seemed mesmerized by the waves and foam, as if they were more real to her than the freedom she could now enjoy.

It was the letdown after the trauma, Sovern assumed, and it would go away.

But when they arrived in Washington, Amelia graciously declined his invitation to a reception for CRG men who had worked on the neo-Nazi problem, saying she was just too exhausted by the ordeal and begging him to understand that she needed time alone. Sovern did not pressure her, and she spent almost a week by herself at Andrews.

Finally Sovern called her to check up. She was feeling better, she told him, but she also revealed her wish to make a private trip to her girlhood home in Atchison.

"When?" Sovern asked.

"Tomorrow," she replied.

Sovern sensed there was something wrong, but didn't pursue the point, knowing Amelia would deny it. She said she would call in two days and told him where she would stay and the assumed name she would use.

Amelia left Andrews as scheduled and flew to Kansas.

Two days passed. There was no call.

Concerned, Sovern phoned the hotel in Atchison and asked for Earhart by her assumed name. He was told she had been registered, but had checked out, leaving no forwarding address.

Alarmed, Sovern contacted hotels, hospitals, and airfields in every town where Amelia might logically have gone. No one recognized her description.

He theorized that she might have returned to her plane for some emotional reason. It had been temporarily stored at a small commercial airfield, and

Earhart had easy access to it. At Sovern's request police checked on the plane.

The Electra was missing.

The airfield was closed nights, with only a dozing watchman to protect the planes, and Sovern guessed that it was during the night that the plane had been taken. He urgently called on other federal agencies to help launch a major search. But no plane had been reported down, and no airport reported the landing of a Lockheed Electra.

A day later, though, Sovern received a letter.

"Dear Richard," it began . . .

I want first of all to tell you how much you've meant to me these last days. I knew from the first that you were the right man to lead our common struggle, and everything you did reinforced that belief. My gratitude to you cannot be expressed in mere words. And you must realize that the world owes you a tremendous debt.

But there is more to one's existence than gratitude and personal good feelings and so, by the time you read this, I will be gone. Please don't try to find me, for it will be of no use. This is your world, Richard, not mine. I have no place here. All that is within me lives in a different time—perhaps, at least for me, a better one.

You really can't live twice. I, of all people, have come to realize that.

I'll only make one request, that you keep this letter a private affair between us, our own secret, our last communication on Earth.

My best to you, Richard Sovern. Maybe, if you believe in those things, we'll meet again.

                                                    Amelia

Sixteen hours after Sovern received the letter, the Coast Guard found parts of the Electra floating in the Pacific. But the cockpit, with Amelia inside, had gone to the bottom.

Richard Sovern respected Amelia's request and never revealed that she had written her note. He lived with the knowledge of what she had done for her country and the world and he had the assurance of the President that her role would be publicly acknowledged and honored.

Amelia was officially listed as "missing, presumed down." Only Sovern would ever know the truth. He alone kept locked within him the answer to the question asked year after year by a generation of Americans: "Whatever happened to Amelia Earhart?"

Dell Bestsellers

BY REASON OF INSANITY

Shane Stevens
author of *Rat Pack* and *Go Down Dead*

"Sensational."—*New York Post*

Thomas Bishop—born of a mindless rape—escapes from an institution for the criminally insane to deluge a nation in blood and horror. Not even Bishop himself knows where—and in what chilling horror—it will end.

"This is Shane Stevens' masterpiece. The most suspenseful novel in years."—Curt Gentry, co-author of *Helter Skelter*

"A masterful suspense thriller steeped in blood, guts and sex."—*The Cincinnati Enquirer*

A Dell Book $2.75   (11028-9)

At your local bookstore or use this handy coupon for ordering:

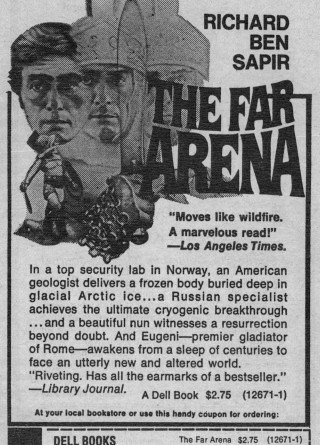

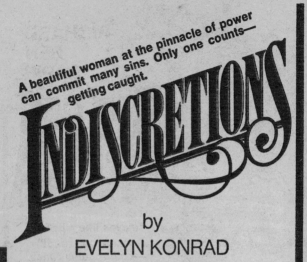